SOLOMON
MOON

VILLARD BOOKS · NEW YORK · 1984

SOLOMON MOON

WILLIAM DARRID

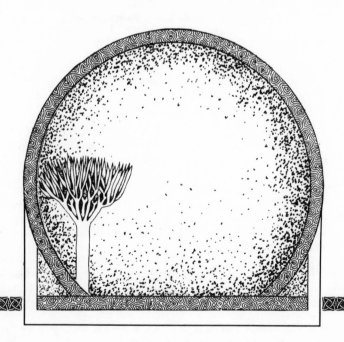

Library of Congress Cataloging in Publication Data

Darrid, William.
Solomon moon.

I. Title.
PS3554.A76S6   1984   813'.54   83-50861
ISBN 0-394-53357-7

Manufactured in the United States of America

9 8 7 6 5 4 3 2

First Edition

BOOK DESIGN BY LILLY LANGOTSKY

Grateful acknowledgment is given to the following for permission to reprint previously published material:

Chappell & Co., Inc: Excerpt from the lyrics to "September Song" by Kurt Weill and Maxwell Anderson. Copyright 1938 by DeSilva, Brown, and Henderson Inc. Copyright renewed; assigned to Chappell & Co., Inc. and Hampshire House Publishing Corp. for USA only. All rights outside the USA controlled by Chappell & Co., Inc. International copyright secured. ALL RIGHTS RESERVED.

Edwin H. Morris and Company: Excerpt from the lyrics to "Buddy Bolden's Blues" by Jelly Roll Morton. Used by permission of Edwin H. Morris and Company, a Division of MPL Communications, Inc.

Morley Music Co.: Excerpt from the lyrics to "Ole Buttermilk Sky" by Hoagy Carmichael and Jack Brooks. Copyright 1946 Morley Music Co. Copyright renewed 1974 Morley Music Co. and Frank Music Corp. International copyright secured. All Rights Reserved. Used by permission.

FOR DIANA
AGAIN, ALWAYS

With or without their knowledge, friends
and family have contributed to this book,
their thoughts gratefully accepted. Where
used well, I thank them. If used badly, only
I am to blame. It is a pleasure to acknowledge my debt to Dr. Elsie Giorgi, Walter
Seltzer, William Whitehead, and to my most
patient editor, Peter Gethers. Most particularly I would like to thank my brother,
John, my sister, Barbara, and my father,
Morton Gustav Blum who, sadly, failed to
recognize the first assassin.

AUGUST 1983
SHERMAN OAKS

CIRCLES
OF
OBSESSION

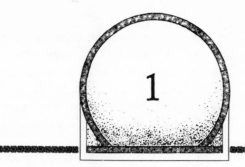

1

Brother Death fluttered his wings.

"Easy, darlin'," the old man whispered. "It's not time."

The old man's long white beard was matted from the falling rain, and as he raised his head to look at the black crow his beard lay like a used napkin on his chest. Above him, the black bird clawed to a branch of an ancient maple, his body a silhouette darker than the night. The old man rose from his kneeling position at the grave. He whistled softly to the bird. The rustle of wings ceased at once. The cold October wind that swept down from the Vermont mountains flapped open the old man's buckskin coat. The coat was blackened from campfire grease, and its rough hem hung to the old man's bare feet, which were covered by the graveyard's dead clover. Neatly sewn inside the coat were twelve squares of cloth, each forming a separate pocket. Across each pocket was a name written in the blood of an animal. They were the names of the apostles, and Riordan Flynn believed that they would be his companions long after he had ceased suffering from his association with men.

Click click click.

The old man whirled.

"Shhhh!" he whispered.

His son, Jubal, crouched under a hazelnut tree in the cemetery. He had retrieved two nuts from the wet grass beneath the tree and he juggled them in his hands. He glanced around at the leaning tombstones and laughed softly. "Can't nobody hear," he said.

"They listen," the old man said. "They always listen. They must listen."

The boy cracked the nuts between his muscular hands. His finger scraped inside a broken shell and he lifted the meat of a nut to his mouth. But before he could suck the sweetness he felt a terrible sting and he tasted the blood that ran from his split lip. He dropped the nut. No matter how often it happened, the boy was always amazed at the swiftness of his father's hands; and he hated him for it. He kept his anger secret, for he was terrified of swift retaliation.

"Ah, Jubal," the old man said gently, his voice only slightly brogued, as if it were difficult to hold on to the memory of an Irish coast. He held an uncommon whip in his hand. It was fourteen feet long and braided from the strands of a bramble bush. Its entire length was studded with wicked thorns. The thorns at the tip of the whip glistened with the boy's blood.

"Ah, Jubal," the old man repeated, his voice still gentle and infinitely patient. His hand twitched and the bramble whip slithered across the wet grass on which it rested. Hastily, Jubal stepped backwards, and immediately regretted it, for his shoulder thumped into the trunk of the hazelnut tree and he knew that even that dull sound might anger the old man. But Riordan pulled the whip toward himself and lifted it from the ground. Underneath his buckskin coat he wore a loose woolen shirt. He raised the flaps of the shirt and slowly coiled the bramble whip around his waist, the thorns puncturing his skin, leaving tiny drops of blood, oozing toward each other until a crimson circle was completed around his belly and his back. He paid no attention to the wounds. He pulled down his shirt and closed the coat around him. Riordan Flynn held a finger to his lips and spoke once more to his son.

"Listen!"

Jubal cocked his head, straining to hear what his father heard. He wished desperately to please the old man, fearful of the consequences if he failed. But there were no sounds unusual to the night. The rain fell steadily, soft wet grass absorbing its sound. Leaves from the hazelnut tree and the maple and the various elms and birches and aspen throughout the small cemetery, no longer able to hold the weight of rain, fell silently to earth. Anxiously, Jubal peered through the wet darkness. He reasoned simply that something strange was in motion and that the old man's keen hearing had detected an alien sound. But even as he turned in a small circle looking for something, anything, he knew he was wrong, for had so much as a shadow moved among the graves Brother Death would have cawed. Jubal turned back toward his father.

"Ain't nuthin'," he said. "Nuthin' but the wind. The wind is all."

"Yes!" Riordan's hiss was quiet but triumphant. "Yes. The wind is all. It is the voice of God. Surely you can hear Him."

"Ayuh!" Jubal said eagerly. He did not wish to see the pleasure vanish from his father's eyes. "Ayuh, I hear Him, Riordan, I hear Him sumthin' fierce."

"And they, too, boy," Riordan said as he gestured at the dark shapes of tombstones. "Do you not see how the stones tilt? All the poor souls listening to the wind, listening to His voice, listening to see if He calls, for they that have not sinned will rise tonight. Look now. Here!"

The old man dropped to his knees in front of a small stone marker. The stone was slightly cracked, its face stained by moss and lichen. Riordan reached inside his voluminous coat and removed a short-bladed sickle he and Jubal had found in the village dump. He whisked the blade across the face of the stone and dislodged the rotting vegetation. Jubal moved closer and through the falling rain saw the carvings that were revealed; and when he saw that the tombstone marked the grave of an infant boy who had died some years ago he smiled and his voice was excited, for he knew they had found what they sought.

"Yeah," he said. "Yeah!"

Quickly, the old man and his son set to work. Riordan whipped off his greatcoat and laid it flat on the ground beside the grave. Still on his knees, he shuffled around the perimeter of what he determined was the size of a small boy's coffin. He moved without hesitation. The measurements were familiar. The blade of his sickle sliced a rectangle into the earth, then he and Jubal rolled back the sod. Riordan nodded to the boy. Jubal moved swiftly to the hazelnut tree. A rusted spade, also retrieved from the village dump, still smelling slightly of manure, leaned against it. The boy returned with it and began to dig, and each time he raised his spade he poured the soil onto the cloak of the Apostles. It was mounded high when Jubal's blade struck the coffin.

The boy was in his middle adolescence but he was as lithe and muscular as a circus acrobat. He was surprised when he slipped on the greasy dirt at the bottom of the grave. Quickly, he regained his balance. He pulled at the coffin lid. The wood was rotted from age and earth and it splintered easily under the boy's strength. He froze at the sound of cracking wood and quickly looked up at his father, who knelt still at the edge of the pit. Riordan raised his hand to calm the boy, then he turned slowly so that he could gaze over the cemetery and beyond it.

Although it was a small graveyard no longer used by the villagers of Down Derry, it was maintained in pristine order, an homage to ancestral connections. The shade trees were pruned. The grass was neatly clipped. The gravel paths, which led to marker after marker, were raked clean of ruts. The old tombstones, cut from a limestone quarry long since abandoned, were of uniform simplicity, slabs of gray rock on which were chiselled names and dates and, occasionally, a few words which implied that he who lay beneath the marker was now warmed in the hands of God.

The cemetery was on a gentle slope of land, bounded on the south by Down Derry's river and on the north by a curving road that gradually widened into a state highway leading easterly toward Springfield and westerly toward the town of Manchester. Riordan gazed across the river at Down Derry's village square, in the center of which was a hexagonal bandstand, its sides constructed of wooden lattice work. Three sides of the village square were flanked by small clapboard houses of traditional New England design. The fourth side, which faced the river, was home to the few commercial enterprises of the village. The old man recognized the outlines of a gas station and the post office and a general store and the larger silhouette of the Silver Spoon, a restaurant converted from an ancient mill. Not far from the mill site was a small clapboard church, distinguished only by its simple steeple, which rose higher than the town's houses. Higher even than the steeple was the bell tower of a Catholic church situated on the outskirts of the village. On the land behind the church was an iron bridge. It crossed the river and led to a narrow footpath that bisected the cemetery.

It was long after midnight and Down Derry was quiet. Only one light was visible to the old man. It burned behind the window of a house on one corner of the village square. Riordan Flynn stood so that he could better see the lighted window. He raised his massive hand and wiped rain from his eyes. He knew that unlike its neighbors, which were of predictable architecture, the house was a cube of reinforced concrete sprayed an absolute white. The front side of its roof, which faced north, was slanted at forty-five degrees and consisted of an enormous skylight. At the second-story level, tall, narrow windows, drapeless, ran the length of the house. There were no windows on the ground floor. The house had been the conceit of an artist. He no longer lived there.

Its present occupant paced slowly behind the window, crossing through the light, disappearing for a moment, then returning, his movements leisurely and seemingly without intent. He paused for a moment, his silhouette no longer in profile but facing forward toward the window. It was as if he were staring across the village square, across the river, and into the cemetery where the old man stood. Riordan knew he was curtained by the rain, invisible in the moonless night, but still he stepped back. The man behind the window puzzled him — had puzzled him for many months.

His name was Wilfred Callahan. He was a sergeant of the Vermont State Police. He had moved into the strangely modern house a year ago. Neither the old man nor his son had ever exchanged a word with Callahan, nor had they even glanced into each others' eyes. But on Sunday mornings when Riordan and Jubal left their home hidden in the mountain woods and attended mass at the Catholic church, they were aware of Callahan's presence. He was a quiet man, tall, lean, with high cheekbones and a long jaw. He dressed invariably in gray, which matched his close-cropped hair and his eyes. His hard, angular body looked as if it might have been carved out of slate, and when Riordan had first seen the man's arm move in the making of the cross and, later, when Callahan had genuflected, the old man had expected to hear a cracking sound as if the joints of Callahan's limbs were unoiled by natural fluids. But there had been no sounds other than the whisper of cloth and, once, a muted sigh.

It was the sigh which had alerted Riordan. The sound was stifled, held back, discouraged. Throughout the litany of the mass, the old man had watched Callahan for other telltale signs of a sinner. For Riordan had no doubt about the meaning of that sigh. It was the sound of a man weary of his faith. It was the sound of an unattended soul.

Riordan Flynn was a hunter of souls. He had to be, for he was the natural heir of God. He did not think this so. He knew it. He waited only for His sign. But while he waited for what he prayed would be the final acknowledgment from Him, the old man agonized over whether he had performed, was still performing, would always perform with sufficient zeal. There were long and awful hours when he was made desperate by the doubt that wormed his soul.

During such times he howled. Whether self-impaled on the thorns of a hawthorn bush or rooted among the wild flowers of his hermit's mountain, his legs bent backwards as if both kneecaps had been cracked apart and then rehinged by some blind physician, he howled. The shriek bulged goiterlike in his throat, burned its way between his black gums, and curled upwards, its fierce spiral forever haunting the scalded sky, and within its echo innocence collapsed.

Then, cleansed by his own agony, he stalked those heretics whom he could deliver to the Father of all fathers; like the villagers of Down Derry, he was paying homage to his ancestral connection.

The policeman's sigh had created a deep suspicion in Riordan, so he was determined to be watchful. Now, standing by the open grave, staring through the falling rain at Callahan, the old man was wary. He stood totally motionless in the lee of the maple and waited for some indication from the man behind the window, some telltale action that would reveal the policeman's purpose for looking into the dark night. But Callahan turned away and disappeared into the unseeable recess of his room. The light went out behind the window. Like the rest of the village, the house was dark.

The old man slid into the grave. He leaned over the rotted coffin. He marveled at the beauty he beheld. The skin and flesh, long since decayed, flaked from the bones of the infant's skeleton, which was partially obscured by the decayed coffin wood. Riordan felt he had never seen such a fragile composition. The gentle curve of bare cranium and kneecap accentuated the harmony of the boy's bare bones. His fingers looked like dried bits of weed petrified to marble. Rain fell through the sockets of his eyes.

Jubal stared in awe. "One bite, that's all he is," he said. "Just a little bitty bite."

"He'll do," Riordan said. "He'll do wondrous fair."

"Won't take but a corner of the kiln," Jubal said.

"Wondrous fair," the old man repeated. And he quivered with the pleasure of the coming burn. For just a fleeting moment he regretted that the woman who had taught him what to do with children's bones was not present to observe the treasure. He sorrowed that the woman would not see the delicate pottery he would make from river clay bound with the ashes of a child. But then he remembered the sweet sight of fish nibbling at the woman's tongue and how he had delivered her unto God, and he no longer felt remorse.

Riordan reached high and hoisted himself to the lip of the grave. A deerhide bag hung down his back. He removed it from around his neck, held it open over the grave, and Jubal filled it with the infant's bones. The boy climbed out of the pit. He and the old man lifted a corner of the apostle's cloak and poured back the dug soil. They tamped it hard. They rolled back the grassy sod, then pressed flat the earth that bordered each slice of the sickle and fluffed the green grass until no cut was revealed. It was time to return to their kiln. The old man smiled and rain ran from the corners of his lips. The boy's pulse quickened and he felt himself short of breath, for he knew he had performed well.

Brother Death cawed.

Both Riordan and Jubal spun at the sound. The old man immediately looked toward the darkened window of the policeman's house. But still there was no light. His gaze swept the river. Nothing moved.

"What, what?" the boy whispered, frightened now by the signal from the crow.

Lightly, the old man laid his hand across the boy's mouth. His eyes swept the landscape. Something dark moved behind a distant tombstone. Riordan heard a snuffling sound and then a scratching as if someone else were digging at a grave. A dog appeared from behind the tombstone, then stopped, one leg still suspended, as he saw the old man and his son. The animal lowered his leg and slowly inched forward, his muzzle close to earth, his ears flat to his head. He growled softly. The dog's body was close to the ground as he slithered across wet grass and leaves. His teeth were bared and there was an ugly rasp in his throat. As he looked at the old man he raised his head. Jubal heard the animal's thin wail and then he heard another sound, and because he knew what it was he sucked in his breath and held it deep inside his lungs so that he could be as quiet as the grass. He turned to the old man.

Riordan's wrist was rotating slowly and in his hand he held a bola. It was a primitive weapon of rawhide thongs. Stones were tied to the end of each leather. Riordan grasped the center of the weapon so that all the cords radiated from his hand and the stones dangled free. His wrist twirled faster, then the motion extended through his arm as he lifted the bola above his head. The stones spun wildly, burning the air, whistling, and just when Jubal thought his lungs would boom from the explosion of his breath, the old man pivoted on his heel and sailed the bola straight at the animal.

The leather cords scissored the dog's neck and the wail ceased. The dog thrashed on the ground, clawing helplessly at his throat. The old man and Jubal moved quickly to the animal. They crouched beside him and as Riordan pulled the rawhide thongs tighter and tighter he sang the praises of the Lord.

The dog died.

"Ave Maria," said the old man.

"Ave Maria," said his son.

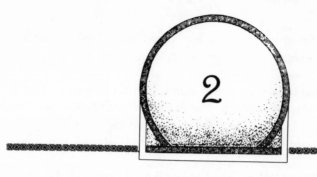

2

Solomon Moon was running out of time. Swiftly, he flipped through the pages of the jungle book that lay open on his desk. He wanted to find a picture of an exotic animal and was frustrated by photographs of common species. He knew his opponent would scoff at a tiger or giraffe, a lion or hyena. He had great respect for the man who would arrive at any moment and in no way did Solomon wish to demean his friend's intelligence. As he thumbed through the book he glanced fitfully at his office window, then down to his desk, where a pocket watch lay by the book. It was an old Ingersoll and its tick was loud, emphasizing the quick passage of the hour.

"Shit," Solomon mumbled.

"I *beg* your pardon!" The voice of Solomon's secretary, Priscilla, resonated through the office intercom.

"Oh, sorry," Solomon said. "Sorry about that." Damn. He'd forgotten to switch off the intercom. Now Priscilla would begin her lecture.

"It has been my experience," her prim little voice continued through the intercom, "that one resorts to profanity only . . ."

"Yeah," Solomon interjected. "Right." He flipped the switch on the intercom and the office was quiet once again. He closed the book of animals, rose from behind his desk, crossed to a bookcase, and knelt before it. The shelves were crammed with film scripts and galley proofs of new novels, newspaper clippings of adventurous deeds, manuscripts of plays both produced and unproduced, articles from domestic and foreign magazines, and biographies of statesmen and athletes, rock stars and pimps. The library did not so much reflect Solomon's eclectic taste as house the tools of his profession.

Solomon was vice-president of creative affairs and head of the New York story department for TransGlobal Films. Although the company maintained its principal offices at its studios in California, its chairman of the board and chief executive officer, Wilton Forest, recognized the need to support a literary department as well as a sales force for motion pictures and television films in New York. Such an arrangement facilitated the constant meetings between TransGlobal personnel and TV network representatives, and it gave access to a literary source of supply offered by publishing firms, writers' agents, and dozens of theatrical producers on and off Broadway. Because office space was at a premium in mid-Manhattan, the company had bought its own building, thus enjoying convenient quarters and a financial reward from its role as landlord.

Solomon's office was on the eighteenth floor. It was a corner office, reflecting the status of his position. It was, as he pointed out modestly to any visitor, a kind of geographical compensation for longevity of service.

Kneeling before the bookcase, he fumbled among the manuscripts until he found what he wanted. He pulled out a beautifully illustrated book of birds. The color plates were superb, and when he swiftly riffled the pages, the iridescent feathers of phalaropes and pheasants flashed in the sunlight from the window as if the birds were rising on their wings.

Solomon's study of birds, his delight in them, was caused not so much by their beauty as by the pattern of their flight. Whether skimming a sea or splitting the sky, even momentarily poised on a telephone wire, they were, it seemed to Solomon, constantly in motion. The spontaneity of their flight was unrestrained, without inhibition, primitive in its beauty; it was as if they were on their way to join a flock whose secret destination was not the end of the trip but the trip itself. Solomon envied them terribly, for he felt that the freedom of their wings allowed them to enter unexpected places and to instinctively explore the surprises of the world until, finally, lifting higher and higher, they would soar into the sun and die well.

Solomon was unable to reveal to others that in his middle years he had gradually succumbed to a feeling that he would *not* die well. He did not fear death, knew it to be the natural future of all men. What gnawed at him was that he could not connect that future with his past. His history had been stolen from him and the absence of it had created a submerged and inarticulate anger in his heart. It disallowed connection to other men. He had no flock with which to fly.

Now, he paused at a picture of a ruby-throated hummingbird. Unlike other birds, they were able to fly backwards. (To their beginnings? Solomon wondered for an instant.) He knew their idiosyncracies. They had weak feet, which prevented them from perching more than momentarily. Oh, yes, he thought, this bird will do!

He rose from his kneeling position and automatically glanced out the window to check the two things on his mind. He studied the gutters far below on Park Avenue to see if any debris was moving. Although in his fifties, Solomon had retained his boyhood fascination with kites, and it was his habit to check the velocity of the wind. He saw that scraps of paper and leaves from the avenue's meridian plantings lay dormant. There was no fair wind for flying. He leaned forward at the waist and peered upwards through the window, but the sharp vertical rise of the building prohibited him from seeing anything except the sky. He turned, but when he heard the bumping sound he knew so well he spun back. The sight of a window washer's scaffolding board only inches above his head galvanized Solomon to action.

He hurried to the door of his office. He edged it open. Except for Priscilla, the long hall that ran the length of the office floor was abandoned — secretarial desks vacant, other doors ajar, revealing the emptiness of the offices beyond. It was lunch hour on Friday and the coming weekend prompted a curious casualness among employees of Trans-Global. It was as if, Solomon thought, the serfs had deserted the kingdom, knowing royalty was at play. Priscilla had not seen him. Quietly, he closed the door and locked it.

He returned to his desk, opened a lower drawer, and removed a high-wattage spotlight bulb. He took out the bulb in his gooseneck desk lamp and replaced it with the new bulb. He turned the lamp to face the wall opposite the window. He flicked on the lamp and the wall was splashed with a hot circle of light. He sat down behind the desk and swiveled his chair to face the window. He hummed to himself. Solomon was happy.

Slowly, the scaffolding descended. The heavy guiding ropes slipped across the gleaming windowpane, which never really looked as if it needed cleaning, and the narrow wooden platform rode downward. It stopped at the lower edge of Solomon's windowframe.

A window washer stood at the center of his board. His name was Harold. Although he and Solomon had never actually met, each knew the other's name, watching each other through the window, they had been friends for years. Harold was a tall, thin elderly black man who sported a luxuriant gray mustache, the ends of which were waxed into needle points. The heavy growth on his lip compensated for the gleaming baldness of his skull, and he knew it gave him a fine military air. Harold snapped his heels together, only slightly rocking the scaffold hanging hundreds of feet above the street, and saluted Solomon. Solomon returned the salute, then spun his chair around to face the wall. As he did so his glance slipped across the framed photograph of his wife, Kendal.

The candid snapshot on Solomon's desk was of a lovely, middle-aged woman kneeling in a rose garden. She was dressed in faded blue jeans and a man's blue chambray shirt that was unbuttoned low enough to reveal the slight swelling of her breasts. Wisps of gray-blond hair curled from beneath a red bandanna tied loosely but with infinite style around her head. Her green eyes were totally without guile. Mud smeared her cheeks and her lips, which were parted in a grin. The pleasure on her face made her look as if she were watching the antics of a clown. For just a moment Solomon wondered what she would think of the game he was about to play. She was wary of any waste of time.

He glanced back at the window. Harold leaned forward, squashing his nose flat against the window pane as he peered in. Even though the glass was bronzed, he could plainly see the hot circle of light on the wall. Solomon started the game. He bent the upper part of his body forward and placed his elbows on the desk so that his raised forearms were directly in front of the spotlight. He folded his hands and lifted one finger. Its dark shadow split the circle of light on the wall. Solomon heard Harold knock three times on the window, acknowledging the clarity of Solomon's shadow play.

Adroitly manipulating his ten fingers, Solomon shadow sketched various animals upon the wall and after each he paused and checked the window. The black man studied the figures and after serious but swift consideration he used a grease pencil to write upon the glass. He wrote backwards so that Solomon could easily read the legend and, because he knew that Solomon was timing him with his Ingersoll, he wrote quickly and in a splendid Spencerian flow as he identified the figures on the wall. This was no game for amateurs. The window washer had only one minute to scribble his answer, and Solomon was diabolically clever with his fingers. He did not insult Harold's imagination by projecting simple shadows.

Solomon's fingers twisted into a complicated pattern and a shadow bounced awkwardly on the wall. The window washer knocked. Solomon turned. The black man wrote on the glass: *One-legged duck.* Solomon glanced at his watch. Boy, he thought, only eight seconds. He thrust five upright fingers in front of the lamp and their shadows stabbed the wall. Slowly, he glided a pencil through his open fingers. There was an instant knock on the window and Solomon turned to see Harold's look of disdain as he wrote across the glass: *Snake in the weeds*. Damn, Solomon muttered, two in a row. But he had one more chance and, referring quickly to the bird book open on his desk, he tasted victory. Simulating the branch of a tree, he held one finger of his left hand on a horizontal level. He bunched the middle fingers of his right hand into a partial fist and let the forefinger and pinky perch lightly on top of the extended finger of his left hand. Suddenly, the forefinger slipped off the simulated branch, and Solomon's bunched hand darted backwards. He repeated this maneuver twice. Certain that Harold would admit defeat, Solomon kept his back to the window. He knew he was smiling and he didn't wish Harold to think him smug. He looked at the Ingersoll and saw the seconds ticking by, and when a full minute had elapsed he turned in triumph.

His smile disappeared. Harold lounged nonchalantly on his scaffold, leaning lightly against the protective railing, the tips of his mustache glistening in the sunlight. Across the window was his answer: *Bad-footed hummingbird flying backwards*.

"Son of a bitch," Solomon said aloud. He shook his head and grinned as he applauded Harold. The window washer bowed. He wiped the letters off the windowpane, then tugged at the hawsers. The scaffolding descended slowly. Solomon watched until only Harold's gleaming pate was visible and then that, too, was gone. The game was done.

"There, you see," Solomon said to the framed photograph of his wife. "It took hardly any time at all."

He checked the Ingersoll and saw that he would have to hurry to catch his train to Westport, where Kendal would pick him up. He had asked Priscilla to cancel any appointments scheduled for the afternoon. He buzzed her on the intercom. There was no answer. He unlocked his door and stepped into the hall. Priscilla's desk was empty. Solomon sighed. His secretary made a fetish of her figure and to maintain its slimness she resorted to diuretics; therefore, she was constantly running to the bathroom. He scribbled a hasty note and left it next to her typewriter. The note said he'd gone to the reading of a new play that he hoped would prove suitable film material. He returned to his office, put away his spotlight, straightened his bookcase, and dusted his desk with his handkerchief so that the marks of his heel would not be visible to Priscilla.

He crossed the office to a large antique armoire. Gently, he eased it away from the wall and reached for something hidden behind it. He removed a slim oblong box of heavy cardboard. He hefted it in his hands, enjoying the weight of it, and when he returned to his desk he was smiling slightly.

On his desk was a film script, its title, *Shadow on the Grass*, printed in bold block letters on the cover. Solomon reached for it and then paused. No, he told himself, it's *my* weekend, not *theirs*. And he reminded himself that the script was excellent and needed very little work. He left it on his desk and moved into the hall, the oblong box under his arm. He leaned over Priscilla's desk and extended his note. *P.S. It's a very long play. I won't be back. Yr. obed. servant.* He crossed out *Yr. obed. servant.* Priscilla would not be amused. He signed it S.M. He crossed out S.M. She might think he were referring to something sadomasochistic. He left the note unsigned.

The thought of being in Vermont in just a few hours cheered him and he was whistling as he rang for the elevator. Stepping into the elevator, he saw that it was occupied by two men in somber suits. They were executives from the West Coast office of TransGlobal. They were talking animatedly about completing a deal for the distribution of a film made by an independent producer. Both nodded at but, concentrating on their verbal celebration, said nothing to Solomon.

Referring to the independent producer, one of the men said, "We got him by the balls."

"Fuck 'm," said the other man.

Solomon studied the floor. He stopped whistling.

He crossed west to Fifth Avenue and hurried downtown. It was a detour to Grand Central but one he took every Friday. He knew if he varied this ritual his two friends would be disappointed. He did not want to violate their trust. Fifth Avenue was crowded with sightseers and window-shoppers, and Solomon weaved expertly through them, occasionally shifting the oblong box he carried from under one arm to another and imagining himself a broken-field runner or a soldier bravely crossing a minefield as he rushed to the rescue of comrades. By the time he reached the library he was breathing heavily from his imagined daring.

There, sitting side by side on the wide steps between the two stone lions who guarded the library were his friends. It was difficult to tell the age of the woman because her head was wrapped in a long scarf which, in turn, was covered by a man's gray fedora, its wide felt brim turned down on all sides and shadowing the woman's face. She was dressed in ragtag clothing and she wore GI boots. She was surrounded by string bags crammed with a varied assortment of junk that had obviously been claimed from trash bins on the streets she'd walked. Next to her was a hulking man with a flattened nose and cauliflower ears, each, like the scar tissue around his eyes, attesting to a ring career that must have ended painfully and many years ago. Resting on the step next to him was a battered suitcase secured by a canvas strap.

Solomon ran up the library steps.

"Hey, Solomon," Clarence greeted him, "you buyin'?"

"Well," Solomon panted, "if you have something nice."

"Nice!" Gloria pulled Clarence's suitcase toward her. She began to unstrap it. "You think he'd stiff ya, Solomon, all these years? Lookit! Clarence, he got this deal with a jobber. I mean, lookit!"

She opened the suitcase. It was filled with men's ties. Most of them were designed in garish colors, with oversized polka dots and zigzagged stripes, but they were not stained nor torn. They were new. They were stolen. Solomon knew they were stolen. Both Gloria and Clarence knew that Solomon knew. None of them had ever thought it necessary to point out the obvious.

On an afternoon some years ago when Solomon had decided to skip lunch and take a walk instead, he had strolled by the library steps and seen Gloria and Clarence playing jacks, their little red rubber ball bouncing in the sunlight. Impulsively, he had asked if he might join them. They had been so pleasant that when they showed him the ties and suggested that he might want to replenish his wardrobe, he'd been unable to resist. It was apparent that the ties represented the only source of income between them and it pleased Solomon that he was able to help. It had become a Friday ritual.

"Gee," Solomon said, "this is a beaut." He removed a tie whose green background was laced with orange stripes. He ran his hands across the cheap material. "I don't know. Looks expensive."

"Ya could have it what it cost," Clarence said.

Solomon nodded. "Must have set you back, huh?"

"Well, yeah, wattaya think? Stuff like this, it don't come from no junkie."

"Right," Gloria said. "You could see this ain't no sweatshop item."

"I don't know," Solomon repeated. It was all part of the ceremony and he knew that it made them feel as if they had to work hard to make a living.

"Hey," Clarence said, holding his arms wide, his hands upturned as if he were about to embrace Solomon. "You an' me, we go back, huh? Ya got a fin, I take a fin."

"Boy," Solomon said, "that's pretty good. Okay." He gave Clarence a five-dollar bill. Automatically, the big man tore it in two, pocketed one half, and gave the other to Gloria.

"We fight," Gloria explained for the hundredth time to Solomon, "he don't walk out."

"I gotta run," Solomon said, folding the tie into his jacket pocket.

"Hey, yeah," Clarence said. "Take care of ya'self, ya know?"

Outside of Grand Central, Solomon threw away the tie and hurried into the station. He reached for a copy of the New York *Post* on a newsstand but a young man in Levi's edged past him and whisked the paper off the pile.

"Sorry," Solomon said as he stepped aside.

The young man ignored him. He tossed coins onto the pile of newspapers and ran for his train. Solomon lifted the coins the young man had thrown and proferred them to the news vendor behind his stand.

"Jus' leave 'em, buddy, okay?" the vendor said, obviously irritated by Solomon's action.

"Oh," Solomon said. "Sorry." He removed a five-dollar bill from his wallet. "The *Post*, please."

"Huh?" the vendor asked.

"The *Post*. The New York *Post*?"

The vendor stared at the five-dollar bill. "Ya don't got change?"

"I don't think so," Solomon said. He quickly patted his pockets but could feel no coins. "That's funny," he said as he continued the search. "I almost always have —"

"C'mon c'mon c'mon," snapped the vendor, "ya holdin' up traffic." He snatched the bill from Solomon's hand and began to make change.

"If it would help any," Solomon said apologetically, "I'll take a pack of cigarettes."

"Hey," the vendor barked, "gimme a break, willya? Jus' tell me what you want, huh?"

"Well, I really just want the *Post*."

"So take the fuckin' *Post*, okay? C'mon a'ready!"

"Yeah. Sure," Solomon said. He took a copy of the paper. The vendor slapped change into Solomon's hand and shook his head in disgust. "Jee-eez."

A few customers stood behind Solomon, waiting impatiently for the sale to be concluded. Solomon was embarrassed by what he felt had been his foolish attempt to find rapport with such a surly man and he wondered what would happen if he opened the oblong box under his arm. But he wasn't sure what the legal ramifications would be if he exposed the contents in a public place. He decided a lightly mocking tone might be best and so, neatly folding the newspaper under his arm, he turned away from the newsstand and smiled at a woman behind him.

"He's charming, isn't he?" he said as he nodded toward the vendor. "Isn't he charming?"

"Please," the woman said. "I don't know you, mister."

"Oh, boy," Solomon said.

As he walked into the tunnel to board his train, he hummed *New York, New York, it's a helluva town.* He was glad he lived in Connecticut. He was even happier that he had recently purchased a hundred acres and an old farmhouse in Down Derry. He was certain that the pastoral peace of that quiet, little Vermont village would provide a necessary retreat from the clang and clamor of Manhattan. This weekend he planned to explore every corner of his new land and, perhaps, beyond to the mountain ridges in the north. He hoped it would rain. He liked to walk in the rain. Kendal did, too.

It was too early in the day for the average commuter to return home, so the train was uncrowded. Solomon took a window seat in the rear car, a smoker. He tapped out a low-tar filtered menthol cigarette from his pack. He tore off the filter and put the undamaged end of the cigarette in his mouth. He removed a wooden kitchen match from a vest pocket, struck its head with his thumbnail, and was pleased to see an immediate spurt of flame. It was a gesture he'd copied from western heroes of cinematic fame. As a boy he'd practiced it until he became proficient. He inhaled deeply and exhaled through his nose. He liked the sting in his nostrils. The expertise of his gestures reminded him of the one he had not perfected. He removed his cigarette from his mouth and placed two fingers of one hand between his lips. He paused. He didn't want to disturb anyone.

He shifted in his seat and looked behind him in the railroad car. A heavyset woman with frizzy hair, dressed in a man's stained raincoat, hunched in a rear seat. Her eyes were closed and her head bowed over a large paper bag that filled her lap. The bag overflowed with scraps of torn cloth. Each time the woman breathed, a thin strip of black velvet fluttered beneath her nose. It reminded Solomon of the trembling of a blackbird's wings, the preliminary quiver of a crow's flight. He turned away from the woman and glanced upwards. The oblong box rested securely on an overhead rack. Solomon's mouth twitched in a secret smile; and he was startled to feel the fingers he'd left between his lips. He'd almost forgotten what he'd wanted to practice. He placed his fingers in the exact center of his mouth, leaving just a quarter of an inch between them. He curled his tongue backwards so that the tip touched his palate. He took a deep breath. He blew it out between his fingers. But he failed to whistle. The only sound he heard was a rush of air. He tried again. He failed again. He shook his head. He could not understand how whistling through his fingers could prove so difficult.

The train started. As it lurched forward and picked up speed, the wheels clacking through the dark tunnel, Solomon studied his own reflection in the window. He hoped he might discover that he had positioned his fingers in some strange way that prevented whistling but he saw that to all outward appearances his technique was accurate. He kept trying until saliva began to seep from between his lips and he was hyperventilating. He stopped when the train emerged from the tunnel and instead of his image on the window all he could see was the sad landscape.

The train stopped right outside the tunnel. Solomon's view of tenements was unobstructed. There were rows of squat brick buildings, their stone defaced by graffiti messages of anger and despair, their street gutters polka-dotted with used condoms and banana peels, and each street looked like a graveyard for abandoned cars. It was a mean horizon offering little comfort to its observer and even less to those who dwelled there.

Solomon saw a small black boy roller-skating down the center of a street and he marveled at the smile on the boy's face. He had a sudden impulse to break the train window and shout at the boy.

"What is it," he wanted to call, "what is it that you know?"

A pigeon exploded out of one of the paneless windows of a tenement. Solomon turned in his seat to watch the bird's flight. It skimmed the rooftops, weaving through steely woods of broken television antennas, and then sailed above the ghetto as if to wash its feathers in the sun. Solomon twisted further in his seat; he didn't want to lose sight of the bird. He hoped the bird was wild, unbanded, independent of man, soaring with no purpose other than to test the glory of its wings. But the bird flew a circle in the sky and then plunged toward the building from which it had escaped. Its wings spread and braked against the air. It landed daintily on the rooftop and strutted proudly across the asphalt, its body puffed and its head bobbing with superfluous knowledge. Its wings beat again and the bird rose abruptly. The pigeon landed on a strange edifice, which puzzled Solomon. As he studied it, an elderly man walked into view.

Good Lord, Solomon thought and leaned forward in his seat, I know him! Solomon pressed his face close to the window but quickly realized that he was wrong. The man sported a pure-white beard and white earlocks that contrasted sharply with his traditional black garb of the Hasidim. It was the vivid contrast of black and white which had stirred Solomon's sense of recognition. He searched his memory and recalled a rainy morning when he was a boy. Forbidden by his mother and father to play in the wet weather, his father at work, his mother shopping, he'd spent the morning wandering throughout the rooms of their New York apartment, searching for some amusement to pass the hours. Like most boys, he was curious about the secrets that might be hidden in his father's chest of drawers, so, his head cocked for the sound of a front door opening, he rummaged through his father's things. Disappointed at the mundane content of the drawers, he'd closed all but one, was about to push that shut, too, when something caught his eye. It lay under his father's shirts. Solomon pulled it out. It was a photograph; old, faded, brown with age. It showed what looked like a very young man, not much older than a boy, really, standing in an empty field. Solomon turned it over. Written across the back of the photograph was a name: Rafael Fernandez Muñoz. Solomon looked again at the picture, held it up to the light, but it was difficult to discern more than the silhouette of the man and the flatness of the field. Although his name was rarely spoken, Solomon had learned that Rafael Fernandez Muñoz was his grandfather, who'd been dead for many years. He wished he knew more about him, wished that he could see the features of his face. And then a thought struck him.

He put the picture in his pocket, donned a raincoat, left a note for his mother, telling her that he had gone to the public library for books he needed to complete his homework, and left the apartment.

At a photographer's shop the clerk assured him that he could make a negative of the photo, then print it in clear black and white. The following day, Solomon picked up both the original photo and the new print, the latter startling in its clarity and revealing that the young man stood in a clearing surrounded by what looked like olive trees. Unfortunately, the man's features were still muddied, and all Solomon could see was that he squinted against the sun and that he wore a cheap black broadcloth suit and a collarless white shirt and the heavy shoes of a workingman.

Solomon replaced the original photo beneath his father's shirts. He kept the other one. During the day, not wanting his father to know that he'd searched his drawers, Solomon hid the print. But at night, when he was alone, he stuck it between the glass and frame of his bureau's mirror and compared his own face to that of the man in the field, the grandfather about whom he knew so little.

One morning he forgot to remove it, and when he returned from school it was no longer in the mirror. Angry, no longer caring that his deception had been revealed, he demanded to know what had become of it. His parents professed ignorance, his father warning Solomon to mind his manners, his mother cautioning him not to get overly upset, both treating the disappearance of the photograph as trivial.

Solomon never did discover what happened to the photographic print and when, soon afterward, he sneaked into his father's room, he found nothing beneath the shirts. The original, too, was gone.

As the years passed and Solomon grew older, the memory of the photograph faded, and he accepted his father's point of view that familial history was of no great import.

Then why now, Solomon asked himself as he stared through the train's window at the elderly Jew on the rooftop, do I feel such a return of anger? Certainly there was no connection between himself and the old man with a white beard — even less than there was between him and the shadowy figure who stood in the field, his eyes squinted at the sun.

In a reflex action, Solomon, too, squinted at the structure on which the pigeon rested. Two canvas sheets had been attached to the brick side of a chimney. A distance of three or four feet separated them. The two sides of canvas, each some five feet high, were held stiffly perpendicular to the asphalt flooring of the roof by thin battens. The elderly Jew, crouching slightly between the canvas walls, was placing narrow wooden slats in a continuous row along the top of the three-sided room. He finished making his roof and then took great care that each slat was slightly separated from the next one. It was obvious to Solomon that anyone taking refuge in such an awkward shelter would be drenched by rain.

The Jew adjusted the last slat on his roof and stepped out of the make-shift cubicle. He stood quietly and admired his handiwork. A look of absolute delight crossed his face. He smiled at the pigeon, which remained perched on the corner of the strange little house. The Hasid clapped his hands and did a little jig of joy. He stooped and opened a brown paper bag. He removed two pomegranates and three bunches of green grapes. A long piece of butcher's string was tied to each grape cluster and to each of the pomegranates. The Jew moved back into his shelter and began to tie the fruit so that it dangled from various slats on the roof. As he turned back in the direction of his paper bag, a pomegranate, tied too loosely to its slat, dropped behind him and began to roll toward the edge of the roof.

Solomon was so taken with the scene that he quickly raised his hand to wave at the man, to warn him, but he succeeded only in cracking his knuckles against the window pane. He held his breath. The pomegranate gathered speed as it rolled toward the roof's edge. The pigeon flapped its wings and lifted from its slatted perch. Even though he knew the train's window was permanently sealed, Solomon tugged at it, banged at it with the heel of his hand, and was relieved to see the old man, alerted by the sound of the bird's beating wings, scurry forward and rescue the pomegranate from its final roll. The pigeon flew back to its roost and Solomon wondered if the bird had actually warned the old man about the potential loss of his pomegranate or whether it had been about to attack the fruit.

The Hasid spit lightly on his pomegranate and rubbed it on his black coat, slowly turning it in his hand, examining it for blemishes. When he was satisfied that no damage had been done, he returned to his little house and tied the fruit securely to a slat.

Solomon heard the metallic squeal of wheels, and the train rolled forward. Now kneeling in his seat, he saw that the Jew was mouthing words to the pigeon, which sat only inches from the man's head. The Hasid plucked a grape from its cluster and held it on the palm of his hand. The pigeon dropped from its roost, landed on the man's wrist, and speared the grape with its beak. The bird rose in flight and, in an instant, was lost to sight. Solomon slid back into his seat. Unable to explain his own desire, he wished he had been able to join the Jew under his slatted roof so that, together, they might spend the day polishing pomegranates and exchanging words with the winged world that nested in the cruel, cold chimneys of Harlem.

He opened the newspaper that lay flat on his lap, and stared at the day's stories: events of gratuitous violence, national and international, made shockless by repetition. Lulled by the monotony of clacking wheels, Solomon slowly closed his eyes and fell asleep. Like most commuters, he didn't worry about missing his station. Long years of riding the train through Westchester and into Fairfield County had enabled him to set an automatic clock in his mind. An imaginary alarm would sound at the appropriate time for disembarking.

He opened his eyes at Stamford. Refreshed by his nap, he began his ritual of approaching freedom. He loosened his tie. He removed his jacket. He untied the laces of his shoes. He unbuckled his belt. He shrugged out of his vest.

Westpooooort! Westport! Through the train's loudspeaker, the conductor announced the station.

Solomon stood, tugged the shirt out of his trousers, and removed his shoes. He heard a gasp and looked toward the rear of the train to see the frizzy-haired woman watching him. He smiled politely. He didn't want her to think he was a flasher. He gathered up his jacket and vest and shoes, pulled the oblong box from its rack, and, shirt tails flapping, marched in his stockinged feet toward the door of the train.

The train slid to a stop. The doors rolled open. Solomon plunged through them, and as he ran along the station platform, artfully dodging the few other passengers who had disembarked and who were staring at him in some astonishment, he felt such a sense of liberation that he ripped at his shirt and popped his buttons, the small disks sailing through the sunlight. He sped down the steps to the parking lot, taking them two at a time, and raced toward a bright red convertible moving slowly toward him. It was a 1966 Mustang lovingly cared for by Solomon. Behind its wheel was Kendal. He saw that she was waving wildly and that in her hand she held a pair of khaki trousers and a man's old blue workshirt. His legs pumping, he sprinted toward the car, and when the wind created by his own velocity whipped back his shirt, he laughed with pleasure and sucked in his belly so that Kendal could see he was still reasonably flat and hard.

"Okay, sweetheart," he shouted, his lips curled back like Bogart's, "let's hit it!"

Kendal gunned the engine and swerved the car around so that as Solomon reached it, he was running alongside the slowly moving car. Solomon was panting and sweat ran down his face. Galloping beside the open convertible, he tossed his clothes and the oblong box into the rear seat and then, one hand clutching the chassis, vaulted into the car, sprawling across the passenger seat, his face flat in Kendal's lap.

He bit her belly.

"Oh, God, Solomon," she cried, "you're crazy. You're certifiably crazy!"

"And you love it," he grinned at her as he twisted his head in her lap and looked up at her clear green eyes.

"Yes," she said. "Yes, I love it!"

She slammed into a higher gear and the car surged ahead. In a moment they had crossed the parking lot and raced up the entrance ramp of the Connecticut Turnpike. They sped toward Vermont.

Solomon eased back into the passenger seat. He reached down to the floorboards and lifted the crumpled khaki trousers, the blue workshirt, and a pair of dirty white sneakers into which Kendal had stuffed rolled sweat socks. He shoved them into the space between his and Kendal's seats. He tore off his buttonless shirt and let the wind slap his bare chest. He pulled off the trousers of his suit. He unsnapped his garters, ripped off his calf-length socks. He crossed his legs under him and sat in his blue boxer shorts, and the sight of her almost naked husband perched like a Buddha in the open convertible filled Kendal with delight. But when he reached behind him and removed an object from the oblong box her eyes darkened with surprise and she cried out.

"Jesus, Solomon. Jesus!"

Solomon grinned as he raised the shotgun in his hands.

3

Pow pow!'' Solomon said as he sighted down the twin barrels of the shotgun. He swung it in an arc as he followed the imaginary flight of a bird. When he completed the sweeping motion, the gun pointed toward a car passing on the right. Shocked at the sight of the weapon, the driver whipped his wheel over and his car swerved sharply, rocked for an instant on two wheels, then spurted ahead in a burst of speed.

"There," Kendal said, "you see?"

"He's not supposed to pass on the right," Solomon said indignantly. "I ought to take his license number."

"Darling, do put your pants on," Kendal said. Soon they would approach the outskirts of New Haven, and Kendal waved vaguely in the direction of the university. "What would they think of you at Yale?"

"It would depend on who saw me," Solomon answered thoughtfully. "I mean, if they have a large gay community . . ."

"Bugger off." Kendal's expletive had a curious ring. Although for many years she had been a naturalized citizen of the United States, her voice was still tinged with British overtones. Not obvious in casual conversation, it resonated when she resorted to exclamations, obscenities, or remembered lullabies of the music hall, and it was most apparent during any flash of passion. She had a remarkable ability to make vulgarities sound like the start of a sonnet.

"Okay," Solomon said. "I will put on my pants."

He twisted in his seat and placed the shotgun back in its oblong box. He pulled the crumpled clothing from between the front seats and proceeded to dress.

"I packed a lovely Camembert," Kendal said, "and seeded rye and some Anjou pears and a bottle of that Chardonnay you like so much, and now look.''

" 'And now look,' " Solomon repeated as he leaned forward and tied the laces of his sneakers. He wasn't mocking her. He was in the habit of repeating phrases Kendal used to complete thoughts which were clear to her but unfathomable to him. " 'And now look,' " he said again and frowned. "Sorry, darling. I'm not quite following you."

"We can't have a picnic with a cannon in the car."

"We can leave it in the car and we'll get out."

"But we'll know it's there. Why did you get the damn thing, anyway?"

"Because," Solomon said, "I want to take a walk with it."

"You what?"

"I want to take a walk with it."

"What ever are you going to do with it?"

"I don't know. Put it over my shoulder. Carry it under my arm. Wave it around. I don't know. Whatever a hunter does with a gun."

"Oh, Solomon, you're not going hunting? You're not going to shoot something?"

"Well, no," Solomon said. "No, I'm not really going to shoot anything. I'm just going hunting."

"You're not making the least bit of sense."

"Yes, I am. I mean, it's all very simple. It's sort of a game I've made up. Like map-reading. What do we do when we take a walk?"

"We don't *do* anything. We just take a walk."

"Exactly," Solomon said. "That's the thing. We just sort of amble, don't we?"

"I think that's nice."

"So do I. But not always. Not every time. Now and then we should make a game of it. One of us could hide something in the woods and then give the other a map to show where it's hidden. Then you'd have to learn how to follow the coordinates of the map, so that —"

"Why can't I hide the thing and you follow the coordinates?"

"We'll take turns."

"You don't need a gun to follow a map. That's dumb."

Solomon sighed. "The gun is another game. We can pretend we're hunters, you see, and we have to find something to eat."

"We have plenty to eat."

"Jesus, Kendal," Solomon said, "will you let me finish?"

"Well, I'm not going to eat it. I don't care what you shoot, I'm just bloody well not going to eat it."

"I'm not going to shoot anything," Solomon said patiently. "I'm just going to pretend. But you can't pretend unless you do it all the way. I mean, you have to give authenticity to the game. That's why I got the gun. There are a lot of grouse in our woods and . . ."

"They're darling," Kendal said. "They're darling birds."

"Yes," Solomon said, "they're darling birds. I'm going into the woods and —"

"Shoot them. I think that's awful."

There was a long pause before Solomon spoke again.

"Would you like some Camembert?" he asked.

"Yes, please," Kendal said.

As they picnicked on ripe Camembert that Solomon slathered generously on slices of heavily seeded rye bread, they left the cities of Connecticut behind them, and by the time they had crossed the Massachusetts border and entered Vermont, they had consumed the chilled Chardonnay. It put them both into a splendid mood, and there was no more discussion of the hunting game. Together, they admired the brilliant crimson and golden hues of turning leaves and they breathed deeply of the cool, clean air. The early October sun was hot and Solomon leaned back against his seat. He rested one hand on Kendal's thigh. She covered it with hers. They drove many miles in companionable silence.

As they moved deeper into the Green Mountains, Solomon studied the lands on either side of the state highway and wondered idly why it was that this landscape gave him so much pleasure. He was born and bred a city boy, at home in Manhattan's streets, at ease with urban mechanization. He was not, he reminded himself, a man who stood in fields, squinting at the sun. And yet he lusted for woodland and meadow. The sight of wildflowers cracking through a granite slab filled him with awe. Such a tender triumph never ceased to amaze him. It was as if the natural phenomena of the land proved all things belonged to each other — as if each flower, each tree, each stone were driven to seek its rightful place and that, together, they formed a secret community, a gossamer tissue invisible to man. Invisible and perhaps, Solomon mused, secretly inviolate. He tried to imagine some great hand from above lifting that tissue, much like a man taking hold of the center of a giant spiderweb and gently raising it to the sky.

But something white slandered the sky. Solomon sat up, opened his eyes wide, and raised his head. A junco flew across the pasture, its white tail feathers flashing. Its flight carried the bird across the path of the moving car and as it blazed above Solomon's head he heard the bird's swift trilling, the sound so like stones striking together that Solomon expected to see sparks ignite the air.

"Darling, look!" Kendal cried.

He glanced swiftly at her, expecting to see that she, too, was watching the bird, puzzled then when he saw that she was staring straight ahead. He looked forward.

They were nearing an old covered bridge. It spanned the river that eventually curled alongside Down Derry. The bridge was one of few that remained in this area of southern Vermont. Because it enhanced the legendary rural nature of the state, it had been restored and, along with the yearly arrival of autumn foliage, the cold trout streams, the mountain ski resorts, the antique shops, and the beauty of the Green Mountains themselves, it assumed its rightful place as a tourist attraction. The bridge was only a few miles from the village of Down Derry. Sitting by the shadowed entrance of the bridge were an old man with a white beard and an adolescent boy. Charmed, Kendal thought they looked like a benign sorcerer and his apprentice. In the boy's lap was an Irish harp and the music he was playing was as sweet as the junco's song. Displayed on the ground in front of the old man were a dozen pieces of pottery. Although the ware varied in shape and glaze, all the pots and vases and bowls were of exquisite design.

"Oh, let's get one for Darby," Kendal said, referring to their daughter. "She adores these things."

"Sure," Solomon said, glancing at his watch. He was worried that Jabez Tuttle, their handyman, would not wait for what Solomon had planned before the sun went down. "Only let's not get into a long blah-blah-blah about the technical aspects of the craft."

"Why would I do that?"

"I know the curlicues of your mind."

"Didn't you like the wine?" Kendal asked.

" 'Didn't you like the wine?' " Solomon repeated softly and then shrugged, not really wishing to explore the non sequitur. "The wine was good. It was very, very good."

"All right, then," Kendal said, ending the matter.

She braked to a stop only a few feet from the pottery and leaned over the side of the car. "Hi."

"Shhh," Riordan Flynn said and pointed to his son. "He's playing for you, don't you see?"

"How lovely," Kendal said. "Isn't that lovely, Solomon?"

"Lovely. You bet." Solomon was still thinking about Jabez Tuttle.

Jubal smiled at the Moons and then lowered his eyes so that he could watch his fingers as he plucked at the strings of his harp. Although his hands were broad and muscular, his fingers were unusually long and slender and beautifully shaped, and Jubal took care of them. After any menial task the old man might assign him, such as digging a grave or scraping out the intestines of an owl, Jubal made sure to wash his fingers carefully, clean his nails and pare them with the old man's beaver-tooth knife. With a pumice rock he would then smooth the hard calluses he had developed and rub his fingers with bear grease so that the flesh remained supple, the skin smooth. In this way he made certain that each time he played the harp his fingers would respond swiftly and surely to the music in his head.

For it was in the songs he dreamed that Jubal imagined tales of wonder. Each note he struck, each chord he strummed, conjured up shadowy figures from the strange world of his pretense. It was a world inhabited by men and women unlike any he had actually known. Undefined, lacking in specific shape, always in shadow, these figures drifted through an undulating sky. The sky was golden and its ripples were like the sea; the figures, faceless in their drift, moved constantly toward each other, through each other, and returned to what Jubal imagined was their circle of affection. He was not sure of this. He had no experience with affection or what he conjectured was affection. He knew only that the men and women in his musically dreamed world reached out even in their shadowy fashion and touched each other as they circled the golden sky. Their touchings caused ripples of the sky to curl like waves, but before these waves could crest and fall into foamy surf the figures had passed through each other and continued their drift, endless and silent save for the notes of the harp. Jubal always held his breath at such moments, for he was sure that if only he could arrest the drifting figures, the golden waves would crest and the surf would break and at that moment it would be possible for his fingers to invent a new form of music, a melody so pure and fine, so wondrous, that the sea would slide inside him and he, too, would turn golden.

The waves were rising now as he played for the strangers in their red convertible, but before the sea crested Jubal heard the man speak.

"Kendal," Solomon said, "we're going to be late."

Jubal stopped playing. Kendal left the car and crouched alongside of Riordan Flynn. She lifted a bowl from the ground.

"Did you make these?" she asked.

"I did."

"They're beautiful," Kendal said.

"Yes," said Riordan.

Kendal smiled at the old man, amused at his apparent reticence. "I'm sorry. I'm not trying to pry out your secrets, you know. It's just that they're so . . . so . . . ."

"Beautiful," said Riordan.

"Yes," Kendal said.

Solomon checked his watch. He got out of the car and walked over to the old man and Kendal. "Kendal."

"I know, I know." She edged closer to Riordan. "How long do you fire your clay?"

"As long as I need," Riordan said.

Solomon, impatient, shifted his weight and absentmindedly chewed his thumbnail.

"I've never seen such delicate colors," Kendal said. "They're so pale. I'd think they'd wash out in the kiln."

"Jesus," Solomon muttered. He saw the old man's eyes flick toward him. He didn't wish to hurt the old man's feelings but he knew that Jabez would not wait forever. He spit a sliver of his thumbnail onto the ground and then, without thinking, ran his sneaker over it, covering it with dust. When he looked up he saw that Riordan was staring at him and that the old man's gaze was as bright as a bird's, and when Riordan shifted his gaze from Solomon's face and stared at the tiny mound of dust which covered the splinter of thumbnail Solomon suddenly felt like a small boy about to be chastised by his father. He resented the old man's implied criticism and so deliberately stepped on the mound of dust and turned to Kendal.

"Darling," Solomon said, "why don't you buy one of the bowls? And then we can go."

Kendal rested the bowl in the palm of her hands and held it up against the sunlight. "How much is this?" she asked Riordan.

"Whatever you wish," Riordan said softly, his eyes still on the ground beneath Solomon's foot. Jubal glanced quickly at the old man but said nothing.

"Oh, dear," Kendal said. "I really don't know what it's worth to you."

"Whatever it's worth to *you*," Riordan said, finally looking up from the ground. "That's the thing of it, isn't it?"

"Well, yes, I suppose." Kendal felt uneasy. She didn't like to bargain; nor did she want to underpay such a gentle old man. She knew that pottery similar to this sold in Westport boutiques for ten or fifteen dollars; and yet, she thought, this really is special. "Would twenty dollars be all right?" she asked hesitantly.

"Whatever it's worth to you," Riordan repeated.

"Yes. Well," Kendal said. Her purse was still in the car, so she turned to Solomon. "Darling, I think twenty-five, don't you?"

"Sure," Solomon said, anxious to depart for the farm. He removed his wallet, took out the appropriate sum and held it out to Riordan. But the old man did not even see the money. His gaze had returned to the mound of dust on which Solomon stood. Jubal looked at his father and then at Solomon and laid down his harp. He moved to Solomon and took the money.

"Thanks," Solomon said.

The boy just nodded.

Kendal and Solomon returned to the car. Holding the bowl in her lap while Solomon drove, Kendal waved to the boy as the car entered the covered bridge.

Jubal nodded again. The car disappeared, its tires clacking over the wooden planks of the bridge. It reemerged on the other side of the bridge and then was shortly out of sight on the road curving toward Down Derry.

Jubal turned back to his father. The old man, his weight still lowered onto his haunches, shuffled forward a few paces and stared closely at the ground where Solomon had stood. He reached out and ran one finger through the mound of dust, scraping gently at it, sifting it, until he had uncovered the tiny splinter of thumbnail. His father's actions puzzled Jubal and he was about to speak, but he saw that Riordan's whole body had begun to shake. Slowly, the old man rose and quieted himself. He stood very still. He made the sign of the cross. He turned to the boy and spoke, his voice almost without breath.

"Why does this man call on Jesus and yet not raise his eyes to the Lord? Why does this man spit his filth upon the ground?"

Riordan turned. His gaze moved across the wooden bridge, beyond to where the road stretched toward Down Derry, and beyond Down Derry to the mountain where he and his son dwelled in their cave.

"Why does he come to this place?" Riordan whispered. "Why does he blaspheme the ground on which we walk? Why?"

The litany of questions was spoken in such a musical cadence that Jubal knew he need not answer even if he could — knew that, much as he, Jubal, strummed his fingers on the strings of his harp, Riordan, too, was listening to a song only he heard.

The old man knew what he had to do. He closed his eyes so that a black curtain shielded him from a casual view of his surroundings, and so that when he looked again at God's province, he would be able to detect the slightest sign that would indicate his mission. Refreshed by this momentary blindness, he opened his eyes, certain now that his bright stare would be a connecting tunnel to the Father's vision. He studied the gentle landscape of flanking meadows, aspen and birch bending slightly before the wind, wildflowers fluttering, the quiver of grass. He turned to the river running beneath the bridge. He watched the flow of water and prayed for revelation.

Early autumn rains had raised the level of the river and it rushed swiftly between its sandy banks, cascading whitely over rocks, spitting at tree stumps, hissing softly like a snake awakened. But Riordan ignored this natural flow. He concentrated on a movement of water at variance with the central current, for he believed that it was in the opposition of things that he would find his answer. Beneath the bright glass of the sunlit river he saw the serpent twist of an errant eddy, clashing with the rhythm of the river, and in its angled course he saw a shadow quiver. The dark shape was a trout and Riordan knew it was sucking greedily on insects washed loose from the river's banks. The fish, camouflaged by the black turbulence of the chaotic eddy, was swallowing the life of the river. The words of the Psalm came to Riordan.

He made darkness his secret place.

And when he turned back to Jubal, the old man's voice was so light he might have been singing with an angel.

"That's it, boyo," he sang to Jubal, "that's it. A secret lies in the darkness of the stranger's soul; and we, you and I, graced by the mercy of His hand, must lay it bare!"

Riordan's hands plunged inside the cloak of the Apostles. He pulled at the bramble whip until it hung loose below his waist, then he clutched the strands and swiftly ran his hands across the wicked thorns, forward and back, forward and back, forward and back, until in less than a minute his skin was ripped and blood ran freely from his fingers. When Jubal saw the exaltation in his father's face he felt the muscles quiver across his back. He was not sure whether the trembling came from excitement or from fear. He knew only that once again they would ride on the wind of the Lord.

4

They passed the general store in Down Derry, then turned right onto a gravel road that led to the farm. The road rose sharply up a hill; as they crested it, they both silently acknowledged the single blackened pine tree that marked Ray Poole's place.

It was a sad landmark, for Ray's grown son and daughter-in-law had been killed by the tree. A summer storm, whipping swiftly through the mountains, had caught them in the fields. When they ran for the house, they passed under the pine tree as it was struck by lightning. The top twenty feet was severed and the two who were fleeing from the storm were crushed under the weight, one broken branch puncturing the jugular of Ray's son. The tree was black from burn now, its remaining branches without needles, but Ray refused to cut it down. He said it filled him with hate and that hate was as life-giving as love.

Poole had retired as the village postmaster and spent most of his hours silently casting homemade flies into a beaver pond close by the road under whose western bank grew roots of the tree of hate. There were some in the village who thought that Ray was really fishing for the ghost of his children.

After the beavers had abandoned the pond, Ray, with the help of his grandson, Andy, had cleaned out the fallen birch trees and ripped a path through the mud dam, so that the stream which crossed his land and the Moons' could run freely and its temperature would be lower, making it habitable to trout. On many Sunday mornings, Andy would walk the two miles up the road to the Moons' farm and shyly present them with a breakfast of fresh fish. He rarely said anything on these occasions, but if Darby were present he would linger a little, shuffling awkwardly from foot to foot, content to look with sidelong glances at the young woman so different from the farm girls he had known that she might have been from an alien star. What fascinated Andy was Darby's spontaneity. When he'd learned that city people had bought Jabez Tuttle's farm and that they had a daughter still in her twenties, he had fully expected to meet someone who would epitomize the chic, brittle young women who paraded through the films Andy was fond of watching on television. Based on these films, Andy assumed that those young men and women who dressed in designer jeans and Gucci shoes were sexually nimble and in constant search of ambidextrous partners. At fifteen he had become acquainted with lustful fumblings in a pickup truck, but he fantasized about tender wrestlings beneath satin sheets. The Sunday morning when he had first seen Darby was gray and humid, and tiny black deerflies swarmed across the graveled drive to the Moons' farmhouse. Holding his grandfather's trout in a damp newspaper in one hand, slapping at flies with the other, he had kicked softly at the screened kitchen door at the rear of the house.

"C'mon in!" she'd shouted.

He pushed through the door and his mouth fell open. Sweat pouring down her face, her arms folded beneath her head, Darby stood upside down in the center of the kitchen floor.

"Gimme a minute," she panted.

Andy was speechless. Expecting to meet a young woman all in velvet, he had stumbled upon a sweat-stained doll. Darby had inherited the curly dark hair of her father and the fine bones of her mother. But she looked like neither one of them. She was a tiny girl, all angle and curiosity. Her mouth was uncommonly wide, almost as if a ventriloquist had carved too deeply in his dummy. Her lips curved upwards at the ends, giving her face a clownlike appearance but, strangely, also giving it pleasing balance. Those who observed her for the first time were always surprised to discover the mischief of her mouth. These contradictions of her face were the external manifestations of her nature. She was an elusive and unpredictable girl whose very spirit of independence dictated the attention of strangers.

"It's supposed to put you on the path to wisdom," she groaned, her body straining with the effort to remain upright. And then: "Fuck it, I'll stay dumb." Andy blushed. Darby toppled over backwards and lay flat on the floor, drawing in deep breaths, then, abruptly, she somersaulted to a standing position. Her man's gray woolen sweat suit was drenched from exercise, and she was barefooted. She leaned against the sink and worked the long handle of an old-fashioned pump. Although the sink had modern faucets, Solomon had refused to remove the pump. Water gushed forth and Darby thrust her head under the spout then turned her face so that water ran into her mouth. She straightened and ran one hand over her face, blinking water out of her eyes. Andy had not moved. She glanced into the wet newspaper he held.

"Oh, God," she said as she saw the trout, "they're beautiful."

"Just some trout is all," Andy said. "My granddaddy thought you might like 'em."

"Fantastic," Darby exclaimed. She moved closer to Andy and the boy was terribly conscious of the musky fragrance of her warm body. He backed away an inch. He didn't think she'd want to handle the fish anyway, but to his surprise she reached out and lifted one of the trout, holding it up so that its scales regained their luminosity in the pale light from the window. "Gee," she said, "his eyes are so dead."

"The whole thing's dead," Andy said. "You was to want, I'd gut 'em."

"Well," she said, "if I'm gonna eat 'em, I guess I ought to gut 'em myself. Could you show me how?"

"Ayuh."

After introducing themselves, they moved outside to the kitchen porch and spread newspapers on a rickety redwood table. Andy showed her how to gut the trout and was amazed that she didn't flinch at cutting open the belly or, using two fingers as he had demonstrated, scraping out the entrails. He could hardly believe this was a city girl.

Neither by gesture nor inflection did she ever insinuate sexual possibilities and, to his surprise, the lack of sexual tension between them made her even more attractive to Andy, creating an intimacy he'd not experienced before. He was, however, puzzled by the questions she asked. It was as if she couldn't get enough information about his life and his grandfather's life and his grandfather's grandfather's life. She seemed absorbed by the history of his family. It was not until he'd said good-bye and was halfway down the road to his own home that he realized that he had asked her nothing, nor had he learned anything about her. All he knew was that he would wait impatiently for each week to pass so that on Sundays he could deliver his granddaddy's trout.

As the red convertible swerved around potholes in the graveled road that was the entrance to the farm, Kendal cradled the bowl in her lap and glanced at Solomon. She smiled to herself as she saw the pleasure on his face. During the last year, Kendal had sensed an insidious pattern to

Solomon's behavior. He seemed lacking in purpose, caught in a web of hesitation, the unseen strings of that web capriciously pulling him into shifting attitudes alien to that which had previously served him well. He talked little about his work, yawned too often at the mention of social engagements, became unexpectedly irritable during casual discussions of contemporary issues, and laughed too little. There were moments when Kendal thought he resented the age in which he lived, and she perceived that more and more he was inventing a nostalgic plot within which he cast himself in the leading role. It was as if he were devising an ancient character whose robes he could wear. The persona he sought troubled Kendal, for she felt he was moving further and further away from her. She became acutely conscious of the fact that the things which seemed to afford Solomon the most pleasure were strangely anachronistic.

Unlike his neighbors in Westport, who conquered ennui by playing golf or tennis, Solomon built and flew kites, occasionally chased butterflies, or churned buttermilk or tossed horseshoes by himself. At first charming, these actions later made Kendal uneasy as she suspected they implied a retreat from contact with others. These incidental and solitary choices of Solomon's seemed to Kendal to serve little purpose, and because she believed that men and women were happier if they could behold the fruits of their efforts she suggested that they look for a piece of land on which they could retire for weekends or holidays, a summer, perhaps forever. What she really intended was to find some place where Solomon could apply his creative energies. Solomon thought it a splendid idea. They searched the regions of New England that could conveniently be reached by car from their Westport home.

They found Jabez Tuttle's farm in Down Derry. Tuttle was a tall, thin man whose sunken chest was circled by a long white scar where a scythe might have slipped. His age was uncertain, but the dark stubble of his beard was salted white and he walked as if drained of destination. He wore dung-smeared boots and faded overalls whose shoulder straps hung loosely from his bare and narrow shoulders. The overalls billowed in the faintest wind, revealing the scar and the fact that Tuttle wore no underwear. He constantly plucked the cloth of his overalls from between his buttocks, and when relieved of the irritation he broke wind and then spat a thin stream of tobacco juice onto the ground.

The Moons had formed a symbiotic relationship with Tuttle. Using as few words as possible, he explained that he wished to sell his land because he no longer wanted to farm. He'd sold his herd of dairy cows and, with the profit realized, purchased a silver-metaled mobile home and a nine-hundred-dollar television console. He had no intention of trailing his new home behind his battered pickup truck. At the distant end of the farm land, isolated by surrounding woods, the mobile home was perched on cornerstones of concrete block. Tuttle had an artesian well drilled nearby. He paid the county to string electric wire down the farm's subsidiary road. A telephone line was installed. He heated by propane gas, flushed into his new septic tank, subsisted on sardines, condensed milk, and boiled potatoes, and made an occasional Sunday visit to the Catholic church in the village. On weekdays he sat in his Sears catalogue-ordered reclining chair and watched soap operas. He wanted nothing more.

It was Kendal who explained to Tuttle that the inflationary rates of this decade would gradually erode his capital and that he would be wise to find another source of income.

"Don't know," Tuttle muttered as he fingered the overalls from between his buttocks, "don't know if'n I'll live long 'nough to need it." And he spat windward, neatly dodging the returned spray of his sour juice.

Kendal ignored his pragmatism. Because she hated waste, she was appalled that the land would no longer be put to use; and she hoped that Solomon would become excited about the possibilities of a working farm. She was convinced that if he addressed himself to the purpose of the land he would discover a newly focused pleasure. She suggested that Tuttle become the Moons' caretaker and asked if he would dig a vegetable garden for them to maintain while he raised chickens and daily milked the one dairy cow she would purchase. She thought, also, that he might resow the large mowing in hay. In turn, he could take whatever fresh produce he wanted and keep the profits from any hay sold.

"Well," he said, "I guess."

Although Solomon approved of Kendal's decisions, he did not participate in them. Kendal planted the vegetables. Kendal gathered eggs. Kendal spent hours drawing plans to redesign the barn so that eventually it could incorporate a separate study for Solomon. Kendal read voraciously of architectural digests, trying to discover imaginative uses for the chicken coop and the fenced corral and the silo.

Solomon walked the woods and studied the flora and fauna of the land. He talked of Indians and Ethan Allen's boys, and he drove many miles through the countryside looking for and buying old wooden sap buckets with which, he told Kendal, he planned to sugar maples the following spring. But the iron bands that held the buckets' wooden staves were loose and the buckets leaked. Kendal did not comment. As she didn't wish to furnish the farmhouse with the kind of expensive antiques in their Westport home, Kendal purchased sturdy wooden furniture from local craft shops in Townsend. She bought beautifully lathed and highly functional bowls and trays from the Weston Bowl Mill. Cups and saucers and platters she found in Bennington potteries. Her concentration was on utilitarian objects.

Solomon's was not. On numerous occasions, he would return home from one of his many countryside wanderings with objects from the past: a broken spinning wheel, antiquated and rusted farm implements missing vital cogs or gears, half of a hand-carved yoke for oxen, squared and dented coffee and flour tins embossed with advertisements from the previous century, a gumball machine. It was obvious to Kendal that Solomon remained wistful about days long past, and that she was not able to provide a palatable present.

None of Solomon's collected items were expensive or in good repair, but when Kendal suggested that Solomon restore them he declined. He said that they didn't really belong to him, that he was just borrowing them from the men who'd made them years ago. This metaphysical logic seemed to Kendal an overly romantic concept foreign to Solomon's nature, so she pursued it a step further. She strolled around the barn loft where Solomon hoarded his collection.

"If we removed the rust . . ." she began.

"I like rust," Solomon said. "It's natural. It's what happens to us." He paused for a moment, looking a little puzzled by his own words, and then continued. "I mean, to things."

"Do you think the men who made these would approve of their going to waste?" Kendal asked.

Solomon removed a wooden haying fork from the barn wall. Two tines were missing. His hands slid up and down the weathered handle. "It would be nice to know what they'd think," he said thoughtfully, "but we can't, can we? I mean, we weren't part of it."

"Part of what?"

"Part of that time." Using the fork, he mimed pitching hay into a wagon, then rested the handle of the fork on the floor and pointed out the small hexagonal window at the end of the loft. The window faced east onto a mowing that was high in grass. He smiled at Kendal. "You ever think what it must have been like then? The whole village, maybe thirty or forty people, all of them planting together, haying together, raising roofs together, fighting Indians, I'll bet. It must have been a helluva time."

"Well," Kendal said, "I can't promise you any Indians, but if you fixed that pitchfork you could still use it to hay."

"No," Solomon said, his tone melancholy, "I don't belong to it." And as Solomon carefully rehung the haying fork, Kendal could not help but think that he continued to mourn an artificial history to which he could lay no claim.

Now, holding the bowl she'd bought from the old man with a white beard, she remembered the incident of the haying fork and Solomon's inexplicable sadness, and she turned to him in the car and lightly touched his cheek.

"I love you," she said.

"I know." He kissed her fingers. He braked the red convertible in front of the farmhouse. He and Kendal got out of the car and started for the house, but Solomon paused as he glanced toward the barn. The wide double doors were open.

"Where's Darby's truck?" he asked.

"I guess she's been delayed," Kendal answered lightly.

"What do you mean, delayed?"

"Maybe she got a late start or ran into traffic. It's Friday. I don't know."

"You told me she had this big thing about getting here early this weekend," Solomon said. "I had Jabez open the house just for her. Can't she ever be on time?"

"You know Darby. She's unpredictable."

"Unreliable," Solomon said tartly.

"Unpredictable. There's a difference."

Solomon's glance moved swiftly from the barn to the chicken house and over to the fenced corral. There was no one in sight. "Jabez isn't here. Jesus, he's probably pissed off that he had to open up early and he's gone back to his trailer. Darby's not a child anymore, Kendal. You'd think she'd have some goddamn consideration for —"

"Oh, c'mon, darling," Kendal said. "That's enough. The chrysanthemums are huge!"

" 'The chrysanthemums are huge,' " Solomon muttered darkly and walked into the farmhouse.

Jabez Tuttle lay on the sofa in the living room. On his belly, he stretched out over the end of the sofa and twiddled with the dial on a small television set. Solomon knew that Jabez was intrigued with the sexual complications and the complex behavior of deceit dramatized in the network soap operas. He gave no credence to the evening news and was bored with prime-time car chases and sophomoric farce; therefore, Solomon had felt it was no imposition to call on the services of his caretaker during the coming twilight hours.

"How are you, Jabez?" Solomon asked cheerfully, hoping that his own enthusiasm would influence the mood of his dour caretaker. It didn't.

"Opened up early like you asked," Jabez said. "Missed *General Hospital.* Missed the whole dang thing, and Luke, he's in a mess of trouble." Irritation made Jabez loquacious.

"Gee," Solomon said, "I'm sorry. You get the tin cans?"

"You asked me to, didn't you?"

"Right. You get the shells?"

"You asked me to, didn't you?"

"Yeah."

"Well, don't seem no need to ask, then. Them shells and the cans, they're down to the mowin'."

"Great," Solomon said. "You ready?"

"Don't see no point in hangin' 'round here," Tuttle said as he continued to dial the television. "Ain't nuthin' but news, anyways." He turned off the set, slowly rose to his feet, and looked balefully at Solomon.

"If you don't mind," Solomon said, "we'd better go to the mowing now before the sun sets."

"Be better tomorrow."

"I'd like to go now," Solomon said stubbornly.

Jabez nodded. He opened a glass jar on the coffee table. He scooped out a handful of peanuts and popped them into his mouth. He chewed hungrily, and little beads of saliva formed on the whisker stubble around his mouth. "Pistachios are better." He brushed by Solomon and walked out of the farmhouse. "Ought to get pistachios," he said over his shoulder.

Solomon peered through the window. Kendal was crouched by a small rock garden, clippers in hand. She was cutting back the green stalks of iris. When Jabez passed her, she waved to him. He flicked a finger in acknowledgment. For a moment Solomon worried that Jabez was going to return to his trailer but then he saw the caretaker turn toward the barn, pass it, and continue on to the mowing. Solomon hurried outside to the car. He reached in and removed the shotgun from its oblong box. Carrying it under his arm, he moved quickly after Jabez.

"I'll be at the mowing," he called to Kendal. "We'll do a steak outside, okay?" He didn't wait for an answer. He shifted the gun to his hand and broke into a trot.

Kendal looked up from her gardening and watched Solomon disappear behind the barn. Then she turned to scan the driveway. She frowned. She knew the special thing that Darby had planned for this evening, the secret that she, Kendal, had promised not to reveal. It worried her. She was not at all sure that Solomon would be pleased.

"Damn," she muttered, and stabbed the ground with a trowel. She looked at her fading autumn garden, and as she snipped at the mums' rusted heads she wished she knew a way to close the distance that had developed between Solomon and Darby. She was certain that they loved each other, but neither was able to freely communicate this. It was as if both felt that if they baldly revealed their feelings toward each other, a penalty would incur. So they warily circled each other, their uncommunicated love encased in a protective patina and only occasionally revealed by some oblique action chosen for demonstrative purposes — such as, Kendal thought, the secret Darby planned for today's twilight hours. Father and daughter were, Kendal mused as she continued her garden clipping, in the words of the poet, *confused among chrysanthemums.*

The boom of the shotgun crashed into her thoughts and she looked up sharply. Another shot was fired, its echo reverberating among the mountains. Kendal dropped her garden tool and moved swiftly toward the mowing. The pastureland on which Jabez Tuttle and Solomon stood sloped gently upward to the rear of the barn, so Kendal had a clear vision as she looked down at the two men. It was a small mowing, not worthy of seeding, and the grass, which Jabez had ignored, was summer tall.

"Pull!" Solomon shouted.

Tuttle threw a tin can in a long curved arc over Solomon's shoulder. Solomon whirled, snapped the butt of his shotgun to his shoulder, and fired at the can as it reached the height of its curve. He missed.

"Pull!" Solomon shouted again.

Tuttle hurled a second can so that it simulated a bird's flight from left to right in front of Solomon. Solomon fired. Kendal heard the sharp ping of pellets and the tin can jumped in the air and then plummeted to earth. She saw Solomon grin and, looking for approbation, he turned toward Jabez. The farmer's words floated through the thin mountain air and reached Kendal at the barn.

" 'T ain't a pa'tridge," he said.

Bloody bastard, Kendal said to herself, annoyed that the farmer was unable to acknowledge Solomon's perfect shot. The thought surprised her. Solomon had never mentioned any familiarity with guns, but as she watched she recognized that he handled the weapon with expertise. She saw something else. She saw that the farmer was deliberately trying to frustrate Solomon. Invariably, Tuttle hurled the targets so that they flew in front of the dying sun or high into the bending branches of a nearby tree. The shape and speed of his tin cans was lost in the land-scape. Kendal wondered why Solomon did not complain about the awkward pattern of the farmer's toss. She thought it must be difficult to aim through the failing light and fire above the confusing shadows on the land, but Solomon never said a word. It puzzled Kendal that Solomon seemed content to accommodate the perversity of the farmer but when she saw the joy on Solomon's face as he listened to the consistent rattle of pellets against the tin cans and watched the targets tumble from the sky she turned and started back to her garden, unhappy only that Solomon's eye might soon turn from tin to the warm flesh of a bird. Such a possibility saddened Kendal for it represented a repugnant waste in a world already stenched by inexcusable consumption.

The telephone rang in the farmhouse. She moved slowly, hoping that the ring would cease. She thought Mr. Bell's genius had provided one of the more irritating implements of progress. She recognized the facility with which one could deliver messages or arrange appointments or dis-cuss crises through the use of a phone, but she resented its function as an exchange of gossip or small talk or pleasantries: another waste of time. It rang again. And again. The bell was persistent.

"Damn," she muttered and walked into the kitchen. She picked up the telephone.

"Yes?" she asked abruptly, purposely inhospitable.

"Hello, sweetheart."

Kendal winced. The voice on the telephone belonged to Ben Brindig, vice-president in charge of production for TransGlobal Films. He was, Kendal knew, Solomon's *bête noire*. He was a crude, ruthless man who, having survived the many struggles for power within the company, op-erated in a strangely archaic fashion to insure his sphere of influence. Most high executives in motion picture companies were aware that the bullying tactics employed by yesterdays' moguls were no longer accepted by the creative talents upon whom the companies reluctantly relied. Because of this bitter knowledge, they were forced to employ a shrewder strategy in order to seduce the producers or directors or writers they needed. They cajoled and flattered and charmed them, promising them a certain degree of independent action and choice, and fattening these promises by offering financial participation in any net profits realized from the films conceived by these talents. However, the recent exposures of some studios' creative bookkeeping practices, in which net profits were seldom recorded, thus guaranteeing the meaninglessness of participation, had tainted the system and made it suspect. Brindig was fully aware of this, and used this knowledge in a wily way. His approach to talent was simple and direct. Assuming the attitude of an honest and concerned man, he pointed out to the individual producer or director or writer with whom he was in negotiation that financial participation represented an unfair risk on the part of talent and therefore he, Brindig, was prepared to eliminate such risk and pay, *up front*, a larger-than-ordinary sum for the talent's efforts. Because Trans-Global had an extraordinary cash flow, such an approach posed no difficulties. There were other rewards for the company. Should the film in question prove to be a large financial success, the ensuing profits would not have to be shared. Should the film fail at the box office, the monies paid to talent would be incorporated into a legitimate tax loss for the studio. Brindig's proposals were rooted in the knowledge that the creative talents who labored in the film industry were continuously caught in an economic vise and that immediate cash was an attraction not easily dismissed. What pleased Brindig the most was that after such a deal had been accepted, he felt no obligation to coddle the man or woman who, in his terms, had been bought. Their willingness to enter such an arrangement was proof positive to Brindig that every man had his price. He had never doubted it. Because he felt the same way about the men and women employed within the corporate structure of TransGlobal, he felt no necessity to treat them with respect. His enjoyment came from accentuating his vulgarity, aware that it offended his employees and just as aware that few had the courage or economic resources to challenge the coarseness he projected. What hardly anyone suspected, and only his wife, Brenda, knew, was that Brindig revered courage and, because he constantly searched for its manifestation in any form, whether physical or moral, was driven to test all those with whom he came in contact.

"Hello, Ben," Kendal said, cradling the telephone between her head and shoulder and immediately picking up a pencil and message pad. "Solomon's busy. Can I have him call you back?"

"What," Brindig said, "he's painting the house?"

"Where are you calling from?"

"With what I pay him, you can't afford a painter?"

"Are you at the studio?" Kendal asked patiently.

"Where else? Please, tell him to get off the ladder, okay? Be a nice girl."

"He can call you back."

"What do we got here, a bad connection?"

"Ben . . ."

"I got a garbage problem here, Kendal, a real serious garbage problem. I need the genius to sweep it up. You understand what I'm saying?"

"Yes, Ben," Kendal answered. "I understand what you're saying. Hold on."

As she walked down to the mowing, Kendal wished there were a way not to interrupt Solomon at what he was enjoying so much, but the reality of his job dictated that he take the call from Brindig. She knew what Brindig was referring to when he mentioned garbage. It was the term he used for film scripts under consideration by the studio. His perverse pleasure at demeaning a writer's efforts was a legend at the studio, and more often than not Solomon was the first recipient of this perversity. She stood on the rise of the mowing and saw that the grass was now littered with spent shells from the shotgun. Falling sunlight glinted off the pierced tin cans scattered throughout the grass. Flushed with pleasure, Solomon was reloading.

"Darling," Kendal called through her cupped hands, "Ben's on the phone."

Solomon turned to her, a frown crossing his face. "Tell him I'm out," he called back to her.

"He says it's important."

"Bullshit."

"He's waiting."

"He'll hang up."

"He won't hang up."

"Goddamn it."

"Solomon, will you *please* get the phone."

Solomon stared at her and then, angrily, ejected the shells from the shotgun. Leaving the chambers empty, he leaned the weapon against the nearby tree and turned to Jabez.

"I'll be back in a — "

"Sun's almost down," Tuttle said.

"It'll just take a — "

"No point to it now," Tuttle said. " 'Sides, I got to have my supper. Got to eat early so's I don't get gas durin' the night. I get a lot of gas." As if to emphasize the point, he shifted his weight onto one foot, lifted one buttock, and farted.

"You're a real pleasure, Jabez," Solomon said. "A real pleasure."

"Well," Tuttle said, "I do my best."

Solomon deliberately walked as slowly as possible across the farm-yard and into the house. As he started to pick up the phone he noticed that he had gun oil on his hands. He wiped them with his handkerchief and then held the linen close to his nose so that he could smell the oil and the faint fragrance of cordite that clung to his skin. They were pleasing odors and vitiated some of his annoyance at the interruption.

"Hi, Ben."

"You finish your painting?" Ben asked.

"What? Finish what?" Solomon was perplexed.

"Nothing," Ben said. "A joke. Forget it. Don't get your tit in a wringer. Not over that, anyway. Your worry is product, Solomon. We need product, not the goddamn garbage you sent me."

Product.

Solomon grimaced. What an inglorious word for the magic of men's minds. He thought of all the legends, myths, chronicles, and narratives devised by the poets of the past, and of the biographies and fictional adventures and romances hammered into form by storytellers, of plots twisted into logic, topics researched, characters delineated, structures changed and rechanged, atmospheres sketched, words chosen — and all these labors performed in honor of imagination. The fanciful flights of men's minds, carefully polished from observation and memory, had been stripped of wings by small men who demeaned the process with their base label: *product*.

Nowhere was product more appreciated than in the offices of TransGlobal Films. Although the production values of motion pictures and television films made and distributed by TransGlobal were of high caliber, the stories presented within these productions reflected the manipulative whims of dishonest creativity and resulted in celluloid lies. This was a fact recognized by the publishing companies and Broadway producers and writers' agents, the triumvirate primarily responsible for a continuing source of supply; therefore, those sources submitted material for Solomon's consideration with the tacit understanding that they were offering manuscripts which more often than not had been rejected previously by rival film companies, or which were distinguished by ineptness or salaciousness or unjustified violence, or all three. The paradox of this situation was that the same material that had been deprecated by others often generated enormous box-office receipts for TransGlobal.

Wilton Forest, the small, gray, neat president of TransGlobal, had remarked once to Solomon that it was an identifiable fact that the mass of filmgoing public thirsted for stories about only two things: fighting and fornication. Solomon had smiled. Now, some years after his initial employment, he thought perhaps Wilton had been right. What Solomon had absolutely no doubt about was that TransGlobal would continue to pander to the lowest common denominator of public taste, and had no wish to alter that taste, as long as it could be equated with the ring of a cash register.

During his years of employment, Solomon had often provided the studio with material for successful films, and he knew that Wilton relied on his taste and astuteness. But he had become increasingly aware that he held a position with limited power. He would discover a book or play or an original screenplay about which he would become genuinely enthusiastic. Excited by its film potential, he would send it to Brindig or, on occasion, prodded by his eagerness to consummate the purchase of the manuscript before his competitors outbid him, he would fly to TransGlobal's California studio and, hands damp with excitement, present it personally.

Because Brindig's interest did not include the complexities or subtleties, the moods and shadings of the written piece, Solomon would have to define these elements, and show how they related to the potential success of a film, within a matter of minutes. He was, in a sense, a verbal butcher artfully stripping flesh from bone and finally offering a polished skeleton. The trick of the butcher was not to bleed on Brindig.

But Solomon was no magician. He bled. He was, in those early days, drugged by the splendor of the written word, and he could not refrain from sharing his addiction. Such an impulse, he learned, was a grave miscalculation of Brindig's sensibilities, for after pouring forth his passion, Solomon was invariably confronted by Brindig's single refrain:

"Hey, kid, don't get your tit in a wringer."

Recently, Solomon had concocted a plan to circumvent this *leitmotif.*

His daughter, Darby, had introduced him to an off-Broadway playwright named Charles Manzinni. He had presented what Solomon considered a fine idea for a screenplay. Using funds available to him as the head of the story department, Solomon had contracted Manzinni to develop the idea into a first-draft screenplay called *Shadow on the Grass.* Solomon thought it splendid.

Manzinni's script was based on an old German legend. In the legend, a woodcutter named Peter Schlemiel — the original of the slang term — sold his shadow to the Devil in exchange for wealth and power and the domination of beautiful women. But as his life progressed, a life incorporating the external trappings of success, Schlemiel discovered that a man without a shadow is anathema to all those he encounters, and the paradoxical relationship between shadow and substance culminates in tragedy. Both Manzinni and Solomon had recognized that the story's Faustian aspects might preclude acceptance by Brindig, so they had masked its esoteric nature by setting it in a contemporary framework which embodied a legitimate terror of the supernatural. It was a genuinely frightening story, but Manzinni and Solomon had meticulously eliminated any elements that might lead to gratuitous titillation and had focused on the terrible consequences of any man's bargain with the Devil. Brindig had called it a risky undertaking, but he had been seduced by the fact that the script offered a highly appealing role for a major actor and that its dazzling optical illusions would appeal to a youthful audience. What worried Solomon was that TransGlobal might want to bolster the film's chance for success by compromising its thematic values and stressing its inherent violence. He had little doubt that this was the subject of Brindig's call. The thought filled him with a sudden weariness.

"What's the problem, Ben?" Solomon asked, and held his handkerchief to his nose so that he could sniff again the gun oil and cordite, as if he were clearing his head for the coming conflict.

"You kiddin' me?" Brindig barked through the phone. "What the hell do you think the problem is?"

"I'm sure you can solve it."

"Not me, buster, you. You bought this garbage; you clean it up."

"What garbage are you referring to, Ben?"

"Don't be a shmuck, Solly, you know goddamn well what I'm talkin' about. *Shadow on the Grass* is what I'm talkin' about. Garbage is what I'm talkin' about. Harry West is what I'm talkin' about."

"Harry West?" Solomon knew that West was a major star whose presence in a film almost guaranteed enormous box-office return.

"We bought this shit," Brindig went on, " 'cause we got a pay-or-play with Harry West, and Harry West is a little son of a bitch but when he stars in a picture the picture has legs, and this same little Harry West does not want to look unsympathetic on the big screen, you understand what I'm sayin'?"

"I'm not sure, Ben."

"The dodo who wrote this picture didn't give the hero any balls. You think Harry West is going to play a guy with no balls? Jesus, Solly, use your head."

"The thing is," Solomon said, "psychologically, the hero — "

"Psychologically the hero can stick it up his ass," Brindig snapped. "Monday, Solomon."

Solomon blinked. "I'm not following you, Ben. On Monday the hero has to have balls?"

"Jesus Christ. Monday I want you and the writer in your office. I want to hear how you're going to fix this garbage. You got that?"

"You're coming in on Monday?"

"You got it. So if I were you, I'd get hold of this Marconni — "

"Manzinni."

"— and spend the weekend cleaning up his garbage. What the hell, who asked you to paint your house anyway, you know what I mean?"

Brindig hung up. So did Solomon. He had a headache. He walked across the kitchen and leaned against the sink. He worked the lever of the hand pump. He lowered his head and let cold water run across the back of his neck. It didn't help. He soaked his handkerchief, and when he wiped his face he smelled again the gun oil and cordite, but it no longer gave him pleasure. He stared out the window and saw that shadows lay across the ridge of mountains in the north. Although the sun was in a steep decline, the sky still held a graying brightness. A bird, more streak than form, arrowed through the glow and then rose in widening circles until it was a dark silhouette flying black patterns in the sky. The bird was too distant to identify. At first Solomon thought it was a crow but then remembered that such birds are prone to fly in flock. The flight of this dark and silent bird fascinated Solomon. Its pattern of concentric circles seemed totally without purpose.

And then it plunged, its descent so swift and startling that Solomon sharply drew in his breath. The bird was gone.

As if, Solomon thought, it had been summoned by some command-ing call.

It was a bitter reminder of his own response to Ben Brindig. Solomon opened a kitchen cabinet. He removed a bottle of Johnny Walker Black Label. He poured scotch into an empty jelly glass, then topped it with cold water from the pump. He drained the glass. He placed two fingers in his mouth and tried to whistle. All he heard was the sound of his own breath.

"Shit," he said.

He decided to get drunk.

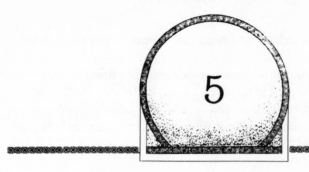

5

Sergeant Wilfred Callahan was amused at himself. He'd been off duty all day and had taken advantage of the free time to drive deep into the mountains where, previously, he had discovered a small waterfall which fell into an icy stream below. It was an ideal place to picnic and to paint. Callahan was a gourmet cook and an amateur painter. After he set up his easel, but before he mixed his oils, he lunched on a cold quiche he had baked. It was filled with asparagus and tarragon and hot crushed pepper, and it was even more savory when washed down with sips of iced espresso. When he finished the delicacy, he wrapped his paper plate and plastic utensils in a sheet of aluminum foil and, together with his thermos, stored them neatly on the floor of his Jeep. The autumn sun was unusually warm and so he removed his clothes and folded them, too, neatly into the Jeep. Naked, he lay on the grassy bank of the stream and closed his eyes. He was in no hurry to paint. He wanted to wait for the afternoon light to strike the surrounding mountains. The elusive quality of the light appealed to him and he was determined to capture it on canvas. He decided to sleep for an hour. Like many men whose work is often dictated by emergencies, he was used to catnapping.

At the end of an hour, he opened his eyes, rose swiftly, and dived into the icy stream. He swam under the waterfall and then stood against the rock ledge behind it. He looked through the curtain of falling water and wondered if Bierstadt or Moran had ever been tempted to paint their Hudson River landscapes from this point of view. He swam back to the bank, dressed, and mixed his oils. He painted for the rest of the afternoon, but when he finished he gazed ruefully at his own work. He had tried to depict the subtle tints of rose and yellow that seemed to shimmer off the mountainside, but the result was too bold, too primitive to catch what he had seen. There was no mystery in his painting; because the mysterious nature of things was what attracted him, he knew he had failed. Well, he said to a squirrel who had come to watch, it's not the first time. He thought fleetingly of an earlier failure in his life and then quickly dismissed the memory.

He removed a cigar from his pocket, cut it in half, returned one half to the pocket, and placed the remaining half between his lips. He didn't light the cigar, rather he chewed it, relishing the pungent bite of tobacco. He returned to the Jeep and drove home to Down Derry.

As he parked on the road between his house and the village green, he glanced up toward the mountains and paused. A bird — a hawk perhaps, or a crow — was slowly circling near a mountain ridge, its dark silhouette flat against the sky. As primitive, Callahan thought, as my painting. He took from his paint box a tube of black paint and a palette knife and, carrying the painting of the mountain sky, he climbed onto the hood of his Jeep. He sat cross-legged, the canvas resting in his lap, and edged in the lines of a black crow.

He wore hiking boots and faded jeans and a checkered cotton shirt whose sleeves were rolled up high on his arms. A long welt, white and puckered, ran the length of his left forearm. It was a bullet scar. Although the wound was old it had left Callahan with a slight stiffness in the forearm's muscle, so, unconsciously, he had developed a habit of occasionally flexing the fingers of his left hand. This occurred most often when he was under stress or when he was on the verge of some discovery that excited him. These discoveries were not necessarily related to crime. Although he was a quiet man who rarely displayed excessive reactions, all revelations excited him, for he believed that the more man knew about the human condition the less he understood it; therefore, the correlation to that theorem seemed clear to him: man must continue to unmask the commonplace and give credence to the unknown.

He studied the crow he had just drawn and, as with the rest of the painting, was dissatisfied with it. There was no sense of flight. As he picked up a wipe rag, he heard a distant squeal of brakes. He looked up. A few cars were parked around the village green but because the autumn foliage had not reached its peak there was little tourist traffic. Those who might wish to dine at the Silver Spoon had not yet arrived. Farmers' wives had done their shopping for the day and no one either entered or left the country store. There was another squeal of brakes. This time it was closer. Callahan thought it had to be a car traveling west on the road to Down Derry. He saw Ray Poole come out of the rear door of the post office holding two clear plastic bags in his hand. They were filled with multicolored feathers Ray used to tie his flies. Callahan guessed that the L.L. Bean store had sent them. Ray was too busy studying them to notice Callahan. As Poole started across the road to where his car was parked, a small pickup truck sped into sight at the far end of the village. It was approaching the hill road that led to Poole's farm. The driver, Darby Moon, obviously saw the turn, whipped the wheel over hard and applied her brakes, but the pressure was too much. The truck spun and skidded into a one-hundred-and-eighty-degree turn, grazed a tree at the corner of the road, richocheted onto the main road, and veered straight across the village green. Ray Poole leaped out of the way and dropped to the grass, spilling his plastic bags of feathers. As Callahan jumped from the hood where he sat, the truck sideslipped to a stop only inches from his Jeep. Darby thrust her head out of the window and cried out to Callahan.

"Oh, my God, I killed you!"

"No," Callahan said, flicking shreds of tobacco from his lips, "but you ruined a good cigar." He stepped toward Darby but stopped as she rammed her shoulder against the door and burst out of the truck. She was dressed in a white silk blouse and a long plaid skirt that reached her bare feet. The blouse was stained scarlet and clung to her breasts.

Good Lord, Callahan thought, she's bleeding, but as she lifted her skirts and ran by him he caught the unmistakable odor of wine. Darby raced across the village green toward Ray, who was on his hands and knees groping for the scattered feathers.

"Are you all right, Mr. Poole?" Darby shouted. "Did I hit your chickens?"

"Peacock feathers is all," Poole said. He was as composed as if he leaped from death every day.

When Callahan reached them, both Poole and Darby were sitting calmly in the grass as they stuffed feathers back into the plastic bags. Darby's skirt was hitched high on her thighs and the outlines of her nipples were clear under the wet blouse, but even as Callahan noticed this he felt that she was unaware of the sexuality she projected.

"Have you ever seen anything lovelier than this?" Darby asked, holding up one of the peacock feathers.

"I'd like to see your license," Callahan said.

"Now, Wilfred," Poole said as he rose, the two plastic bags almost filled again and in his hands, "she didn't hurt nuthin', did she?"

"Not yet," Callahan said.

Aware of his tone, Darby stood up. "You're sore, aren't you? I don't blame you. I mean I practically cut off your ass. I'm awfully sorry, I really am. It's just I've got to get home before the bad angel."

Poole and Callahan exchanged a look.

"This here is Darby Moon," Poole said. "Belongs to the folks bought Tuttle's place. My boy says she's real down-to-earth."

"Uh-huh," Callahan said, and then addressed himself once again to Darby. "I'd like to see your license."

"You going to make a citizen's arrest?" Darby asked.

"Say hello to Sergeant Callahan," Poole said. "Sergeant Wilfred Callahan."

"Oh, boy," Darby said.

"Don't think she meant no harm, Wilfred," Poole said.

"About time for the evening hatch, isn't it, Ray?" Callahan's hint that it would be appropriate for Ray to go fishing now was not lost on the Vermonter.

"Ayuh. Sun, she's 'bout down now. You take care." Ray crossed the green, got into his car, and drove slowly by the other two, leaning out the window as he passed. "Soakin' wet the way she is, Wilfred, she gonna catch her death 'less you send her on her way." He winked at Darby and drove on.

"Listen," Darby said urgently to Callahan, "could you arrest me later? I mean, I won't run away or anything, but I'm in an awful hurry."

"I can see that," Callahan said. "What with the 'bad angel' and everything."

"Yeah. Right." Darby began to trot across the green to her pickup truck. She stopped and spun around. "Oh. That sounds kooky, doesn't it?"

"Why would you think that?" Callahan asked innocently. Regardless of her reckless driving, he found himself intrigued by a girl who drove a truck while attired in evening dress.

"Would you just look in my truck, please?" Darby asked.

As Callahan approached the truck, Darby swung open the door. The floorboards of the truck were littered with the spilled contents of cardboard boxes and the seat was drenched in red wine from a broken bottle. A heady fragrance permeated the truck's cab.

"Isn't that awful?" Darby asked as she stared at the mess. "Isn't that just goddamn awful!"

"Take it easy now," Callahan said. He saw that there were tears in Darby's eyes and that she was biting her lips to keep from crying. "The general store's still open."

"You think they have gefiltefish?" Darby asked, her eyes brightening.

Callahan laughed. "I doubt it."

"It was so special," Darby said. "I had it all worked out to surprise Daddy. I mean, everything's there. Gefiltefish, chicken soup with real matzoh balls, sour pickles. I got those from Em's. He does them in some special way, but I baked the challah myself. You ever see more beautiful challah than this?" She reached under the clutch pedal and pulled out a baking tray covered by a wet napkin. She uncovered two small loaves of twisted bread. Their crusts were damp from pickle juice. "Shit," Darby said.

"We'll wipe them off," Callahan said. He removed a handkerchief from his jeans pocket and began to scrub at the bread.

"It probably won't make any difference now," Darby said mournfully as she looked toward the western sky where the sun was steadily lowering. "She's probably there by now."

"Who?"

"The Queen, that's who. The Sabbath Queen."

"Ah," Callahan said. "You're Jewish."

"Yeah," Darby said. "Kind of."

"That explains the 'bad angel.' "

"You know about that? I mean, Callahan doesn't exactly sound . . ."

"If I remember correctly," Callahan said, sniffing a little at the challah to see if he had succeeded in removing the briny smell, "on Friday nights, on *Shabbis,* there are two angels who go with a man on his way home from the synagogue. A good angel and a bad angel, right?"

"Right."

"The two angels go into the house before the man does, and if the house isn't just right, if it isn't spotless and if the table hasn't been set with a feast, and the candles lit . . ." He peered into the cab of the truck. "You bring any candles?"

"They're under the pastrami," Darby said.

"Well," Callahan said, "they ought to smell good when they burn. Anyway, if the people in the house aren't really prepared to greet the . . . uh . . ."

"Sabbath Queen."

"Yes, the Sabbath Queen. Forgive me, I'm a little rusty at this. If they're not ready, why then, the bad angel puts a sort of curse on the house, isn't that it?"

"Something like that," Darby said.

"It's a nice story," Callahan said.

"Yes," Darby agreed.

"Yes." Although Callahan continued to wipe dry the challah, his eyes were on Darby, and he was acutely conscious of her body so clearly outlined under the wet blouse, and he knew instinctively that she recognized his reaction. Unconsciously, he began to flex the fingers of his left hand.

Darby studied him. Although she was attracted by his calm, his reserve, she sensed that he was a man drawn to emergencies, to danger, waiting with infinite patience to reveal his strength.

"Do you know the legend of the waxing moon?" she asked softly.

"No."

"You'd like it."

"Really."

"Ummmm."

There was a long silence between them before Callahan spoke again. "I think," he said, "you might just make it in time for the good angel." He handed her the bread, now dry.

"Thanks," she said. She edged past him and climbed behind the wheel of the truck. "God, I'm sitting in the horseradish."

"Good *yontif*," Callahan said.

"You're sure you wouldn't like to arrest me?"

Callahan stared for a moment at the front left tire. The treads were worn thin. "Drive carefully, please."

"I promise." Darby remained motionless.

"It helps," Callahan said, "if you turn the key."

Darby stared at the scar on his arm. "Does that hurt a lot?"

"No."

"I'm glad." She turned on the ignition, shifted into a low gear, and slowly accelerated. Callahan watched until the truck had turned up the hill road and was lost to sight. He glanced up at the sky and saw that the black bird was gone. For some inexplicable reason, he wondered if the bird were flying with the bad angel. The sergeant grinned at his own nonsense and picked up the fallen canvas. As he walked toward his house, he studied the painting. He suspected that Darby might like waterfalls. He wondered what she'd think of an ex-priest turned cop.

. . .

The warmth was gone from the twilight sky and Kendal felt an October chill on the land. Her hands felt suddenly cold from digging in the earth and she laid down her tools and blew into her fingers. Solomon had been in the house for a long time. She hoped he had laid a fire. She glanced toward the front porch, where weekend logs were stacked by Tuttle. The pile did not seem diminished. She rose from the garden and moved up to the porch. As she lifted small logs, she heard the sound of a scratchy phonograph record and then the voice of Hoagy Carmichael. *Ole buttermilk sky, I'm keeping my eye fixed on you.* Balancing the logs in her arms, she kicked open the front door.

A jelly glass of whiskey in his hand, his eyes closed, Solomon was dancing in the living room.

"Hi," Kendal said.

"Listen," Solomon said, his voice only slightly slurred. "Why doesn't anyone dip anymore? It's a great step. You've got to be very, very graceful to do the dip. Did you know that?"

"I knew that," Kendal answered as she deposited the logs on the stone hearth of the fireplace.

"Don't you think the dip is a very, very great step?"

"I think the dip is a very, very great step," Kendal said. "And I think you're getting quite pissed."

"Possible," Solomon said.

What's the good news tonight, is it going to be cloudy or bright?

"You remember when . . ." Solomon began.

"Yes."

"When we . . ."

"Yes."

Kendal smiled and moved into Solomon's arms. She remembered. And, as always, she marveled at how two strangers meet.

Born in the small village of Bagshot, Surrey, England, Kendal had spent her infancy playing in the gardens of her parents and of their neighbors. Her earliest memories were centered around horticultural activity: digging, seeding, pruning, grafting, and the final reward of flowering fragrance. Later, as a very young girl, she spent hours roaming the lovely paths of nearby Windsor Park. She was not a particularly gregarious child and the park suited her well. It was an arena for the imagination, and she delighted in the invention of her own games. On any given day she might choose to be Mary, Queen of Scots, racing among the chestnut trees on her way to a tryst with her lover Bothwell, or a fair and brave maiden, dressed in doublet and hose, climbing the branches of a maple so that she might look down on any foes of Robin Hood, her own sweet prince. There was no limit to her imagination and she played happily alone.

Her father, Colonel Oliver Darby, recognized Kendal's penchant for solitude, and it worried him. He feared she had inherited it from him. Outwardly jovial, the colonel was a brooding man. The major battles and fierce small skirmishes in which he had participated over the years of army service had diminished his faith in the sanity of men, and had made him too vulnerable to the death of comrades. He did not question the validity of his service, did not delude himself with the promise of utopian fields over which no conflict would wage again, but gradually he eased behind a self-protective wall. He chose to dissociate himself from the emotionality of relationships. He sought distance from the heart. He was unsuccessful. Oliver Darby discovered that to separate oneself from the sharing of others' grief or yearning or anger or love was a restless and dishonest death. It lacked quiet.

He did not wish this for his daughter. He knew she must relate to the company of others. The decision to effect this societal entrance was made for him. When Kendal was eight years old, her mother rode in a fox hunt. Her great gray gelding balked at a privet hedge and Kendal's mother somersaulted into the Sussex sky. She jackknifed to the ground and her neck snapped. She died listening to the baying of hounds.

Colonel Darby enrolled Kendal at Upper Chine school on the Isle of Wight. There, too, the gardens were lovely and the long lonely sweep of sea vista was soothing to a mourning child. At first, made rebellious by her loss, she refused to participate in any activities not demanded by rules of the school. Contrary to her father's wishes, she did not seek the companionship of her peers.

Then she was befriended by an extraordinary woman.

Miss Turnbull, a gentle, gray-haired woman who wore comfortable shoes, was the English mistress at Upper Chine. She was sympathetic to Kendal's lamentation but knew that the girl's inward retreat was self-destructive, and she determined to rescue Kendal from melancholy. She closely watched the girl and observed that Kendal sustained herself by fanciful flights of the imagination. Miss Turnbull decided to introduce Kendal to a more positive world of collective illusion. She started by inviting Kendal to her small cottage in the village of Shanklin, where she and the girl would share tea. Over crumpets or cinnamon toast or delicate sandwiches, Miss Turnbull read aloud from the great dramatists. It was not long before Kendal was beguiled by the histories of Shakespeare, the biting wit of Wilde, the nonsense of Sheridan's fops, and the marvel of Goethe's mind. Soon she yearned to participate more actively in drama. Within a matter of months, Kendal's own imagination found focus. Determined to become an actress, she willingly joined the school's dramatic society. The collaborative efforts of production released her from solitude and taught her the pleasures of sharing. The colonel's wishes were fulfilled.

When war was declared, it was feared that Shanklin would be the stepping-stone for a possible German invasion. Upper Chine was moved to High Wycombe, a village north of London. Kendal graduated and elected not to attend college. The colonel was unhappy with this choice but was too busily engaged to offer any definitive colloquy of dissent. He was chasing Rommel across the sands of Africa.

Although never in doubt about the validity of the Allied cause, Kendal dreaded reading the daily lists of dead and missing. She had suffered from the early death of her mother, from a life wasted, and it pained her deeply to learn that so many young men with whom she was acquainted would never return, would never have the chance to step into the future they had planned. She saw how swiftly dreams were shattered and she resolved never to squander opportunity. She deplored those who hoarded their energy, their talent, their affection, frittering away their hours, seemingly to wait for some mysterious signal which would finally provoke them into a useful life.

She threw herself boldly into a theatrical career and it blossomed under the shriek of German bombs. Unlike many actresses, her energy was not funneled in the direction of stardom. She wanted to use herself fully, stretch whatever capabilities she had. She was content to play anything, anywhere, and because of that was constantly employed. When peace finally returned to Britain, she was an established player. An American producer saw her perform in an intimate revue in which she sang, danced, and told ribald tales. The producer was so taken with the production that he arranged to present it in New York.

On Kendal's opening night, she joined the traditional party at Sardi's restaurant. She received a standing ovation from the assembled patrons, most of whom had attended the performance, and in a few short hours, was informed by the producer that he was immediately closing the play. The critics had been vitriolic, condemning the little revue as an unwarranted piece of fluff reflecting the worst of British music hall and a demeaning comment on those who had kept the skies free of Stukas.

Not wishing to participate in failure, the same patrons who had earlier endorsed her pleaded the lateness of the hour and fled.

Alone, Kendal sat at the little horseshoe bar and was comforted by Vincent Sardi, an empiricist who understood the vicissitudes of Broadway openings better than most men, and whose courtesy had consoled legions of actors.

Warmed by wine and words, Kendal left the restaurant. It was snowing and there were few pedestrians about. It was quiet and windless and the air was as soft as the falling snow. It was a night for walking. Kendal crossed east to Fifth Avenue and proceeded north toward her hotel, on Fifty-Eighth Street between Fifth and Sixth avenues. She was exhilarated by the weather and she noted with delight that she was making virgin tracks. The snow was untrampled and she felt like the first explorer of Manhattan. Her pace quickened and, because her thin-soled shoes were swiftly soaked, she removed them and began to run in her stocking feet, unmindful of the cold. Occasionally, she bent low even as she ran, scooping a handful of fresh snow, rubbing it on her face and in her hair, and chewing fistfuls of it.

As she skidded around the corner of Fifty-Eighth Street, she was quite certain that she had fallen through a looking glass — for surely what she saw was the Mad Hatter and his friend the Dormouse.

Drawn up outside the entrance of the Plaza Hotel was a small wagon such as peddlers might have used many years ago on the rutted roads of Europe. Hitched to it was a very old horse. Two benches had been anchored onto the open bed of the wagon. Sitting on the carriage seat forward of the wagon were two young men, both dressed in the uniforms of the United States Army. One of them was small and skinny, and he wore a long row of battle ribbons on his chest. Like the Mad Hatter, he sported a tall stovepipe hat, its crown battered, its silken sheath in tatters. Next to him, dozing peacefully, chin pinned to his chest, was a younger man with the crispest, blackest hair Kendal had ever seen. The Mad Hatter gnawed on a carrot, then placed the tip of it to the Dormouse's lips. Even though apparently asleep, the younger man nibbled courteously. But as he did, he tilted forward.

"He's going to fall!" Kendal cried.

Slowly, the younger man slipped off his seat and into the snow.

"Hoo ha!" shouted the Mad Hatter. He leaped off the wagon and as he leaned over his friend, Kendal joined him.

"Is he all right?" Kendal was genuinely worried.

"Well," said the Mad Hatter, whose name, Kendal would learn later, was Mousey Blum, "let's discover." He removed his stovepipe hat and gently fanned the fallen man's face, but it was not until Kendal rubbed Solomon's face with snow that he opened his eyes. He blinked when he saw her and then his eyes filled with joy as he sang.

"*Ole buttermilk sky, I'm keeping my eye fixed on you./What's the good news tonight, is it going to be cloudy or bright?*" Solomon twanged like Hoagy.

"Would you like to get up now?" Kendal asked.

"I don't think so," Solomon replied.

"I'll tell you the truth," Mouse said. "He looks comfortable."

"Well, yes," Kendal said. "Yes, he does."

"Maybe we should join him," Mouse suggested.

"My feet are awfully cold," Kendal said.

"Put them in my pocket," Solomon said.

"Now?" Kendal asked.

"Forever," Solomon said.

She did.

Not long after that snowy midnight Kendal discovered that, recently discharged from the army, Solomon was waiting for his friend, Emilio Ho, to convert the back room of his delicatessen into a nighttime bar where Solomon would play the piano. Because they shared an enthusiasm for New Orleans jazz, she and Solomon would cruise the night streets of Greenwich Village, where they searched for the sinuous rhythms of marvelous men — men like Wild Bill Davison and Big Sid Catlett, Baby Dodds and Pleasant Joe and Pops Foster, Kaiser Marshall, Danny Barker; trumpeters, bassists, sax men, drummers, the caressers of clarinets, celebrants of the blues. And at each club, where they listened to what Solomon called the sound of blue smoke, they talked between the musicians' sets. They talked as urgently as strangers on a train, each secretly fearful that the other would disembark before the journey was complete. Because they were falling in love, their communication was unrestrained, shaped uniquely by an immediate acceptance of each other's dreams, given form by desire. They exchanged opinions on everything. Nothing was trivial between them. Each thought revealed, every reaction exposed, was a discovery of delight. Small things they had in common were greeted with exclamations of enchantment.

"I hate beets," Solomon declared.

"Oh, my God," Kendal cried. "That's fantastic!"

Their pleasure in each other was overwhelming and they could not bear to witness the sadness of others. At Nick's, where Eddie Condon strummed, they sat next to a single black man at a small round table. He had a long nose and wet eyes, and the flesh of his face lay limply in descending folds. He looked like a basset. On the table in front of him was a neat semicircle of one-ounce shotglasses, each filled with brandy, and he was weeping into them. Kendal turned to him.

"Are you all right?" she asked.

"Great God A'mighty," the man wept, "I missed it."

"Missed what?" Kendal and Solomon spoke simultaneously.

"What he done, man. What Sidney done!" The hound-faced man lifted a shotglass and downed the brandy in one gulp. "Bechet," he continued. "He is formidable, you dig it? That man, he hate a sloppy cat. He settin' up there with his band and this horn man, this sloppy cat is spittin' through his brass sumpin' awful to hear. I mean, it racked up your goddamn ears. Well, it gonna pain Sidney, ain't it? Ain't it gonna pain Sidney?"

"Well, certainly," Kendal said.

"You bet," said Solomon.

The sad-featured man lifted a shotglass in each hand and downed one after the other. "Oh," he said, "the pain. I can feel the pain! Sidney, he get so riled he jus' up an' got. He sets hisself at a table in front of this cat an' he orders hisself some pretty little brandies, an' each time he throw one down, *wham*, he sets that empty glass flyin' at the cat with no ears. *Wham! Wham!* Oh, Sidney, he is formidable. Oh, he is my *man!* An' I missed it!"

"Wow," Solomon said. "He just kept throwing the glasses at this horn player?"

"Wham! Wham!" said the basset.

"Where did he do this? Where was he?" Kendal asked.

"Shee-eet, man," the man said, "if I know'ed where he was at, would I have fuckin' missed it? Jesuu-uus!" In quick succession he drank the last of the brandies. "Wham," he wept. "Wham. Wham." And then he snatched one of the empty glasses from the table, spun around in his chair to face the wall, and hurled the glass. Even before the glass shattered, he had plucked another one from the table and hurled it.

"Wham!" he yelled.

The glasses shattered over the heads of two Marines who were cozied with their pretty young ladies. Splinters fell into steins of foaming beer. The Marines leaped up and in their rush to get to the sad-faced man, they overturned their table. They crunched and skidded through wet pretzels, struggling to reach the man who, in his sad fury, continued to fling his glasses, tears rivering down his folded face.

"Wham wham!"

A burly chief petty officer, his navy uniform combat-ribboned, smashed a beer bottle, the broken shards a wicked weapon in his hand as he charged toward the Marines. Hurdling the outstretched legs of customers, two waiters ran to intercept him. Kendal ducked under the flailing arms of the basset man and swept the remaining shotglasses into her open purse. Young men and women, many still in their uniforms of the recent war, shoved backwards from the frenzy, toppling chairs and tables, stumbling over wine glasses and half-eaten sandwiches, shouting at each other to get the hell out of there. Solomon grabbed Kendal by the hand and, their bodies bent low, they duck-waddled through the melee. But by the time they reached the door of the club they heard laughter and the twang of Condon's guitar. They spun around and saw that Condon and Peewee Russell had moved onto the bandstand and that Russell's stringbean body twisted in ecstasy as he blew whispers from his clarinet. Applauding him was the chief petty officer, who now sat with the Marines and their ladies. Sandwiched between the ladies, nestled in their benevolent embrace, was the basset man, his eyes closed, his face wreathed in a dreamy smile. His lips moved in a soundless word.

"Wham!"

Later, after they had made love in his one-room apartment on Cornelia Street, Solomon removed a small frame from one wall. It was a simple frame and it held a single piece of paper on which was scrawled a penciled paragraph. Solomon returned to bed and, his head on Kendal's naked belly, he held up the frame for her to see.

"One night," Solomon told her, "I met this guy who knew Bechet. Actually knew him. And he told me something that Bechet had said and I wrote it down. Listen to this. You'll like it."

"I like what you just did," she said. "A lot."

"You've got a one-track mind."

"Is that bad?"

"That is not bad," he said, "but I want you to hear something. It's important."

"To us?"

"Us," Solomon repeated softly. "Oh, God, what a marvelous word." He turned his head and kissed the golden hair which rose below her belly. He felt her muscles spasm with pleasure. "I love you." She leaned forward and cradled his head between her breasts and ran her tongue over his eyelids.

"Read," she said.

Before he read the framed passage, Solomon explained to Kendal that Bechet, whom Solomon thought to be the greatest soprano saxophonist of all, was obsessed with excellence. He, Bechet, recognized his own irascibility, his impatience with men of lesser talent, but he justified that impatience by his single-minded veneration of the melodies he played.

"What's so goddamn wonderful," Solomon said, "is the respect a guy can have for one thing, the pleasure he gets from it, like riding a balloon that floats forever. It's just so goddamn wonderful."

"I love you," Kendal said.

"Listen to this," he said, and he read the passage.

" 'Oh, I can be mean. I know that. But not to the music. That's a thing you gotta trust. You gotta mean it, and you gotta treat it gentle. The music, it's that road. There's good things alongside it, and there's miseries. You stop by the way and you can't ever be sure what you're going to find waiting. But the music itself, the road itself, there's no stopping that. It goes on all the time. It's the thing that brings you to everything else.' "

Solomon lowered the framed passage. He turned on his side and cupped Kendal's breast and kissed her nipple. "What do you think?"

"I think it's goddamn wonderful," she said. "I think you're goddamn wonderful."

Solomon released her breast and pulled himself up to lie flat against her, and they were so close that when he whispered to her his lips moved against hers.

"I don't like secrets," he said.

"Neither do I."

"So I'm going to tell you something and after I say it, I don't want to talk about it. Not now, not ever. Okay?"

"Okay."

Solomon took a slow, deep breath and because of the proximity of their mouths Kendal felt as if he were drawing air from her own lungs, and that if he continued she would be breathless until he replenished her.

"What you saw tonight, it's what I am," Solomon said softly. "I'm a rinky-dink piano player in lousy bars. I'm not good and I'm never going to get any better. I know that and it doesn't make any difference because playing that piano, that's my balloon, that's the balloon I ride on. That's all I want."

"That's *all?*" Kendal asked and, as she knew it would be, her voice was without breath.

"That's all."

"Darling," Kendal said and then paused. It was the first time either had used the word and the sound of it was sweetly rich with commitment. She felt Solomon slowly harden. "Darling," she said again, her voice overly gentle as if trying to soften her unease, "there's so much waste in the world, so much awful waste. Let's not be part of it."

" 'The music,' " Solomon murmured, " 'it's that road. It's the thing that brings you to everything else.' " Gently, he bit her ear. "Okay?"

"Okay," she said and guided him into her. But even as they moved in the slow lazy rhythm of their love, Kendal worried about the waste of things, the waste of men, the waste of a rinky-dink piano player.

During the early years of their marriage, Kendal had continued to work in the theater and Solomon played in the little back room of Emilio's delicatessen. The deli's patronage expanded, became more sophisticated, attracted the many night people of Manhattan. Among them were theatrical associates of Kendal's: producers, directors, writers. The nights were spent in heated discussions about the merits or frailties of Broadway productions, regardless of their success or failure. It was not long before many of the participants of these discussions realized that Solomon had a great deal of critical insight. He became a favorite sounding board. It was a natural progression for many of those who listened to his judgments to suggest that he find a way to become more than an observer. Solomon would wink at his friend Mousey Blum and continue to experiment with left-handed chords.

One night, Kendal gave him a script. It was a contemporary satire incorporating song and dance. Solomon liked the combination of bitterness and charm. Kendal had been offered a role in the production but the producer lacked complete financing. A patron of the nightly sessions in the bar, he was an admirer of Solomon's and had pleaded with Kendal to ask Solomon to co-produce.

"Once," Kendal urged Solomon, "just try it once. You'll be good at it, terribly, fantastically good at it. You'll set them on their bums! I mean, God, darling, you can't spend your whole life playing the fucking piano!"

By the time Solomon was forty, he had produced a number of Broadway plays. Most were critically acclaimed. Each was a financial failure. But his record of achievement had not gone unnoticed by TransGlobal. Eventually, it led to his employment.

Now, in the Vermont farmhouse, dancing slowly in Solomon's arms, Kendal thought how swiftly the years had passed. Mellowed by memory and music, she pressed her cheek against Solomon's.

"Hey, mister," she whispered, "wanna make out?"

"Watch it, guys," Darby's voice intruded. "You got company."

Kendal pulled away from Solomon and started across the room. She saw her daughter's red-stained blouse. "My, God, Darby, what —"

"It's okay, Mom, honest. It's just wine."

As Kendal and Darby hugged each other, Solomon moved to the phonograph and lifted the needle.

"Don't stop, Daddy," Darby said. "It's sweet."

Solomon stared at her, then lifted his jelly glass and drained his drink. "Nice of you to come."

"I'm sorry I'm late. I couldn't help it."

Solomon knew that his daughter was truly contrite and he was annoyed at himself that he'd let his irritation show. He realized that Brindig's call had turned the evening sour. He had no wish to blame his daughter for his own foul mood.

" 'S okay," he mumbled through the whiskey. "C'mere."

Darby grinned at him, stepped across the room, and hugged him. He ran his hand gently down her cheek. "You're a good lookin' broad."

"I got good genes."

"I miss you," Solomon said.

"Me, too," Darby said.

"But I'm still hungry, kiddo." Solomon waggled his finger at her, stepped away, and turned toward the kitchen. "I'll go fix the steak."

"Oh, Solomon, don't!" Kendal's voice was urgent. Solomon saw a look pass between Kendal and Darby.

"Wha's the matter," he asked politely, "you guys become vegetarians?" When they didn't answer, he shrugged. "Well, tha's okay. I mean, *chacun à son goût*. Ask Jabez for some fresh vegetables, he won't mind. I mean, if he's there. Which I doubt. He's pro'ly hitched his trailer an' driven to General Hospital or Greenwich, where the clocks run on time." He frowned and blinked at his own words.

He was, Kendal realized, definitely drunk. She watched him run a finger around the inside of his jelly glass, then suck on the finger and smack his lips. He turned to her. "That's wrong, isn't it? I mean, the clocks are set in Greenwich, England, not Greenwich, Connecticut, right?"

"Greenwich, England," Kendal said.

"Well, then," Solomon continued, "how could he drive to England? There's all that water."

"I don't think he went to England," Kendal said.

"Well, I'm not gonna go either," Solomon said.

"No," Kendal said.

"I'm going to Scotland." Solomon winked and tapped his empty jelly glass.

"Would you like some coffee?" Kendal asked.

"In Scotland?" Solomon asked. "They don't drink coffee in Scotland. The Scots in Scotland drink scotch. That's the way it should be, you know. It has form to it. Everything should have form to it. Isn't that what you tell me, Kendal? When form goes, all goes? I'm going to Scotland where they have form." He was weaving a little as he walked out of the living room and into the kitchen. Darby looked questioningly at her mother.

"Mr. Brindig called," Kendal explained.

"Why doesn't Daddy tell Mr. Brindig to fuck off?"

"It's not that simple, dear."

"Isn't it?" Darby looked questioningly at her mother.

"Did you stop at Em's?" Kendal avoided Darby's question.

"Uh-huh."

"Did you get what you wanted?"

"It's in the truck. What's left of it."

"Then let's set it up outside. We'll eat under the trees."

"It'll be too cold outside."

"For heaven's sake, Darby, you've planned this all week. Let's not ruin it."

"I don't think Daddy's in the mood for surprises."

"Then we'll change his mood. Now let's go."

By the time Darby had run upstairs and changed her clothes, Kendal had rescued what she could from the truck. She spread a paper tablecloth on a picnic table in the apple orchard. She put Darby's candles in red clay flowerpots and placed them at the end of the table that was sheltered from the evening breeze. As she removed the food which was still in reasonable condition from its cardboard containers and ladled it into paper picnic dishes, Darby joined her. She was in one of Solomon's old shirts and a pair of jeans and sandals.

"You're supposed to dress in the nicest things you have, but this was all I could find," Darby said.

"You look beautiful," Kendal said.

"What I really like about you," Darby smiled, "is that you're so objective. You have any Mogen David wine?"

"Will you settle for a good Margaux?"

"You mean that'll make Daddy happier?"

"If he can still taste anything. I'll get some glasses."

"No," Darby said, "we'll share this." She had been standing with one hand behind her back and now she brought forth a beautiful silver goblet cast in the shape of a tulip.

"Darby!"

"It's a *Kiddush* cup. Mouse gave it to me. He told me how to do this whole thing. When we're all ready, you step up to the table because you're the mother and cover your head and light the candles and say a prayer. Here, I brought it for you." Darby took a small piece of paper from her jeans. A prayer was typed on it. She handed it to Kendal. "Then Daddy blesses the children — well, in this case, it's just me — and then everybody gets quiet and feels good because they know that the Sabbath Queen has come into the room, or, I guess, out here in the woods. I mean, you can't see her or anything, but you just know." She paused and looked shyly at her mother. "Does all this sound silly?"

"It's lovely," Kendal said. "It's absolutely lovely."

"There're some great stories, legends sort of, for the Sabbath." Darby hesitated for a moment. "Maybe Daddy'll tell some."

"I don't think," Kendal said slowly, "that we should count on that. I'll go get him."

When Kendal entered the kitchen, Solomon was stripped to his underwear. He was sitting in the huge kitchen sink, pumping cold water over himself.

"This isn't much fun, you know," he said, shivering under the icy flow.

"Poor baby," Kendal said, trying very hard to stifle her laughter. She appreciated Solomon's brave attempt to sober up.

"When I see him on Monday, I'm going to bite Brindig's ass."

"Yes, darling," Kendal said. She opened a kitchen cabinet, removed a bottle of Margaux and uncorked it.

"You don't think I'll bite his ass?" Solomon demanded.

"You want some help?" Kendal asked.

"In biting his ass?"

"In getting out of the sink."

"Am I getting out of the sink?"

"I think it would be nice. Darby's waiting."

"I did this before, you know," Solomon said proudly. "This isn't the first time I've sat in a sink. No siree-bob."

Kendal took Solomon's hand and helped him climb out of the sink and lower himself to the floor. He stood in his soaking boxer shorts and dripped onto the linoleum.

"Take your shorts off, darling," Kendal said. She reached under the kitchen sink and removed a handful of dishtowels from a rack.

"That's what she said."

"Who?" Kendal asked.

"The lady I sat in the sink with," Solomon said. "I mean the lady with whom I sat in the sink."

"Here," Kendal said. She gave him the dishtowels. He pulled off his shorts and used the towels to scrub his body dry as she picked up his shirt and pants from the kitchen floor.

"Boy," he said, "I'm really hungry."

"Good," Kendal said. "Darby's brought a wonderful dinner. Put your pants on."

"You say that a lot." He slipped into his shirt and pulled on his pants. He slid his bare feet into sneakers.

Kendal stepped close to him, smoothed back his wet hair, then lightly held his face between her hands. "Listen to me, Solomon. Your daughter has a surprise for you. It's a very nice surprise. Be good, okay?" She took him by the hand and led him out of the kitchen, down the slope to the apple orchard. Dusk had fallen and the wind was down. The moon was swollen in the western sky. Although the air was chilly it did not yet hint of a November bite.

Slowly, Darby rose from her bench at the picnic table, her body slightly awkward with tension. When she spoke it was as if she were asking a question.

"Good *yontif*," she said. "Good *yontif*, Daddy."

Solomon said nothing. He looked at his daughter, then at his wife. Then he stared at the table. He frowned. He opened his mouth as though to speak, but no words came out. He sighed. Finally, he spoke.

"Why didn't you tell me?"

"Tell you what?" Darby asked tentatively.

"That we were having deli. I *love* deli." He reached down, plucked a slice of pastrami from a plate, and lifted it toward his mouth.

Kendal breathed a sigh of relief. For the moment, at least, Solomon seemed able to accept Darby's involvement with Judaic ritual. She knew that Solomon's attitude reflected only an indulgence, but even that pleased her for she was aware that theological matters irritated Solomon, made him uncomfortable. Kendal's own religious beliefs were centered in a quiet faith which she felt no need of sharing or exposing. Such things were personal, private, and required no exposure. That she was an Episcopalian and Solomon a Jew were simple facts — accepted, acknowledged, and, she believed, nonintrusive to their relationship.

"Wait a minute," she said, taking the meat from Solomon's fingers, replacing it on the platter. "Don't be greedy. There's a ceremony first. Isn't that right, Darby?"

"Uh-huh." Darby gave a handkerchief and the printed prayer to her mother and instructed her in the Sabbath procedure. "You cover your head with the hanky and light the candle and then say it."

"What is this stuff?" Solomon wanted to know. He pointed to a large dish of gefiltefish.

"Solomon," Kendal said, "pay attention."

"I don't like the way it feels," he said, poking the gefiltefish with one finger.

"Daddy, please," Darby requested, "listen to Mom."

"May I listen sitting down?"

"Not yet. It's your turn next."

Solomon looked at her blankly. Kendal had asked him to be good. He was going to be good. "Whatever you say, honey."

Kendal unfolded the handkerchief and draped it over her head. She had an instant memory of accompanying her father to the Church of England and of the small lace scarf he had given her to cover her head and of their voices raised joyously together in the singing of psalms. She wished suddenly that she and Solomon had introduced Darby to the warmth of religious ritual and, looking at her daughter, she felt quite certain that Darby wished it, too.

"Now?" she asked.

"Now," Darby answered.

Kendal lighted the candles and in their flickering light she read the prayer.

"Blessed art Thou, O Lord, our God, King of the Universe, Who has made us holy by Thy Commandments, and Who commands us to kindle the Sabbath lights."

Solomon wished his feeling of discomfort would disappear. His hand edged toward the pastrami but he saw Kendal glance sharply at him. He withdrew his hand.

"Perfect, Mom!" Darby turned to her father. "Now you bless your child. I'm a girl, so —"

"I can see that."

"— you put your hand over my head," Darby continued, "and you say, 'May God make you like Sarah, Rebekah, Rachel, and Leah,' and then you get to pour the wine and recite *Kiddush: I will lift up the cup of salvation and call upon the name of the Lord.*"

Solomon wished it would storm so that claps of thunder and streaks of lightning would divert his daughter from the ceremony she had begun. Although never denying his Judaic roots, he felt isolated from them. They were part of a past in which he'd never shared; nor had he infused Darby with any sense of tradition. For either of them to give credence to Hebraic matters was, he thought, an act of hyprocrisy. He knew that Kendal was aware of his feelings and it angered him that she had participated in sham.

"C'mon, Daddy," his daughter repeated. "Say, *I will lift up the cup of salvation and —*"

"I don't think so," Solomon said quietly.

"Solomon," Kendal said.

"Aren't you carrying this a little far?" Solomon asked slowly. His voice now had none of the drunken foolishness of moments before. He stared at Kendal. "I don't understand you. I really don't. What conceivable reason would you have for doing this?"

"Really, Solomon," Kendal said, an edge to her voice, "we haven't hatched some awful plot."

"It was my idea," Darby said quickly.

"Well, I don't like it," Solomon said to her. "I don't want to offend you, but if you and your mother want to indulge in some kind of . . . of . . ." He sought for the right words. "Some kind of religious fantasy, that's your privilege. I'd appreciate it if you'd grant me the privilege of not being part of it."

"I hardly think fantasy is the right word," Kendal said.

"Don't you? What would you call it?"

"For God's sake, Solomon, it's a simple ceremony."

"It's artificial piety, is what it is," Solomon retorted sharply. "Pure and simple."

From somewhere down the road a farm dog wailed and Darby turned toward the sound. She spoke softly. "There's a legend that if you hear a cry on *Shabbis* it means the Angel of Death is in town."

"That's foolish," Solomon said.

"Mouse doesn't think so."

"Mouse?" Solomon looked at his daughter in surprise. He couldn't picture his best friend, Mousey Blum, listening to the Angel of Death. Laugh at him, yes, but not listen to him. But then a small suspicion grew in Solomon's mind. "Did Mouse put you up to all of this?" he asked his daughter.

"He didn't 'put me up to' anything," she replied. "He taught me some things, that's all. Like what to do at a *Shabbis* dinner. I think it's beautiful. I thought you'd think so, too. Is that so awful?"

"No. No, it isn't awful. It's just . . . presumptuous."

"God, Daddy, how can you say that? You're a Jew, aren't you? I'm a Jew."

"Well," Solomon said, fidgeting with the paper tablecloth, tearing little pieces of it with his fingers.

"Why does that make you so uncomfortable?" Darby pressed on. "I'd like to know that, I really would."

"Darby, that's enough," Kendal said.

Solomon ripped the tablecloth. His voice was quiet but intense. "What do you want, Darby, a medal? Do you really think you're something special?"

"Yes," Darby cried. "I am something special."

"Bullshit," Solomon said. He told himself to be quiet, to discontinue this conversation, to just walk back to the house, but he couldn't. "That's what's wrong with the whole goddamn world. Everybody's special. Everybody's better than the next guy. Can't you see how lousy that is? How you get trapped in that?" He crumpled the torn piece of tablecloth in his hand and threw it to the ground. "It's like walking into a cage without any doors."

"You've got it backwards, don't you, Dad?" Darby asked. "I found the door. Mouse opened it. What about you? Where's your door?" She grabbed the *Kiddush* cup, spun away from the table, and strode angrily to her truck. "You can keep the food," she shouted. Then the truck's engine roared and the tires spun and Darby sped away. After a long silence, Solomon spoke.

"Good *yontif*," he said bitterly.

"Solomon . . . Solomon . . ." Kendal paused.

"Go ahead, say it."

"Nothing," she said. "Nothing." Wearily, she left the apple orchard and walked slowly to the farmhouse. Solomon didn't watch her but he heard her say "we never gave her the pottery," and then the slap of the

screen door shutting behind her. He wet his fingers and pinched out the
flame of one candle but when he realized how swiftly the night had descended he let the second candle burn, its flame a yellow thumb in the
darkness.

He stared at the flame, sightless as a blind man, his vision turned in-
wards toward an examination of his guilt. The guilt was mixed with irritation, for Solomon thought of himself as a man liberated from what he
considered the strictures of religious affiliation. He did not deny that
both his mother and father had been Jews and, in the eyes of society he,
too, was a Jew. But he believed that such categorical definition was a
form of sophistry and he resented it. He was a product of parents who
had been made uncomfortable with the consequence of faith and who
had attempted to defuse the combustible and prejudicial pressures ex-
erted by those who judged Jews. Deliberately, they had made no effort
to inform Solomon of his roots so that he could fit better into the world
they perceived. Neither Hebrew nor Yiddish had been spoken in his
house. Dietary laws were unknown, the rituals of holidays unobserved.
Solomon was not bar-mitzvahed. Not once had he stepped through the
doors of a temple. He had not read the Torah, nor studied the Talmud.
He was ignorant of Hebraic legend. Though he was an uninformed Jew,
his conscience, nevertheless, was pricked by the history of diaspora and,
because of the uneasiness caused by this knowledge, like his father and
his father's father, he had attempted to absolve himself from any linkage
with his past. The ensuing paradox was his constant but unconscious
search for some community, some connection, to which he could
pledge his allegiance.

Distressed by what he felt was Darby's arbitrary, and seemingly sentimental, quest for Judaic roots, he stared at the now-sodden Sabbath dinner that lay before him. Slowly, plate by plastic plate, he swept the food
into a garbage bag. He brushed crumbs to the ground with the sleeve of
his shirt, the cotton absorbing both pickle brine and flecks of spiced fish.
He pinched out the remaining candle flame. He sat in the darkness, listening to the cry of owls and the tiny click of cicadas.

He felt a drop of rain and then another. He looked up and saw that
now the moon was hidden. A northern wind whipped the apple trees,
and leaves fell silently to earth. He rose and as he stepped toward the
farmhouse he heard a sound so strange, so frightful, it was as if a demon
had shrieked.

Distant, thin and high, borne by the northern wind, the mournful cry
tunneled down from the mountain top, cycloned in its own anguish.

Under the rain that pelted his skin, Solomon stared toward the mountains. He saw nothing but the blackened sky. The cry, drowned beneath the rain, was gone. Solomon turned and saw a light in his bedroom. Kendal stood at the window and as Solomon looked up at her he was certain that she, too, heard the echo of Darby's words.

The Angel of Death is in town.

6

At first Callahan thought it was a thirty ought six, the shot exploding, then echoing in the village square, but when he hurried to the window he saw Darby's truck careering across the grass, its front left tire a circle of shreds from the blowout. Darby was fighting the wheel, just managing to stop the truck from tipping and spilling on its side. It slid to a stop only feet from the bandstand.

When Callahan ran outside he saw that Darby was hunched over the wheel, pounding the spokes with her fists. She looked more angry than frightened. She paid little attention to him as he moved closer, just kept slamming her small hands against the wheel and mouthing silent oaths.

"You punishing the truck?" Callahan asked. "Or yourself?"

"God," she said, "neither of us is much good!"

Callahan reached up and helped her out of the truck. Together, they examined the ripped tire.

"You're lucky," Callahan said. "You got a spare?"

"No. And please don't tell me how dumb I am. I know that. Boy, do I know that."

Callahan realized that she was not really referring to the lack of foresight in not carrying a spare tire. She was accusing herself of something else, and as he watched her kneeling by the truck, her slim figure lost in the voluminous folds of a man's shirt, he wanted very much to know what troubled her.

"I'm a man of very strange habits," he said. "About this hour every night I have some hot chocolate. I love hot chocolate. Would you care to join me?"

"I'm a terrible nuisance, aren't I? Maybe there's a garage open where I can . . ."

"There's nothing open. Not till morning. You've never tasted hot chocolate like mine. I guarantee it."

She stood and smiled at him. "You're very nice."

"No. Just proud of my chocolate."

Darby was intrigued at Callahan's house. It consisted of a huge single room, incorporating a kitchen, and soaring to a skylight, its walls interrupted only by a balcony loft that ran along all four sides. Attached to steel beams and girders, which had been left exposed, were track lights, their metal cones focused individually on paintings and graphics, posters and icons, all conveying the eclectic taste of Wilfred Callahan.

But the outstanding feature of the room was a group of four oil paintings, seemingly identical. They hung in a horizontal row on the loft wall at the far end of the room. The paintings showed the figure of Death holding a scythe mounted on a racing horse. Darby recognized the work as Albert Pinkham Ryder's acclaimed *Death on a Pale Horse*, but the fact that there were four identical paintings startled her. Surely, a Vermont sergeant of police could not afford such a priceless work. And how could there be four? She turned and saw that Callahan was watching her.

"Forgeries," he said.

"Forgeries!" Darby was incredulous.

"Umm-mm," he said, with no further explanation. He stood in front of the stove stirring a wooden spoon through a richly thick mixture of milk and melted chocolate steaming in a pot. Two spice jars stood open on the counter next to him. He dropped a large pinch from each into the pot. Darby sniffed the spicy scent of nutmeg and cinnamon. Callahan whisked his spoon through the mixture and lifted it to his lips.

"Ah," he said and held it out to Darby.

As she sipped from the spoon, Darby was aware of the intimacy of that sharing, and she made no effort to dissipate the moment. She savored the rich, sweet taste of the chocolate and her gaze slowly swept the room, lingering over fine leather furniture, hand-woven rugs, and the fine paintings. She looked again at Callahan and saw that he was still savoring his taste of chocolate, his face glowing with pleasure.

"You're a sensuous man, aren't you?" she asked.

Callahan didn't answer. He poured the hot chocolate into two heavy mugs, set them on a butcher-block table, returned to the stove, and removed an oblong object encased in aluminum foil. He unwrapped it and placed two pastries on a plate and brought them to the table. They sat at opposite ends of the table. Callahan lifted one of the pastries and studied its light-brown glaze.

"Brioche," he said. "If it's not flaky, I've failed."

"I have a feeling you don't fail at anything," Darby said and bit into her brioche. "No," she said, relishing the delectable flavor, "you haven't failed."

In silence, they ate slowly, enjoying the light repast, Darby feeling terribly at ease with this quiet man, Callahan wondering what it was that troubled her.

"Tell me," he finally asked, "how was your Sabbath dinner?"

"It wasn't," she replied, her eyes on her plate.

"No Good Angel?"

"No Good Angel."

"Oh," he said. "I'm sorry."

"Me, too." She glanced quickly at him, then back to her plate. "My father doesn't believe in the Good Angel . . . or *Shabbis* . . . or . . . a lot of things. He doesn't believe in a lot of things." She stopped. She was attracted to Callahan, found it easy to talk to him, but she neither wanted to elicit his sympathy, nor, because he was still a stranger, did she want to be disloyal to her father. She had removed the topknot of the brioche, then separated the bread along its flutings. Now she placed the four equal pieces in front of her and studied them.

"Which one will live the longest?" Callahan asked.

"My God," she exclaimed, not hiding her surprise, "how'd you know what I was doing?"

"When I was a little boy," Callahan said, "I used to play a game with the peas on my plate. I pretended they were soldiers of Christ and I was their God." He saw her puzzled look but he wasn't yet prepared to tell her that he'd been a priest. "One by one, I would send each pea out to battle, and because I was all-powerful, all-knowing, I would decide which would live and which would die. It was a very complicated game because as I pushed them around on my plate, as I watched them roll around, some hiding under the beef or taking refuge among potatoes, I'd become inordinately fond of one or another of the peas and it would make me quite unhappy to gobble them up. There were times I was unable to make the decision and I'd rescue one, slip it into the pocket of my jacket so that it might live happily forever after. The trick, of course, was to perform this sleight of hand without my father seeing it."

"Would he have disapproved?"

"He would have thought it foolish." He sipped from his mug of chocolate. "And very sacrilegious."

"Because you made the peas soldiers of Christ?"

"No. Because I assumed the role of God. But then that's common, isn't it?"

"I think," Darby grinned, "that anyone who assumes the role of God has to be flakier than this brioche."

Callahan laughed. "No, I mean it's common for fathers to think their children are foolish. Don't you agree?"

"You're tricky," Darby said.

"Oh?"

"You want to talk about my father."

"Fathers are interesting. That's just a simple fact, isn't it? I believe in facts."

"Is that why you're a cop?"

Callahan left the table, then returned to it with a box of cigars and a lighter. "I normally just chew these," he said to Darby, "but there are times I can't resist temptation." Carefully, making a small ritual out of it, he lit his cigar and watched the smoke from it curl upwards. Darby followed his gaze, and when she saw the drifting patterns she almost believe this quiet man was painting in smoke.

"I became a policeman," Callahan said quietly, "because I think that the prize of salvation we seek in heaven is less essential than how we perform here. Here and now. You should understand that."

"Why?"

"Because that's the philosophy of Jews. It must have been what you were taught."

"No," Darby said. "I wasn't taught that. I wasn't taught anything. I mean anything about being a Jew." Suddenly, she laughed. "God," she said, "you're doing it, aren't you? You're getting me to talk about my father. You're dangerous, Wilfred."

"Would you like a cigar?" He smiled.

"Sure. Why not?"

Callahan removed another cigar from the box and started to cut a cross in it at the rounded, closed end, but Darby took the cigar and the knife from him.

"If I'm going to do it," she said, "let me do the whole thing."

"Why didn't your father introduce you to any religious training?"

"I'm not sure," Darby said as she concentrated on preparing her cigar. "I think he decided that if I wasn't taught anything about it, it would just go away. Being Jewish, I mean."

"Don't cut too deeply," Callahan instructed her as he watched her working on the cigar. "You just want enough to let the smoke through. And did it?"

"Did what?"

"Did being Jewish go away?"

"You're kidding," Darby said. "With this nose how can it go away, for God's sake?" She put down the knife and held the cigar in front of her. She held it gingerly in two fingers. "Do I have to wet the end? I don't want it to get all mushy."

"Don't put it in your mouth yet. Hold it over the flame, an inch above it, and let the tobacco catch the heat. When there's a little ash on it you can begin to smoke."

Darby did as she was instructed and as a tiny band of white ash grew on the end of the cigar, she said, "It smells wonderful."

"It should," Callahan said. "A friend of mine smuggled it in from Havana. You were talking about your nose."

"Yeah," Darby said. "You'd have to admit this is a Jewish nose."

"I would say that it is."

"So did all the other kids. At school." She took her first drag on the cigar. "It tastes as good as it smells. It's funny. I looked through an album of pictures once. There were a lot of my mother's father but none of the other side of the family. I asked my father if he had any and he said there was one, a long time ago, but he didn't know what happened to it. I wanted to find out if maybe his father or his grandfather had a nose like mine. I mean, my father doesn't. I guess it skips a generation. I used to wish it had skipped me."

"But no longer?"

"No. No longer. But then, boy! I used to get hassled a lot as a kid. You know the worst thing about it?"

"No."

"It's all so boring, so goddamn boring."

"Is that what you felt?" Callahan asked, studying her. "Bored?"

"Yeah. Bored." Darby took another drag on her cigar. "That's a lie. I'm lying. I just wanted to sound adjusted. No, I wasn't bored. I hated it. And I was frightened. I was frightened that one day they'd beat me up." She looked away from her cigar and grinned mischievously. "So I did something to stop them." She tossed her head back and laughed. "Oh, boy, I was crazy!"

"What'd you do?"

"Well, I thought that if I could show all those kids how tough I was, they'd leave me alone. One day — it was in the winter and very cold — I waited until we all had to go out for recess and run around the playground. God, I never could figure out why grown-ups think it's good for the soul to freeze your ass off. You think that's good for the soul?"

"Not particularly. I'd rather sit by the fire and drink hot chocolate."

"We would have had fun if we'd been kids together," Darby said.

"Yes," Callahan said.

With no self-consciousness, their hands slid along the table and their fingers touched, just touched, no more than that. It was as if each was acknowledging the beginning of something new between them.

"Anyway," Darby said after a long moment, "we were all out there and I climbed the ladder to the slide and then lay on my stomach on the slide, with my feet hooked over the top of the ladder. That way, no one could use it. I knew it would make everyone mad and they'd all come around and start yelling at me and everything. I waited until every goddamn kid was watching and yelling at me, the little Jew girl, and then I did it. I opened my mouth and I put my tongue against the metal of the slide. The steel was so cold that my tongue froze to it, and when I pulled my tongue away, some of it, some of my tongue, stayed on the slide and I began to bleed and I couldn't stop it and when my mouth was full of blood I spit. I spit at all the kids who were standing below me."

"That's a terrible story," Callahan said. "Terrible."

"I never told it to anybody before." She shook her head a little as if trying to dislodge the memory, then tried to smile. "I couldn't. My tongue was too sore."

"You never told your father, your mother?"

"No. Well, I did tell somebody. I told the Mouse."

"You told *who?*"

"Oh, sorry, you don't know him, of course. Mouse. Mousey Blum. He's a friend of the family. He's terrific."

"And what did . . . did . . . Mouse say?" Callahan tried to picture the man about whom Darby spoke but images failed him.

"He said I was victim of narcissism. He reads a lot."

"I don't understand."

"There's this guy, this Viennese psychoanalyst, Dr. Kohut, who developed a theory. He says that if a child doesn't feel accepted, doesn't feel worthwhile, maybe even lonely, then that kid'll do things to get attention. The kid wants so much to be appreciated that he'll do anything, no matter how dangerous it is."

"Could you understand that as a child?"

Darby laughed. "Hell, no. If I'd understood it, I wouldn't have kept doing it."

"You kept putting your tongue on the slide?"

"No." Darby's mischievous grin disappeared, her eyes darkened, and slowly she pulled her hand away so that her fingers were no longer touching Callahan's. "I did other things."

Callahan wanted terribly to know what those other things were, but from her tone, her whole physical attitude, he knew she had withdrawn and that to pry her with further questions would not only be unfair but might intrude on the warm feelings that were growing between them. But his own past drove him to make one more inquiry.

"Darby," he asked, "are you religious?"

"I'm not sure how to answer that," she said. "The thing is, I didn't know where I belonged. Mouse helped me with that. He helped me a lot. He taught me what a Jew is. At least, he's teaching me. I'm not sure you ever know all of it. But I do know that I'm a Jew. And I'm glad of it. I'm proud of it. What I've learned from Mouse doesn't really have anything particular to do with God. I mean, if you believe in Him, great, but what I think I was looking for was some sense of the past, some idea of where everything I am began. Some feeling of tradition, I guess. Does that make sense to you?"

"Yes, of course. It's happening more and more."

"What do you mean?"

"It would be impossible for any Christian today to deny that the time we live in is not exemplified by acts of morality. By Christian I don't mean Gentile as opposed to Jew. I mean any who acknowledge that there's a validity in the teachings of Christ, the philosophy of Christ. Any sane observer is forced to give credence to the fact that there is a deep fracture in our ethical behavior. There really isn't any ambiguity in what we see; therefore, it's only natural to seek solace in what we would like to believe was a better time. We all hope that what we discover in or of our past will inform us of who we are today. We pray that it'll animate our present condition. There is, of course, a terrible danger in that."

"Why?"

"Because we assume that the past was less troubled — more genuine, if you will — and that in our journey backwards we'll be able to recapture innocence. When we do that, we're using nostalgia as a panacea, and it can never be."

The few drops of chocolate in her cup were cold and Darby frowned as she stirred the remaining liquid, then left the spoon in the cup, clicked it a few times against the sides of the cup, then spoke quietly.

"May I ask you something personal, Wilfred?"

"Sure."

"Do you believe in God?"

"I'm a Catholic," he answered simply, but still unable to reveal his past priesthood.

"Then don't you find pleasure, something that moves you, that has meaning for you, when you observe the traditions of the Church?"

"I'm not disputing that. There is more than pleasure in participating in the liturgy. There is a deep consolation. And, yes, I relate to the history of who I am when I kneel before the cross or celebrate the Eucharist or listen to the Te Deum. These things are all part of a ritual and I think man derives great solace from ritual. It is not, however, a substitute for moral action. We can't alleviate the discomfort in ourselves until we accept the consequences of our choices, and by accepting them perhaps we'll elect to do that which allows us to live happily."

"I wish my father understood that."

"By that you mean he's not a happy man."

"No. He's not."

"Does he know it?"

"I think so. It's hard to tell with him. He's a very private man. It's difficult for him to reveal things."

"Perhaps," Callahan said, "he's like you were. He doesn't know where he belongs . . . who he is . . . what he is."

"God," Darby said, "I hope he finds out, don't you?"

Not replying, Callahan rose, took the two empty cups and the plate, put them in the sink, then crossed to the door of the house. "I'd like you to stay here tonight. You're too tired to drive and you can't get a tire till morning anyway."

"Where are you going?"

"I'm on duty tonight. I'll be back in the morning. Will you stay?"

"Thank you. I'd like that. What time will you be back in the morning?"

"After you're gone." He smiled at her.

She returned the smile. They both understood that the intimacy of the evening might lead to other things but neither wanted to force it.

Darby waited until he was half out of the door before she asked him her question again.

"Wilfred?"

"Uh-huh?"

"You didn't answer me. Wouldn't it be good if Dad could just find out who he is — *what* he is?"

"Some men," he answered slowly, "have a hard time with that. They discover things they don't like. Things they can't handle. It makes them . . . angry . . . very angry, and they . . ." He stopped, obviously not wanting to say more.

"What?" Darby asked. "They what?"

"They do what you did," he answered softly. "They do crazy things." He stepped out of the house and closed the door.

Darby ground out the butt of her cigar. She felt cold. Callahan's words had chilled her. She looked around the room and saw the door to a closet. She opened it and removed a woolen mackinaw. She draped it over her shoulders, then lay down on the sofa. She stared up at the four forged paintings. She would have to ask Wilfred about them. She knew she'd see him again.

As she closed her eyes, she wondered if lives, too, could be forged.

7

Warmed by the flesh of his wife, whose sleeping body curled around him, Solomon opened his eyes and stared through the open window of the bedroom. A wind blew down from the mountains and brought with it the fragrance of cinnamon fern. Solomon saw hemlock branches beat against the sky. A hawk, red-shouldered and swift, swept toward an unsuspecting prey. Solomon watched a spider walk a silver web across the windowpane. A moth shuddered against the cold window glass and slipped to the waiting web.

Next to Solomon, Kendal stirred uneasily as if she were aware of the day's quickening and its attendant carnage. She pressed closer to Solomon, flattening her breasts against his back. Her hand sought the warmth of his thigh. As always, Solomon was astonished at how the touch of lover's fingers on lover's flesh brought surcease to pain. He turned and lightly touched his lips against hers. Her breath was sweet.

"Mm-mm," she murmured, but he knew she still slept.

A gust of wind pulsated the windowpane and the moth trembled within the silken mesh of its captor's web. Solomon eased out from beneath the blankets, careful not to disturb Kendal. Wincing from the touch of cold floorboards against his bare feet, he crossed the room and stood at the window. He saw that last night's bitter rain had prematurely stripped deciduous trees of their foliage. His gaze moved past the apple orchard that marked the northern boundary of his land and he looked toward the huge maple that stood between the house and barn. He stared at the tree for a long moment. He was puzzled. There was something not quite right. And then he knew because he saw the leaf. Suspended. Splendid. Alone. The sugar maple was a miracle of dying color;

of wine and tarnished pink, of ghostly yellow. But from a narrow limb
which strained toward the sky hung one green leaf. The other leaves
were in their final fade. Many, defeated by the vanished storm, had
dropped to earth. But this one leaf, this thin emerald, unwounded by
the wind, refused its future. Defiant, it held dominion in the woods.

Looking at the leaf, Solomon was saddened that the coming cold
would flush it from its sly position, would fire it to a ruby flake. It
would bleed gently and flutter to an obscure death.

As he turned from the window he saw the moth's wings tremble in
the web. He smiled to himself. It was as if he had been presented with
an opportunity to balance nature's struggle. Gently, he pulled at the fine
strands of spider silk until he was able to free the moth. Placing it in the
palm of one hand, he carried it out of the room, through the kitchen,
out into the snap of morning air. Lifting his hand toward his mouth, he
blew the moth away and watched its rise and fall of flight, watched until
the shape of wings was lost among the crooked limbs of an apple tree.

Solomon returned to the kitchen. He filled a copper kettle with water
and placed it on a burner of the stove. While he waited for the water to
boil, he discarded his pajamas and dressed in the stiffly new clothes he
had ordered L.L. Bean to send in care of Tuttle. The caretaker had hung
them in the downstairs closet. He pulled on a pair of ankle-length red
woolen underwear and a red woolen top to match, then slipped into a
pair of khaki twill trousers. Two pairs of woolen socks came next, and
over them he laced a pair of calf-length leather boots.

The copper kettle whistled and steam rose from its spout. Solomon
made instant coffee. He placed it by the sink where he could sip it as he
shaved. From a small cabinet next to the sink, he removed a straight razor, an Arkansas honing stone, a china shaving mug, and a shaving
brush made of fine beaver bristles. He honed the blade of his old-
fashioned razor with swift, sure strokes, stropped it six times on either
side on a long piece of leather which hung from the sink, dipped his
brush into the porcelain bowl, lathered it, and began to soap his face. He
was fully aware that in these days of safety razors and instant lathers, his
ritual was archaic but it gave him great pleasure, made him feel closer to
those men who, so long ago, had risen on a thousand dawns to work the
land together. This imagined bond was the catalyst of this morning's
hunt. Solomon wanted to experience the history of this landscape and in
the experience he hoped to find community with those forgotten men.
For he had found it nowhere else.

Each morning of his summer weekends in Vermont, Solomon had

wandered through the woods and pastures nearby and marked in memory those places which offered likely possibilities of grouse. There were special areas: hardwood stands which had been timbered long ago but which were still dotted with tall evergreens, and isolated sunlit patches where green shoots sprouted, and along one section of the stream which zigzagged the farm, an abundance of thick green fern. The land was rich with birch and beechnut and aspen. Hemlock was profuse.

Once, Solomon had stayed in the woods all day. As the sun lowered in the sky, he stumbled through a greenbriar thicket and cursed softly as he pulled thorns from his skin. It was on that day that he heard his first drumming. Distant at first, then growing closer as if a marching band were approaching, then receding like the thunder of a passing summer storm, the sound swelled, faded, rose again in repeated beats, the dusk-dark woods enveloping the echo. Solomon was thrilled. It was the drumming of a grouse. Trying to locate the source of sound, he thrashed through the thicket, unmindful of thorns puncturing his flesh, and raced under the bending hemlock until he reached a clearing in the woods. In the center of the clearing were the foundation ruins of a house. All that was left were huge stones tumbled one against another into a long-forgotten cellar. A pitchfork, its wooden handle broken and bleached, its tines dissolved into rust, lay half hidden under one of the stones. Tucked into the soil next to it was the eyeless skull of a celluloid doll.

What man had lived here, Solomon wondered, and for what purpose had he pitched his fork? Had he turned the earth to plant seeds or had he dug the grave of his child?

He thought of his daughter Darby. As a child she had amassed an extensive collection of dolls, most of them representative of the people of foreign lands. At first, Solomon had thought that she was attracted to their exotic costumes but one day he overheard her speaking to them in a strange tongue, not unlike the jabberwocky of Lewis Carroll.

"What are you saying to them, honey?" he asked.

"Things," she replied.

"What things?"

"Things."

"Is that a special language?"

"Umm-hmm."

"What does it mean?"

"I can't tell you."

"Why?"

" 'Cause then it wouldn't be mine," she said.

Unreasonably annoyed at what he felt was her premature sense of privacy, by an act that frayed connection, Solomon left the room. Behind him, he heard the whisper of her alien language. It was as if she were sharing a secret with her family of dolls. Solomon did not inquire again. The celluloid doll reminded him that his daughter and he still did not share their secrets, nor their lives. Although occasionally weekending with her parents in Westport or Vermont, Darby lived alone in New York City. Inspired perhaps by the past theatrical backgrounds of both Solomon and Kendal, Darby was a stage manager for an off-Broadway repertory company. The company had a penchant for presenting the translated works of little-known foreign playwrights. The esoteric nature of these works caused Solomon to wonder if Darby were not merely extending her family of dolls. He made no mention of this notion for fear that the thread that still connected him and his daughter might further fray. At best, his relationship with Darby was tenuous. For many years he'd felt she'd wanted something from him — something unspoken, elusive. It had started, of course, with that letter. That goddamn letter.

Solomon turned away from the bruised, eyeless doll and saw, at the far end of the clearing, a long stump fence constructed from the wrenched-out roots of massive trees. Years ago it had defined a border between the clearing and a mowing that stretched several hundred yards to the north before it disappeared into the woods and rising hills beyond. The long-neglected mowing was now punctuated with a second growth of birch and aspen and elm, and greened with pine. But what drew Solomon's attention was what he saw along the fence of stumps. Threading through and cascading over the gnarled butts was a vine of wild fox grape, the berries still luminous in the dusk and emitting a faint fragrance of wine. Because he had read voraciously of the habits of the wild, bursting birds of Vermont, Solomon knew that fox grape was their favorite food. He had little doubt that the drumroll of the grouse had come from this place. He knew where he would hunt.

Now, remembering that evening of fox-grape fragrance, Solomon turned from the kitchen sink and glanced toward the corner where he had propped his shotgun. It was a twenty-gauge double-barreled gun with improved and modified chokes, a light weapon appropriate for the killing of small birds. Because of his early army training, Solomon was a skilled shot with small arms, but he had no intention of actually killing a bird. He wished Kendal had understood that. He wished that she had understood that to validate the experience of hunting he had to carry a loaded weapon. He did not doubt that he would fire it, for he liked the feel of the butt thudding into his shoulder and the sound of the crack and the smell of cordite; but his target would be a tree or a bush or the empty sky. He had no wish to see or handle the mutilated remains of a bird. He wanted only to enjoy the sense of his skill.

As he finished shaving, he hummed into the oval mirror over the sink. The mirror delighted Solomon. Its graceful shape pleased him but he particularly admired the mirror itself, its flawed surface. The glass was marred by a rough and rippled surface, and all images reflected from it were diffused, all objects distorted. The face in the glass that stared at Solomon had little reference to the external realities of Solomon's true features. His face was not deeply lined. His nose was short and uncommonly straight, his mouth wide and unbowed. His dark hair, only slightly flecked with gray, was crisp and unruly as a boy's. But his eyes were not young. They were gray and gentle and, although they often hinted at a sadness as if he had looked too long at something he did not wish to see, on this morning they were as bright as stream-washed granite.

But this flawed mirror showed none of these things, for the face it reflected was adrift in scars, as if the man to whom it belonged had taken many risks. Solomon enjoyed the illusion.

Solomon finished shaving. He washed out his cup. He put on a light flannel shirt and a canvas jacket. On either side of the jacket was a large bellows pocket to hold shells. Sewed inside the rear of the jacket was a rubberized pocket where a hunter could put his game. The game pocket was unstained by blood. The jacket had never been worn. Solomon slipped a box of shells into each side pocket.

He walked upstairs and entered the bedroom. Kendal had rolled herself tightly within a blanket and her eyes were closed. Solomon leaned over and kissed the tip of her nose.

"Mmmmmm," she said. But this time Solomon knew she was not asleep. He hoped she would open her eyes. He wanted her to admire his appearance, wanted her to see the image of the primitive man who had stared back at him from the flawed mirror. Her eyes remained closed, however. He turned and left the room.

Pulled forward by the marvelous memory of drumming, Solomon moved cautiously across the land, his boot heels deep into the October stubble. He walked over patches of wild raspberries and through clumps of stag-horn sumac and stumbled only once, on a hidden vine of deadly nightshade. As he dreamed of birds plunging noiselessly, silence quivered over the grieving ground of autumn.

The twin muzzles of his gun held high, Solomon's fingers moved restlessly over his gun, touching and tapping the stock, breech, and trigger in anticipation of the coming oiled precision. He waded through his creek and thought of the Iroquois, who had hollowed trees from the land; he imagined himself a raiding Indian crossing the Wantasequet. He reached the far bank of the stream, and as he climbed it his boots crushed the leaves of wild bergamot and he breathed deeply of the sudden scent of mint. A single crabapple tree studded the final pasture of his land. Solomon picked an apple from its branch and bit into it. It was as tart as a witch's kiss and Solomon hurled it upwards.

The apple was a scarlet globe against the pale October sky. Suddenly, high overhead, higher than the apple's climb, came the honking: the great sad sound of geese. A huge wedge of black-necked birds traced southward, racing away from winter.

"Pow pow," Solomon whispered, not bothering to raise his gun. And staring at the sky whitened with wings, he failed to see the boy who stalked him.

Standing in a high mountain glade that overlooked the woods toward which Solomon moved was Riordan Flynn. He believed that the mountain on which he stood, the woods below it, the river that descended through those woods, and the surrounding green land made fertile by that river were all parts of his domain. He did not welcome strangers. But as he watched the scene below him, the intensity of his concern diminished and was replaced by curiosity and pleasure.

Riordan saw the blasphemer of the road, and he saw that Jubal had turned hunter into prey. Swiftly, and without sound, Riordan moved down the mountainside.

Jubal was camouflaged by brush bordering the thin woods. Underneath his torn shirt, faded from many river washings, his back and arms were ribboned with muscle, which twitched and spasmed in excitement as he spied on Solomon and saw that the hunter was not without cunning. He saw that Solomon walked stealthily but with no attempt to disguise the rhythm of his pace. He walked into the wind. Jubal saw that the hunter understood that unnatural sounds would alert most wily birds and would keep them in their sanctuary, and that their sanctuary on days of hinted storm would be among the fallen leaves and jagged rocks and clumps of moss into which their plumage would blend. He noted with approval that the man in khaki clothes only occasionally gazed toward the high treetops of conifers, where a flushed bird would hide before his flight to freedom. He wondered where the hunter had developed his skill.

"Shh-hh," whispered Riordan, who slipped into the brush beside him.

Unexpectedly, Solomon's first grouse burst from a leafy cover, its wings thundering against the air as it exploded toward the trees. Startled, Solomon whipped up his gun and tracked the bird, his gun painting an arc across the sky. The bird swooped high and was lost behind a pine.

"He had the fucker," Jubal whispered to his father, but the old man's fingers dug hard into Jubal's shoulder and the boy was quiet.

Solomon laughed out loud and turned, swinging his shotgun toward another pine. He fired one barrel then the other, and spiny needles of the pine ripped from their branches. Their free float encased no feathers nor claw nor beak, for the tree was without birds. He reloaded and fired again. Methodically repeating these actions, Solomon depleted the contents of one box of shells. Not once had he waited for a bird to rise, and now the air was rank with cordite.

Jubal grunted. He could not understand the foolishness he watched. He had seen that the shotgun was fitted with an upraised rib, the thin strip of corrugated metal over which a gunner sights. He knew that, unventilated, the rib would grow fiercely hot from excess firing and that the ensuing waves of heat would warp the gunner's sight. He thought the hunter would have a difficult time should another grouse be flushed.

Riordan thought something else. He thought the man who had fired willfully at the tree might not have lost the ability to make war. And he wondered why.

Solomon walked into the woods.

The old man and his son followed.

When Solomon finally stepped into the clearing that held the ruins of the house and the vines of fox grapes, Riordan and Jubal slipped behind the stump fence. They crawled up a gentle rise of the northern mowing and lay in the tall grass, spying upon their prey. The sun rose higher in the sky, burning the mist off the land, and burning the backs of Riordan's and Jubal's necks. The ants sucked on their sweat, and the stones under their bellies pricked their flesh, but neither the old man nor the boy moved. Not one word passed between them.

His gun loaded once again, Solomon paced the perimeter of the clearing and waited for the sight of wings that drummed, but all he saw was a flight of sullen crows that cawed mockingly above him and then flew into the glaring sun. He was sorry that he had dressed so warmly. He discarded his canvas coat, removed his shirt and the top of his underwear. Sweat ran down his chest. He saw that a corner of the ruins was partially in shadow, so he picked his way through the tumbled rocks and came again upon the eyeless doll. He turned it over with the toe of his boot. Solomon could have sworn that the eyes of the skull were opening and closing, opening and closing, the eyes of ghosts awakening from their corporeal sleep. He had a terrible feeling that if those eyes succeeded in remaining open they would gleam with accusation. It was as if the eyes belonged to someone he knew: Darby, perhaps, or Kendal. Brindig.

Or were they the eyes of his father?

Solomon remembered his father, Ralph Moon, as a man who looked with sidelong glances for improbable assassins. An undeclared Jew, he was a man of ancient fractures, made desperate by his own pretense, made awkward by any flow of sentiment, made suspicious by possibilities. His eyes were shielded and unblinking behind bifocals, the rimless glass dustless, dry, octagonal. But once, Solomon had seen the wind whip past the hard bones of his father's face and lodge something in his eye. His father had reached up, a gesture of controlled annoyance (so typical of him, Solomon thought), had reached up and removed his glasses so that he could extract the offending dust, and in that swift second Ralph Moon had been unshielded. Solomon had seen eyes that told the truth. The wind had unmasked him. Rage and apprehension filled the mucous circles in his father's skull. At that moment, Solomon had had the strange sensation that perhaps his father had lived one day too long; that, weary of his public passivity, his father knew that his life was just one step after another toward the final accommodation. Death.

Dying, therefore, had been a simple experience for his father. He did it every day. On one sunless morning he simply failed to lift his eyes. Bifocaled, he stumbled out of life, affection still unspoken. His death made no statement that his life had not made before.

Now, staring into the imagined eyes of the doll, Solomon suddenly felt he had been accused of maintaining the passive accommodations of his father's life, and he knew the indictment was not without merit.

Suddenly, he felt an awful *thing* inside him. He felt the tiny teeth of an animal biting into the pulsating sacs of his lungs and as he felt *the thing's* razored teeth ripping at his spleen, a gray-winged junco sailed toward the north. Solomon whirled, slapped the butt of his shotgun to his shoulder, and fired. His shot was high and wide. The boom of fire bounced against the mountains, then slowly faded away and joined the silence of the retreating bird.

The black pellets of the shotgun, spent of their velocity, rattled harmlessly against Riordan's buckskin coat. He did not move. Neither did his son. But Riordan's eyes glittered, for he had seen a partial unmasking of the hunter in his khaki killing clothes.

The old man looked at things in a special way. He had the eyesight of a madman, and so observed only the interior life and death of things. With his focus on a leaf, he saw not the shape or color or movement of its blade, but its sapless veins and disintegrating tissue and the exposed walls of surface cells. He saw the fulminating abscess of God's work and it filled him with veneration. So, too, did he look at a man. He saw neither limb nor muscle nor pigmentation. He saw the soul.

The barrels of his shotgun were not as hot as the awful thing of claws that scratched and burned inside his belly, so Solomon opened wide his mouth and sucked air into his lungs as if to provide a path of breath on which the animal might climb free. But the perfume of sun-warmed fox grape drifted toward him, engulfed him, and in that moment he believed that he must have swallowed the musky scent, for its sweetness was in his mouth and chest and belly and *the thing* was gone.

Riordan knew better.

Solomon viciously kicked the eyeless doll, then sank down among the tumbled stones of the cellar. He was frightened. He thought of himself as a man in control of his own actions. He took pride in discipline. He admired restraint. Why had he fired at the harmless junco?

Numbed by his own conduct, Solomon leaned wearily against the stones. He closed his eyes. A warm wind carried the soft cry of mourning doves hidden somewhere in the distance. Solomon slept.

The old man and his son remained motionless in the grass.

The chill of twilight awakened Solomon. He looked down and saw the doll at his feet. He picked it up and held it gently in his hands. Long years of weathering had rubberized its texture. The doll's face was wrinkled and rain stain gave it the appearance of a child whose tears had dried but failed to disappear. Solomon stared at the doll for a long moment and then lifted his gaze to the landscape. When he saw how the trees arched in gloom and how the autumn season had drained red mulleins of their color and how dusk had dyed the sky gray, he was overwhelmed with sorrow and the recognition that there were fewer and fewer corners of his life around which he could turn. He thought of a cage without doors.

And then he heard the bell. It was a faint tinkle, echoless and vagrant, as if some wanderer roved the woods and gently juggled silver. Again, softly, the bell's note was struck. Solomon shivered. He was alarmed by the bell. It was as if God had struck one more note to sound sorrow on the land.

He peered across the clearing at the northern mowing of tall grass but saw nothing to reveal the gypsy sound. He turned and looked into the woods behind him and, for just one moment, thought he saw the shape of doors, but when he blinked he saw that the suspected doors were only the leaning shape of trees. He let the doll slip from his fingers, rose from the cellar's stones, and lifted his double-barreled gun.

The bell struck.

Solomon whirled toward the fence of massive roots. Fox grapes bulged with venom, their juice hissing through their skins and releasing a cathedral stench of terror. Something white fluttered in the vine and Solomon dug the butt of his gun deep into his shoulder. Once more he heard the bell. It came from the patch of white. A wood thrush flew from among the fox grapes, its breast startling white against its olive feathers. From its beak came the lovely silver tinkle of a bell.

And *the thing* crawled inside Solomon. It *was* alive. A *thing* of a thousand feet, all clawed and tearing at the soft fibers of Solomon's belly and now ripping upwards inside his chest, gnawing at his lungs, choking him.

"Now," whispered the old man hiding in the grass.

Solomon fired and blew the wood thrush out of the sky.

His legs trembling, Solomon ran, stumbled across the clearing until he stood over the dead thrush. He leaned to lift the bird, but at the sight of its torn and bleeding body Solomon felt a terrible rush of heat course through him and then his stomach spasmed painfully. His head jerked sharply forward and he retched. He lost his balance and fell to his hands and knees. His mouth hung open weakly as he vomited on the dead bird, and the foul mess below him caused him to spew further until, at last, he disgorged his final bile. Sweat stung his eyes and he reached out blindly for support. His fingers closed on the tangled vines of fox grape; as he pulled himself erect he crushed the fruit and the juices flowed warmly down his hand, across his wrist and dripped into the ground. He knew the color of the grape and wished desperately that the dead bird's eyes would unglaze so that it could see that he, Solomon, was bleeding, too.

He stood. His eyes closed, he pulled long breaths deep into his lungs until the nausea disappeared and his body no longer heaved. He opened his eyes and forced himself to look down at the mutilated thrush. He lifted his shotgun from the ground. Slowly, using the stock of his gun as a shovel, he began to dig a shallow trench alongside the bird. When it was finished, Solomon gritted his teeth against the return of sickness and, still using the gun's stock, pushed the vomit-coated bird into the trench, then scraped dead leaves and dried moss and the skins of crushed grapes over it.

Bewildered by the hunter's action, Jubal turned to his father for an answer, but when he saw what the old man was doing he was unable to speak. Riordan had shoved a flat stone between his teeth and he was grinding so hard that little flecks of flint splintered from the stone and mixed with the saliva in the corners of his mouth. A terrible soft moaning came from him. The boy realized that Riordan was stifling the howl that must have gathered in his throat, his body trembling with the effort. Mesmerized, the boy stared at him, not knowing what to do, but then the hunter staggered across the clearing, vanished into the woods, and gradually, the old man's shaking ceased. The stone dropped from his mouth. Like a wounded dog, he rubbed his torn lips in the grass below him. Slowly, Riordan raised his hand and pointed toward the woods.

"Do not lose him, boy," he said in an awful whisper. "Do not lose him!"

Jubal did not hesitate. He crouched low and sped across the pasture, leaped the tree-root fence, and disappeared among the trees. Riordan turned his body, lay belly up in the grass, and stared into the sky, where he knew his Father watched. He rose to his knees and bowed his head and gave thanks to the Lord, for he suspected why the hunter in the woods could still make war.

The reason thrilled him.

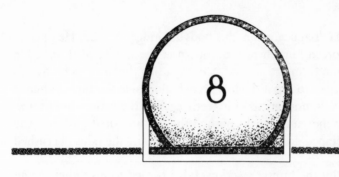

8

After Solomon joined Trans-Global, it had been pointed out to him that executives were expected to dress in attire appropriate to their position. The casual sport jackets and baggy flannel pants he was fond of wearing, the crepe-soled shoes, gave way to vested suits and polished brogans, each suit cut exactly alike and each pair of shoes highly polished. At first reluctant to observe this sartorial request, Solomon now found a certain pleasure in assuming the conservative plumage so common among those who commuted from Fairfield County to Manhattan. It helped to legitimize his membership in the club.

Having brushed his teeth with salt, forced forty pushups on the cold tiles of his bathroom floor, stepped in and out of an icy shower, and stropped and shaved, he chose a soft brown tweed whose wool smelled faintly of tobacco. Before he put on the tweed, he dressed in a pair of blue boxer shorts, a pale-yellow button-down oxford shirt whose weave was not corrupted with any trace of polyester, dark-brown socks held calf-high by garters, and cordovan shoes with heavy soles. He splashed a few drops of Caswell-Massey cologne into the center of a white handkerchief and tucked it neatly into the breast pocket of his jacket. He wore only bowties of a butterfly cut. He chose one with a paisley print of quiet browns and yellows.

"Darling," Kendal shouted from downstairs, "you're going to be late."

"Down in a minute," Solomon called back. He glanced out of the window to see if his ride had come, but all he saw was the early morning fog that rolled in from Long Island Sound. He opened the window and inhaled deeply and swallowed the fog. He thought it tasted of ocean salt and clams. He liked the taste. He moved to Kendal's dressing table and stood in front of the mirror, bending a little as he knotted his tie. He paused. Overlapped in the first loose knot, the ends of his tie looked like the wings of a fallen bird. Solomon felt a spasm in his belly and feared he would be sick. Was it only forty-eight hours since he had killed the wood thrush? He moved back to the window and once again drew the cool sea mist into his lungs. Not wanting to return to the mirror, he stood at the window and finished tying his tie, no longer caring whether it was neatly bowed.

He turned and glanced down at his shoes, almost expecting to see his own vomit and fox-grape skins covering the leather, and felt a sudden need to polish them. He returned to his closet, pulled out a cardboard box, and removed its lid. Inside the box was a small brush and a can of shoe polish. There was also an assortment of junk — some broken plastic collar stays, brass blazer buttons, a strapless wristwatch whose crystal was cracked and which had long ceased ticking, two onyx marbles, a torn advertisement for an inflatable kayak. Solomon stared into the box. He lifted out a tiny wooden case. The case was beautifully hand-carved in delicate, swirling scrollwork. A strip of parchment was visible through a small opening in the upper part of the scrolled case. Printed on the parchment were three Hebrew letters. They spelled *Shaddai*. Almighty.

The case was a mezuzah. Traditionally, it was attached to a doorpost where it could be kissed before entering a man's home. Inscribed on the other side of the parchment was a prayer of affirmation. This particular mezuzah had been a gift from Solomon's friend Mousey Blum. The Mouse had presented it many years ago on the day the Moons had purchased their home. Although Solomon considered himself an agnostic, he had no wish to offend his friend; and during the Mouse's first weekend visit the little scrolled case hung on the doorpost. When the Mouse departed, the mezuzah was relegated to Solomon's cardboard box. On subsequent visits Mouse never referred to its absence, but once Solomon had surreptitiously observed his friend, hand in hand with Darby, who was very young then, lightly touching that place where the mezuzah had hung. Darby had smiled and, standing on tiptoe, kissed the Mouse. It was such a private moment that Solomon had quickly turned away and pretended that he had seen nothing.

The pretense epitomized the relationship with his daughter. It wasn't as if they did not share things. Each loved mischievous humor, jigsaw puzzles and chess, old movies, Bach rather than Tchaikovsky, raw onions, and moonlight; but Solomon was uneasily aware that often they participated in these pleasures in order to avoid confrontation. It was as if each donned a mask to avoid revealing what was underneath. Solomon suspected that he had instigated this Punch-and-Judy show.

Even as a little girl Darby had scorned any admonition of caution. Her extraordinary sense of curiosity had vitiated any natural prudence. She had been an audacious adolescent, never hesitating before the challenge of adventure. Her impetuosity had often provoked Solomon into parental lectures, but he discovered that his words of advice brought only polite withdrawal on Darby's part. Her dark eyes growing even darker as she listened to her father's lecture; Solomon would note that at the end her eyes were almost without light and she seemed far away. He did not really wish to damage her ebullience, so his criticism became sporadic, discreet, softened, and gradually ceased. This self-censorship on his part created a strange situation within which they functioned. Solomon resorted to written communication. Darby followed his lead.

With only a glancing knowledge of each other's heart, they continued to chat easily of unimportant things, shared reactions toward trivia, joined in bawdy humor, and, like nervous birds of flight, camouflaged their true colors by the speed of their flight.

Now he juggled the mezuzah in his hand. Replacing it in the cardboard box, his hand struck something else, which he pulled free. It was a folded piece of foolscap, its edges yellowed, its crease slightly torn from many unfoldings, many readings. Solomon stared bleakly at it, wanting to return it to the box, unable to. He opened the letter. The goddamn letter.

Dear Daddy,

This is as difficult for me to write as it will be for you to read. I am suddenly conscious of how often you quote Baudelaire's advice. "Simplify! Simplify!" It sounds so easy but we both know it isn't. I'll try.

It's obvious that what you saw when you walked into my room shocked you. I am sorry about that. I am truly sorry. But I am not sorry about what I was doing. There is nothing unnatural about making love. You and Mom taught me that — or, at least, I always thought that's how you felt. Thinking about that now, I'm not sure. I'm not sure how you feel about a lot of things. I'm not sure what makes you glad or sad or angry. You hide, Daddy. You make people look for you. You've hidden so long that I think you must be very tired. I know I am. (I don't mean that disrespectfully.)

Maybe when you walked into the room you should have yelled or thrown something or hit me or hit Samuel or something. Daddy, anything, but I don't think just looking, just looking and turning away and saying nothing, just walking away like you did, like you'd just stepped into something and had to wipe it off your foot. I don't really think that's an answer to anything, to anything at all. Ever.

I think it's sad that we write so many notes to each other. I know it's my fault as much as yours but I guess that's the only way we can "talk." I wonder why that is.

Are we afraid of each other, Daddy?

You probably won't believe this, but I love you.

Darby

Carefully, Solomon refolded the letter and placed it under the mezuzah. He wondered what a fifteen-year-old girl had known about fear. It pained him to think that fear had been and might still be the root of her unrest. Was that the cause of her fumblings with Judaic ritual? Did she hope for theological relief? Remembering his own anger at her Sabbath surprise, he wished he'd been more gentle, so that he might have persuaded her to relinquish her search for panaceas. He decided to call her today.

He heard Kendal whistle and realized that, after all, he didn't have time to polish his shoes. He closed the cardboard box, returned it to the closet, left the bedroom, and trotted downstairs and into the large front hall of the colonial house.

Kendal stood at the open front door, squinting against the sea mist, holding a trowel in her hand. She turned when she heard Solomon and pointed at him with the trowel. A clump of soil dropped to the wide pine boards of the hall.

"You ought to wear your blazer, darling; that way you won't have to change for the party."

"What party?"

"You know, Susie Mitford's."

"I don't know Susie Mitford."

"Of course you do. It's some outdoor do for local artists. She called weeks ago and you said yes. You'll have to get an early train."

"I do not know any Susie Mitford."

"Darling, I think you're going mental."

"Why do you always say mental?"

"I don't *always* say anything."

"Mental is an adjective," Solomon said. "It's used to qualify a noun. People don't think people are mental. People think people are lunatics. Lunatic is a noun. I wish you'd get that straight."

"You're very testy this morning."

"You burned the kippers."

"I didn't burn the kippers."

"And the toast was soggy."

"You didn't eat any toast."

"Of course I didn't eat any toast," Solomon said. "It was just lying there. Dead."

Kendal stared at her husband. It was not like him to be petty. Ever since he had returned from his hunting walk in Vermont, he had been in a strange mood, but when she'd questioned him about it, he had refrained from comment. Then she remembered the phone call and thought she knew why his morning was sour.

"It's the meeting, isn't it?" Kendal asked, her tone self-reproaching. "You're meeting with Brindig today."

"That's right," Solomon said. "Me and King Shit."

"Is shit a noun?"

They looked at each other. They both laughed. Gently, Kendal ran a fingernail down one side of Solomon's nose. "It'll be okay. You'll see."

"Sure."

"Tell him you have to leave early."

"For what?"

Impatiently, Kendal kicked the clump of soil toward the doorjamb. "For Susie Mitford's."

"Why do we have to go to a party for a bunch of goddamn dilettantes?"

"Because you accepted the invitation, that's why. We're obligated. Jesus, Solomon."

"*I thought I heard Buddy Bolden shout,*" Solomon sung.

"Not this time," Kendal said irritably.

"*Open up that window and let the bad air out,*" sang Solomon.

"It won't work this time," Kendal said.

She was referring to the song. In the first flush of their affair after World War II, when Solomon played piano in the back room of Emilio Ho's delicatessen, Kendal had remained active in the Broadway theater. After performances, she would join him every night and, together with Em and their mutual friend, the Mouse, listen for hours as Solomon played one request after another. It had been a youthful and exuberant time, the night hours pulsating with Solomon's rhythms, blues, and scat, the long lazy mornings warmed by sunlight and passion. Occasionally, strained by the employment vagaries of her profession, Kendal's good nature would splinter and she would find fault with little things, unimportant things, and, her voice rising in English pique, demand that a bath towel be folded thrice, not twice, or that a soft-boiled egg be eaten from a scissored aperture on its top and never, never cracked in two. Little things. Unimportant things. During those times, because it pained him to know of the daily rejections encountered by and inherent in the life of any actor, Solomon refrained from overt criticism. Instead, he sang in a perfect hoarse imitation of Jelly Roll Morton: *"I thought I heard Buddy Bolden shout,/Open up that window and let the bad air out!"*

At which point Kendal would no longer care how a towel was folded or an egg was cracked and she would welcome Solomon's mouth on her neck. Or anywhere else.

But that was many years ago and now, as she stood in the open doorway of their house, she was truly annoyed. "I didn't want to go to the damn party. You're the one who said yes."

"Okay."

"Does it ever occur to you that we do a helluva lot of things we don't want to do?" Kendal asked.

A horn sounded outside. Both Solomon and Kendal turned. A black Cadillac Seville was pulling into the driveway. Its driver, a large florid-faced man, leaned out of the driver's window and pumped the bulb of a custom-mounted horn. He played the first bar of *Pomp and Circumstance*.

"Bugger off!" Kendal snapped it out as she turned back quickly toward Solomon.

"He bought it specially for you." Solomon grinned. "I think he wants your body."

"Well," Kendal asked, ignoring Solomon's sexual reference, "are we going to the party or not?"

"I guess we have to, right?"

Kendal didn't answer.

"We'll go to the party," Solomon said and he stepped out into the rolling mist. As he moved toward the Cadillac, he neither waved nor looked back, and his head was lowered, his gaze on the gravel driveway as if he were looking for something lost.

As he got into the Cadillac he heard Kendal slam the door. He took a deep breath and regretted it immediately as he was assailed with the sweet odor of Sen-Sen. The sickening smell rode the breath of the car's driver, and it was accompanied by the man's finger drilling into Solomon's shoulder.

John Luckey was the comptroller for TransGlobal Films. And John

Luckey was a toucher. He was unable to carry on a conversation without constantly jabbing his stiff forefinger into some part of the anatomy of the man or woman he was talking to. It was not so much a gesture of emphasis as it was a desperate attempt to establish contact; it was as if he needed to prove to himself that his partner in dialogue was not a phantom. To indulge in verbal intercourse with Luckey was a painful experience which demanded the physical dexterity of an acrobat. The problem was further heightened because the comptroller constantly sucked on Sen-Sen. This posed a particular puzzle for the man or woman being addressed. He or she could avert his head and therefore escape the malodor of licorice, but such evasion meant that the listener who chose that course would be blinded to the approach of Luckey's terrible finger. Solomon found it an insoluble dilemma.

"You [peck] will [peck] ruin it [peck peck peck] for all of us!" said Luckey and his finger. "It's just not fair!"

Solomon knew immediately that Luckey was referring to his, Solomon's, expense account. He submitted these accounts once a month and, after approval by the comptroller, was reimbursed for monies spent in the pursuit of business. Such an arrangement was an accepted practice among most major corporations, and it was a constant source of irritation between Solomon and Luckey. They vehemently disagreed about the philosophy underlying this custom. The origin of their long dispute was reflected in the expense-account sheet Luckey was waving frantically under Solomon's nose.

"Solomon!" Luckey was so overwrought that he spit little black pieces of Sen-Sen onto Solomon's jacket. Solomon flicked them off. "You could not possibly have spent so little."

"I swear, John."

"It just won't pass muster. Now, please, let's go over it again."

"Sure."

"What was the purpose of the trip?"

"I went up to New Haven to see if a play at the Yale Repertory Company had any film potential."

"A legitimate reason, right?"

"Yeah, but a lousy play."

"It doesn't make any difference."

"Oh, yeah? How would you like to sit for three goddamn hours watching an Albanian fairy tale?"

"You drove to New Haven."

"Right."

"And it cost you three dollars and twenty cents?"

"Uh-huh."

"That's ridiculous." Luckey belched and Solomon shifted away from the cloud of licorice.

"You've got the receipt."

"I don't want the receipt." Luckey's voice was shrill. "I don't want to look at the receipt. I hate the receipt!"

"John, I think you're getting paranoid."

"Okay, okay, we get on the train, I'll prove it to you."

"Prove what?"

"You don't understand figures, Solomon. You're just very dumb about figures." And with that, the comptroller lapsed into a sulky silence.

They drove past the Longshore Country Club, turned onto Riverside Avenue; Solomon watched the seagulls swooping over the Saugatuck River. The graceful arc of their flight could not hide the fact that they were scavengers in pursuit of filth and dead matter.

Like me, thought Solomon. In pursuit of *product*.

"Gotcha!"

"What? What?" Solomon was startled by the broken silence in the Cadillac.

Luckey's voice was a triumphant rattle of speed. "The very shortest route from our office to New Haven is the F.D.R. Drive to Bruckner Expressway to the Hutchinson River Parkway and up Route Ninety-Five, and that is approximately seventy-five miles, which multiplied by the twelve cents a mile you're allowed comes to nine dollars I repeat nine dollars and not three dollars and twenty cents!" The comptroller whipped his Cadillac into a parking space at the railroad station and braked to a victorious halt.

"I didn't leave from the office," Solomon said. "I drove from my home in Westport and only used three dollars and twenty cents' worth of gas."

"Solomon, don't do this to me!" Luckey's finger thudded into Solomon's ribs. "You want to be some kind of anarchist, for God's sakes? I mean, they'll kill you."

"Who'll kill me?"

"The guys, that's who'll kill you. Everybody who puts in an expense account, that's who."

Luckey slammed out of the car and Solomon followed. The morning train to New York City was pulling in and both men hurried up the stairs to the station platform. It was crowded with the legion of daily commuters. The majority of the men carried a briefcase and folded newspaper in one hand and a plastic container of coffee in the other. Other than an occasional nod or wave of the hand, there was very little communication among the commuters. Although it was not an unfriendly crowd, years of traveling back and forth on the same trains had erased any necessity for casual courtesy, and few dared to make a simple inquiry about a compatriot's mental, moral, or physical state. They feared the answers.

Because each commuter was long accustomed to taking a specific seat in a specific car — such location determined by a desire to smoke or not to smoke, to stretch legs in an aisle or to huddle by a window and stare morosely at the passing landscape, to sit forward in order to avoid the crush of disembarkment or to sit in the rear of the train so that one might tarry legitimately before beginning the daily grind — there was little jostling among the men and women as they entered the train and prepared for the hour's journey to Grand Central.

Both Solomon and Luckey were smokers. Side by side, they sat in their customary seats. Solomon withdrew a wooden kitchen match from among others in his vest pocket and struck it on his thumbnail. He inhaled deeply, savoring the day's first acrid bite of tobacco.

"It's not just the mileage, Solomon, it's how you eat," said Luckey as he stared hard at the expense account he still held.

Solomon sighed. "You mean the fork in my left hand? It's an English custom. I picked it up from Kendal."

"I don't give a damn if you eat with your fingers. I'm talking about *where* you eat. Morey's, for chrissake, you ate at Morey's."

"The director of the show invited me."

"You should have taken *him*. What kind of an impression can you make if you freeload? That's not the way this company does business. I'm going to put down that you took him to the Rathskeller."

"Suppose he doesn't like pot roast?"

"He doesn't have to eat the goddamn pot roast. He can eat anything he wants." Luckey began to scribble marginal notes on the expense sheet. "Let's see. You had, say, one or two martinis at two dollars and fifty cents a pop, which is ten dollars, and then you probably had . . ."

"Can't drink martinis anymore. They give me a hard-on."

"Listen, don't knock it. Sixteen-ounce sirloin would be about right." Luckey continued his notes. "Say twelve seventy-five apiece, 'cause I don't like to round off the numbers — it looks phony — and maybe two cheesecakes, they make it great there, and two coffees with, uh, brandy or Cointreau or something — and, oh yeah, I forgot the bottle of wine. Okay. So, with tip you spent fifty-one dollars and twenty-six cents. Hey, that's more like it, Solomon. Now, fifty-one dollars and twenty-six cents plus nine dollars transportation and, uh, seventeen bucks and thirty-seven cents this and that, together with . . ."

"This and that?"

"You know, miscellaneous."

"Oh. Sure."

"Together with two tickets at ten per — "

"What tickets?"

"To the show, for you and Kendal."

"They were freebies. And Kendal didn't go."

"Course she went. Wives always go. That's the rule." With a flourish of his pencil, the comptroller finished his arithmetic and, as he beamed at the result, he exhaled a suffocating haze of Sen-Sen. "Ninety-seven dollars and sixty-three cents we owe you."

Solomon couldn't reply. He was coughing from the smell of licorice. Luckey smiled sympathetically. "Listen," he said. "That's a bad cough. Was it raining in New Haven? Sure, it's always raining in New Haven. Never mind, I'll add eighteen forty-one for medical expenses. Goddamn cost of drugs is terrible." He did some quick figures. "Excellent. A hundred and sixteen dollars and four cents. Now that, Solomon, that's class!"

Clickety clack clickety clack look at me Mac clickety clack look at me Mac clickety clack clickety clack.

Solomon listened to the soothing monotony of train wheels racing over their tracks. He often used the sound as a kind of morning mantra, a quiet preamble to the dissonance and deceits of his work. He stared out the window at the curve of Connecticut's shore and watched a lobsterman heading in from the sound in a small lapstrake boat whose gunwales were low in the water from the weight of collected pots. The sea was choppy and the rise and fall of the boat's bow was erratic, but Solomon wished he were on it so that he might listen to the cry of gulls rather than to the insistent voice of John Luckey. His cigarette tasted bitter and he stubbed it out in the crevice between windowpane and sill and, because he knew what the comptroller was about to ask, he rubbed his fingers in the dead gray ashes.

"Sign it," demanded Luckey.

"What the hell," Solomon said quietly; he took his expense sheet and the proffered pen from Luckey's hand. He signed his account. When he returned it to Luckey, the paper was bisected by long black smudges, but Solomon's dirty fingerprints of protest were ignored by the comptroller. Luckey neatly folded the expense sheet and placed it inside his briefcase. A smile of satisfaction on his face, he leaned back in his seat, closed his eyes, and immediately went to sleep.

Clickety clack look at me Mac clickety clack clickety clack clickety clack.

Solomon's fingers drummed restlessly on the windowsill. He wished he had a copy of *Shadow on the Grass* with him so that he could study it before the coming meeting with Brindig. In his mind, he turned the pages of the script, looking for elements that could be adjusted to please the executive and yet not destroy the story. He knew it was a hopeless task. Ben Brindig would blemish it page by page until the story had been scarred beyond repair; and if the writer, Charles Manzinni, objected, Brindig would insist on the final infamy. He would demand that Solomon exercise the *cutoff.*

Like most writers who had not achieved either power or fame, Manzinni had been forced to accept a contract which stipulated that if TransGlobal was displeased with his first draft, the studio had the right to cancel his services and employ another writer. That the story originated with Manzinni made no difference. It was the price a writer paid for his employment. Faced with the threat of a cutoff, many writers unconsciously adjusted their story-telling techniques in order to please those who ultimately would judge their work, and in this accommodation quality was destroyed. This ritual of destruction was not unique. Solomon had reason to know . . .

Wilton Forest, president of TransGlobal Films, was obsessed with the constant growth of his company, and therefore assumed that there might be a market for products of greater quality. He understood that the only way to discover the truth of this assumption was to explore its possibilities. He was not interested in arbitrarily presenting films of virtue and goodness; but if there were stories that explored the complexities of the human condition rather than skimmed its surface, and if these stories could attract a paying audience, he wanted his share. Fully aware of his company's reputation, he realized that he would have to secure the services of some qualified person previously untainted by any mercenary involvement with the company; a person whose reputation was not besmirched by the legacy of TransGlobal, one whose image would be seductive to reputable agents and allow them, in clear conscience, to submit stories of quality. What he needed, he realized, was a sort of house intellectual. A sort of Judas goat.

A quiet search led to Solomon Moon. While still a Broadway producer, Solomon was made uneasy by the need to raise money from backers to whom he could not guarantee return. He was disheartened by the observation that such return might be better insured by the presentation of trivia, and thus was disenchanted with the theatrical scene. He was further troubled by the knowledge that his labors had not led to security for his wife and the daughter whose birth had prompted Kendal to retire from the stage. The fact that neither Kendal nor Darby ever complained of this increased Solomon's anxiety. There were times he felt that theirs was a conspiracy of silence, and this silence was the garden in which Solomon's guilt flowered. His peers had talked so often about the realistic need to compromise that Solomon began to give credence to this distorted dogma. He wondered if his quest for moral independence was the act of a selfish man.

He had optioned a brilliant biography of an American homosexual poet. It was a tragic story of an artist whose excesses and vulnerabilities ultimately led to suicide. Solomon realized that the only way he would be able to raise money for this Broadway venture would be to secure the services of a major film star whose popularity would compensate for the riskiness of such an undertaking. He failed. He found no star willing to portray the poet. But in his quest, Solomon's project received wide attention from Hollywood studios and ultimately led to an offer of a paid assignment from TransGlobal. The offer pointed a new direction in Solomon's life and he was grateful.

The company owned a best-selling novel about murder in a gay bar, but they had not assigned a producer to develop the material into a film. An executive at TransGlobal knew of Solomon's interest in the biography of the homosexual poet and assumed that he might be interested in developing this story. Although Solomon thought the tale of murder was grotesque, he was determined to give service to the theory of compromise. A standard contract was negotiated between him and the studio. His terms were simple. He would function as a producer and, working with a New York writer assigned by the studio, would develop a first-draft screenplay. It did not escape his attention that after submitting the screenplay, both he and the writer would be subject to the cutoff should the studio wish to exercise it. He made a calculated choice. He decided that if it were essential to sacrifice quality in order to please TransGlobal he would do so. When the first draft was completed, he sent it to the studio and a week later was asked to fly west and meet with Wilton Forest. He was surprised. He had been told of Ben Brindig and had assumed that any discussion of the script would be with him. He did not understand why the president of the company wished to see him.

He was even more confused when he was ushered into Forest's office. He thought he had stepped into a jungle, for wherever he looked he saw leaves and vines and bent branches. Cautiously, he sniffed. He expected to encounter the aroma of damp earth and exotic flowers, but he could discern only an unfamiliar fragrance, a subtle shading of spice and lime.

"Do you like it?" asked a man with a thin, high voice. The voice came from behind a dozen leafy plants.

"What is it?" asked Solomon.

"Spice and lime," said the man and then his hands pushed aside two enormous plants and Solomon saw the president of the company. He sat behind a marble desk on which the plants rested. He was a small man, immaculately groomed and tailored and manicured. He held an atomizer made of fine glass in his hand. He squeezed the bulb. A spray of scent drifted toward Solomon.

"I'll be darned," said Solomon.

"I have it specially prepared in Bermuda. The herbs are indigenous to the island. So are the limes. The cologne bottles are handblown. They're quite lovely. Would you like to see one?"

"That would be nice."

Forest gestured in such a way that Solomon knew he was expected to move around the desk. The gesture, simple and graceful, reminded Solomon of royalty. As he crossed the office he was struck by a single painting on one wall. It was an oil portrait of a woman, done in bold, primitive strokes. The artist had posed the woman in an old Boston rocker, which had been placed in the center of an enormous wheatfield. Neither house nor horizon was depicted. There was just the woman and the wheat. The field of grain was a golden stubble and the woman was faceless. She sat prim and still in her rocker, her gray hair pulled back tightly in a bun, her blunt-toed black shoes only slightly visible from under a knitted afghan that fell in loose folds from her lap to the field. The afghan's linked squares of wool were in muted earth colors that blended unobtrusively with the soft gold of the wheat, with the severe black dress the woman wore, and with her silvering hair. At a first glance, Solomon was impressed with the peaceful solitude of the painting, but as he

studied it further his eyes wavered from the wheat to the afghan and finally to the face which had no features. He was made uneasy by the implication of its mystery. Solomon had heard about this painting. He
knew that many visitors had remarked about this singular aspect of it
and had asked Forest to explain its purpose but, always, the thin, quiet
man had smiled politely and turned the conversation away from their
inquiries. There were a few who thought they recognized something familiar about the woman, but they could not put a name to her.

His eyes on the painting, Solomon stumbled against the leg of a chair
that had been drawn up close to Forest. The neat little man held up the
atomizer. It was a small bottle holding no more than four ounces of liquid. It was bell shaped and tinted a beautiful blue; the handle of the bell
was made of heavy silver. The feathery silhouette of a tree was etched
on either side of the bottle.

"Yes," Solomon said, "it is indeed quite lovely."

"Of course," Forest said. "I said so and I never lie."

"What is the tree?" Solomon asked. He admired the delicacy of the
etching.

"That is a cedar tree. Won't you sit down?" Forest leaned back in his
chair, hands together under his chin, fingertips pressed against each
other in the triangle of a child's steeple. He looks, Solomon thought as
he took his seat, like a holy man at prayer. "Look around you, Mr.
Moon," Forest said. "What do you see?"

"Plants. Vines. Greenery."

"They're beautiful, are they not?"

"Yes."

"Have you seen such plants before?"

"I've seen plants."

"These plants?"

"I'm not sure."

"You have not."

"I have not?"

"You have not. These are rare ferns, Mr. Moon, collected by me at
considerable expense and with great effort. Do you know why?"

"No, sir."

"Because they are originals. That is to say, they cannot be duplicated
by some cheap, artificial crossing of spores by ambitious horticulturists.
They are true to their own form and they are odorless. They do not depend on a seductive fragrance to call attention to their beauty. They are

what they are. As were the cedars of Bermuda. Until we pollinated them with rot."

"We?"

"Man. In this instance, one man. His name has long since been lost to history, but his calamitous deed is evidenced throughout that lovely island."

"Bermuda?"

"Yes. Until that unwise man performed his malevolent magic, the island was a haven of cedars. They were everywhere. On the beaches, high on the hills, in the valleys, everywhere. But this — this ignominious fellow was not content to gaze upon the simple splendor of the cedar. He was immune to its perfection and so, discontent with that which was *original,* mark the word, Mr. Moon, discontented with that which was original to the island, he introduced to her shores another tree. A California redwood. And imbedded in that redwood was an alien virus which needed only the stiff salt breezes of Bermuda to be carried to the cedars. In a matter of a few short years the cedars were diseased. The groves were decimated. The trees died. And now, when you look at the hills and the valleys and the beaches, your eye meets a sea of stumps."

"That's a very sad story."

" 'Ugly' might be a more appropriate word. As ugly as that sea of stumps. You perceive the meaning, of course."

"Don't throw dice with God," Solomon said.

"I like you, Mr. Moon. You have a civilized mind."

"Well," said Solomon. He blushed.

"We will do well together, you and I."

"I'm sorry?" Solomon was startled at Forest's remark.

"This vile man who gazed upon the cedars had no reverence for their nativeness, their uniqueness, their . . ."

"Originality," Solomon supplied.

"Exactly. Well said. Truly understood. But then, I could hardly expect otherwise from you, as it is apparent that you have something in common with my ferns and those poor dead cedars."

"I do?"

"You do. You, too, Mr. Moon, are an original."

"I'll be darned," said Solomon.

"Are you quite comfortable?" asked Forest solicitously.

"Oh, yes," Solomon replied, snuggling deeper into the soft chair and glancing upwards at the bower of greenery. "And I like the view."

"It is a peaceful office."

"Yes."

"I like peace."

"Me, too."

They smiled at each other. Wilton Forest rocked back in his chair. It was a grand chair, high-backed, ornately carved, thronelike. The desk was a massive slab of marble; besides the ferns, there was only one object on it — the first-draft screenplay about the murder in a gay bar. Forest ran a finger across the title page of the manuscript.

"Remarkable," he said.

Solomon felt a rush of warmth through his body. He felt at ease in this truly peaceful office and he could not remember meeting a man with such instant perception as had his new friend.

"Do you like it?" he asked modestly.

"No," Forest said.

"The writer and I did our best," Solomon said stiffly.

"On the contrary," Forest said. "I suspect you did your worst. Do not misunderstand me, Mr. Moon, I do not accuse you of intentional malingering. I think, rather, that you have been an unwitting accomplice to what we at TransGlobal imposed on you. What I have learned about you is that you are a man of genuine talent, a man of curiosity and compassion who is blessed with psychological insight and honest skills." He tapped the cover of the manuscript. "But I do not see you on these pages. I do not hear you. I hear a stranger. I hear a man who walks so lightly that he leaves no footprints. He has unweighted himself of all substance and has become alien to his own talent. The irony, of course, is that you did exactly what was asked of you. You did faithfully serve the novel which we assigned you. And the novel, Mr. Moon, is vile."

"You really hate that book?" Solomon asked.

"I loathe it."

"But your company bought it."

"Yes."

"It was a best-seller."

"Yes."

"It must have been very expensive."

"Yes."

"I mean, you must have spent a great deal of money."

"We spent a great deal of money."

"But you hate the book."

"I hate the book."

"Then who decided to buy it?"

"I did."

"I think my eye is twitching," said Solomon.

"Yes," Forest said. "I can see it."

"I hope it stops. I don't like the feeling."

"No. It must be most unpleasant."

"I hope it stops soon."

"Perhaps I've confused you."

"That's a possibility. That's a real possibility."

"Forgive me."

"Would you repeat that, please?"

"Forgive me."

"No, I mean the part about the book. The part about who bought it."

"I did."

"Honest to God?"

"I told you, Mr. Moon, I never lie."

"Oh, right. Sorry, it slipped my mind."

"I would prefer that you remember it."

"I will."

"Good. You'll find it a beneficial shortcut in our relationship. I do not welcome liars to the family."

"The family?"

"TransGlobal Films. Which you are about to join. On your own terms, naturally."

Slowly, Solomon sat up. He let his gaze shift over the foliage, then deliberately drew in a long deep breath and savored the pungency of spice and lime. No one, he thought, has ever asked me to join anything, to belong to anything. No one. Ever. Anywhere.

"May I ask, sir, why you wish me to join your company?"

"I need you, Mr. Moon," Wilton Forest said simply.

"Don't you think you should call me Solomon?"

"My father was a Victorian man and we were raised with a certain formality. We learned to address a gentleman by his first name only after receiving permission. Such formalities, I have discovered, are not strictures on our behavior but rather an insurance of grace, an acknowledgment of respect. Such as a woman covering her head in church. Or the liturgy sung in Latin." He frowned for a moment, then continued. "Those delicacies have disappeared. It's a shame, really, that even our theologies have become so casual."

Wilton glanced toward the faceless painting on the wall and was silent. Solomon thought how fine it was to be in the company of such a thoughtful man, and he felt ashamed that in the past he had so blithely categorized the mentality of Hollywood moguls.

"I would be happy if you would call me Solomon," he said.

"Thank you. And please know me as Wilton." Wilton Forest inclined his head forward. It was a precise little gesture which, Solomon thought, would be best accompanied by the clicking of heels and, perhaps, the rattling of swords.

"Why do you need me, Wilton?"

"Simply put, Solomon," the thin, quiet, nasal voice continued, "TransGlobal Films is only one part of TransGlobal Enterprises, which is a public corporation listed on the Exchange. As chairman of the board, it is incumbent upon me to act responsibly toward our shareholders. Such responsibility encompasses many things, not the least of which is the show of profit. And profit, Solomon, justifies — indeed dictates — the purchase of such material as this." Wilton's forefinger flicked the manuscript on his desk and then curled back into its own hand as if seeking refuge from filth. "The majority of filmgoers today seek instant gratification — titillation, if you will — and by presenting such material as this we are not only supplying their demand, we give them the opportunity to indulge their voyeuristic fantasies in the safety of a darkened theater. There are, as you must know, eminent psychologists who believe that the role-playing we see on film is not essentially different from the role-playing of the viewer. The extreme example might be the man who watches a film in which a murder is enacted. It is entirely conceivable that, given the pressures and anxiety to which the average man is subjected today he, too, has murder in his heart. But when seated in the quiet darkness of our theaters, that average man watches our little drama of death and empathizes with our celluloid killer, and in that way gives vent to his rage. He will, in a manner of speaking, have safely committed his murder; when he returns to the street he will have been purged of his own violence. In short, Solomon, in exchange for profit, we offer a sort of spiritual benediction. It is, one might be tempted to say, a symbiosis of silver and soul."

Solomon was confused. The sequential logic uttered by Wilton Forest sounded cool and sane and yet, Solomon thought, there was something wrong here. He had an uneasy feeling that he was being lulled by the subtle recitation of a wicked rationale.

"If, in point of fact, TransGlobal Films is performing a kind of moral service, Wilton, in its choice of presentations," Solomon inquired, "what is it you need me to do?"

"I said before that the show of profit is only one aspect of responsibility. There is another that concerns me a great deal, and that is the obligation to quality. It is, I feel, an area to which we have not sufficiently addressed ourselves — and it is the area in which you, Solomon, could perform with remarkable success."

"I don't like palm trees," Solomon said. "I don't like them at all."

Wilton laughed. It was a strange laugh. Soundless. A series of indrawn breaths, swiftly swallowed and lost somewhere in his lungs.

"There would be no need for you to come to California, other than occasional visits, of course. What we need is a man in New York, a man of quality and taste and sensitivity, a man whose judgment would be respected by those who have not previously submitted material for our consideration. We need a man who will find and develop that material. We need a man who will bring excellence to fruition. We need you, Solomon."

"I don't know what to say," Solomon said.

"Say 'yes.' "

"Yes," Solomon said softly, "yes."

The details were settled swiftly. Solomon Moon would be the executive head of the New York story department for TransGlobal Films. Above and beyond a comfortable salary, he would be entitled to a large expense account, a bonus at the end of each fiscal year, freedom to operate his department as he saw fit, and a corner office. Made buoyant by the coming possibilities, Solomon shook Wilton Forest's hand and left the office.

During his years of employment, it became increasingly apparent to Solomon that his real authority was limited. He was an actor in a charade directed by Ben Brindig. Stories or plays or ideas recommended by Solomon were purchased, but fewer and fewer were turned into motion pictures. Once, when his frustration became acute, Solomon sought an audience with Wilton Forest. He complained about Brindig's crude responses, his lack of insight, his impatience with quality, and he suggested to Wilton that he, Solomon, was not fulfilling the job for which he had been hired. He thought it best that Wilton replace him. Wilton's response was immediate. He would not think of Solomon's leaving. He persuaded Solomon to exercise patience and convinced him that he was functioning well; and he revealed a special program of films that he contemplated TransGlobal making one day — a program which he wanted

Solomon to supervise. He talked quietly of this program, which would explore the nature of religious experience, and Solomon was strangely touched. Wilton stood in front of the painting of the faceless woman and discoursed on grace and charity among men and the urgent need to reawaken society to the benefits of faith. It will be a program, he said, in which you, Solomon, will be proud to participate. He spoke with such sincerity that Solomon found himself unable to expose his own lack of religiosity, for he felt it might be interpreted as a personal attack on the man who had befriended him.

He remained with the company, and as the years progressed a convenient liaison was established between Solomon and those who were willing and able to supply him with story material. There was a tacit agreement among them which justified the perpetuation of the myth designed to continue the quest for quality. It was taken for granted that Solomon would be supplied with occasional works of merit, but the obligation inherent in this transaction was his promise to give equal consideration to manuscripts more obviously applicable to the immediate and pecuniary motives of TransGlobal Films.

Clickety clack clickety clack clickety clack.

And then: *Click-eteeee click click click whoooosh.* Silence.

Solomon's reverie was interrupted by a chorus of quiet moans which rose from among the commuters as the train slid to a stop some distance from the tunnel into Grand Central Station. Although here and there an epithet was whispered, these sounds of protest were mild and uttered without feeling. Little activity was interrupted. Crossword puzzles continued to be solved. Liar's poker persevered. Newspapers crackled into the commuter's special fold. Bile was generated, watches were checked, feet shuffled, but the men and women who daily rode these trains were acclimated to the idiosyncracies of their railroad: faulty air conditioners in summer, no heat in winter, dim lights at night, endless delays, all stemming from power shortages, was the price paid for a commuter's franchise on the Connecticut shore. To some, it was a mark of status; to others, it was a dubious privilege.

To Solomon, it was just one more adjustment in a long line of accommodations. Much as he liked Westport, there were times he regretted that he had not kept the old apartment on Cornelia Street as a pied-à-terre. Kendal had thought that such an arrangement would be a waste of money. She had further suggested that if they had their own Manhattan quarters, they would surely be tempted to spend a great number of nights in the city instead of returning to Connecticut where their daughter waited. She felt the obligations of parenthood far outweighed convenience.

Nervous about the coming Brindig meeting, Solomon lighted another cigarette. He glanced at John Luckey. The man still slept, little bubbles popping at his lips as he breathed in and out. Solomon looked out the window. Suddenly, he sat up straight for he saw, once again, the crude structure on the tarred roof of the tenement. The old Jew was nowhere in sight, but perched on the slatted roof of the little outdoor room was the pigeon. Solomon could not be sure that it was the same pigeon to which the Hasid had fed grapes, but he chose to believe it was. It pleased him. He watched as the bird tucked its head under one wing and pecked at mites. He hoped this action was a signal of discomfort and not hunger, for the morning sun slanted onto the rows of fruit tied to the latticed roof, and Solomon thought it would be a pity if their glossy roundness and shiny skins were marred by the bird's beak in the absence of the old man. The bird hopped off a slat and swiftly flew to another. Its head cocked to one side and then to the other side as it seemed to study a bunch of grapes hanging below him. Solomon held his breath. The bird retreated, flapped its wings, and flew away. Solomon applauded.

He was genuinely surprised to hear the clapping of other hands. He looked around, pleased that others had been witness to the bird's act of honor, but saw immediately that he had misinterpreted. No one peered out the window; the applause was a sardonic response to the restarting of the train's engine. Steel wheels ground on their rails, and soon the train entered the long dark tunnel to the station. Guided by habit, commuters stirred from their sleep, hawked phlegm, collected bets, closed briefcases, crushed cigar butts, applied lipstick, reached for parcels and coats, and began the shuffle forward preliminary to departure.

John Luckey, refreshed from his sleep, poured bits of Sen-Sen into his hand and popped them into his mouth. He jabbed Solomon with his finger and suggested they share a taxi on the ride uptown.

"What the hell," he said, "you're probably going to some meeting out of the office, right? Put it on your account."

"I like to walk," Solomon said.

"Dumb," Luckey said. "Dumb." He strode down the aisle of the train.

Solomon remained motionless in his seat. He closed his eyes. He wanted to recall the image of the Hasid doing his spontaneous dance of joy and of the pigeon feeding on a grape. But as Solomon tried to recreate these visions, the picture in his mind distorted. The pale green grapes lost their sunlit luminosity, darkened into tiny blood-red globes, and when the pigeon opened its beak Solomon heard the tinkle of a silver bell. It filled him with remorse and he vowed never again to raise his gun. He would walk instead in those places where he could listen to the wind and where the woods were empty. He thought of areas he had not explored, places near his farm, and he remembered Jabez Tuttle talking of hidden caves high in the steep inclines of the northern mountains and hidden by hawthorne. The thought of hiking on this isolated land, untrodden in recent years but surely a past ground for the Iroquois or a hiding place for the boys who fought with Ethan Allen, elated Solomon and it caused him once again to wonder why only in the solitude of landscape did he feel at home, did he belong. Perhaps, he thought, I am only one more part of that connective tissue that lies over the land. The thought was strangely exhilarating.

He turned in his seat and looked up and down the aisles. The train was empty. He placed two fingers in his mouth and blew out his breath. He whistled!

A member of the cleaning crew stepped through the door of the car. "Good morning, sir," he said.

"You bet your ass," Solomon grinned and then laughed out loud.

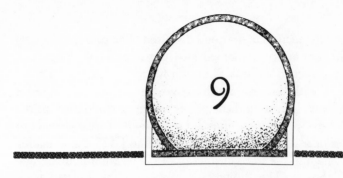

9

Riordan Flynn was not inconvenienced by God. He was, after all, His heir. The old man truly believed this. He believed also that time was meaningless. He thought of time as a vast sea, ebbing and flowing, always present, forever delivering flotsam in its surge. Man was the flotsam, cresting sometimes, riding high in the spindrift, but doomed one day to drown. It was, he thought, a rewarding future. For some it demanded nothing but a passive drift, a voyage of sweet monotony never ending, bereft of corporeal wound. For others, it was a trial during which the unredeemed must earn his freedom from pain if he was to be rewarded with that quiet float that was God's gift.

Riordan was wholly filled with God; and since God is love, Riordan too was filled with love, and he expressed this love through many acts of mysterious mercy. By the means of certain painful works he offered redemption to sinners. He lighted the path to their salvation. He erased darkness from the night. He determined that the way to salvation was to walk through dust and pierce the heart of the Devil. Because he wished no man a journey to hell, nor a purgatorial pause, he extended a hand toward those who truly sought grace, and he provided the heretic the means to die singing. As a man of mercy he, Riordan Flynn, heir to God, could do little else.

He was truly mad.

He was the bastard son of an Irish woman who had squatted among the periwinkles on a deserted beach off the coast near Dingle and dropped him from her womb. She was a scrawny woman with pancake breasts and stringy thighs whose flesh was forever on fire. Her lust was insatiable and she bedded indiscriminately with fisherman or farmer. She neither knew nor cared who fathered Riordan.

They lived in a strange rock-domed dwelling that resembled a beehive, which had been used long ago by a forgotten order of monks. Visited by a succession of men, they were never lonely; nor did they want for food or drink. The mother's sexual partners provided them with slabs of bacon and loaves of crusty bread, a snared rabbit, eggs, and an occasional jar of gin.

Like Saint Theresa, Riordan's mother could be bribed with a sardine.

When he was just a little boy, Riordan learned to anticipate a coming copulation, for his mother would begin to moan softly and as she mouthed obscenities to herself her wet tongue flicked in and out, moistening her fingers, and then she would lift her dress and slide those fingers into her vagina, her excited eyes gleaming at the boy, and the moaning would grow as loud as a storm wind in the rigging of a ship. It was at this point that Riordan would always hear the approaching footfall of a fisherman and know that he must depart. He learned to hide in the dune grass until the man had entered the strange house where monks had dwelled.

And he learned that the strange house was laced with narrow chinks through which he could spy. He was mesmerized by the slippery collaboration between his mother and her partner and studiously informed himself of those efficient acts which led to gratification. Often, he was in danger of being consumed by his own sexual tapeworm, but because he had observed the contortions of pleasure he knew how to appease his desire.

He roamed the lonely hills until he spied a sheep that had strayed from its flock. He approached the animal slowly, with infinite patience, clucked softly to it and soothed it with gentle sounds, ran his fingers through its wool, then hobbled its rear feet with short lengths of hemp tied to stakes he stomped into the damp soil. Then he sodomized the sheep.

Once, a neighboring farmer, a hulking man who smelled of pig shit, visited his mother and stayed throughout the night, leaving Riordan with no place to bed. He stole into the farmer's chicken yard and took a hen. It was a large bird wonderfully feathered; Riordan carried it into the hills. He unbuttoned his trousers and, holding the hen in front of his loins, he wrung its neck. Riordan fucked the hen as it thrashed wildly to its death.

The boy had no difficulties finding bestial companionship. He had a way with animals.

After each sexual encounter, Riordan's mother required certain services of her son, for she was a devout woman who understood that the penalty of sin was penance. She stood naked in the center of the beehive house and made her son scourge her flesh with a hickory whip. As the cruel branch tore her skin into bloody scars her voice would drone a cleansing liturgy.

I will wash my hands among the innocent and will encompass Thy altar, O Lord, that I may hear the voice of Thy praise and tell of all Thy wondrous works. I have loved, O Lord, the beauty of Thy house and the place where Thy glory dwelleth. Take not away my soul, O God, with the wicked, nor my life with men of blood. In whose hands are iniquities; their right hand is filled with gifts. But as for me, I have walked in my innocence: redeem me and have mercy on me. My foot hath stood in the direct way: in the churches I will bless thee, O Lord. Glory be to the Father and to the Son and to the Holy Ghost: As it was in the beginning, is now, and ever shall be, world without end. Amen.

When the whipping ended, the woman fainted. Riordan would drag her across the packed-earth floor of the house and, not troubled by the wispy weight of her limbs, place her upon a thin horse-hair mattress that was stained by sexual sweat. He crossed her arms upon her breast, and as she lay in sweet repose he sat on his heels next to her, keening in a thin high voice as he had heard the fishermen do when they shrouded a corpse washed in by the sea, and he waited for the words he knew would come. She never failed to utter them. After an interval, the length of which was determined by the energy expended in her previous fornication, the woman would open her eyes and she would talk softly of the secret between them. She warned him that throughout the days of his life he must never reveal her true identity, nor his. For I, she whispered, repeating the confidence again and again, for I am Mary, who has smothered sin by birthing the redeemer of fallen men, and you, boy, are the new Adam and a slayer of snakes.

There was no reason for the boy to disbelieve.

She died masturbating with a crucifix. When the boy found her, only the head of Christ protruded from her womb. She had seemingly drowned in His own blood.

Riordan said:

Hail Mary, full of Grace. The Lord is with thee. Blessed art thou amongst women and blessed is the fruit of thy womb. Holy Mary, Mother of God, pray for us sinners now and at the hour of our death. Amen.

The boy summoned a village priest, who stared with horror at the dried body of the woman and tried to comfort Riordan by reminding him that the blood of martyrs is the seed of Christians; but when the priest, too, said *Hail Mary,* the boy became suspicious that the priest had eavesdropped through the chinks of the beehive house and gained forbidden knowledge of their true identities. So Riordan determined to leave behind the winkles upon which he was born and cross the seas to a fresh land that might welcome the new Adam.

In fact, Riordan was no longer a boy when he departed the desolate coast of Ireland. He was a fully grown man armed with an extraordinarily muscular body and a peculiar potpourri of religious dogma. During the many years of his mother's self-imposed flagellation, he had listened to her wild-eyed recitations of the lives of saints and the words of apostles, and all through the rush of words he never dreamed that the woman abused the logic of these good and learned men. Simply and truly, he believed in the literalness of those unharmonious thoughts she spewed forth, and, in good faith, he accepted the random rhetoric of her witless theology. Obsessed by an archaic Catholicism, he enlisted the aid of a local priest. He learned to read. Even before puberty, his cronies were Benedict and Augustine and Ignatius Loyola, and he could mouth their words as eloquently as if they were his own. He took from them those things his mother told, and he tattooed them on his soul. And throughout the long nights under the moon, which he knew to be the eye of God, the saints whispered to him.

Man was created for a certain end, said Saint Ignatius, *and this end is to praise, to reverence, and to serve the Lord God, and by this means to arrive at eternal salvation. All other beings and objects which surround us on the earth were created to be useful to him as means to his final end; hence his obligation to use or abstain from use of these creatures according as they bring him nearer that end or tend to separate him from it. Hence we must above all else endeavor to establish in ourselves a complete indifference toward all created things, not giving any preference to health over sickness, riches over poverty, honor over humiliation, a long life over a short. But we must desire and choose definitively in every thing what will lead us to the end of our creation.*

And hiding in the wet dune grass, Riordan heard Augustine.

To be gone from the Kingdom of God, to be an exile from God's city, to be without the manifold sweetness of God is so mighty a punishment that no torments we know can be compared to it.

And the boy nodded in agreement as he scourged his mother and keened to himself and listened to the words of Francis.

Brother Ass, the body, must be tamed before he can be ridden to God's work.

Riordan was thrilled to learn about Tomás de Torquemada, the Grand Inquisitor of Spain. The Inquisitor's standard of severity in the persecution of heretics pleased and excited the boy and he pledged his future to the same standard of excellence.

Riordan's attraction to Torquemada was a result of the convolutions of his mother's mind. She never tired of explaining to the boy that God was the first Inquisitor and that his first tribunal had been conducted secretly in the Garden of Eden, from whence he had banned the fallen man. Was not Adam the father of all heretics? she would continue. Are not infidels shaped in his stain? Her eyes would glisten wetly at the thought, reminding Riordan of approaching footfall and fuck, and as her fingers scratched open the dried leaves of her Bible she would warp the words of Aquinas, who told her that heretics are infidels and they are to be compelled physically so that they do as they had promised, and then her scratching finger would linger on the passage of proof from Luke, who instructed men to *go out and compel them to come in that my house be filled.*

There were times when, spitting the taste of some man's flesh from her mouth, her bony knees pushing hard into the earthen floor of the beehive house as her skin split under the stinging hickory lash and blood ran down her flanks, there were those times she would pull her treasured book of Bernard Gui from beneath her mattress and read aloud from it in order to stifle a scream of pain.

" 'The object of the Inquisition,' " she read shrilly, " 'is the destruction of heresy, and heresy cannot be destroyed unless their defenders are destroyed; and this is effected in two ways, when they are converted to the true Catholic faith or they are corporally burned.' "

The readings from the fourteenth-century churchman were never long. They were cut short by the woman's piercing shriek and a burst of vomit into which she fainted. When the boy washed up his mother's mess so, too, did he wash his mind clean of sin. It would be days before he once again sought a sheep or a hen, and during those intervals of innocence he would appear at the always-unlocked door of the parish house and, entering it, mark himself with holy water, then slip silently from pew to pew, his fingers fluttering over the hard edges of prayerbooks, until he knelt in front of the altar and waited for the village priest. The priest, who never fancied that one day he would be terror-haunted by a womb-blooded head of Christ, became accustomed to the sight of a kneeling Riordan, and he learned that what the boy truly sought was entrance to the tiny, book-lined study at the rear of the church. There Riordan studied the scholarship of early Christian writers and the history of a medieval church, its function and its form. With his fingernail, he underlined only those passages which corresponded to the teachings of his mother. Sometimes he pressed so hard against a page that he tore the paper, and this increased the pleasure of his reading, for when he saw the flutter of black ink against the white paper, it reminded him of thunder in the sky. Behind the thunder, he saw God.

He did not imagine this. He *saw* Him. For Riordan Flynn had trained his eyes to let God's light in, and, at long last, when he departed from his Irish beach, he assumed a quiet profession in keeping with the harsh and wicked fiction fed him by a whoring mother.

He became a hunter of souls.

His spiritual voyage was flawed by a terrible legacy, for he inherited his mother's temptations. As he wandered from city to city, he was unable to extinguish the fire on his flesh. He rutted like a pig in the dark alleys of Dublin, was unrestrained in Rome, and when he crossed his final sea, he was unshackled in the shadows of New York. Seeing the dreadful frenzy in Riordan's eyes, the lonely men and women who roamed squalid streets would tremble and silently present either buttock or mouth in response to his request. It seemed a safer thing to do. After each mad ride on his carnal carousel, Riordan would look for a wide place in the road which might lead to that silent country he sought where, among the rise of hills or along a riverbank, he could find course and contemplation and a bramble bush. Reveling in his own vexation, he rolled among the thorns and renewed his friendship with God.

On one such diversion, he discovered a New Hampshire beach, and beneath the ebbing tide he saw a sea of grass which reminded him of earlier dunes. The receding ocean uncovered a string of blue mussels. He crunched the mollusks under his heel, scraped out their meat, chewed on it, and washed it down by sipping briny fluid from a mussel shell. He poked tiny holes in the shells, laced them together with dried seaweed, and placed them around his neck. When he walked the beach he did not hear the jingle of shells, he heard the music of an angel.

He did not imagine this. He heard it. He had come home.

Once again, he hid among the dunes, feeding himself from the sea and low-lying blueberry bushes. Occasionally he would snatch a gull from the crest of a wave and hold it in front of his loins as he rung its neck. Neatly, he buried his fecal matter from the sight of strangers, and if he were alarmed by an unexpected hum of voices signaling an approach of visitors, he retreated to the safety of coastal caves. There he would listen to the boom of waves, which he recognized as the pounding drum of a papal court; he would genuflect before the sound, knowing it was a call to arms.

Every dawn and every dusk he spoke a High Mass for the birds and the fish and the blowing wind.

For some months he held sway over this secret dominion. During that time his flame receded into an acceptable glow and he no longer lusted.

Until the woman appeared.

She wore broken boots and carried a bag of orange peels; she threw rocks at the swooping gulls, driving them away from what she herself wanted to scavenge. From his hiding place, Riordan watched her walk into the sea and lower her body three times. Each time a wave roiled over her head, and each time as she lifted herself clear, cursing the cold, she held a clam in her hand, which she tossed to the beach. But Riordan was blind to the clams. What he saw was a woman submerging herself three times, and he saw her lips move and knew she was calling to God to breathe His spirit on the water. Riordan knew she was freshly baptized and therefore he loved her as he had loved his mother. They fornicated for many hours, grinding sand between their teeth, until they both lay exhausted and entwined in seaweed.

He was a marvelous fuck, so she stayed to love with him on the beach and among the dunes and in the wet caves along the coast.

She was not satisfied with a simple diet of crawfish and berries. She wanted more. She knew how to get it. She taught Riordan how to build a kiln and one night when the thunder rolled and the sky was cracked with fire, they crept into the cemetery of a nearby village and, squinting against the rain, moved among the headstones until they found the grave of a child. They uncovered the child and carried its skeleton back to be cremated in the kiln. They fired clay made from the silica of eroding rock and sand and sea water, and bound it with the ashes of the child. They spun urns and vases and some shallow dishes and they sat together on the side of a distant highway, selling their pottery to travelers, who would always exclaim over the beauty of the clay. The money allowed the woman to buy more sophisticated fodder than mussel chowder or fried sea grass.

It was a happy time and, because it was, it diminished Riordan. He was unprepared for a lightness in his soul and he worried lest God disapprove. He compensated for his uneasiness by daily journeys to the surrounding foothills, where he rolled among the thorns and recited his catechisms. But still he was uneasy.

He awakened one night to hear the squalling of an infant. He opened his eyes and in the shadows of a cave saw his woman severing her umbilical cord with the sharp edge of a clamshell. At the end of that cord was a wailing boy.

A son had been born to the heir of God, and it was Riordan's undoing. The rapture which surged through him stifled him with guilt, and he knew the time of penance had arrived. He waited patiently until the infant was weaned and then, under the fading moon that was God's eye, Riordan drove the woman from the cave. In an act of ultimate mercy, he pounded her into the sea.

He was made chaste again when at last her mouth filled with mussel shells and small fish nibbled at her tongue.

Silently he bid farewell to the beach, to the caves, to the dunes. He strapped the potter's wheel across his back and, under one arm, he tucked an urn spun from children's bones. Under the other arm, he carried his son.

He called him Jubal, after the son of Lamech. For according to Genesis, Jubal was the father of all such who handle the harp. Because Riordan knew that the years ahead would surely be filled with strife, he was determined to teach his son how to pluck the strings of a lyre, so that the boy could play sweetly for those who would die in the flames.

Clothed in his mildewed cloak of the Apostles, hand in hand with Jubal, Riordan wandered the paths of New England. He had a knack for finding isolated places that provided shelter. Along the northern coast, overturned hulls of abandoned dinghies were made snug with pitch. Deep in the Maine woods the black boughs of lightning-scorched trees were gathered together and, by the use of hanging vines, tied into lodges. The rural landscape of New England was undergoing great change. Its utilitarian purpose was falling into neglect as farms gave way to vacation homes for city dwellers and creekbeds were dredged for summer camps and barns were converted to ski lodges. Riordan and his son did not find it difficult to discover abandoned chicken coops and potato cellars, and here and there a horseless stall.

No matter where they roamed, Riordan reconnoitered the area to make certain that a cemetery was nearby, for he needed the ashes of a child to bind his clay. He instructed his son in the fine art of pottery, and soon the boy was as expert as he. Like his mother who died with fish in her mouth, Jubal joined his father on the roadsides. They were a striking pair as they hunched on either side of their earthenware, the old man's beard as soft and white as flowing cream, the small boy softly strumming the strings of an Irish harp Riordan had stolen from an antique shop in the Berkshires. Men and women gazing out of their car windows at the autumn foliage of New England hills saw Riordan and his son and were charmed. They stopped their cars and, after listening to the boy's lovely songs, they hefted urns and bowls in their hands and talked admiringly of their singular beauty. They almost always purchased a piece or two. Sometimes skiers would stop, astonished at the sight of Riordan and his son resting comfortably within the hollow of a snowbank. Summer travelers often thought about offering a chilled can of soda or a slice of watermelon to the old man and the boy who sat motionless under a noon sun, but when they approached they saw that neither man nor boy seemed the least bothered by the heat. Embarrassed by their own vulnerability to weather, they would leave the soft drink or fruit in their cars and buy a bowl or two or three.

There were seasons of storm when it was useless to set their pottery along the roadsides as no cars would stop. During these times, man and boy satisfied their appetites by snaring the wildlife of the woods and drinking from mountain springs. Occasionally, when they hungered for different fare, they waited for nightfall and, with one swift blow from a stone, crushed the brain of a farmer's strayed calf, or wrung the neck of a chicken.

They did not bleed the chicken. They were not Jews.

Once, as he watched a chicken thrash in Jubal's hands, Riordan felt himself grow hard but he quickly turned away and, with the coarse sand from a running stream, scourged his skin until he bled. Then he was no longer hard. The incident occurred during the time he knew that Jubal, too, was beginning to feel a stirring in his loins. Riordan reasoned that he would have to teach the boy how to resist his sexual yearnings, how to sublimate them.

Later, when he saw the boy fumbling with himself, the old man wove a belt of thorns and tied it around Jubal's waist. He ordered the boy to press the thorns deep into the flesh of his body until the thorns punctured his skin and bled profusely. Jubal cried out in pain but the old man only made him press harder. The blood dripped down Jubal's belly and ran into his groin. It stained his penis. But it was not until the boy begged for mercy that Riordan let him cease the torture.

The old man was so taken by his own invention that he began wearing the belt under his cloak, around his own belly. He cut slits on either side of the cloak so that he could thrust his hands through them and reach the thorns. Each day at noon, when the sun was centered in the sky, Riordan inserted his hands through the convenient slits and he slid his fingers back and forth along the bramble belt until his flesh was lacerated and wet with blood. Then he would remove his hands from the protection of the cloak and raise his arms, his palms parallel to the sky, and exhort God to send His stinging insects for a visitation. Attracted to the sticky rivers that laced Riordan's fingers, a tiny winged world flew to feast on his blood. Black deerflies and small gnats and a wasp or two whirled around Riordan's head and then dived at the crimson juice of his flesh, all stinging his fingers before they drank. But Riordan's love of God narcotized the pain, and this paradox worried him. He searched for means to prolong his agony in order to give credibility to his piety.

His search ended in the noonlight of a summer's day. He and Jubal crouched on the banks of a muddy pond on a farmer's field. They had walked through much of the previous night on their way to the higher reaches of the southern mountains in Vermont. Now they paused to rest. They had eaten green kernels from July corn in the field behind them and, while Jubal lay quietly among the stalks, Riordan collected the anise-scented leaves of sweet goldenrod, which he would later dry and make into a tonic.

Jubal watched a viceroy butterfly swoop from a stalk and flutter to the muddy waters of the pond.

"What gives her color, Riordan?" he asked, his eyes intent on the butterfly.

Riordan paused among the goldenrod and glanced at the butterfly.

"God paints her, boy."

"She's pretty. She's real pretty." The boy's gaze drifted to a stand of birch trees at the far end of the pond. He squinted toward the uppermost branches and began to giggle. "Old devil, he seen her. He gonna feed himself true."

Riordan peered up at the tree. A hugh black crow was perched on a curving limb. The bird was motionless, but its beady eyes were directed toward the pond below, toward the butterfly.

"Hooie," Jubal declared as he studied the black bird. "Ain't he gonna bust his belly!"

The old man smiled as he stuffed goldenrod into his pockets and then came over and sank down next to Jubal.

"No, darlin'," Riordan said. "Brother Death won't flutter a wing. He knows. That is to say, he thinks he knows."

"What? What's he know?"

Riordan sighed. "You're not listening, me bravo. I said he thinks he knows. There's a difference, don't you see?"

Jubal looked dumbly at the old man. Then he looked back and forth between the glistening crow and the viceroy butterfly whose vertical wings shimmered in the sunlight striking the waters of the pond.

Jubal shut his eyes for a moment so that he could better imagine the swift plunge of the bird and so that he could better hear the snap of the bird's wicked beak as it closed around the body of the unsuspecting butterfly. But when the boy opened his eyes again, he saw that neither bird nor butterfly had moved. He was disappointed.

"Mr. Crow — " he began.

"Brother Death," said Riordan.

"Brother Death. He's takin' his sweet time 'fore he grabs holt of that fucker."

"He don't want that butterfly, Jubal, he don't want her 'tall."

"He don't?"

"Look close at the little thing," Riordan said, pointing to the butterfly which still quivered on the water. "See how lovely she's marked. See how the black stripes kiss the orange curve of her wings. Mark you the sweet white spots on her. Isn't she a wonder, boy?"

"Won't make no nevermind to Mr. Crow if'n he — "

"Brother Death."

"Ayuh, Brother Death. Won't make no nevermind what she looks like if'n Brother Death, he sees fit to gobble her."

"Ah, Jubal, you fail to see the marvel of it. That butterfly, that little lady all of a quiver, she's one of nature's lies, don't you see? She's one thing pretendin' to be another, and she's safe in her own lie, she's safe from the beak of Brother Death."

Jubal frowned. He knew the old man never lied to him, but the words the old man spoke were confusing. The boy's sense of order was violated. Looking from tree to pond, from bird to butterfly, the boy saw predator and prey, each tied to the other by that invisible wire which twanged between hunter and hunted. In Jubal's mind, it actually *was* a wire, which when plucked by the fortunate, hummed the high music of a kill. It made him uneasy to think that the wire between butterfly and bird would remain silent.

"But, Riordan," he said obstinately.

"Listen to me, darlin', so that you can get the straight of it," Riordan said and reached for the boy's hand so that he could reassure Jubal that all he, the old man, had previously told the boy about the natural rhythms of predator and prey were true, but locked within those rhythms were spasms of a cunning camouflage.

Riordan explained the protectiveness of mimicry. He pointed out that the butterfly hovering over the pond was a viceroy, but that it had almost the same markings as a monarch, which all birds shunned because of its displeasing taste. Therefore, God in his wisdom had given the viceroy a similar coloration, thus to avoid the punishment of beak and talon.

The old man's voice was quiet as he spoke of the duplicity of nature, but Jubal sensed a strange intensity in Riordan's lecture. It was as if the recitation were only a preamble to some other thought that stirred within the old man's brain. The growing heat of Riordan's words enraptured the boy, for he suspected that something important was going to be said, some secret revealed. Riordan continued. He spoke of fish in the Sargasso Sea that resembled seaweed and therefore were not destroyed by the jaws of sharks; and he spoke of the caterpillars that had adapted the ways of ants and which, when threatened by a marauding blue jay, would spray an acid — similar to the formic acid of ants — from its glands, which frightened the jay and drove it away; and he spoke of the bright bandings of the wasp, which warns of a repulsive feast; and he spoke of the pine hawk moth whose green body blends, blurs, and then disappears against the needles of a spruce. As the old man spoke there was a rising timbre to his voice that reminded Jubal of steel striking stone, and the boy felt sure that fire would soon spurt from Riordan's mouth.

Riordan paused. He rose and walked down the bank of the pond. He walked into the water until it was waist deep and then he lowered himself three times. Each time when he lifted high of the pond, Jubal saw that water ran across the old man's eyes, which remained open and unblinking and black with internal vision.

Across the pond, the butterfly trembled.

The black crow was still.

Slowly, Riordan lifted his arm and pointed at the viceroy.

"And this deception," he said to Jubal, "is one more mystery of God that must be unraveled by His apostles, for the continuance of this deception provides a hiding place for the children of lies."

Riordan thrust his hands inside his cloak. He grasped his belt of thorns tighter than he had ever done before; the thorns ripped his fingers again and again. When he felt the coursing of his blood, he yanked his hands free so swiftly that he tore loose the inner pocket which was marked with the name of St. Paul. His arms stabbed upwards as if to pull the sky around him and then he wailed at God.

"There is another who hides behind his markings. There is a great deceiver. There is a Jew!"

Palms parallel to the sky, Riordan bled.

The black bird plunged.

The crow's beak sunk into Riordan's fingers and tore loose a strip of ravaged skin. The bird's black wings beat against the old man's beard. And when he was savaged, Riordan Flynn's search was done. He had found the instrument of pain that would prove his piety.

Brother Death was his salvation.

The crow satisfied his appetite on a feast of Riordan's bleeding fingers and then sat quietly on the wounded hand. Riordan was in ecstasy. The bird was more than a vehicle for the old man's veneration. It was a symbol of God's will; a sign of good things to come, a direction from Him that here, among the green hills, was the place for Riordan to erect his tabernacle. For had not a small black bird plucked the poisoned loaf of bread from the cave of Subiaco and rescued St. Benedict from a premature death? And had not Benedict, studying the beat of the small bird's wings, thrown himself into a coil of hawthorn and released himself from temptation?

It came as no surprise to the old man that, later in the day, he and Jubal, together weaving a rough path through the heavy mountain undergrowth, Brother Death perched on the old man's shoulder, discovered the cave that became their home. And it came as no surprise when, that night, reconnoitering the outer regions of what would be his praying fields, Riordan stepped onto an abandoned logging road. He followed it. It angled southward through the woods and eventually crossed a wider graveled road; Riordan turned onto that road, too, and followed it.

As he walked under the moonlight, Riordan was aware that gradually the roadbed became firmer under his feet and he knew that the surface had been packed under the weight of vehicles. The landscape changed. Woodland gave way to pasture. A dog barked. Riordan saw the light of a farmhouse. He walked on. He heard a waterfall. He crossed a narrow, wood-planked bridge.

At the bend of the river, Riordan saw an ancient grain mill, its huge lower and upper millstones still in place and attached to several sets of gears and a waterwheel. The stones were chipped and dry and the gears rusted, and though the wheel turned slowly in the rush of river water below it, the action was without utility. It was obvious that many years had passed since the millstones ground wheat or rye into flour. For a moment, Riordan's heart quickened because in the white path of the moon he saw that the building had been fitted with stained-glass windows. But anger quickly displaced delight as he recognized that the palleted panes were abstract and bore no relevance to things godly. The mill had been made into a restaurant.

Nailed to the barnsiding above the door was a wide plank into which letters had been burned: *The Silver Spoon.* Just below the center of the sign, wood had been gouged out; imbedded firmly in the cavity was a silver spoon. It was a tiny spoon such as is often used to dip jam from a crystal jar. The head of the spoon was a delicate triangle. Under the moonglow, the spoon resembled a silver arrow and Riordan, always alert to the mysticism of moments, decided to continue his exploration in the direction the little arrow pointed. He left the shadows of the mill, passed the post office and a garage, and saw the iron bridge that crossed the river on his left. He picked a pebble from the road, tossed it onto the bridge. When he heard the sweet ping he knew it was the cry of an angel. He did not imagine this. He heard it. And he knew he was on the verge of marvel.

As Riordan stepped forward, moonlight struck the face of Christ.

For many months, those who heard the ensuing sound would debate its source. The men and women who slept behind the doors of the village, the farmers and their families who had retired early in their homes, the children who were dreaming, all would talk in whispers of mountain cats and strangled deer and wild coyotes and ancient hangings, but none could say for certain what it was they heard on that awful summer's night.

It was the howling man.

The moon-splashed face of Christ under which Riordan howled was part of a simple stone carving of the crucifixion. It adorned the granite facing over the central door of Down Derry's Catholic church. The sight of Him enraptured Riordan, filled him with such felicity that his response was automatic. His howling was an act of supreme blessedness.

Once, when Jubal had been privy to that awful sound, he had asked the old man what it meant. Riordan had compared his long wail to a sort of canon and, upon seeing that the boy did not comprehend, offered further explanation.

"It is the sound of my soul," he told the boy, "and it mirrors the cry of Christ. It is like a canon, because it is an ecclesiastical melody sung together by the Redeemer and me. Can you not see that, darlin'?''

"Ayuh," answered Jubal, not seeing, not caring really.

The fact that Riordan discovered the church on the same day he witnessed the camouflaged butterfly and found Brother Death convinced him to set up his own sanctuary in the woods as a place from which he and Jubal could journey toward other uncoverings. That night he retraced his steps around the converted mill, glancing gratefully at the tiny silver spoon that had shown him his destination, then recrossed the wooden bridge to step onto the graveled road. After some miles, he veered onto the abandoned logging path until he reached the hawthorn-hidden cave.

It took many months to carve the niches into the stone face of the wall and many more months to collect the natural pigments and then paint the faces and figures of all but Judas. But Riordan was a patient man. He was comforted by the knowledge that when he was ready his hunt would be rewarded with sufficient quarry.

Somewhere within the walls of the Catholic church a Jew would be hiding.

History had taught him this. And he taught it to Jubal.

Arranged on a stone shelf in Riordan's cave was a row of ancient books, each corseted in cracked leather. They were kept separate from the old man's illuminated Bible because he did not wish to taint the gospels. And it was not coincidence that Brother Death, that blackest of birds, made his perch above these books.

During each long night of that first winter in the woods, Riordan pulled one or another of those cracked leather books from its shelf and read aloud to Jubal. The boy was genuinely interested in the contents, for he knew that when he had learned, understood the texts, he and the old man would join in the hunt.

The titles of the books indicated their cohesiveness. One was called *Declaration of the Ceremonies of the Judaic Rites.* Another was *Audience with a Self-Confessed Jew.* The old man's favorite was *Censure and Confutation of the Talmud.* Jubal particularly enjoyed the *Alboraico,* a slim, beautifully published volume which employed exquisite metaphors to characterize the Jew according to specific parts of Mohammed's mythical horse, *al-Burak,* from whom the author derived his title.

All of these tomes had a common heritage and a similar purpose. They were written in the fifteenth century under the aegis of Tomás de Torquemada, confessor to Ferdinand and Isabella, Inquisitor General of

Castile and Aragon, charged with the centralization of the Spanish Inquisition. And all were used to identify and ferret out Conversos, those Jews who, submitting to baptism, professed their newly attained Christian faith but secretly engaged in Judaic practice. Once exposed, these *villains* of Spain were subject to the niceties of Torquemada's torture and, ultimately, were consumed in the fires of his autos-da-fé.

The written rules of identification were stunning in their simplicity. Neither dullard nor oaf nor vagabond strolling the orange-scented streets of Seville could fail to recognize a Converso, or Marrano as they were more often called. The Christian citizens of Spain derived much pleasure in this latter appellation, as *marrano* was the word for swine.

And so, under the light of his flickering winter candles, Riordan tutored the boy who was his familiar, his bravo, his human ferret. He made Jubal repeat endlessly the maxims from the works of Jew-Roasters. The boy learned well the vile rituals of heretics. He committed to memory those things which the secret Jew performed. And he was suitably repelled as he listened to Riordan's fervid pronouncements.

The hidden Hebrew, the old man intoned in the cold cave air, recites the Psalm of David without *gloria patri*, and at night he drops his hand before his face, begging forgiveness of another but failing to cross himself because this is the benediction which Jacob offered the sons of Joseph. The Jew rips off his fingernails and hides them in the ground so that they may be gathered up on that day when all things will be called to account. Jews light nine candles one by one and then pinch out the flame as they intone their prayers. They let no smoke rise from their chimneys on Saturday, the day before the *true* Sabbath. They eat fowl only if its neck has been severed to allow the free draining of blood. They shun rabbits because the animal is without a cloven hoof. They turn their faces to the wall when death approaches, and in the mouth of the dead is placed a pearl. They doubt the Immaculate Conception. They go barefoot on fasting days.

The infamous litany was endless and without mystery. It provided clear clues to those who had violated the baptismal celebration, and Riordan assumed that those who knelt before the altar in Down Derry's church had received that blessed sacrament. It followed naturally that any of the Catholic congregation who were discovered covertly engaged in one or more of these Judaic vilifications were falsifiers of the True Faith and were to be treated accordingly.

The Marranos, Riordan explained carefully to Jubal, are not unlike the darlin' little butterflies who pretend to be what they are not and thus avoid the beak of Brother Death. It is an intolerable pretense. Paul's epistle to the Romans explains that, regardless of his or her age, of his or her sinful past, the neophyte who willingly accepts an immersion in the waters has been accorded a share in the death and resurrection of Christ and is forever joined in holy membership; and the abuse of this membership is surely grounds for pursuit. But, Riordan warned the boy, the goal of this pursuit is not, must never be, vengeance. Indeed, me boyo, the old man said, it is only through God's grace that we enjoy the privileges *ex auctoriate apostolica*, apostolic authority, but so too must we accept its responsibility. We must hold the Relapser to our bosoms and return him to the way of the light.

"We must," the old man softly spoke, "sing to them in the sight of angels."

And he said: The way to light is through temporal suffering.

And he said: One must not be so given up to contemplation as to neglect the good of his neighbor.

Riordan was a pragmatic madman.

The winter lessons done, the body of Torquemada's texts committed to memory, Riordan and his bravo welcomed the softer days of spring and every week walked through the woods to Sunday mass, each a secret missionary of mercy. At first, the small Catholic congregation was puzzled at the sight of the old man and the boy, but the taciturn Green Mountain villagers in their pews were reluctant to disturb those they saw deep in prayer. They did not wish to invade the privacy of worship, nor did they think it fitting to make casual inquiry of strangers who asked nothing of them and who behaved with sweet propriety.

The villagers were not familiar with either Riordan or his son. Riordan had seen to that. During the times when his search for lesser men drove him relentlessly from place to place, he had made certain to set up his kiln and to sell his pottery at some distance from the temporary shelters within which he and Jubal lived; and on those occasions when he chose not to feed from the wilderness, he and the boy journeyed far afield to make their purchases.

At Down Derry's church, Riordan's schedule of arrival and departure afforded little opportunity to exchange pleasantries. He and Jubal slipped through the doors of the church moments after the service had begun and slipped out again moments before mass was done. The old man and his silent son stayed only long enough to watch the parishioners for any signs of disbelief or doubt, or subtle indications of heretical manner. It was many months before their vigil was rewarded.

On an early summer morning, a young man who was dressed in old clothes and a rough fishing vest and who sported a fine black beard hurried into the church. He slipped a knapsack from his back and let it rest on the stone floor. He dipped a finger into the font of holy water and crossed himself. He genuflected before the altar. He took his place in a pew.

Riordan saw that the young man's eyes were red-rimmed from lack of sleep and that during the recitation of mass his body bent with fatigue. Then Riordan saw something else. When the young man opened his mouth to receive communion he let the wafer slip from his tongue, thus desecrating the body of Christ and denying mystical union with the Crucified Savior.

The old man remembered John the Baptist's report that the Jews had murmured at Him because He said *I am the bread which came from heaven. Doth this offend you?*

Looking at the damp wafer lying on the stone floor, Riordan saw the discarded body of the Lord. He crossed himself and was filled with woe for the sinner who had refused the Host. When, later in the liturgy, that same sinner recited the first three phrases of the *Paternoster* but then closed his eyes, let his head droop wearily, and lapsed into silence over the prayer's remainder, Riordan's flesh tingled. He became short of breath and his eyes were hot, for he knew well that the only words uttered by the sinner paralleled the opening words of the *Kaddish*, an ancient prayer of the Jews.

The old man had flushed his prey.

Riordan touched his son and they left the church. Jubal told his father that he, too, had seen the manifestations of a heretic. Jubal's voice was without resonance, high and twanging like the invisible wire between hunter and hunted. He knew that he was about to enter the service of Tomás de Torquemada, an experience he had longed for.

When the mass was over, the young man with the fine black beard left the church. Once again he wore his knapsack. He walked down the steps of the church, crossed the highway, and turned west to follow the horseshoe bend of the river. It had been a dry spring and the level of the water was low as the young man waded through it. He climbed the river's bank and entered the bordering flat fields then disappeared into the thin woods of bending birch.

Remaining at a discreet distance, Riordan and Jubal followed.

In less than a mile the woods thickened and the young man stepped onto a narrow path that led to the long Appalachian Trail. He turned north on the trail. Riordan was momentarily worried. He feared the young man was returning to one of the open campsites available to any pilgrim who wandered the woods, so it was with some relief that he saw the young man veer off the marked trail and turn west again. Now the woods were thick with conifers, their branches so heavy and spread so wide that they blocked the passage of the sun. The ground underfoot was deep in moss so footfall was silent. Occasionally, Riordan notched a tree with his beaver-toothed knife, but when he heard a distant run of water he pocketed the knife, as he was certain that the young man's journey was almost done. He was right.

The young man made a final turn and stepped into a small clearing. In the center of the clearing was a rolled sleeping bag and a circle of stones within which was a mound of dead ashes. Neatly stacked next to the stones were tin plates, a tin cup, a stainless-steel knife and fork and spoon. A macramé bag hung from the lower branch of a pine tree. Within the bag were plastic pouches of dehydrated food. Hanging from an adjacent branch were beaver pelts.

The clearing was confined on one side by dense woods and on the far side by a narrow stream whose waters flowed slowly into the lattice-work of a beaver dam. The sides of the dam that bisected the stream were packed roughly with mud and stones and small sticks. The top of the dam was crowned with a crosswork of gnawed tree limbs. Upstream of the dam was a wide pond.

Short iron stakes were driven into the ground above the pond. Secured to them were long thin chains of steel. The chains descended into the pond. Although they were hidden, Riordan knew that the submerged ends of the chains held the steel teeth of snares. They were set to spring and clamp onto the body of a curious beaver.

The young man laid his knapsack on the ground and walked to the water's edge. One by one, he pulled up his chains. The steel vise at the end of each was empty. He replaced the chains into the pond. He moved around the campsite, gathering dry clumps of moss and placing them and some small strips of dried birchbark within the circle of stones. He scattered twigs over them and then picked up a handful of slender fallen branches and triangulated them over his bed of moss and bark. He struck a match and lit his fire. When it was burning nicely, he returned to his knapsack and removed a store-wrapped slab of bacon. He used his hunting knife to cut thick slices from it. He placed the slices of bacon in a tin skillet and set that on a portable grill of steel bars. He moved back to the fire. The flames of the dry wood had risen quickly but were lowering now, and the young man balanced the grill on the stones that circled the fire. In just a moment the fragrance of frying bacon pervaded the woods.

How pitiful, Riordan thought, that the young Jew's deception even encompassed the eating of pork. Riordan smiled at the irony of what the heretic had chosen for his Last Supper.

Little rain came that summer. The stream thinned to a trickle, then dried. Water slowly receded from the pond. The beavers left. It was not until early October that a hiker strayed off the Appalachian Trail and roamed through the flanking woods in quest of the season's last wild flowers. He found something else.

He found an empty beaver pond, its sides cracked and dry from the rainless season. Lying against the dusty side of one end of the pond was a skeleton. Attached to each wrist and to his ankles were the steel jaws of a beaver trap, the end of their long chains driven deep into embankments that had earlier been covered with water. The hiker's vision of the dead man's posture would haunt him forever.

His arms were outflung. His feet were together. He was clamped in the posture of the Crucifixion.

Two years passed before Riordan Flynn came across another man whom he suspected might be worthy of the Lord's investigation. For when Riordan had seen Solomon Moon bury his own vomit in the woods, the old man remembered that which was written in the book of his enemies:

And thou shalt have a paddle upon thy weapon; and it shall be, when thou wilt ease thyself abroad, thou shalt dig therewith, and cover that which cometh from thee.

10

"Johnny Walker, please. Black. Double."

The bartender nodded, poured three fingers of whiskey into a cheap tumbler, and slid it toward Solomon, whose fingers closed lightly around the glass. He toyed with it, moving it in little circles, then up and down, then in little sideway paths. His eyes remained focused on the shimmering liquid, his concentration so intense it was as if he were first discovering the color amber. It was a false preoccupation but it was one in which all men at this bar indulged. It prevented each man from looking at another. Recognition would have meant that an unspoken edict had been violated, for nowhere was the territorial imperative more respected than in this place. It was a small and undistinguished tavern that smelled of stale beer and urine. The wall behind the bar was covered with framed photographs of antiquated athletes and coy, bosomy girls who had danced in long-forgotten choruses. There were booths along the opposite wall. Their tables were made of thick wood that had darkened from years of the grease spill of french fries and sirloin fat. The bench seats were made from real leather but the fabric was stiff and cracked and revealed little pockets of old cotton stuffing. It made no difference; none of the booths was occupied. The men at the bar were not here to rest. They were the morning commuters, and each man stood in his own space, eyes focused on the single glass of spirits he would suck into his soul before marching toward corporate battle. Never was a word exchanged, nor a gesture of conviviality extended. The tintinnabulation of ice cubes was the only morning music.

The saloon was on Lexington Avenue, a single block from Grand

Central. It was a convenient way station for those who sought comfort or courage for coming confrontations.

Solomon stared into his whiskey and thought about Ben Brindig. Brindig was a masterful tactician who, in his sixty years, had seen little to dispel the idea that men behaved according to their appetites. He was suspicious of any who disclaimed greed. He seduced the unwary with promises, dangled rewards over the heads of the unsuspecting, and was amused at the spectacle of lesser men straining toward an elusive future. Exploiting the frailties of others, he stood near the apex of the corporate hierarchy. What made him unique among the vice-presidents of production in film companies was that Ben Brindig had never made a film. That was his ultimate triumph. Cognizant of the vagaries of creative choice, he had sidestepped all responsibility for the filmed product of his company. He surrounded himself with men who dared to give celluloid reality to their fantasies but he remained passive in the face of their passion, and in that manner absolved himself from their performances.

"What do I know?" Brindig would say. "A Jew from Wilkes-Barre. You think I know from the *cinemaa-aah?* In a rooster's ass."

He had a way with words.

And with the corporate pocketbook. He bought and sold talent with the sureness of a commodity dealer in the wheat pits of Chicago. The roster of talent on the books of TransGlobal Films was legend in the industry. This was Brindig's genius. He assumed that each man had his price and, willingly, Brindig paid it. He lured the best to the studio. Those who succeeded in making profitable pictures were wooed and wined. Those who faltered were purged. It was a simple process. Should a producer or director or actor be so indiscreet as to hint that the failure of a film might be attributed, at least partially, to Brindig's lack of commitment, that producer or director or actor would find his future foreclosed. The same was true among the executives within the company. Few wished to get off the merry-go-round and abandon the hope of grabbing the gold ring. Rather than defy Brindig, they chose to accommodate him. They closed their eyes to their self-inflicted humiliation.

But Solomon suspected something else. He felt that juggling the lives of weaker men had lost its tang for Brindig. The hatchet man was becoming archaic so, to restore the tingle of action, Brindig resorted to tiny provocations. He incited minor skirmishes. He sought combatants.

He sought Solomon.

Solomon instinctively knew this, but because he thought of himself as a man born into the age of reason, his defense was pallid. He resorted to the assumptions that pettiness could be countered by patience, disputation by logic, meanness by humor. Because he suffered from the pride of civilization, he remained an apprehensive victim.

He threw the whiskey down his throat and walked out of the bar. Surprised to see that the sun had paled and that a northeast wind pushed clouds across the sky, he paused outside the saloon and peered into the gutters of Lexington Avenue. When he saw the wind lift a scrap of paper he was happy. It was a splendid day for flying a kite. As he walked uptown Solomon continued to watch the swirl of guttered debris and he began to fashion his day around it. But he knew that all would depend on his meeting with Brindig and Manzinni. He wondered if Brindig had ever flown a kite. He wondered if Brindig had ever been a little boy. He doubted it.

"Hoo ha," shouted the Mouse. "What a nice horse! What a good horse!"

Solomon looked up sharply. The morning brightened at the sight of his friend. Mousey Blum stood in the street, feeding a cucumber to the animal attached to the Mouse's phaeton cab. He rubbed the animal's long ears, talking to it, reassuring it that it looked like a horse and, as if to confirm this fact, Mouse ran his hands along the blotches of white he had painted on strategic spots of the animal in order to duplicate the markings of a pinto pony. He was aware that the paint had turned a dirty gray under the constant onslaught of the city's soot but he felt certain that the animal was colorblind and therefore would feel no chagrin at the image that might be reflected from rainy pavements.

The animal was a mule but under Mouse's coaxing, believed himself a stallion. He was partially deaf. He wore a headdress of Indian feathers and his bridle was studded with an assortment of pins. Each of the pins was a disk of round white metal on which was embossed an individual name. They were the names of Mousey's heroes. Franklin Delano Roosevelt. Lou Gehrig. Jelly Roll Morton. Fiorella LaGuardia. Hoot Gibson. Maimonides. There were many, many disks. The Mouse had eclectic taste.

Like his mule, the Mouse was outfitted in a fashion that mirrored his eccentricities. He was a skinny man with wrists and ankles no larger round than a horseradish. It was easy to see this because his jacket sleeves rode high on his forearms and the legs of his trousers barely descended to his ankle bone. Like the rest of his apparel, these items had been rescued or bartered from his customers, the customers he encountered during the hours he practiced his profession. The Mouse was a tour guide.

He carried the permit of his profession in his purse. The purse also had been acquired from his clientele. It was a small remnant of multi-colored carpet that had been sewn into a soft square, which was opened and closed by a rusty clasp, such as one might find on a widow's handbag. The purse lodged in the inside pocket of Mouse's prized possession, a shooting jacket of heavy Irish tweed. Although the jacket was narrow in the shoulders and too short in the sleeves, the tweed itself was beautiful. It was woven of wool whose colors reflected the blue-gray mist of an Irish sea, the dark brown of a peat bog, and the heather of untoiled fields. The cloth was rubbed soft by age and here and there a thread poked loose, but its dark buttons still shone. They looked like miniature black dahlias, their little leather leaves turned inward in perfect clusters. But the things that filled the Mouse with joy were the pockets. On each side of the jacket was a bellows pocket, and within the pockets were circular loops sewn to the side. They were designed to hold shotgun shells, but the Mouse had redefined their purpose.

Mousey Blum loved raw vegetables. He loved everything about them. Their shapes and colors and smells and consistencies. The feel of them in his hands. The crunchiness between his teeth. The fragrance of their roots, especially if they had been freshly plucked from the ground. All day long, riding on his carriage seat as he toured the parks, the Mouse nibbled. He was a connoisseur of beans, beets, celery, cucumber, turnips, zucchini, carrots, chive, and endive, and because he was acutely aware of the individuality of each vegetable, he deplored those who made a casual grab bag of this produce. He refused to rub carrots against celery, perch beans on zucchini, entwine chives with a turnip. The rows of cloth loops sewn inside his pockets provided a neat solution. He could insert a single vegetable of his choice into each individual loop and thus protect the singular identity of each.

This belief in the *singleness* of things was shared by his friends Solomon Moon and Emilio Ho, in front of whose delicatessen he was parked. It was the core of their friendship.

The three men formed an unusual triumvirate. They had served together in the army during the last year of World War II, and that common experience had triumphed over their disparate backgrounds. They truly enjoyed each other's company, and this was so because never did one demand something of the other. Their mutual attachment was without intrigue.

In Solomon's case this was particularly important, for during the last few years of employment with TransGlobal, and the business relationships it entailed, he had begun to doubt the innocence of friendship. Regardless of their sophisticated patina, their subtle rhetoric, the majority of men and women with whom he dealt extended their regard proportionate to the penalties exacted. More and more, he relied on the companionship of Emilio and the Mouse.

Each man accepted the others for what they were. None denied the differences among them. Their harmony was rooted in a tacit understanding that friends should not violate the privilege of affection. Their companionship was sustained by candor, each treasuring the fact that none had to camouflage his curiosity about the other or feign approval or seek accord through spurious reaction. Each felt quite certain that their harmonious companionship could not be threatened by dissent. They were not honey-mouthed together, neither were they disparaging. Any criticism leveled was not an arrow of aspersion but, rather, an unrancored inquiry into motive. Because the cement that bonded them together was their mutual admiration of the separateness of men, they refrained from fingering each other's soul. Unless requested, none delved into the other's dream or discontent.

"Mouse," Solomon said as he stepped close to the mule who thought he was a horse, "he shouldn't eat cucumbers. They'll give him gas."

"Nah," Mouse said. He winked at Solomon. "Only mules get gas."

Solomon shook his head. "One day, he's going to find out and you'll be in a lot of trouble."

"You better eat a pickle."

"What?"

"You better eat a pickle."

Solomon cupped his hands in front of his mouth and blew into them. "You can smell it, huh?"

"Yeah. Johnny Walker?"

"Black. The best."

"You better eat a pickle."

"Yeah."

The Mouse reached up to the floor of the carriage and removed an old metal fireman's helmet. Two holes had been bored through the sides and a strap inserted through them. The helmet was half filled with a mixture of molasses and oats. Solomon helped the Mouse fix the strap over the mule's ears. The helmet dangled below the mule's muzzle and became a feeding bucket. The two men turned and entered Emilio Ho's delicatessen.

Emilio Ho had been born to a Chinese father and an Italian mother. He inherited almond eyes and an olive skin and his parents' culinary skills. He had heavy shoulders and a wrestler's thick neck, and his forearms bulged with muscle. He had a voracious appetite for any ethnic food and an equal hunger for the dance floor. A bachelor, he frequented many social clubs of Manhattan, and Saturday nights were spent at Roseland. There were no intricate steps he could not perform. He was as familiar with the tarantella and a pachanga as he was with a Viennese waltz.

His mother and father had run the delicatessen all through the war years, and even though their fare often consisted of Spam rather than pastrami, the store's clientele never wavered in its loyalty. When Emilio was discharged from the service, Mr. and Mrs. Ho presented the keys of the store to him. They retired to Mrs. Ho's native Palermo, where Mr. Ho introduced Chinese checkers to his new friends, with whom he sipped wine and sat in the sun.

Emilio's love of food had found a professional channel, and when he converted the back room into an intimate and informal piano bar, his pleasures were complete. He constantly hummed to himself and even as he sliced bologna or fileted whitefish, his feet tapped the quiet rhythms in his head. Listening to the world's music had created a vast calm within him, and he believed that men were truly good. He smiled a lot.

It was too early for his usual customers, so Emilio had moved out from behind the long glass counter of displays and was seated on a small wire ice cream chair, the morning newspaper spread before him on a round marble table. He looked up when he heard Solomon and the Mouse enter the store.

"It ain't nice they print stuff like this, ya know?" Emilio said as he tapped one huge finger pad against the tabloid.

"You got a pickle?" Solomon asked.

"Third shelf inna glass jar. There's wax paper next it." He shook his head sadly and held up the paper. He pointed to a large photograph of a dancing girl clad in a tight-fitting leotard, her body stretched in the flight of an arabesque. The Mouse leaned over the table and examined the picture.

"She's pretty."

"Well, sure," Emilio said. "But lookit. You could see the nips."

"Everybody's got 'em, Em," Solomon said as he wrapped a large sour pickle in a sheet of waxed paper, then bit off the protruding end.

"How'd you like it this was Darby, huh? Huh?" Emilio asked indignantly.

Remembering his surprise that Mouse had instructed his daughter in the *Shabbis* ritual, Solomon studied his friend. He spoke carefully. "I don't know, I guess it'd be up to her. Everybody has to make his own decision, isn't that right, Mouse? I mean, you wouldn't like it if someone told you what to do, right?"

"When you're right, you're right," Mouse answered, obviously unaware of any particular tone to Solomon's voice. He sat in a chair across from Emilio. "Listen," he said. "The wind's kicking up."

"For real?" Emilio quickly closed the tabloid. "What you think, Solomon?"

A thin stream of brine trickled down Solomon's chin. He wiped it away with his forefinger. He wanted to ask Mouse what had prompted him to impose a Judaic ritual on his daughter, but much as he loved Emilio, he didn't think this was the time to introduce what might turn into a contentious discussion. "Terrific pickle, Em," he said. "Really terrific."

"I give it a good shot o' black mustard seed. I mean, lotsa guys, they're like cheapos, ya know? They take maybe a pinch, a pinch an' a half . . ."

"Are you listening to me?" the Mouse asked.

"Yeah, yeah," Emilio answered. "The wind."

"So?" the Mouse asked. "Do we fly the kites or do we not fly the kites?"

"We fly," said Emilio.

"I love it," said the Mouse.

"I'd like to, but I don't know," Solomon said. "It depends."

"What are ya' talkin'?" Emilio wanted to know.

"Brindig," Solomon apologized. "I got a meeting with Brindig."

Mouse saw how uncomfortable Solomon looked. "Hey, what the hell, we'll fly tomorrow, day after, whenever. Right, Em?"

"Yeah, Mouse, sure. What the hell."

"No, no," Solomon said. "You guys go ahead. Really. It's okay." He was saddened by the thought of a day with Brindig, but he had no intention of visiting his own plight onto his two best friends. He took the last bite of his pickle, crumpled the little piece of waxed paper, and neatly placed it in an ashtray on the round marble table where Emilio and the Mouse sat. "I'll just go check the mule, okay? Oh, sorry, Mouse, I mean the horse." He walked out of the deli.

"He oughta quit," Emilio said.

"*You* tell him," the Mouse said. "You got the ice?"

"Yeah." Emilio rose from the table and, crossing behind his counter, opened a refrigerator door. He took out a plastic bag of ice cubes. "This enough?"

"Sure," Mousey said. *"Zei gezunt."*

"Es iz geven a fargenigen tsu eich zen." Emilio beamed. "Pretty good, huh?"

"I love it." The Mouse chuckled. He took the bag of ice and started for the door.

"Hey, Mouse." Emilio turned back to the open refrigerator and removed something else. The object was hidden in his enormous hands. "I got sumthin' else. It's like a, ya know, uh, like a present." And Emilio actually blushed as he uncovered the object in his hands. It was a pomegranate. The Mouse stared at it. He walked back to Emilio. Gently, he took the pomegranate from his friend's hands.

"You're a sweet son of a bitch, do you know that?" the Mouse said softly. "You are really one sweet son of a bitch." He lifted the pomegranate and held it under the light of a fluorescent bar. He slowly turned it in his hand. Its bright red skin was as shiny as a Christmas ball.

"Will you do me a favor, Em?" Mouse spoke quietly. "Will you come down tonight? Will you come down and hang it for me tonight?"

"I was hopin'," Emilio said shyly.

The Mouse smiled. "I'll see you in the park."

"Which one are you gonna fly?"

"The big one."

"She needs a good lift."

"It's blowin' from the northeast," Mouse said.

"Yeah. Oughta be stiff say four, five o'clock."

"You got it." Holding the bag of ice in one hand, the pomegranate in the other, Mouse left the store.

Solomon had unstrapped the feeding bucket from the mule and placed it on the floorboards under the carriage seat. He had climbed up onto the seat and was clucking softly to the mule, which moved restlessly, his shod hooves clicking against the street, his head bobbing and jiggling the false eagle feathers which adorned it. Out of the corner of his eye, Solomon watched Mouse approach. Solomon felt an overwhelming desire to talk to his friend — to ask him about Darby; to tell him what a rotten man Brindig was; to inform him of the killing of the thrush; and to reveal that strange moment in the woods when *the thing* had clawed in his belly. He felt somehow that all these things were related, but he didn't understand why. But when Mouse put the bag of ice on the floorboards next to a small ice cooler, Solomon glanced at him and saw the pomegranate.

"I'll be damned," Solomon said, remembering the Hasid and his pigeon.

"What's the matter?"

"Nothing. It's just this is the second . . ." Solomon stopped. He was looking at Mousey's hands. He winced at the sight. The knuckles on both of the Mouse's hands were swollen and hard and as white as celery knobs, and his fingers were curled into tight half-circles. "Jesus, Mouse, they look awful."

"Yeah. Well."

The mule brayed and kicked backwards with his left leg.

"Hey hey hey!" The Mouse yanked sharply on the reins.

"Boy, he wants to go," Solomon said. "Maybe you'd better let him."

"I fed him, right?"

"Yeah, sure."

"Would you call that a gratifying experience?"

"If you like molasses, yeah."

"Okay," the Mouse said. "Tit for tat." He leaned down and opened the ice cooler. He removed an eyebrow tweezer and a Mason jar filled with buzzing bees.

"Oh, Mouse," Solomon said, "I hate this."

"Pretend it's Brindig." The Mouse grinned. He gave the jar and tweezers to Solomon then pulled an ice cube from the plastic bag. As he held the cube to a knuckle on his hand, he stared at a newspaper folded on the floorboards. It was the *Jewish Daily Forward.* His concentration was immediate.

Mouse believed deeply in the responsibility of pleasure. Although an admirer of Schopenhauer, he was not a genuine pessimist. He did not subscribe to the theory that pleasure was simply an absence of pain; rather, he thought of pleasure as a button on the soul which, when pushed, set the heart quivering and the eyes on fire. He was convinced that a moral obligation existed among all living things, an obligation to exchange pleasure and joy.

He did not discriminate between men or women, children or beasts;

and therefore concluded with Talmudic logic that as his offering of molasses and oats had provided pleasure to his mule it was only fair that the
mule reciprocate and stand patiently as he, the Mouse, fed with pleasure
on the philosophy of scholars. He was engrossed in the written disputation between two rabbis, each claiming a different interpretation of the
Talmud. The central argument concerned the meaning of the words: *repent one day before thy death*. The first rabbi questioned the wisdom of
such an admonition, as it implied that a man must know the day on
which he is to die in order to spend the previous day in repentance. The
second rabbi took grave issue with such a literal interpretation and insisted that the virtue of the warning was its inherent enigma. In what the
Mouse thought was a rather bellicose tone, that rabbi postulated that
since man can never know the exactness of his final hour, it behooves
him to assume the posture of a penitent all the days of his week and (the
rabbi was a military man) do double time on *Shabbis*.

"Hoo ha," said the Mouse, "this I have to think about. But first, the
fingers." He turned to Solomon. "Okay, let's do it." He threw the ice
cube he'd been holding against his knuckle into the fireman's helmet between his feet. He held out the frozen knuckle. "Go!"

Solomon unscrewed the lid from the Mason jar. Holding the eyebrow tweezers, he reached into the jar. As gently as possible, he clamped
the tweezers around the thorax of one of the buzzing bees and lifted the
bee out of the jar. He looked at the Mouse. The Mouse nodded. Solomon lowered the bee's behind onto the extended knuckle. The insect's
stinger plunged into the skin and the bee collapsed in death. It fell into
the bucket next to the melting ice cube. The tiny black stinger vibrated
deeper and deeper into the Mouse's flesh.

"Christ," Solomon muttered.

The Mouse smiled at him. He seemed immune to the pain of the
stinger. Years of arthritic anguish had caused him to deeply research the
problem. He had tried myriad remedies. None had worked. One day, a
tourist left a book under the seat in the phaeton cab. It was called *Bees
Don't Get Arthritis*. It was a well-researched tome on the curative value
of bee venom and it advocated the stinging of a painful joint. From that
day forward, Mousey Blum collected bees and stung himself and was rewarded with relief. When his fingers were particularly stiff, he requested
help. Both Solomon and Emilio were reluctant experts.

It took another twenty minutes for Mouse to freeze his remaining
knuckles and for Solomon to sting them. When each knuckle was

adorned with its quivering stinger, Mouse turned the reins of the mule over to Solomon and asked him to drive.

Driving the phaeton cab was not a new experience for Solomon. He and Emilio had become, on the Mouse's arthritic occasions, adept at the necessary skills. Although Emilio approached these random rides purely as a requirement to get from point A to point B, Solomon enjoyed the experience on a more personal level. He liked the feel of leather reins between his fingers and he was pleasured by the sweet sweat smell of the mule and the ringing sound of the animal's steel-shod hooves. More importantly, he enjoyed a subtle sense of power while perched high on the carriage seat.

Because he was genuinely affected by the landscape through which he moved, Solomon guided the cab westward on a neighboring street and then turned north on Park Avenue. He enjoyed the width of that avenue and the strip of center plantings which divided the two lanes of traffic. The anachronistic sight of a mule-pulled wagon provoked waves and smiles from pedestrians and sporadic cheerful honking from vehicles. A pretty girl standing outside the entrance to the Waldorf-Astoria blew Solomon a kiss.

"How do, ma'am," he called and tugged his forelock in acknowledgment. He was, by this time, imagining himself the driver of a Wells-Fargo stagecoach embarked on a dangerous journey across the western badlands, and when he shifted his weight on the carriage seat it was to ease the position of the mythical .44 Colt strapped to his waist. He glanced at his companion to check that a shotgun was riding on his lap and, because he was immersed in his own image, was truly surprised at the absence of a weapon. The only thing in Mouse's lap were his hands. He held them stiffly and watched the bees' black stingers screw into his flesh. The hands fluttered for one brief moment, as if in protest to unacknowledged pain, and the fingers' spastic movement reminded Solomon of the final fluttering of the thrush's wings.

"Mouse," he said softly, "I did something yesterday. I did something crazy."

"So who doesn't?" The Mouse spoke through clenched teeth as he stared at the boring stingers.

"I mean really crazy," Solomon said.

"Listen," the Mouse said. "I think you'd better pull 'em."

"Sure," Solomon said. He signaled to the traffic behind and then tugged twice on the reins. When the mule halted, Solomon saw that the cab was only half a block from the TransGlobal building. He was no longer a western hero. He tied off the reins then picked up the eyebrow tweezers. Mouse extended his hands. Slowly, one by one, Solomon plucked out the stingers from the Mouse's knuckles. The Mouse sighed with relief.

"Hoo hah," he said. "Sometimes I don't know."

"Yeah." Solomon climbed down from the carriage seat. "About the kites. I'll try to make it."

"I know." The Mouse pulled a carrot from his pocket. He brushed it against his jacket sleeve and then held it out to Solomon. "A *bissel nosh?*"

"Maybe one bite," Solomon said. He didn't like carrots but he wanted to please his friend. "After you."

"Please," Mouse said, holding out the carrot. "Take the tip. The tip is sweet."

"Yeah," said Solomon.

"Yeah," said the Mouse.

They smiled at each other. Solomon bit the tip off of the carrot and then returned the rest to Mousey.

"We'll meet around four, okay?" the Mouse asked.

"If I can make it."

"Don't be late. Sun goes down early these days."

"You afraid of the dark?"

The Mouse laughed, then spoke casually. "Sundown today, we got Sukkot."

"What's Sukkot?"

The Mouse grinned and shook his head. "What the hell am I going to do about you? Sukkot's a holiday, dummy. The Festival of Booths. It's a big time, a wingding. A little dancing, a little wine, you know." He picked up the pomegranate and rubbed it lovingly in his hands. "To tell you the truth, it's a lot of dancing, a lot of wine. I mean, it's a pisser, Solomon. Maybe you'd like to join us?"

"No thanks."

"Darby's coming."

"Is she really?" Solomon realized that he was not surprised. Nor pleased. Solomon glanced toward the TransGlobal building. He knew he was late. "Listen, Mouse," he said, trying to keep the edge out of his voice, "I think you and I, we'd better talk a little. This thing with you and Darby, it doesn't really thrill me."

"You sound sore."

"I'm trying not to be. I don't tell you how to run your life and I don't think it's a number one hot idea for you to tell her."

"If she asks questions, Solomon, someone better answer." The two men were silent for a moment, then Mouse continued. "Why don't you come down tonight? I bet you'd like it. It's a helluva celebration."

"What's she got to celebrate?" Solomon was honestly perplexed.

"Same as you and me, kiddo. Those long, long years of wandering in the wilderness. Amen."

"Oh, c'mon, Mouse. That's old news, for chrissake."

There was another silence between the men. Mouse studied Solomon's face so carefully that he might have been a doctor searching for a sign of melanoma.

"Is it?" the Mouse asked quietly. Then he turned his gaze from Solomon, lifted the reins, slapped them lightly along the back of his mule, and lurched slightly on his seat as the phaeton cab edged into traffic. "See ya," he said as he waved his hand, still holding the pomegranate. As the cab entered the flow of traffic, Mouse turned suddenly on his seat and looked back.

"What crazy thing," he called. "What crazy thing did you do?"

But Solomon was lost among the sidewalk pedestrians. The phaeton cab turned west at the next corner and headed toward Central Park, where Mouse would station himself to wait patiently for some stranger who wished to ride behind a painted mule.

He hoped it would be a long wait. He wanted to polish his pomegranate.

Solomon hurried toward his office. The TransGlobal Film building was sheathed in bronzed glass and steel. As he approached it he could see his mirrored reflection and that of others who passed by. Because the sun was pale behind the clouds and the sky had faded into the color of dirty linen, the glass had lost its light and reflected only dimly. The mirrored images of men and women were merely silhouettes, faceless and without purpose as they drifted across the glassed horizon.

He saw the image of a truck double-parked in a loading zone directly in front of the TransGlobal building. He turned. Darby was standing in the open bed of the truck, waving at him. At her feet, and scattered all over the floor of the truckbed, was an odd assortment of old clothes. Solomon walked over to the truck.

"Hi, Daddy."

"You collecting for the Salvation Army?" Solomon asked.

"I want to talk to you."

"Good. I want to talk to you. But you're in a no-parking zone, you know that?"

"Yeah, I know. I'm sorry about Friday night. I didn't mean to upset you."

"Honey, it's a two-way street. I think we both took the wrong turn."

"No." Darby frowned. "It's not really as simple as that."

"I'm not trying to make it simple, Darby. Please understand that. But you're getting into something you don't know anything about."

"That's why I'm getting into it. Maybe you should, too."

"Let's not start again, okay?"

"You know what'd be swell?"

"No."

"Let's go to the park one day," Darby said. "Just you and me. You know, hang out. Go to the zoo, maybe, and . . ."

"Talk to the seals?" Solomon smiled, reached up, gently squeezed her leg, warmed by the remembrance of when Darby was a little girl and their physical gestures, their touchings, had been unencumbered by complexity. "You're on, kiddo."

"No," Darby said, "talk to me, not the seals. Tell me about my grandfather. I'd really like to know about my grandfather. And his father. You know, all the way back."

In his mind, Solomon saw the photograph of the young man in the field and he knew there was little he could tell his daughter. There was no legacy to share.

"You'd be disappointed."

"I don't think so."

Solomon was silent. He was tempted to tell Darby that life was not like a television show, not like *Roots*. Not all men and women had exotic ancestors like Kunte Kinte. But he feared that this would spark another argument. He stared into the truckbed.

"What are you doing with all the old clothes?" he asked.

"They're costumes. We're doing an old Yiddish play down at the theater. Have you ever read *The Dybbuk*?"

"Yes."

"It's wonderful. The evil spirit of a dead man has entered the soul of someone living and he has to drive it out. It's exciting as hell."

"I know."

"It'd make a good show for cable."

"Well . . ."

"It would. Think about it. You could get some marvelous actors, and it's really only one set and . . ."

"This is not an academic judgment, I gather."

Darby grinned. "No. We need help."

"Ah."

"The woman who's producing it hasn't raised all the money. Now don't get mad, but I told her maybe I could arrange for you to have lunch with her today. I mean, your company is looking for stuff for cable, right?"

"I wouldn't say we were panting for it. The profits are limited."

"But you're getting into it."

"Sure. Everybody is."

"If you helped finance our show, maybe you could tape it right at the theater. You'd have first refusal, at least."

"You know all the terms, don't you?"

"Will you meet with her, Daddy?"

"Of course, this is just an afterthought, isn't it?" Solomon asked, annoyed at being manipulated by his daughter. "You didn't really come here to talk about this, did you?"

"She's awful nice."

"I'm not worried about nice. The woods are full of nice. The woods are full of amateurs."

"She's not an amateur. She's a very serious producer. She's done a lot."

"I don't know."

"She says she knows you."

"Sure. Listen, honey, I'd like to help but . . ."

"Her name's Rena. Rena Nussbaum."

Solomon stared at his daughter. He found it hard to believe what he'd heard. "Jesus Christ," he said softly.

"You know her?" Darby asked.

"Yes," Solomon said, "I know her."

"Well, will you have lunch with her?"

"Jesus Christ," Solomon repeated.

"Daddy," Darby grinned, "you're blushing."

"Don't be silly."

Darby hopped out of the truck and reached into a pocket of her jeans. She pressed a piece of paper into Solomon's hand. "That's her address. She said to tell you that one o'clock would be good but she'd feel better about it if you didn't bring any little strangers."

"Oh, boy," Solomon said.

"Why would you bring a stranger, anyway?" Darby asked. They both heard a whistle from down the avenue and when they looked south they saw a policeman moving toward them, gesturing with his nightstick. "Damn," Darby said, "I'd better get out of here." She leaned forward and kissed Solomon. "Please, Daddy, it's just lunch. How much could that hurt?"

Solomon couldn't answer. He was thinking of Rena Nussbaum and what she meant when she referred to a little stranger. Darby leaped into the truck and gunned the engine. She waved again to Solomon and the truck slipped swiftly into the morning traffic.

As Solomon approached the glass doors of TransGlobal, he noted with some surprise that the image of his face in the darkened glass was not unlike the image reflected in the flawed mirror of his Vermont kitchen. It was the image of a man capable of taking risks. He thought it strange that he had never noticed this before. He smiled wryly. The illusionary man, captive within the glass, would welcome intrigue. Would not hesitate to have lunch with Rena Nussbaum. When he pushed through the doors, he could not help but wonder if he and Rena were still agile enough to climb naked into a sink and sit together in a sea of suds.

He thought it best not to find out.

TransGlobal Films occupied six floors of an office building that towered over Manhattan's Park Avenue. Each of the building's sixty-five stories was sheathed in bronzed glass windows individually outlined in wide strips of burnished steel. Although the structure was a paean to geometrical precision, it was an architectural paradox, for when a passerby raised his eyes to examine the broad expanse of glass through which he could see nothing, his senses were momentarily soothed by the mystery of reflections; but this sensory sedation was swiftly displaced by pain, for the sun that polished thousands of steel strips ricocheted swords of light that seared the eye. Those who looked quickly turned away.

In this way, no uninvited eye was privy to the mischief of men who played their games beyond the glass. Perhaps that was why the building was seductive to its tenants. The majority of them were linked together irrevocably by their common concern with *communication*, that twentieth-century catechism which promises all things to all men. Prominently displayed in the lobby of the building was an alphabetical name board which identified all the occupants and the nature of their interests: public-relations firms, the executive offices of an independent television station, a publishing house, a scattering of press agents, theatrical agencies, travel agencies, advertising agencies, a record company, concert-booking managers, three small magazines of esoteric content and one devoted to purient pleasures, and various other enterprises either central or peripheral to the supply and demand of entertainment, knowledge, titillation.

But the listing of personnel under the banner of TransGlobal Films dwarfed the manifesto in the lobby. TransGlobal was the major domo of this glass house. It was proper, for the company owned the building. It was, as Wilton Forest was pleased to explain, another form of diversifying one's interest. The company also owned an Alabama bank, a Vermont ski resort, a Chicago paperback publisher, a Bermuda cottage colony, and, the root of its proliferating income, a Hollywood studio magnificently equipped for producing motion-picture and television films.

TransGlobal was quoted on the big board at fifty-eight and a quarter and, in this time of recreation and leisure, there were few who believed that the next graph would indicate anything but a rising line. In the arena of bulls and bears, the company's common and preferred were both considered portfolio plums.

Acknowledging the company's record of astute management, reflected by soaring profits and the constant search for acquisitions to enhance those profits no stockholder was disturbed by Wilton Forest's eccentricities.

The broad hall running the length of the eighteenth floor reflected, if not the eccentricity, at least the nonconformity and eclecticism of Wilton's mind. Having demanded of his architect a building whose exterior was a rigid shimmer of glass and steel, Forest deliberately contradicted the effect by designing his company's quarters to resemble a Georgian manor house. The central hall was twenty feet wide, flanked by two walls of doors opening into offices of company executives. Two parallel rows of secretarial desks, placed at right angles to corresponding executive doors, ran the length of the floor. Hanging on the walls of the hall, in fruitwood frames, were prized antique prints of a sporting world whose central concern was hunting and racing, horses and dogs, deer and partridge. At the far end of the hall was a bank of elevators. The space in front of them was decorated to create the effect of a drawing room offering a warm welcome to visitors. Here the visitor was treated to the pastoral simplicity of an English countryside as mirrored in the landscapes of Bonington and Crome. For any who came to call there were authentic Hepplewhite chairs, Duncan Phyfe sofas, a Sheraton sideboard on which was placed for the discriminating a rare collection of scrimshaw and snuffboxes, porcelain and pewterware, and hanging on one wall near a splendid watercolor of the Thames was a Chippendale mirror.

In the Chippendale mirror, Ben Brindig examined the cluster of gray hairs in his nostrils. He was depressed. He felt old. He felt in the need of a prostate tickle. His feet were still swollen from the all-night flight from the coast, his arches ached, and he wondered if his wife Brenda would remain faithful to him while he was rescuing one more project for the *goyim.*

For that is how he felt about Forest and Forest's wife, Sarah. Two neat little people who never perspired. Two Christians carved of ice. Together, they owned the controlling shares of TransGlobal and, as a pair, they dispensed the largess of money or power within the company. They did not hesitate in rewarding bonus or position to any employee who demonstrated unwavering allegiance to the corporation, nor did they pause before extinguishing any fire of opposition. They presented public faces of compassion but Brindig knew they were as callous as coal. They functioned on the principle of friction, creating situations within the company which forced an executive to become the natural enemy of his neighbor. One man looked upon another as an obstacle with which he would collide and over which he must hurdle if he were to ascend the corporate ladder. Predictably, during these *mano y mano* confrontations, one man would rise in triumph while the other would become a fugitive from pride.

"It is," Forest said on these occasions, "the natural order of things."

He was fond of Darwin.

Brindig, too, believed in the survival of the fittest, so he felt that the time had come for Wilton Forest to assume the figurehead position of chairman of the board and appoint him, Brindig, president of the company.

As he stared into the Chippendale mirror, he saw the elevator door slide open behind him. Solomon hurried out.

A *putz*, Brindig muttered to himself as he gently plucked a hair from one nostril, a *putz* with no balls.

"I'm sorry, Ben." Solomon's voice was apprehensive. "I got delayed. The train — "

"It's gray," Brindig said as he studied the strand of hair he'd plucked from his nostril. "Like the pubes."

"Yeah, well," Solomon said. "It happens."

"Wonderful." Brindig's eyes narrowed as he stared at Solomon. "I'm up all night on the red-eye, sitting next to some pussy smoking shit, and I get waltzed around at the Sherry 'cause my room isn't ready and — "

"I'm sorry, Ben."

"Don't interrupt. I don't like that."

"Sorry." Oh, Jesus, Solomon thought, and we haven't even begun to talk business.

"Soon I could have a bald cock and you tell me 'it happens.' Wonderful. Just what I need. A philosopher. You think one day you won't have a bald cock? What are you, crazy?"

Solomon glanced at the watercolor of the Thames and he wished he were standing on the Embankment and that the water was real and that he could dive into it and drown. He sighed.

"Sometimes," Solomon said softly, "I think that's a real possibility."

Sensitive to Solomon's tone, Brindig stepped closer and put his arm around Solomon's shoulders. He enjoyed baiting Solomon Moon, playing him like a fish, but he didn't want to hook him and make him bleed. Not yet.

"C'mon, kid," Brindig said. "Don't get your tit in a wringer." He squeezed the smaller man's shoulder and propelled him down the center aisle of the floor. Together, they turned into Solomon's office.

Brindig sank into the supple folds of maroon leather that covered a massive wing chair and he smiled benignly at Solomon. Solomon avoided his eyes. He was trying to think of a wise way to approach the subject of their meeting. He did not want young Charlie Manzinni hurt. *Shadow on the Grass* deserved respect, not the scorn of vulgar men. Solomon sat in his swivel chair behind his desk. He picked up the script. He belched softly.

"Say listen," Brindig said. "This early in the morning, you already ate deli?"

Solomon said up straight behind his desk. "What?" he asked.

"You smell like a pickle," Brindig said.

Solomon wished he'd worn a lighter suit. He could feel the rivulets of sweat running down from his armpits along his sides. He reached under his jacket and pulled the damp shirt away from his flesh. The sweat burned against the rash in his left armpit, and he made a mental note to switch his deodorant to one with less chlorohydrate.

"Oh," he said. "Well. Yeah. Sure."

Brindig's eyes opened wider as he stared at Solomon.

"Just like that?" he asked. "What, you think it's an ordinary thing for a man to smell like a pickle? Believe me, only a *pisher* smells like a pickle."

"The thing is," Solomon said, forcing himself not to avert his eyes from Brindig's, "the thing is, there's this Chinese guy I know who sells pickles, and . . ."

"Back up."

"What?"

"Back up. A Chink sells you pickles?"

"Yeah."

"This is a fact?"

"Yeah."

"He a commie?"

"You asking if he's a communist?"

"No, I'm asking if he plays polo. What's with you, for chrissake?"

"How the hell would I know if he's a communist?"

"Kosher or not?"

"A kosher communist?"

"Pickles, Solly, kosher pickles! Does the Chink sell kosher?"

"How would I know?"

"What, Solly Moon is a Mongolian? You know from kosher."

Solomon let his gaze drift to the handsomely framed English horse prints that decorated the walls of his office. He wondered if he were too old to take up steeplechasing. He wondered if jockeys had to have a glass of whiskey before taking *their* hurdles.

"Hey, boychick," Brindig said, "don't go away."

"What?"

"The finger in the ear. You got your finger in your ear. I know you. You stick a finger in your ear an' you go bye-bye."

"That's crazy."

"*Emmis.*"

"Why would I stick a finger in my ear?" Solomon asked as he removed the finger from his ear.

"Jesus," Brindig said, "this is a very confusing morning. I think we'd better get to the subject at hand."

"Oh, sure," Solomon said, his eyes drifting once more to the English horse-racing prints. For just an instant his pulse fluttered because he saw that one of the painted jockeys in the picture had the face of a middle-aged man, but Solomon's pulse quieted and returned to normal when he realized that the artist's intent was not to depict age but to show the ravages of weather.

"So, okay," Brindig said. He flicked a finger toward the manuscript. "The dodo who wrote this thing, you talk to him?"

"Not yet."

Brindig stared at him. He smiled. "You're putting me on, right?"

"What you want, Ben," Solomon spoke carefully, "I don't think Charlie would agree to it."

"Christ, Solly, you never learn, do you? We bought the story, right?"

"Right."

"Then we do what we want. This Marconi doesn't like — "

"Manzinni."

"Whatever. He doesn't like it, fuck him. Use the cutoff. What the hell do you think it's for?"

Well, Solomon thought, there it is. The *cutoff*. The quick answer to all things complex. Don't solve the problem, slice it off. The process of emasculation was so swift. He had a sudden picture of Brindig holding a knife in his hand and gelding a stallion.

"Ben," he said, "you ever see a stallion, I mean a really wild horse, a wonderful horse — "

"Please, Solly, don't get fancy with me, huh? Harry West is not gonna play some dipsy-doodle who pisses his pants and runs away, 'cause if he does, the picture goes down the toilet. Do I make myself clear, Mr. Moon? Shit, I should of worn a pinstripe."

Solomon blinked. He was used to Brindig's non sequiturs but this one baffled him. Brindig was dressed in his usual conservatively cut, expensive black mohair suit with an accompanying black silk tie dividing the broad expanse of his starched white shirt.

"Why would you want to wear a pinstripe, Ben?"

"A pinstripe, Solly, a pinstripe is what you wear when you have to listen to shmucks. And you, Solly, you are a shmuck!"

Solomon pressed hard on the blotter of his desk. He forced his fingers to remain flat and quiet. A series of quick little pictures flashed through his mind: the unpaid bills on Kendal's desk, the balance figure in his savings bankbook, the mortgage notes on Westport and Vermont, the moth fluttering helplessly among the silver threads of its captor's web. Surely, he thought, those are the wings I feel trembling in my belly. He did not want to believe it was *the thing*, the awful thing, stirring once again.

"You're beautiful, Ben," he said quietly. "You're really beautiful."

There was a sharp rap on the door, then it swung open and Charles Manzinni hopped into the room. He was a short, beaming, bearded man dressed in a faded denim shirt and dungarees, one leg of which was doubled up and pinned to his hip. His long black hair tumbled down to his shoulders but was held back from his eyes by a red bandanna. He used a crutch under one arm.

"Hey, baby," he sang out cheerfully, "what's happenin'?" He pivoted swiftly on his one good leg and, with the stump of the other, rammed the door shut behind him, threw the crutch into a corner of the office, bounced across the room and perched lightly on the edge of Solomon's desk.

Solomon waved a hand between the two men. "Charlie Manzinni, Ben Brindig."

"Oh, yeah," Manzinni grinned, "you're the guy who owns the store, right?" His single leg swung idly back and forth so that the leather heel of his boot thumped in a soft and steady rhythm against the bottom of Solomon's desk.

For a moment, Brindig seemed mesmerized by the metronome rhythm of the writer's leg, then he smiled at Manzinni. He kept smiling until the writer smiled back. Solomon didn't smile. He knew what was coming.

"So," Brindig said, "here's what we gotta do, Mr. Marconi."

"Manzinni," the writer said.

"Right," Brindig said, still smiling. "Since Solomon's already bought your garbage, what we gotta do, we gotta figure out how to make it smell good."

"Hey, wait a minute," Manzinni said. His leg no longer swung back and forth.

"Take it easy, Charlie," Solomon said hastily. "What Ben means —"

"What Ben means, Ben will tell," Brindig interrupted. "Now you gentlemen listen to me." He paused, flicked a handkerchief from his breast pocket and patted his lips dry. "This weekend, Harry West will join my wife Brenda and me for a little tennis. It is not just a social occasion. What I promised Harry is that this . . . this . . ." His eyes swept distastefully over Manzinni. ". . . this *winner* here would have done something wonderful to the hero Harry West is gonna play, the picture shouldn't go down the toilet. Do I make myself clear?"

Solomon looked at the writer and saw the rigid cords in his neck, the hostility in his eyes. "The thing is, Charlie," he said in a placating tone, "we don't really want to change the story; it's a question of fiddling with a few things."

"What the fuck!" Manzinni twisted around on the desk and Solomon could see the writer's stump pointed directly at his heart. "I spent five goddamn months on this script and you got the balls to tell me how to —" He wheeled toward Brindig. "What right's Solomon got to fuck around with my script?"

"You wanna take the feathers off a hen, you get a chicken plucker, right?" Brindig kept smiling.

"It's a little early to get upset, isn't it, Charlie?" Solomon interjected. "All Ben wants is to make the script a little, you know, better. Isn't that right, Ben?"

"That is right, Solomon." Again, Brindig patted his lips dry but the smile had left his face and his eyes were cold as he stared at Manzinni. "Because without 'better' we got no choice. We cut you off."

"Oh, shit," Manzinni said.

"So, Solly? Let's say Thursday," Brindig said as he rose and crossed the office to the door. "You'll work with this nice feller and give me the script Thursday and Harry West, he'll bless you." He bowed in a strangely formal manner to the two men. "Gentlemen." He walked out of the office and closed the door softly behind him.

"And that," Solomon said quietly, "is the way the world turns."

"Really," Manzinni said tightly.

"Charlie, I'm sorry. I really am. I don't like it any better than you do but my hands are tied. The son of a bitch runs the store."

"Like hell he does. What's his name, he runs the store. You know, Forest, Wilton Forest."

"I can't go over Brindig's head."

"Why not?"

Solomon picked up a pencil and inserted the tip under one thumbnail and started to color it black. He knew why he wouldn't call Wilton. Suppose he was wrong about the script and Brindig was right? Solomon was no longer sure of his own judgment and he didn't want to fail in the eyes of Wilton Forest. With a shock he realized that Brindig did not fear such failure. Solomon forced the pencil tip so deep under his nail that it punctured his skin and drew blood. He watched the blood grow into a small bubble under the nail.

"Well," he said, "I'll think about it."

Charlie was so quiet that Solomon finally looked up. The writer's eyes were downcast. He appeared puzzled, as if he were looking for his absent leg. He pushed himself off the desk, bounced slowly across the room, retrieved his crutch, and made his way to the door.

"Solomon," he said softly, "you suck."

Solomon turned away from the closing door. When he heard it click shut, it reminded him of the sound of a trigger hammer falling into the

empty breech of a rifle. He looked toward the window, hoping that a
bird would wing across the city's sky so that he could raise an imaginary
gun and blow it away. Angered at his own compromises, he shook loose
a cigarette from his pack and reached into a vest pocket for a kitchen
match. His fingers struck a piece of paper and he pulled it from his
pocket. Typed on the paper was the address and telephone number of
Rena Nussbaum.

He picked up the phone.

12

Riordan Flynn and his son had watched Solomon bury his wood thrush, and then followed him out of the woods. They tracked him to the farmhouse. Their bellies tight to the ground, they lay among a cluster of fallen apples in the orchard; the sweet cidery smell reminded Jubal that he had not eaten all day and, although he kept his eyes on the door of the house, he stirred restlessly. The old man sensed his son's discomfort. He split an apple with his knife and gave one half to Jubal.

"Patience, darlin'," the old man said.

Eyes closed, Jubal thought of fireflies that lit the night. The ritual of their death excited him and because Riordan had instructed him well he was able to imagine each formal act played out before him. He saw the flashing signal from a female and knew the light came from her luminescent belly, and he closed his eyes to better visualize the coming slaughter. He saw the male, taunted by the passionate fire of the female, fly to a final embrace. At that moment, Jubal would have sworn that he heard the crunch of tiny teeth as the female devoured the male, leaving only his eyes and feet and wings.

He heard the sharp intake of Riordan's breath. Opening his eyes he followed the old man's gaze.

A man came out of the farmhouse. It was not the hunter. It was a tall, thin man in torn overalls. He gathered an armload of kindling and returned to the house. The old man touched Jubal.

"Do you remember, boy?" he asked softly. "Can you throw your mind back?"

"In the church," the boy whispered in excitement, "we seen him in the church!"

"Aye," Riordan said, "and it puzzles me. Truly." Without another word or even a signal, he rose into a crouch and moved away so swiftly that Jubal only glimpsed his shadow on a moonlit path among the trees and then the shadow, too, was gone. Jubal scrambled to his feet and followed.

For the rest of that night and all through the following day, even though it was Sunday and a time to worship, and through that night, too, the old man and his son stayed in their cave, Riordan studying his books and Jubal supplying them both with bits of jerky on which to chew and water from clay pots they had spun from the bones of children.

The cave was a high stone vault empty of either stalactite or stalagmite. The limestone walls rounded softly into a natural dome. A wide ledge, two feet high, had been hewn out of the curving rock face at the far end of the cave and formed a long and graceful arc. In front of the ledge, and simulating its curve, was a massive stone table. A huge candle stood on the table, sealed to the stone by its own drippings. Its flame wavered slightly from the draft of the cave's tunnel entrance but its light was sufficient to reveal twelve narrow niches carved into the limestone wall behind the table and above the circling ledge. The wall within one of the niches was blank, but on the other eleven niched walls were painted the faces and figures of Christ's disciples.

It was a limestone mural of the first Eucharist.

The unpainted niche was where the figure of Judas might have leaned.

Throughout the two nights twinkling with the death of fireflies, and the day that passed without either man or boy knowing that the earth had warmed and cooled again, Riordan sat on the ledge behind the center of the stone table. He occupied the niche of Christ. In front of him were delicate shapes of pottery and a stone mortar and pestle. Each bowl held natural substances from which he could grind his pigments. There was a crock of yellow oxide and bowls of blue gentians and a vase overflowing with rusted flakes of discarded iron and a shallow terra-cotta shell heaped with charcoal from long-burned wood and an oval plate on which rested pads of moss to be used to apply his paint. Farther down the table, other bowls held those things the old man could use to bind his pigments and turn into paint. There were vessels of marble dust and rendered rabbit fat and pine sap and, precisely separated, the albumen and yolk of partridge eggs.

There was one other object on the table. It was a Bible, its binding leather tooled, it pages illuminated. The old man used it in a special way. He would rise from his stone ledge, cross the cave to his library of ancient books, and after perusing one or more of them he would return to the table and, with a black feather shed by Brother Death, would mark a passage in the Bible. During the course of two days he marked so many that the edge of his Bible looked like one wing of a crow.

Although Jubal wished he were free to run in the woods and strum his harp so that he might conjure up the faceless strangers of his dreams, figures drifting silently in their circle of affection, he remained with the old man, for he sensed that Riordan was troubled in a way which he, Jubal, had never seen before. It was, therefore, with great expectancy that at last he heard his father speak.

"Mark me, boy, and say if I speak the truth." Riordan leaned back against the cold wall of the stone niche, his head resting against the painted robes of Christ, and closed his eyes. "When the hunter bought our bowl did he not call the name Jesus?"

"He did!" Jubal was eager to learn what his father was after.

"Was it not in a blasphemous manner?"

"It was."

"Did he not bite off the nail of his thumb and spit it into the dust?"

"Yeah."

"It is stated in the *Alboraico* that a Jew rips off his fingernails and hides them in the ground so that they may be gathered up on that day when all things will be called to account." The old man was silent for a moment, and then continued. "Did not the hunter bury his vomit in the earth?"

"He did, Riordan. I seen him!"

"It is written thus in the Jews' *Torah:* 'And thou shalt have a paddle upon thy weapon; and it shall be, when thou wilt ease thyself abroad, thou shalt dig therewith, and cover that which cometh from thee.' " Riordan opened his eyes and leaned forward, his arms resting only inches from the illuminated Bible on the table. "Is this man a Jew?"

"It's got to be, Riordan, it's just got to be, don't it?"

"Why then does he harbor a man who kneels before our God?"

"You mean the tall man, come out of his house?"

"I mean the tall man," Riordan said. "Is he a true believer? For what reason does he seek refuge with the killers of Christ? Which one taints the other?"

"I don't follow, Riordan." Jubal spoke nervously. He knew the penalty for not understanding matters about which his father cared. He glanced at the old man's hand and was relieved to see that Riordan was not reaching under his great cloak for the bramble whip.

"Do you remember the butterfly, boy?"

"Well, sure."

"How did he hide from danger?"

"He got this camouflage on him, that's how. He appears to be something he ain't, that's how."

"Who else is camouflaged?"

"Jews. Yes, sir, Jews."

"What kind of Jews?"

"You know, Riordan, them Marranos. They's the ones take the baptism to make us believe they's one of us, but it's a lie, ain't it? 'Cause all the time they's still doin' them Jew things. They's hidin' behind the baptism so's they can't get caught out, ain't that right?"

"That's right, Jubal," Riordan said. "They are hiding from the justice of the Lord. But which one, boy, which one is the sinner? Does the hunter teach the tall man or is it turned the other way?"

"I don't rightly know, Riordan." Avoiding his father's eyes, Jubal scratched a scab from his knee.

" 'Be vigilant; because your adversary the Devil, as a roaring lion, walketh about, seeking whom he may devour.' " The old man spoke softly.

"Chapter five, Peter," Jubal said quickly.

" 'Blessed is he that watcheth,' " said Riordan.

"Revelations!" The boy almost shouted.

"I love you," said the old man. "Now go."

The message was not lost on Jubal. He understood that he was to spy on the farmhouse and report to Riordan any suspicious actions taken by the hunter or the tall thin man who had come out of the hunter's house. He hoped that one or both of the men would perform some heretical deed so that in the hearing of it the old man would admire his son.

When he reached the farm, Jubal slithered through the tall grass of the mowing and crept up the rise until the house and the barn and the outbuildings were in clear view. He had expected to see the red car the hunter had driven across the bridge but it was nowhere in sight. He wondered where the man and woman had gone and if their house was empty. He tried to imagine what things filled the rooms and if there were things of value to either him or Riordan. He had about decided to investigate the house when he heard the rusty hinges of a door. He slid deeper into the grass.

Jabez Tuttle shuffled out of the barn, his broken shoes kicking idly at the dust as if he were punishing the earth for not flowering. Rusted wire enclosed a few square yards of the dust and within the enclosure a handful of hens scribbled dry paths along the surface of the land and pecked at windblown grain. The farmer paused at the split log gate of the enclosure and leaned heavily on one of its cedar posts. He chewed tobacco and stared at the hens. He spat. A wet brown glob spattered a hen and the bird squawked and fluttered in fright. The farmer reached behind him and plucked his faded overalls out of the crack between his buttocks and then moved inside the enclosure.

Slowly, Tuttle advanced toward the birds but then, unexpectedly, he stopped. He lifted one leg and bent it across the knee of the other and studied the sole of his shoe which was smeared greenly with fresh droppings. The farmer's lips moved but even though Jubal was downwind he could not hear what the farmer said. The boy was disappointed. He knew that Riordan would wish to be informed if the farmer had blasphemed. Tuttle snatched some mustard grass that grew alongside the wire fence and rubbed the sole of his shoe clean, then, ignoring the birds, rambled around the perimeter of the enclosure, his back to the hens, his eyes sliding across the Vermont hills.

Suddenly he wheeled and in one swift gesture leaned to the land and snared a hen by its legs and lifted it out of the dust. The bird screeched, its pale beak snapping open and shut, closing on air.

Jubal edged forward in the grass.

Tuttle yawned as he carried the bird at arm's length and ambled out of the enclosure toward an oak stump. The bird hung limply from the farmer's hand. Once, its wings flapped but the movement was feeble. The farmer reached the oak stump and when he bent over to lay the bird down on the stump his loose overalls billowed away from his body and Jubal could see the man's sunken chest and his rib cage, which was circled by a long white scar where a scythe might have slipped. Pressing the bird down firmly onto the stump with his left hand, the farmer used his right hand to yank a hatchet loose from where its blade was embedded in the oak. He raised it high over his head.

Quietly, Jubal blew into the grass in front of him and the blades bent under his breath and his view was unimpeded.

The ax still poised, the farmer glared down at the hen. The farmer's jaws worked rapidly. He spit tobacco juice into the bird's eye and then cut off its head.

Jubal made the sign of the cross. For he remembered that in the

Alboraico it was clearly written that Jews eat fowl only if its neck has been severed to allow the free draining of blood.

Tuttle removed his hand from the hen which flopped off the stump and staggered, headless, in the grass. The bird ran a few feet and then fell over. The farmer stood still until he saw that the headless hen ceased pulsating, and then he sauntered over to the corpse and, with two quick swipes of his hatchet, severed the feet and kicked them aside. He raised the body of the bird and let the blood drain from its neck. Carrying it in this fashion, he crossed the farmyard and stepped onto the dirt road that led to his trailer. He walked down the road, leaving behind him a path of scarlet drops.

It was easy for Jubal to follow. By the time Tuttle reached his silvered mobile home he had plucked half the feathers from the hen. He shouldered his way through the trailer's door and was lost to Jubal's view. Jubal slipped through the cover of trees and edged up to a high window in the trailer. Quietly, the boy placed rocks below the window, stepped up on them and looked in. Tuttle was sitting in his reclining chair, the dead bird in his lap. He was removing the last of the feathers and dropping them into a newspaper on the floor. He was watching television. Fascinated, Jubal watched, too. He had seen televisions operating behind store windows in Springfield, but once when he paused to study the fleeting images Riordan had pulled him roughly away and rebuked him for being attracted to idle pleasure. On the television screen in the tall man's trailer a boy about Jubal's age was talking to an older woman. The boy began to cry. The woman walked closer to him and lifted her hand. Jubal waited for her to strike the boy. But she didn't. To Jubal's astonishment, the woman reached out and touched the boy on his cheek, and even through the window, Jubal could tell how gentle the touch was. He wanted to see what was going to happen next but he knew that Riordan waited. He dared not linger.

Bending low, he ran into the deep woods and turned north toward the mountains. He ran swiftly, without effort, finally reaching the clearing in front of the cave. Although the tunnel entrance was only a scant twelve feet long, Jubal was made uneasy by the weight of the rocks above him and he hurried through the passageway, relieved to step into the heart of the cave.

"He done it!" Jubal cried. "He bleeded a hen!"

Riordan sat in his niche of Christ, the illuminated Bible open before him on the stone table. He looked long at Jubal.

"Which man did it?"

"The tall man. I seen him. I swear it. I seen him take the hatchet an' cut her good an' let the blood run. I seen him do it!"

Riordan said, "The number of fools is infinite."

"We gonna do him?" the boy asked, sweating with excitement. "We gonna do him?"

The old man nodded and smiled and then closed his eyes and leaned back against the limestone wall. "Oh, my, yes," he said. "We're going to do him. We are going to let light into the sinner."

Slowly, he reached out and closed the Bible and then pinched out the flame of the candle. In the darkness, the boy heard his father's voice.

"Ah, darlin'," the old man said, "there is a secret Hebrew on the land."

13

Solomon Moon was the grandson of Rafael Fernandez Mu-
ñoz, a Sephardic Jew who, as a young man, had sailed steerage from
Seville and, like so many other immigrants, had mumbled his name incoherently to the authorities awaiting him in the new country. He was
casually christened Moon.

This arbitrary change of name was the first step toward his ultimate
assimilation into a country of strange customs. He had come from a
farming family in Andalusia and had been accustomed to long hot hours
breaking the rock of that dry land. But even as he worked the fields, in
one of which he had posed awkwardly for a photograph, he had been
comforted by orange-scented winds and the fresh running waters of the
Guadalquiver, and always in the distance was the revolving bronze
statue of Faith at the summit of the Giralda. There were, also, long
walks through the winter mists to the Street of Jews.

The ghetto streets of his new home lacked these consoling features.
The sunlight was not voluptuous and when, on rare occasions, the wind
twisted through the tenements it carried with it the stink of rotting fruit
and unwashed bodies; and the shrill cries of peddling men drowned any
ringing of the Angelus.

Rafael Fernandez Moon became Ralph Moon and gave up the ways
of his father. He firmly believed that if he lengthened the distance from
his past, so, too, could he increase the distance from the ghetto.

At night school and in the public libraries he immersed himself in the
literature of early America. Because they too had crossed the sea to an
alien land he was particularly drawn to the experience of the Pilgrims,
and he was thrilled by the hellfire and brimstone rhetoric of the early

ministers. They seemed to be men who knew who they were and what they wanted and how to get it. They were men of direction. Ralph was not interested in the gospel they preached for he had little time for matters theological. What excited him was their passion. The best among them, he felt, was Solomon Stoddard, the raging pastor of Northampton's church. In later years Ralph would regale his son with stories of Stoddard, and before he died he asked his son to name *his* son Solomon. Although Ralph Junior would wince at the Hebraic connotation of the name, he honored the request.

The Andalusian sun only a dim memory, the bells of Seville an echo, Ralph measured his success in terms of his geographical progress through the streets of Manhattan. He equated uptown with the northern regions of blue-eyed people, the men and women he believed could truly call themselves American. Men with direction. Passion. Men like Solomon Stoddard who, Ralph Moon was sure, had blue eyes.

Although he took his first girl in a tenement on Delancey Street, he married in his own two-room cold-water flat at Second Avenue and Forty-Third Street. His son, Ralph Junior, was born in an apartment on the corner of Amsterdam Avenue and Seventy-Fourth Street. When the old man finally died, he was proud of two things: that his final hours were spent in an apartment with three bedrooms, three baths, separate dining room, and a large foyer on One Hundred and First Street and Central Park West, and that his son had never been bar-mitzvahed.

Ralph Junior's life was sexually motivated. At a very early age, he borrowed a pair of pinking shears from his mother. Peeking into his bedroom, she saw that the boy was cutting holes in the pockets of his trousers. The task completed, he put on the trousers. He slipped his hands into the pockets. He played with himself. The results were so satisfactory that he made it a practice thereafter to snip open the pockets of every pair of trousers purchased.

His constant sexual escapades took precedence over any pursuit of formal education, so Ralph quit school after graduating from the eighth grade. He grew a mustache and lied about his age and found employment as a drummer for a shoe concern. He had a particular affinity to shoes. Not only did he delight in looking at his own image in the burnished toes of his ankle-high boots, he respected the quality of leather, always searching for that which would retain its suppleness and be without squeak. These considerations were more than aesthetic. He never knew when he would have to be fleet of foot, nor did he want to find himself in the dangerous position of giving away his location to some early-arriving and unsuspecting husband.

He was a shrewd young man and saw that if he wanted to maintain his record of seductions he would have to have enough capital to impress. He studied the opportunities available and came to an accurate conclusion that there was a great deal of money to be made in real estate. Perfectly aware that his less than grand income would prohibit competition with the giants of industry, he set about on his own clever scheme.

The territory to which he was assigned as a drummer of shoes covered all the Northeast, west to the far boundary of Ohio. He devised a simple routine to enrich himself. Traveling exclusively by rail, he would make sure to arrive at the tank towns he serviced early in the morning. He would check into a cheap hotel. Leaving his salesman trunk safely in his room, he would strike up a conversation with the hotel clerk and soon learn which trolley line ran furthest out of town. He rode to the end of the line and disembarked, telling the conductor of the trolley that he would wait for the next car before returning to town. Alone, he would stand at the end of steel tracks and survey his location. Generally, the site under his gaze was sad and desolate, ground covered by refuse and tumbleweed, the road unmacadamed and diminishing into footpath or cattle track. He would walk exactly a quarter of a mile down that road, his practiced step lengthened to the measure of a single yard, and counting aloud to himself until he reached the required number of four hundred and forty. There, he would sketch what he saw. Sometimes it was empty land. Sometimes the land held a deserted barn. Often it was treeless. On many occasions it was ripe with bramble or vine. Once, a creek ran through it. But always it was purchasable. His sketch folded in his pocket (a jacket pocket, never one in his trousers with the holes cut out), he would return to town and seek an audience with a realtor. He would show his sketch and inquire about the ownership of the land he'd seen. Before he left that town he would have in his possession a signed contract of purchase stating that he had paid a small amount of money as an option on the land and that a transfer of deed would be forthcoming when future payments were complete. Because most of the men or women with whom he dealt lacked his foresight, Ralph managed to accumulate hundreds of options on tiny strips of land. The acreage involved was minimal but he foresaw the inevitable growth of these towns. He knew the day would come when seemingly worthless land would no longer be on the outskirts of activity; it would be the platform of progress. And those who wished to rise to wealth would need to own it.

Ralph Moon was prepared to sell. For his price.

Not all of his hours on the road were spent on real-estate transactions. Nor on selling. His sexual prowess was legendary and women waited at the whistle stops to fortify the fables. But, like many artists, Ralph succumbed to his own reputation and began to believe that his powers of seduction were infallible and that those seductions would always remain penalty-free.

In 1928 his luck ran out. He was traveling by rail through Ohio on his way from Zanesville to Chillicothe. The train broke down at Lancaster. The failure of locomotives did not disturb Ralph, as it provided a quiet time to contemplate the maps he always carried. He studied these maps looking for possible places to visit, areas that might now be pastoral but which he felt would echo in the future to the clang of machines. He looked for the confluence of rivers or a nearby railroad spur or the seat of political maneuvers. Sometimes it was just the ring of a name that attracted him. He was not without a soul. On that day, sitting in the railroad yards at Lancaster, he spotted a name that lifted his heart. A small town northeast of Lancaster was called Hooker. It was an irresistible lure. Conferring with the engineer of his stalled train, Ralph learned that what was to have been a momentary interruption of his journey would be extended through the night.

He visited a local garage. He had no trouble catching the attention of its owner. Ralph struck up a casual conversation and then produced from his pocket a pack of cards for the garage attendant's amusement. It was not an ordinary pack of cards. Although the backs were prettily designed in a floral wreath, the fronts showed no hearts or spades or numerical value. On the fronts of the cards were pictures of Popeye and Olive Oyl, and if one riffled the cards skillfully, it quickly became apparent that the cartoon lovers were engaged in the most intimate and intricate acts of intercourse. The garage attendant was hypnotized by this muscular Kama Sutra but he was clumsy and could not seem to get the hang of a swift riffle. Ralph suggested that he leave the cards overnight with the fellow, which would give him ample time to perfect his technique. The garage man was a fair-minded chap and said that he would certainly appreciate the thoughtfulness but insisted that Ralph receive something in return. Ralph suggested the use of the attendant's small pickup truck, a battered Ford with an open bed in the rear. The attendant hesitated. Ralph improvised a few swift turns of the cards and the exotic postures of Popeye and Olive Oyl convinced the attendant to transfer the keys to the ignition of the old Ford. He even cranked the engine for Ralph.

It was a dusty drive in the Model T, and when Ralph arrived in the tiny hamlet of Hooker his throat was on fire. He was delighted therefore to see that among the advertisements placarded in the village's general store was a notice of free ice with any purchase of a Dr. Pepper or cream soda or sarsparilla.

The store was cool and shadowy, and a wooden fan turned overhead, sweeping away the day's heavy heat. The shelves bulged with stores — woolens, cottons, gewgaws, pots and skillets, nippled glassware, chewing tobacco, and tools — but all these things were of little interest to Ralph because he had eyes for only one thing. A girl stood behind a long wooden counter, her elbows resting on the top, her enormous bosom squashed against the boards. Ralph thought he had never seen such a beautiful weight. She wore a white sailor's blouse and a long dark skirt, and her auburn hair was piled high on her head and her eyes were as steady as an owl's as she watched Ralph's slow walk to the counter.

He was humming *You're the cream in my coffee*.

He was the only customer in the store. She smiled at him and pulled herself straight, and when she did so her breasts rose from the counter and uncovered a thin volume wrapped in plain brown paper. He ordered a sarsparilla, and when she turned her back to fill a glass with crushed ice, he quickly flipped open the book on the counter and sneaked a look at the title. It was dog-eared, and many passages were underlined in pencil. It was a smuggled version of *Lady Chatterley's Lover*.

He hummed *Makin' whoopee*.

The girl introduced herself as Esther Wine, and as Ralph greedily crunched ice between his teeth she told him of her two ambitions. She wanted to see the new film, *Mickey Mouse*, which was delighting American audiences and she wanted to accompany Lindbergh on his next flight across the Atlantic. These pronouncements thrilled Ralph. He reasoned that if he took her to a darkened motion-picture theater he would have the opportunity to instigate a snuggle; and if she dreamed of dangerous adventure it followed that Esther was a daring girl.

He was right on both counts. While Minnie berated Mickey, Ralph blew into Esther's ear, and by the time the cartoon mice were running from a cat, Ralph and Esther were making the truck bed of the Model T rattle under their wild thrashings. Ralph was a firm believer in coitus interruptus, but Esther was more than he had bargained for. When, at the height of their passion, he attempted to withdraw, she clamped her thick thighs around him, her heels drumming against his ass, and in a fleshy and unbreakable vise held him to her.

And that's how Solomon Moon was conceived.

The knowledge of Esther's pregnancy was delivered in person two months later. Unfortunately, in order to impress the girl with heavy breasts, Ralph had told her of his family's good fortune and had described in some detail the affluent apartment on One Hundred and First Street and Central Park West, where he still dwelled. One dreadful night, while Ralph and his father were chewing on Cuban cigars and playing pinochle as they listened to *Amos 'n' Andy*, there was a knock on the apartment door.

Esther arrived with her father, Abraham, who wasted no time on incidental preliminaries. Staring hard at Ralph's father, Mr. Wine patted his daughter's belly and said from such a swelling comes a *kinde* and from a *kinde* comes a ring. In the ensuing and pithy conversation Abraham revealed that his family, too, had had a change of name. Before Wine it was LeVino. The family had come from the shores of Portugal. Although both families had eschewed their heritage, had become enamored of Americanism, the ceaseless reverberation of their common Sephardic past diminished the tension in the room, and soon Abraham Wine and Ralph Moon (nee LeVino and Muñoz) were chatting pleasantly and exchanging "ho ho" and "what else?" and "this is a fact" and "from this I believe" and all sorts of wisely nodded shorthands and even an occasional "oi," a word neither Ralph Junior nor Esther had often heard at home.

Ralph and Esther were married in a hastily arranged civil ceremony. They moved into the third bedroom of the Central Park West flat. Ralph gave up drumming shoes, and through the influence and pocketbook of his father, became a partner in a new business located in a small office on West Forty-Fifth Street just off Fifth Avenue. His ability to sketch served him well. He became a designer of clock faces and display racks, the latter a blossoming business in a country where marketing of goods was fast becoming an art.

And each month he made further payments on the hundred slips of land he hoarded.

Not long after Solomon was born Wall Street brokers trembled and the value of stocks plummeted.

So did Solomon's grandfather.

Ralph Moon leaped from the ledge of his Central Park West apartment, his dive at least as graceful as those of the Gentiles whom he wished to join. His son's future plummeted with him.

Ralph Junior became increasingly aware of a strange approbation accorded the Christian friends of his father, men who had suffered similar losses on the market. Their plunge to death was judged an honorable act, a way of preserving the dignity of their heirs. But the Jews who swan-dived to eternity were accorded different words. Their precipitous departures were labeled cheap tricks, kikey clever, Sheeny shrewdness, or Jew-boy yellow. He began avoiding any gathering of men where he might overhear these condemnations. He stopped riding either bus or trolley to work, so that he would not hear the voices of these men. He had Esther prepare a simple lunch of a sandwich and an apple, which he carried in his sample case along with blueprints of his display racks and mock-ups of the faces of clocks. He wrapped the sandwiches carefully, always fearful that he might inadvertently pull forth a penciled illustration smelling of cheap bologna. Daily, he walked the two and a half miles to his office and back to the northern apartment that had been the symbol of his father's success.

It was these daily walks which finally undid him. No matter how he mapped his pedestrian travel, he imagined a scurrilous refrain. Whether scurrying against the rain or striding briskly on the winter streets, pausing at a red light or lighting a cigar in the wind, he listened for malevolent whispers.

What he feared most was to be identified with these invectives.

He plotted against his fear. He attempted to shed every vestige that might lead men to point him out. The paradox of this adjustment was that it forced Ralph to research his heritage in order to evaluate the aspersions cast upon it, and in the process he became an expert on the views of anti-Semites. He was a student of those characteristics attributed to Jews by many Gentiles; such things as: Jews are pushy, Jews have all the money, Jews eat funny, Jews killed Jesus, all Jewish girls are great pieces of ass, all Jewish men are shrewd, Jews wear too much jewelry, and so forth and so on. Sometimes he wearied of his study because the list seemed to go on forever, but he continued his objective self-instruction and organized his life around it. He devised means to contradict the image of a Hebrew.

He dressed conservatively, without ring or stickpin. He never ate pickles and changed his sandwich filling from bologna or chicken to fat slices of pork, and he made a point of ostentatiously revealing to the men in his office that the bread which held the pork was liberally spread with butter. He placed his aging mother in a Gentile rest home and sent her packages of guava jelly so popular among the Anglo-Saxon ill. Purposely, he assumed a self-effacing role in his business affairs, constantly reiterating that his competitors might be better qualified to undertake proferred contracts and, disregarding the absurdity of his own position, was smugly pleased as liabilities mounted in his ledger. He could prove that he was neither shrewd nor pushy.

One night Ralph Junior removed all his trousers from the closet. He stitched together the holes in his pockets. He had no balls left with which to play.

In 1876, Felix Adler founded the Society for Ethical Culture and announced that its purpose was "to assert the supreme importance of the ethical factor in all relations of life, personal, social, national, and international, apart from any theological or metaphysical considerations." Its membership met for discussion or dance in the society's headquarters on Sixty-Fourth Street and Central Park West.

Ralph discovered that the society's membership consisted of Gentile and Jew, each group seeking to free itself from its parochial past and examine fresh philosophical concepts. The fact that the congregation appeared to devote a great deal of its time to secular matters rather than enervating itself in a search for a specific God appealed to Ralph, for he felt that, under the guise of intellectual inquiry, any member could find a way to unidentify himself with an unwanted past. This sophistry was the legacy he would bequeath his son.

Unidentified with either Jew or Gentile, Solomon accommodated his father's wish for him to participate in the Society for Ethical Culture. He looked forward to his Sunday nights at the society's headquarters because he felt that at least for a few hours he belonged somewhere, to something. He enjoyed sitting on his hard chair in one of the small, unadorned rooms where, with his companions, he engaged in spirited discussions of non-religious themes. It was within these rooms that he first became intrigued with the mystery of Russian literature, the complexities of dialectics, the possibilities of social reform, the delicacy of Haydn, and the bewildering beauty of the female form. The latter subject was not often discussed. It was observed. Most of the adolescent girls who attended the society's Sunday meetings were attired alike in saddle shoes, their white leather appropriately scuffed, mid-calf woolen skirts which firmly hugged the thighs, and soft angora sweaters. It made little difference to Solomon whether the wool was dyed yellow or pink or pale, pale blue. What bewitched Solomon were the wondrous swellings beneath the wool.

Like many boys his age, during that time of splintering innocence, Solomon was a virgin. On occasion, he had broached, with understandable hesitancy, the subject of sex with his father, but his inquiries had been rebuffed in typical fashion. Ralph Moon, who still secretly resented Esther's viselike thighs on the truck bed outside of Hooker, Ohio, gruffly advised his son.

"For chrissake," he said, "use a rubber. Always use a rubber." And if Solomon persisted in his quest for information, the man who had long forgotten the slits he had cut into his trouser pockets would turn to his wife. "You talk to him," he would demand. "He's *your* son."

But Esther Moon could not. Intimate topics embarrassed her and made her giggle, and when she giggled she was inclined to wet her pants. "Stop! Stop!" she would cry upon hearing any reference to private matters and, unable to restrain the natural discharge of tears or urine, she would desperately clamp her legs together and wobble out of a room, trailing her puddle behind her. Chagrined by her incontinence, Esther had perfected a strategy of protection. She avoided all things personal and concentrated on worldly matters beyond her ken. She became a joiner par excellence. She became a member of the League of Women Voters, the Book-of-the-Month Club, the Theater Guild, the Metropolitan Opera Club, the Mercantile Library, and the Socialist Party, the latter because she thought Norman Thomas an uncommonly elegant man. She was flooded with mail from these organizations and her bedside table was piled high with informative pamphlets, announcements of future events, thick political tomes, volumes of obscure poetry, and a dozen periodicals to which she subscribed. She read everything. She understood very little. This was a matter of indifference to Esther, for she did not pretend to be a scholar. She merely wished to accumulate a massive body of information to which she could refer when she felt the need to divert discussion away from intimacy and thus avoid the dreaded discharge of her fluids.

Sympathetic to his mother's frailties, Solomon doubted that she would share his enthusiasm for an investigation of concupiscence, but frustration overrode his caution. Esther was a sickly woman suffering from arteriosclerosis (from which she would die during Solomon's first year in the army) and she was required to spend many hours in bed. It was her habit to retire directly after dinner. On Sunday nights, before setting off to his meetings at the Ethical Culture Society, Solomon would sit on the edge of her bed and feign attention as she discoursed inanely on subjects she misunderstood. After a reasonable amount of time he would rise and bid her adieu. These short visits by her son afforded Esther the only happiness she knew, and Solomon recognized this and therefore never scoffed at the idiosyncracies of her mind. Checking a normal adolescent impatience, he assumed the role of an attentive son. It was, he felt, the least he could do for a woman whose only wishes were to fly across the Atlantic and to be buried in Ohio.

After the dinner at which his father had commanded the use of a condom, Solomon joined his mother in her bedroom. She lay in bed surrounded by tabloids and texts, her vague eyes already blurring from the hard black lines of print. The pink lace peignoir she affected lay partially open across her blue-veined breasts and Solomon immediately averted his gaze. He did not wish to contemplate the mysterious force which he suspected one day would flatten the breasts of the girls he watched covertly at the society.

"Are you all right?" Esther whined. "Are you worried about something?"

"Me? No. Why should I be worried about anything?"

"Well, I don't know. I mean, it's so hard to tell with you. Sometimes I think you hide things. I'm your mother, Solomon, and if there's something bothering you, I want to know."

Solomon stared at the figure in bed. His mother's bare feet protruded from beneath the blankets. Her toes resembled her fingers, all looking like little sausages which had boiled too long, wrinkled and puffed with steam, about to explode their juices. He looked at her face, her thickening skin as inelastic and clotted as the walls of her arteries, her eyes as dull as tobacco, her thin, perpetually grimaced lips haphazardly stained vermillion from the morning's quick slash of lipstick.

"Goodnight, Ma," he said. "I love you."

" 'Mother' is nicer, Solomon. 'Ma' sounds so cheap."

"Sorry," Solomon said and walked out of the room, closing the door behind him.

As he walked toward the door of the apartment, Solomon was sure he heard his mother giggle. He hoped she would not have to change the sheets.

His pace quickened by the need to escape the stultifying atmosphere of his home, Solomon trotted southward on Central Park West and arrived early at the Ethical Culture Society. When he opened the door of the small room designated for the night's discussion of Jungian precepts he found no one. He sat alone organizing a list of questions about myth and ritual, about symbols and masks. He was in the middle of juggling the doctor's postulated arguments justifying the theory of psychic energism when he heard the drum.

It was a muffled sound, distant, and somehow ominous. Solomon held his breath so that he could better listen. The dull thud continued and then was syncopated with a continuing clash of cymbals. Solomon rose from his chair and left the room. He stood in the hall, his head cocked toward the sound. The music came from somewhere below. He moved to the stairway and started down, and on each lower landing the music grew in volume, the accented beats reverberating through the stairwells. As Solomon reached the basement, the drum and cymbals were joined by the lovely piping of a flute. He was enchanted. Two doors were open in the hall of the basement; one led to a kitchen, the other to a large room at the end of which was a makeshift platform. Three girls were dancing on the platform, dressed in close-fitting tights and low-necked, sleeveless garments, with their long flowing hair held away from their foreheads by silk ribbons. Mesmerized, Solomon watched the dancers weave their intricate patterns, sometimes ebbing and flowing to the rhythm of the music, others freezing momentarily or bending sharply in counterpoint, their gestures as slow as snowmelt or as swift as a swallow's flight. As if he were a shred of steel, Solomon was pulled toward the magnet of the music. He edged into the doorway. Suddenly, one of the trio of dancers pirouetted on her toes, froze her position in the middle of her whirl, then slumped to the platform stage.

"Shit," she said. "it won't work."

Solomon gasped.

All in the room turned toward him. In addition to the three girl dancers, there were three young men, holding the instruments they played. The flute player broke the silence. He was a stocky boy with unruly red hair and a wisp of red beard below his lower lip and his voice was as deep as a tomb.

"You Caldwell?"

"Who?" asked Solomon.

"Caldwell," the drummer said. "Thomas Caldwell."

"No."

"Yeah, he's probably Caldwell," said the girl who still sat on the platform. "He just didn't like what he saw. Why should he? It stinks."

Solomon looked at her. Her long ash-blond hair was tossed forward now and half-covered her face, but one bright violet eye gleamed at him. She sat hugging her bent knees to her chest, her chin resting on them, her breasts forced upward, protruding from the low-necked leotard she wore. Tiny beads of sweat lay on her upper lip and her tongue flicked out and wiped them away. When she saw Solomon studying her, she darted her tongue in and out of her mouth with exquisite speed as if she were riposting with a dangerous pink saber. Then she smiled at him.

"Yeah," said Solomon, "I'm Caldwell."

"And you hated it, right?" said the smiling girl. "That's why you don't want to read."

"No, honest, I thought it was terrific. Honest."

"Look, you gonna read or not?" asked the belligerent flute player.

"Oh, sure. Sure, I'll read." Solomon didn't know what the hell he was supposed to read but he knew he would do anything to stay close to the girl with the darting tongue.

Behind a set of elaborate drums a fat boy sighed with exasperation and reached behind him, picking up a sheaf of mimeographed papers held together with brass staples. He tossed it to Solomon.

"Let's go, for chrissake," he muttered. "From the top."

"From the top?" asked Solomon.

"Boy," said the smiling girl. "You're a real asshole."

Solomon died.

But was reborn when the girl floated out of her posture and seemed to drift through the air and then touch down lightly at Solomon's side. She stood so close to him that one breast pressed heavily against his arm. Solomon could hardly hold the sheaf of papers in his hand.

"Listen, Caldwell," the girl said. "What we're doing here is this. We're using music and dance and words to synthesize the American experience. These guys wrote an original score, see, and I choreographed it. All you have to do is follow us as you read. Just stay in sync with us, that's all. I mean, don't go charging ahead if you see we haven't finished some goddamn *entrechat* or something, *capish?*"

"*Entrechat?*"

For the first time, the girl's smile disappeared.

"Hey, are you sure?" she asked suspiciously. "Are you sure you're Caldwell?"

"Damn right!" Solomon was indignant.

The fat drummer beat an irritable riff on the skins and then boomed the bass drum.

"You guys wanna work," he demanded angrily, "or fuck around all night?" His eyes speared the smiling girl. "And don't answer that, Rena!"

Rena answered by squeezing her half-exposed left breast in the direction of the drummer, and once again her furious tongue vibrated between her lips. Solomon felt faint and was amazed that the others ignored the lewd gestures.

It quickly became apparent that the drummer was also the director of this strange production, and he gave Solomon further explanations of the work in progress. The group gathered in the rehearsal hall were members of senior status in the society, all a few years older than Solomon, and they were preparing a work based on poems of Carl Sandburg. Printed on the papers in Solomon's hands were excepts of "Chicago" and "Fish Crier" and "To a Contemporary Bunkshooter" and "Fog." The drummer had conceived of a score to emphasize the linking themes of the poetry, and the dance had been designed for emotional punctuation. It was to be Solomon's task to give a simple, clear reading of the text. His was to be the voice of reason underlying but not igniting the pyrotechnics of music and dance.

Although secretly recognizing the somewhat pretentious approach to the night's dramaturgy, Solomon prudently kept his counsel to himself. Furthermore, he found he was not only enjoying the experience, he was good at his assignment. His natural intelligence and the fine timbre of his voice combined to bring an ease to the reading, and it was not long before the other members of the amateur troupe were treating him with respect and admiration. All but one. Rena did not join in the general approbation. If Solomon stumbled over a difficult passage or paused at an occasional opacity in the verse, she delayed her dancer's flight, thrust sharply downward with her head as if she couldn't bear to see him and, behind the waterfall of her golden hair, muttered darkly.

"Asshole," she said.

The repetition of rehearsals finally paled and the drummer called a halt to the night's proceedings. They all agreed to meet on the following Sunday to continue their exploration of the American experience. They wiped sweat from their bodies, packed their instruments and their ballet slippers, shrugged into jackets and sweaters, and filed out of the room, talking profoundly about the metaphorical disguise of fog which comes on little cat feet.

"Caldwell!"

During the hours of rehearsal Solomon had learned that a boy named Caldwell had signed a notice on the society's bulletin board requesting volunteers for the Sandburg project. Since he had not appeared during the work session, all had assumed the legitimacy of Solomon's false name and he, in turn, had become rather fond of it. He turned in the doorway and looked back into the room. Cross-legged, Rena sat on the low wooden platform, still dressed in her leotard which was soaked with perspiration. She was mopping her face with a small towel.

"You got a record?" she asked.

"A what?"

"A record. A police record."

"Well, no! My God, no, I haven't got any record."

"Oh, I thought maybe you had a record or something."

"Jesus, why'd you think I'd have a record?"

"Well, you're running outta here like you got to report to somebody. I mean, I never saw an asshole move so quick."

"Really?"

"Really."

The burly red-haired flute player, the last of the amateur troupe to leave the hall, sidled past Solomon and spoke softly out of the corner of his mouth.

"Watch it, buddy," he whispered to Solomon, "she'll blow your nuts off." And then he was gone.

Slowly, Solomon closed the door and took one step back into the room. The thought that the information surreptitiously passed on by the flute player might be fact and not fancy made him weak. He gripped the ladderback of a chair so that Rena could not notice his trembling hands. He stared at her. She stared back.

"You got a face," she said, "of a man terribly glad to be selling fish." It was a quote from the poetry he had recently read.

Solomon flushed. He wished he had the aplomb to laugh off the girl's hostility or the courage to just walk across the room and rip off her wet leotard and fuck her. But he wasn't sure how to do either.

"Well," he said. "Well, well, well."

"That's what I'd call smart repartee. Listen, Mr. Coward, you wanna dry me off?"

"What?"

"I'm wet, Caldwell. Can't you see I'm soaking wet? I mean, for chrissake, look at me." She hooked her thumbs under her shoulder straps and pulled down the top of her leotard. Her sweat-glistening breasts quivered from the abrupt motion. "My goddamn tits are drowning. You want that to happen? You want my tits to drown?"

Solomon couldn't speak. He just shook his head and hoped that she would understand that he did not want her tits to drown. She was a bright girl. She understood.

"There's a dry towel in the kitchen," she said. She rose from the stage and, her dancer's turned-out legs gliding effortlessly, spun across the floor, past Solomon, and out into the empty basement hall. Solomon followed. He saw her *glissade* toward the kitchen and then leap through the open doorway.

It was a makeshift kitchen, lighted only by a single bare bulb hanging from a cord over the steel sink. The room was narrow and lined with shelves, on which were set a few random commodities. There was an open box of dry cereal and an unlidded jar of orange marmalade, a basket of loose eggs, and a closed can of Crisco. Flanking the sink were a small refrigerator and a portable two-burner stove. There was neither chair nor table. An opened wall cabinet displayed a handful of glasses and cups and saucers and a few chipped plates. Over the sink a dry, stained dishtowel dangled from its holder.

"Lock it," Rena commanded as Solomon stepped into the kitchen.

"Suppose somebody, you know, suppose somebody . . ." Solomon stammered.

"Suppose somebody what?"

"Nothing," Solomon said, unable to stop staring at the girl's bare breasts as he locked the kitchen door. His erection pressed hard against the inside of his trouser leg and he was terrified of premature ejaculation.

"Jesus," Rena said. "You could pole-vault with that thing." Her eyes were shining wickedly and her tongue snapped back and forth between her lips so swiftly that her mouth looked like a cage of snakes and the fingers of her hands were snapping triggers as she clawed off the remainder of her leotard and then jerked off her woolen tights. She stood naked before Solomon.

"Oh, my God," Solomon said. "Oh, my God!"

Rena whisked the dishtowel off its rack and rubbed it across the mass of tiny golden curls of her pubic hair.

"Dry me," she whispered. "Dry me here."

As Solomon took two quick steps toward her, he was certain that his testicles would explode. He grabbed the towel from her but as he started to rub her vulva she yanked the towel from him and clutched his wrist with both her hands and forced one of his fingers inside her cleft. Half crouched, her legs wide, she tore open Solomon's shirt and her teeth raked the skin of his belly and her warm, wet tongue lathered his flesh as she rode his finger faster and faster, her body flame-impaled and wrenching wildly, and when she climaxed she drowned her own shriek in Solomon's belly, which was sucked inside her mouth.

Her flesh folded and she fell to the floor.

Dizzy, Solomon stumbled to the sink and held on to its steel sides. Blood trickled down his belly and stained his shirt. He was hyperventilating, gasping at the air, which was now redolent with sweat and musk. His penis was so painfully engorged he wanted to cry and he was bewildered when he heard the girl's soft laughter. He ground his knuckles against his groin, trying desperately to alleviate the ache.

"You got to do something," he panted. "Please, you got to do something!"

"What?" the girl asked sweetly, sitting in her satisfied skin, as demure as a nun. "What do I have to do?"

"Something, just something, please!"

"You don't look so good, Caldwell."

"Please!" The pain in his groin lifted into his belly and he doubled over and wrapped his arms around himself and then lowered one hand to his crotch and kneaded his penis.

"Hey," the girl said, "be careful. You're gonna hurt that thing, and then what?"

"Oh, Jesus," Solomon said and he felt his eyes brimming. A single tear spilled from his eyelash, ran down his cheek and across his lips, and he could taste his own salt.

Rena rose onto her knees and slid across the floor until she was directly in front of Solomon, her head level with his crotch. Her face was very serious and her voice was filled with quiet concern as she stared with interest at the bulge in his pants.

"That stranger," she said, applying a peculiar nomenclature to his penis, "that stranger's in trouble. He's just jumping around something awful. You shouldn't treat him like that. You shouldn't lock him up. You gotta let him out, let him look around, show him the lights of the city. Jesus, Caldwell, you're not just an asshole, you're a cruel asshole. That thing is precious, don't you understand that? I mean, they don't just hand those things around. Do something, Caldwell, don't just let him die in there!"

"I'm going to let him out!" Solomon cried. "I'm going to let him out now!"

Frantically, Solomon tugged at the zipper of his pants and Rena leaned further forward.

"He's breathing hard, Caldwell," she cried, looking into his fly. "He's breathing awful hard. I think he's gonna choke!"

Solomon grabbed both sides of the fly on his boxer shorts and ripped them apart. His cock snapped out and whacked Rena in the nose.

"Why that little son of a bitch," she yelled. "I don't even know him!"

Before Solomon could move, the girl bent the middle finger of one hand against her thumb and, with the velocity of a slingshot, snapped it forward against the head of Solomon's cock.

"Owwwww!" The pain was excruciating and *the stranger* collapsed. Doubled over, his teeth clenched against the stinging agony, Solomon reached for Rena, snaring a handful of hair, but when he saw the look on her face, he paused. She was staring with unfeigned astonishment at his limp wounded penis.

"Oh, my God," she cried. "I think I made a mistake! Caldwell, he probably wouldn't be circumcised, right? I mean, a name like that and everything. Hey, who the hell are you?"

"Solomon," he muttered, grateful that the pain was diminishing. "Solomon Moon."

"That's a terrific name," she said. "Listen, get in here!" She jumped up, turned on the water taps, hoisted herself into the sink, and as steam began to rise around her, she explained that she only gave *goys* a shot to the cock. Removing his clothes, painfully lowering himself into the sink beside her, Solomon looked doubtful. As Rena elaborated, she began to soap his body, her hands moving intimately and kindly over all parts of him. "Guys like Caldwell, or Winthrop the third, or whatever, what they're looking for, see, is a great piece of Jewish ass. That's all they think we're good for. So what I do is get 'em all hot an' bothered and then pow! You shouldn't have lied about your name, Solomon. I mean, really! If you'd just — " She stopped talking and stared down into the steaming sink. "Oh, God, Solomon, look! Look at your little stranger!"

Solomon's penis speared upward through the suds.

"Boy," he shouted. "Oh, boy!"

Solomon Moon and Rena Nussbaum became lovers. Their relationship was cemented by Solomon's reluctant acceptance of her casual infidelities and by Rena's pleasure in introducing Solomon into the delights of the world of performing arts.

It was Rena who taught him how to sneak into Broadway theaters before the second-act curtain, and into concert halls during the first intermission. They mingled with the patrons enjoying a sidewalk smoke and then followed them in and stood in the darkness at the rear of the theater. They became experts on the second halves of many plays, and on the encores favored by a dozen concert artists. It was Rena who encouraged him to study the piano on Sunday nights at the society. It was

Rena who showed him where to make love under the boardwalks of the city beaches and beneath flowering bushes in Central Park. Rena taught him to fly kites in Van Cortlandt Park and to skate on the Mall and where to find the best spareribs in Harlem, egg rolls on Mott Street, pastrami on Delancey. Their frivolity was not without purpose, for each was affected by continuing reports of the bloody progress of World War II. However, their attitudes differed. Rena attributed the conflict to the insanity of greed and felt that, regardless of the outcome, the world would forever be a wasteland. Her cynicism justified a relentless pursuit of pleasure. Solomon accused her of simplistic posturing and said they should look upon their merrymaking as the preamble to an inevitable commitment. He cautioned her that they lived in a real world and that they had an obligation to participate.

Once, they accompanied Hamilton, the red-headed flutist, to a meeting of the Young Communist League. Solomon was excited by the passionate discussion of social injustice and suggested that perhaps they should join the league. Rena scoffed at his naïveté and, vulnerable to her mocking, his resolution wavered. He talked of other political organizations and of social groups that addressed themselves to causes but, always, she dissuaded him from joining, implying that his purpose was suspect, that all he really looked for was false fraternity.

They rode the Staten Island ferry a hundred times, and as they stood at the railing they discussed these matters. One night, as they peered over the bow of the ferry approaching its dock in lower Manhattan, he confided to Rena that he planned to enlist on the day of his graduation from high school.

She was silent for a long time, her eyes on the dark, swirling waters of the harbor. Finally, she spoke.

"What do you want," she asked, "a medal?"

"Don't be dumb."

"You know what you'll get for it?"

"I don't want to get anything," he said.

"You'll get dead, that's what you'll get."

"C'mon."

"The problem with you is you want to belong to something," Rena said harshly, "and you don't give a good goddamn what it is."

In a quick, convulsive gesture Solomon's hand closed into a fist. He had an impulse to strike her, then he forced his fingers to relax, for he knew that she had touched at least a partial truth. But he could not fully admit it to either her or himself.

"What the hell are you talking about?" He asked the question tentatively, not certain that he wanted it to be answered and yet unable to let it rest.

"Well, you belong to me," she said. "That's who you belong to!"

"Jesus, Rena."

"Don't write me."

"What?"

"Don't write me. Don't call."

"What's the matter with you?"

"I don't want to hear from a dead man."

Solomon reached out and put an arm across her shoulders. She shrugged him off.

"Don't," she said.

They rode the rest of the way in silence. When the ferry docked Rena moved swiftly away from Solomon, ran down the gangplank, and before Solomon could catch her, was swallowed up in the darkness of the streets.

"Hey," he yelled after her, "I'll see you."

"No," her voice floated back, "you won't."

He never saw her again. While in the service, he wrote twice to her but the letters were neither answered nor returned. Once, on furlough, he called her family's number but was told they no longer lived there, nor was there a forwarding address. He didn't try to contact her after that.

All this was in Solomon's mind as he checked the paper in his hand to verify the address Darby had given him. He stood outside a narrow white-brick townhouse in the east sixties. It smacked of affluence. A polished brass plate was imbedded in the brick next to the door. The number of the residence was etched into the brass but there was no name. Solomon saw that below the brass plate was a buzzer and a tiny intercom grille. He pushed the buzzer. After a moment, he heard Rena's distinctive voice. She sounded older, but the sexual hoarseness was still there.

"Come on up," she said. There was a clicking noise and as Solomon pushed open the door he heard her voice again. "Hey, listen, I've got white carpets."

He craned his neck around the doorjamb and spoke into the exterior grille. "You want a medal?"

"I want you to take your shoes off, Caldwell," she called back. "Asshole."

14

Naked, he walked out of the living room and turned right into her bedroom. Like the rest of the apartment, it was decorated all in white. A huge circular bed was in the center of the room. The ceiling was a mirror. After what had happened on the white-carpeted floor of the living room it didn't surprise Solomon. There was nothing amateur about Rena's fornication skills. And nothing really spontaneous, he realized. She was a courtesan of the old school, using her body with exquisite precision like a finely wrought tool. He suddenly had no wish to handle it again. And now regretted that he had done so at all.

Why, he asked himself, why, you silly son of a bitch, did you wind up on the floor? He stepped into the bathroom, lowered his head over the sink, splashed his face with cold water, then looked at his dripping image in the mirror. Because she wanted to, his reflection answered, and what pleases others you are prepared to give.

"Jesus," he whispered to the mirror. He had a terrible feeling that if he stared long enough at himself he would watch himself decompose, actually see the physical results of what the mirror had spoken; an arm given there, a leg here, bone melted, tissue flaked away, his flesh stripped as an offering to please others, until, finally, the mirror would be empty, for Solomon Moon would be gone. He squeezed his eyes shut and tried to imagine the vacuum of death and was struck painfully by the thought of never holding Kendal again.

"Oh, shit," he muttered, angered at how he had compromised his marriage. He was not a philanderer; had never had need to seek sexual solace from another woman. His fidelity was not based on arbitrary sentiments, for he understood and, indeed, had been tempted at times by available pleasures; but what had stopped him on these occasions was his inescapable feeling that such behavior would irrevocably lead to an erosion of the trust that existed between him and Kendal. Straying from the reservation, as Mouse had once so aptly put it, did not soil the flesh as much as it sullied the soul. Casual fleshy peccadillos, Solomon suspected, would diminish both the memory and the future of a sexual intimacy shared with Kendal.

Then why now?

He looked again into the mirror, faintly hoping that he would see the face of a buccaneer, a pirate, a daredevil whose life was enhanced by risk, but all he saw was Solomon Moon, who belonged to no band of dangerous brothers. He frowned at the thought. Then to whom do I belong? He remembered Rena's words when they were kids.

"You belong to me," she'd said, and walked into the night.

Is that why he'd fucked her? Was it an obligation long overdue?

"No, goddamn it," he said out loud, "I belong to me." But he recognized that his voice lacked timbre. In the mirror he saw the reflected image of a telephone. "And to Kendal," he said to himself. "I belong to Kendal." He drew in a deep breath, for he wasn't sure it was true.

Standing near the open door of the bathroom, he listened carefully to hear if Rena were moving about. He heard nothing so he closed the door and locked it, then turned on the shower and partially closed the shower door. Sitting on the lid of the toilet, he dialed directly to Westport. Knowing that Kendal hated the phone, he hoped that she would answer, then hoped she wouldn't. He cleared his throat and swiveled his head back and forth, easing the tension in his neck. He wanted to sound casual, charming, amusing. Jesus, what would he say? He was about to hang up when he heard the click of a receiver being lifted, then Kendal's voice.

"What?" She asked the question so abruptly that Solomon almost laughed, knowing that she hoped to warn off the caller.

" 'There was a young man named Hensel, whose prick was as sharp as a pencil,' " Solomon quoted, and was immediately appalled that the limerick had popped out of his mouth.

"Darling!" Kendal said.

" 'He went through an actress, two sheets, and a mattress,' " Solomon weakly struggled on, " 'and buggered the pissing utensil.' "

"Oh, that's sweet, Solomon," Kendal said, laughing still, "that's truly sweet. Did you make it up?"

"An Elizabethan ditty," he answered, anxious to change the subject. "Listen . . ."

"Are you all right?"

"What?"

"Are you all right? You sound hoarse."

"Yeah. Well. I get a sore throat when I listen to Brindig."

"How was the meeting?"

"Terrible. The son of a bitch is Machiavellian. He twisted everything around so that poor Charlie thinks it's my fault that we have to fuck around with his script. Which is why I'm going to be late tonight."

"I can't hear you," Kendal said. "There's a funny noise on the line."

Damn, Solomon thought, the shower. He raised his voice. "I said I'm going to be late."

"Oh."

"Very late."

"Great. That means we don't have to go to the party."

"Well," Solomon said. "I think you should but I'll have to work with Manzinni. Ben wants the script as soon as possible."

Standing in the Westport kitchen, Kendal stared at the black paint under her nails. When the phone rang she had been at the barn painting an oil drum she needed to make a solar water system she thought would be practical for showering after a swim in the pool. She cradled the telephone receiver between her head and shoulder and removed a paring knife from a fruit basket. Using the blade, she began scraping away paint from under her fingernails, irritated momentarily — and unreasonably, she thought — that it was a gesture copied from Solomon. The action made a harsh, rasping sound which echoed her feelings. She'd be damned if she was going to the party.

"You're going to stay in all night, is that it?" she asked.

"Well. You know."

Kendal said nothing. They listened to each other's breathing for what seemed to Solomon like an eternity.

"Where are you?" he finally asked.

"In the kitchen."

"Go to the freezer."

"Why?"

"Just go to the freezer."

"Yes, sir!"

"Don't do that."

"What? Would you speak a little louder, please."

"I'm not ordering you to go to the freezer. I'm asking you to, okay?"

"Okay, I'm going to the freezer."

Kendal stopped cleaning her nails and, trailing the long cord of the telephone behind her, she crossed the kitchen to the refrigerator and opened the freezing compartment.

"I'm at the freezer," she said into the telephone. "I'm looking into the freezer."

"Do you see the pork chops?"

"Yes," Kendal sighed, "I see the pork chops."

"Take 'em out." Solomon paused. "Please."

"I'm taking out the pork chops."

"What's next to them?"

"A container of chili."

"Out."

"Out."

"Well?"

"Well, what?"

"Do you like it?"

"Solomon, are you feeling all right? It's a filthy muggy day with more goddamn rain coming and you think I'm going to be turned on by pork chops and chili?"

"I don't want you to eat them. What's behind them?"

"I don't know. Some dumb thing in aluminum foil. Probably old dogfood."

"We don't have a dog, Kendal."

"I know that."

"Then why would we have dogfood in the freezer?"

"How the hell do I know?"

"Will you please take out the dumb thing in the aluminum foil and unwrap it?"

"I don't want any dogfood!"

"Goddamn it, it is not dogfood!"

"I took it out."

"Unwrap it."

Solomon held the telephone close to his ear and he could hear the dry crinkling of aluminum paper. And then Kendal's quick intake of breath.

"Oh, darling," she said.

"Nice?"

"Super. Absolutely super."

Unwrapped of its aluminum foil was a quart bottle of very expensive

Polish vodka with stalks of bisongrass floating inside the liquid. The bottle was icy from the freezer and its sides were coated with a fine layer of frost.

"Your favorite, right?" Solomon asked.

"Mother's milk."

"I wanted to surprise you, but what the hell."

"It's lovely."

"Okay, then."

"I wish . . ." Kendal didn't complete her thought.

"You wish what?"

"I wish it were raining and it was dark and we were sitting on the porch and we were getting drunk. Together. Now. Naked. And afterward . . ."

"After what?"

"After we made love."

"Ah." Solomon winced, hating both himself and Rena Nussbaum.

"We'd talk. We'd talk all night long. In the dark. The way we used to. Would you like that, Solomon?"

"Yes." He'd never meant it more. "Oh, yes, I would like that a lot."

"It's funny how you don't do things you should. I mean, we don't. Everything just rushes by, doesn't it?"

"Yeah. Yeah, I guess."

"If I ask you a question, will you promise not to get angry?"

"Sure."

There was a long pause before she spoke again. "Solomon . . . are we losing each other?"

"Oh, God, Kendal," Solomon said, feeling as if his heart had stopped. "Don't say that."

"I'm sorry. I don't want to upset you. I don't ever want to upset you. But I don't think you're very happy and I don't know why. I don't know what to do about it."

"Christ," Solomon said, "I love you so much."

"I know."

Again, neither of them could speak. Solomon broke the silence. "I'll try to get home. It's just this damn script . . ."

"You do what you have to, darling. What you don't need is some dotty old lady weeping into her vodka."

"Jesus, Kendal, are you crying?"

"No. Just a thought."

"I'll try to get home."

"I'd like that. I'd like that a lot." He heard her sharp intake of breath, then her expletive. "Bugger."

"What's the matter?"

"I stabbed myself with the pear knife."

Solomon grinned. "What'm I gonna do about you?"

"Love me, I guess. 'Bye, darling." She hung up.

Quickly, Solomon showered. He wanted to get out of Rena's apartment, get back to the office, dutifully complete the compromises on Manzinni's script, regardless of his knowledge that he was succumbing to the bidding of others, and return to Kendal.

When he entered the living room he found Rena, dressed in a simple white peignoir, sipping champagne and munching on caviared crackers. She looked strangely vulnerable and lonely, and any anger he had felt toward her was gone. Not speaking, they gazed at each other as he dressed. Her hair, a mass of silvered ash, was tied in a chignon with a white silk ribbon. Solomon felt she had chosen the white peignoir and the white ribbon so that she would not violate the whiteness of the room. It was a stark room, its simplicity a dramatic choice to heighten the contrasting sculptures of Giacometti — twisted, tormented figures of men and women.

"Where'd you get the Giacomettis?" he asked as he finished dressing.

"Where do you think?"

"I don't know. I suppose . . ." He stopped, for suddenly he did know. He had no doubt. "From Thomas Caldwell. From all the Thomas Caldwells in the world."

"Bingo!" She raised her glass of champagne and saluted him. "But I'm not a harlot, Solomon. Isn't that a nice old-fashioned word? None of the men I married ever lodged a complaint with the Fair Trade Commission. None of them pleased me very much either. But not much does." She paused, sipped from her glass, then continued quietly. "I want you to know something. I didn't plan to seduce you. I really didn't."

"Well," Solomon spoke gently, aware of her vulnerability, "it's not the end of the world, is it? And, God knows, you had a partner."

"We had a partnership once, you and I, didn't we? That was nice. That's never happened to me again. You know why?"

"No."

"I've spent my life getting even, Solomon, getting even with all the little Thomas Caldwells of the world. The doctors say I have too goddamn much anger in me. Sometimes . . . sometimes I have this awful urge to kill somebody. The terrible thing is, I don't know who. Have you ever felt anything like that, Solomon?"

The image of the white-breasted wood thrush flashed across Solomon's mind and his shoulder moved imperceptibly as if he were wincing from the recoil of his shotgun.

"Yes," he said quietly.

Rena was studying him carefully. "Darby worries about you. She thinks you've built a fence around yourself, a very tall fence. What puzzles her is that she doesn't know if the fence is to protect you or the people on the other side."

"She's very young."

"It's a very old question."

Uncomfortable with the idea of discussing his relationship with his daughter, Solomon changed the subject. "I'll send someone from the office to look at a rehearsal of your play. Maybe we can help. I know it's tough to get backing these days."

"Hey," she said, "I can always sell a Giacometti."

"It'd be a shame to break up your collection."

They smiled at each other, and were silent. Each knew they had nothing else to say.

"Well," Solomon said.

"Yes."

Solomon turned and walked out of the room. He collected his shoes at the bottom of the stairs, then walked out onto the street. His pace quickened as he turned the corner. The sun had paled behind new-blown clouds, and men and women hurrying along the avenue darted nervous glances toward the sky as if frightened of being caught in a burst of rain, as if the gray sky were something they had never seen before. Wind drifted from the East River and carried with it the foul smell of debris.

As he headed south, Solomon thought of his accommodation with Brindig, and of his foolish fornication on Rena's floor, and of the painful phone call to Kendal.

He felt corrupt as the air.

15

Carrying the bottle of Polish vodka, Kendal left the kitchen and walked into the adjoining dining room. She removed a brandy glass from a corner cabinet, moved through the room and out into the back porch. Placing the vodka bottle and the brandy glass on a wicker table, she sat down on an old glider. She kicked her sneakers off, poured the chilled vodka into the goblet, adjusted her position so that she had an unobstructed view of the willow tree that weeped over a sloping lawn and of the garden that linked barn to house, and took her first sip of the icy liquor. It failed to revive her spirits.

Kendal stared at the weeping willow, seeking solace in its towering grace, but finding none. Her gaze moved slowly across the lawn of Bermuda grass, past the swimming pool and a clump of white birches, over a rock garden which she had accented with tiny mountain laurels, and finally toward a row of dark cedars that served as a boundary to their land. It was a gentle vista from which she usually derived great comfort, but on this darkening autumn day she could not rid herself of a deep disquiet. The conversation with Solomon had made her aware of the growing separateness between them. She thought of last Saturday night after Solomon had returned from the Vermont woods. He had re-mained silent throughout the evening, adrift in his own space. Later, she had awakened in their bed to see him wide-eyed in the darkness as if he were waiting for some mysterious shape to appear before him.

"What?" she asked. "What is it you want?"

"A place to sit with Shelley," he said, the unexpected lyricism flat-tened by his tone, "where elves will whisper in our ears."

"We'll find it, darling," she said, wanting terribly to comfort him. "We'll find it and the elves will sing."

"No," he replied harshly, "we will not find it and they will not sing. They will never sing."

"Why?"

"Because," said Solomon, "I have cut out their tongues."

Now, sitting on the porch glider, its rusty springs creaking and accentuating the memory, Kendal watched the sky blacken and listened to the distant roll of thunder and she felt suddenly isolated, as if she lived in a house of strangers. She sipped again from the vodka and shifted her position, unconsciously searching for a consoling view.

A long narrow garden bisected the graveled parking area, forming a flowered path between the barn and house. A high trellis fence, painted white and fading here and there, ran the length of the garden and ended in matching arbors. The fence and arbors were covered with the dark green leaves of a grape vine. The foliage on the arbor which was attached to the barn was intermingled with delicate branches of a lilac bush which stood nearby. A wisteria vine gracefully entwined the other arbor, its unpruned tendrils reaching out tentatively toward the sun. The border of the garden was planted in orange and yellow marigolds. Between these border plantings and the grape vine was a twenty-foot strip of loam richly fertilized with peat moss and mulched with bark. It ran the entire length of the garden and it was a home of roses. Kendal had cultivated her rose garden with the same exquisite care demonstrated by Caesar and his conquering legions of long ago. She had planted a fragrant rainbow, each rose bush more colorful and exotically named than the next. There were Buccaneers and Irish Gold and Sarabands and Spanish Suns and Mister Lincolns and China Dolls and Sterling Silvers, and in one corner a Kings Ransom brushed against a double Dainty Bess. Although autumn had stripped the bushes of blossom, in her mind's eye Kendal saw a giant canvas of dusty pink and soft gold and dove gray, of scarlet and silver, and blue tints so pale they looked only faintly dyed by the sky. These emblems of England reunited Kendal with her past.

Even the barn, painted a New England red and constructed of vertical battened boards, punctuated Kendal's past and gave root to her history, for set high into one end of the barn's loft was a stained-glass window, a transparent mosaic of colored glass pieces fitted into channeled lead strips which gave definition to a vibrant representation of England's warrior, Saint George, slaying his dragon as he rescued a maiden.

In an unselfconscious gesture of ceremony, a small thing done with no air of flippancy, Kendal raised her glass and saluted the saint. She smiled to herself as she remembered her father's stirring tales of the warrior saint, but the smile disappeared as she wondered if there were a dragon waving his tail within Solomon's soul. She had a sudden and uneasy feeling that if Solomon were trying to slay his dragon he might be less successful than Saint George. He might be consumed in the monster's fire. And fantasizing the metaphor further, staring at the stained-glass window, imagining herself as the maiden in danger, she was disquieted with the thought that Solomon might not wish to rescue her, might instead prefer the brotherhood of dragons.

Damn him, she said to herself, damn him and his withdrawal. She had never thought of Solomon as an emotionally isolated man, but now she was not certain and she resented her own insidious doubts. She was hurt by Solomon's inability to share whatever darkness was within him. She did not admire secrets.

Distressed by her introspection, Kendal poured the vodka in her goblet back into the bottle. She decided to return to the work that had been interrupted by Solomon's phone call. Physical activity usually restored her spirits. She left the porch and moved to the barn.

Using the barn siding as a back wall, she had constructed a rude shed and based on designs she'd studied, had made an outdoor shower to be heated by a breadbox, a simple solar system to provide warm water. A fifty-five gallon oil drum was placed in a large rectangular box on top of the shed. The box was insulated with fiberglass and its top was a hinged panel of double glass which would act as a collector.

Kendal placed a ladder alongside the shed. A long black hose was attached to the barn's outdoor cold water faucet which she now turned on, and crimping it in her hand so that she could block a wasteful flow, climbed the ladder. She removed the loose bung from the oil drum, inserted the hose and let the water run freely. She climbed down the ladder, knowing she would have to wait until a few inches of water layered the drum before she could test the shower head. Sitting in the grass, her eyes on the shed as she admired her own handiwork, Kendal fumbled in an open picnic chest behind her before pulling out a can of beer. She snapped off the aluminum tab and raised the can to her mouth. For a moment, she didn't drink, for she was arrested by the sound of the water running into the drum. There was something faintly familiar about the noise of splashing water muffled by a container. She couldn't place it though, so she shrugged and took a long pull from her beer can.

Impatient, she lowered the can to the grass and rose. She stepped inside the shed. Staying close to one side, she pointed the showerhead away from her and depressed its trigger. Water spurted immediately. Congratulating herself on her own efficiency, she released and depressed the trigger over and over again, delighted by the spasmodic sound of rushing water. Suddenly, she stopped. She recognized the sound of the shower. It was similar to the background noise that had interfered with the telephone call from Solomon.

Kendal Moon stepped out of the shed and slowly walked to the side of the barn. She turned off the faucet. She picked up her can of beer and stared at it. Suddenly, she emptied it into the grass and tried to bend the can in two, using only one hand as she had seen Solomon do. But she didn't have the strength. Frustrated, she tossed it into the open picnic chest. The ice had melted in the chest and the small aluminum tab from the beer can was floating in the ripples she had caused. For a moment she imagined it as a tiny boat at sea, without rudder, without sails, adrift among the aimless waves.

She couldn't have heard a shower. Surely, Solomon had called her from his office. Then why hadn't Priscilla, his secretary, placed the call? Because it was private, of course.

I don't believe you, said Kendal to Kendal. And then reproached herself for where her logic was leading. She abhorred suspicious women and reminded herself that Solomon had never given her cause to doubt his fidelity.

And if she were wrong, what then? We live in a time of unrestricted sexuality, she acknowledged, and it would be unreasonable to assume that Solomon had never been tempted. Surely, their marriage was sound enough to survive some casual dalliance. But the illicit act she projected in her mind was not the root of her distress. What bothered her was the violation of trust. Are we not obligated to those in whom we place our confidence? And how do we address each other when confidence is gone? Do we not then talk as strangers, each politely uncommitted? She could not bear the thought of a relationship based on mutual reticence.

She moved into the house. She was restless and in the storm darkness wandered from room to room, touching a chair occasionally, toeing a chess table into angled juxtaposition with a wall, shuffling through some opera albums but playing none, rescuing her needlepoint from a cushion crack in the sofa but not wielding a needle, pacing barefoot and aimless, unwillingly resentful of what she had convinced herself was Solomon's adultery.

She entered the kitchen, idly glancing around for some clue as to what she should be doing. She closed the pages of a cookbook and replaced it on its shelf. She picked a plum from the fruit basket and took one bite. She threw the rest away in a trash container. With her fingernail, she scraped away a small circle of candlewax that had dripped onto the breakfast table. A framed sampler hung crookedly on the wall over the telephone. Kendal straightened it. It had been delicately embroidered by her great-grandmother when she was a child. Its border, a row of pale violets, circled her great-grandmother's name, Elvira Dill. Inscribed below were four words: Get On With It.

When she was a little girl, Kendal had asked her father the meaning of the words.

"Well," he'd said, "it's a sort of family thing, my darling. Get on with it. Just pull up your socks and get on with it. I mean to say, that's all we can do, isn't it? It's all anyone can do."

He'd made life so simple.

Her gaze moved down to the telephone and to the cork message board glued to the wall nearby. Among recipes and newspaper advertisements and the weekly schedule of films for Westport theaters, another slip of paper was tacked to the board. It was a reminder of this afternoon's artists' benefit at Susie Mitford's.

Kendal ripped it from the board, crumpled it in her fist, and threw it into the trash bin. She damned well was not going to the party. Her irritation returned as she thought of the wasted time in her and Solomon's life. The incidental engagements had assumed a priority out of proportion to their pleasure. Their involvements were superficial.

And what of the involvements with your husband and your daughter? she asked herself. Are they, too, superficial? She thought of Friday night, when Darby had provoked the controversy with her *Shabbis* dinner. What had she, Kendal, done about it? She admitted to the answer and it didn't please her. She had tried to play the great and wise arbiter, keep things on an even keel, placate anger and disappointment. Why? Was she frightened of contention?

She wandered out to the porch, reopened the bottle of vodka, not caring that it no longer was iced, and poured into her glass, her husband's and daughter's disputation greatly on her mind.

It was obvious that Darby's attraction to Judaic ritual had disturbed Solomon, but why the depth of his uneasiness? In their years together,

Kendal had never heard Solomon deny his background, nor had he seemed to attach importance to it. He gave it no weight.

Sipping her drink, Kendal thought of her own childhood. Bedtime prayers, the bells of the Angelus, vespers, Sunday service had all contributed to an uncomplicated reverence. Although she no longer actively participated in the ceremonies of the church, the memories of them comforted her, for she knew she belonged within their structure, within their loveliness.

What comforted Solomon? She wished she knew. She turned and looked toward the barn, toward the stained-glass window of Saint George and his dragon.

Unselfconsciously, the vodka glass still in her hand, she closed her eyes and, silently mouthed a simple prayer.

16

As Solomon stepped out of the elevator on the eighteenth floor of the TransGlobal building, he saw Priscilla waving her hand frantically toward him. She looked like a schoolgirl begging for permission to go to the bathroom, but Solomon knew that she never asked permission to do anything, including changing the punctuation and rhetoric of his dictated letters or shuffling his appointments to better suit her own schedule. He had often thought about firing her but John Luckey had informed him that she had only one more year of employment with the corporation to qualify for a fully vested interest in her pension fund and, Luckey implied, it would be a heartless thing to do. She hurried toward him and met him in the reception room.

"I will not be responsible," she whispered angrily. "It is not my fault."

"Nothing ever is," Solomon said.

"There's no need to be snide, Mr. Moon. It's the mark of a petty man." She glanced quickly toward his office. The door was closed. "I had no authority to stop him. You understand that, don't you?"

"Somebody in my office?"

"Mr. Brindig. He's very upset."

"How do you know?"

"Just listen."

Together, they walked up the central aisle of the office floor and Solomon saw that a number of secretaries at their desks cast surreptitious glances toward him. He reached the office door. From behind the door came sounds of demolition, the thwack of things snapping and cracking together. Priscilla looked smugly at Solomon.

Slowly, Solomon pushed open the door.

Brindig was leaning over the desk, turning over papers and letters and yellow pads and Manzinni's script and brushing all these things abruptly to the floor where he kicked them away. He was frantically searching for something.

"Ben," Solomon said, "I didn't think you were coming back or I'd — "

"This spaghetti," Brindig said urgently, "this mafioso, where'd he go?"

"Who?" Solomon was bewildered as he watched Brindig lower himself to his hands and knees, his fingers roughly brushing through the thick pile carpeting. "Who, where'd who go?"

"Maletti," Brindig barked, his eyes glued to the floor as he continued his search.

"Manzinni. You mean Manzinni. I don't know. He left, that's all, he just left."

Brindig's fingers were tearing now at the carpet, pulling loose great chunks of wool and tossing them into the air. They began to make him sneeze.

"Gezundheit," Solomon said.

"Jesus," Brindig panted as he used a corner of the desk to haul himself to his feet. "You know anything about this guy? Is he a *gonif?*"

"He's a nice guy, Ben. He's a very nice guy."

"I didn't ask from nice!" Brindig spoke through clenched teeth as he squatted next to the wastepaper basket, digging into it, tossing out balled papers, paper clips, and cigarette stubs.

"Did you lose something, Ben?"

Brindig stared at Solomon. "No, shmuck," he said. "I do this for exercise." He raised himself and duck-walked around the maroon leather chair, his hands sweeping under it.

"Tell me what it is," Solomon urged.

Brindig thrust his fingers into the crevice between the chair's seat and backrest, pulled out a nickel, threw it over his shoulder, and dived back into the leather.

"Ben," Solomon said, "if you'd just tell me what — "

"I got it!" Triumphantly, Brindig rose to his feet, one hand curled around something, his face crinkled with pleasure. He stepped toward Solomon. "It must have fallen out when I used my handkerchief. It was in my pocket. Here, see?" He tapped his breast pocket where his handkerchief was folded, and opened his hand. Imbedded in the flesh of his palm was a diamond.

"A cabochon," Brindig said softly. "Twenty-eight thousand bucks."

Solomon peered at the diamond. It was truly beautiful, its simple curved surface polished to an icy brilliance, radiating tiny cold blue flames. Brindig lifted the diamond between his thumb and forefinger, blew on it, then rubbed it against the sleeve of his jacket.

"There's a man," Brindig said, his eyes still on the diamond, "Sidney Labowski, a diamond cutter, a beautiful man. You never saw such a pair of hands. Small, like a lady's, you understand? Pink. Never a hangnail. And the care he gives those hands! He wraps 'em in flannel. But when I give him this —" Brindig rolled the diamond gently between his fingers. "— this beauty, so he can cut it for my wife, he takes all that flannel off and washes and, finger by finger, he blows himself dry. Then, watch out, genius at work!" His gaze lifted from the diamond and he looked at Solomon. "Talking of geniuses, how'd you make out with the Italian boy?"

"He wasn't happy."

"We don't pay him to be happy."

"No shit," Solomon said testily.

Brindig's lips pursed and his face was thoughtful as he stared at Solomon. "Solomon, you bother me."

"Why? Because I like Manzinni's script? Did it ever occur to you that I might be right?"

"So how come you didn't speak up?"

"Oh, c'mon, Ben, every time I open my mouth you shove your foot in it. You know it and I know it."

"Is that a fact?"

"Yeah. Yeah, that's a fact."

"It was me," Brindig said, his eyes glowing, "I'd tell you to go fuck yourself. What about it, Solly, you want to tell me to go fuck myself?"

The muscles quivered in Solomon's cheeks and his fingers curled around a steel letter opener, his knuckles whiter than snow. "Goddamn you," he whispered. His hand spasmed. He jerked the letter opener free of the desk. And the terrible *thing* with a thousand feet scratched inside him. It furrowed upwards through his chest, sprang into his mouth, whirling, tearing at his tongue. Solomon gagged and dropped the knife. He whipped a handkerchief from his pocket, held it to his mouth for an instant, then withdrew it, staring into its folds, fully expecting *the thing* would be clawing wildly, shredding the linen. But there was nothing. Absolutely nothing. Not even his spittle. "Forget it," he said to Brindig, his voice tired and flat. "Just forget it."

"Maybe," Brindig said after a long silence, "maybe a little time off. Take Kendal someplace good and blow a few grand. What the hell, pull the diamond outta your ass."

Solomon stared at him and slowly shook his head. "Jesus, Ben, what the hell is that?"

Brindig's eyes opened wider. He was honestly surprised. "You don't know about that?" He held up his precious diamond. "You don't know how many assholes closed on such a beauty? I'll tell you something, Solly, always keep the sphincter in good shape. It's the only muscle could save your life. It saved mine."

Solomon couldn't help but laugh. "Sure."

"*Emmis,*" Brindig said. "See, there was this old man, so old that even if he didn't want, he'd piss in his pants, you understand? On the other hand, maybe it wasn't his years, maybe it was all the whips across his kidneys."

"You want this fixed," Solomon said, tapping Manzinni's script which rested on his desk. "Maybe we'd better hold the once-upon-a-time."

"Hey," Brindig said, "gimme a break. This is a good story. My father told me. Listen. You'll like it. You'll maybe learn something."

Solomon remembered that his father had never told him a story and he wished suddenly that he'd had the experience. It would have been nice. "Okay," he said.

"So," Brindig continued. "The old man walked with his eyes on the ground, he shouldn't have to look up and see the world around him. Who can blame him? In the *shtetl* where he lived a man didn't dream of the Czar's caviar. No, he dreamed something else. He dreamed he could fly. This old man who pissed his pants dreamed that one day, God willing, he could sit on the branch of a tree, put out his arms, kick his feet, and whoosh! he would be a sparrow in the sky. That'd be nice, huh, Solly?"

In his mind, Solomon pulled the trigger and the white-breasted thrush plummeted to the ground.

"I don't know," he said.

"What are you talking?" Brindig said. "How could it hurt to be a sparrow? So, anyway, the old man figured that when the next pogrom came, and there is always a next pogrom, Solly, this you'd better —"

"Not always."

"Always," Brindig said. "You'd better believe it. See, that's what the old man knew, so he dreamed that when it came, he'd fly high over the heads of the Cossacks, high up in the air where the whips couldn't get him and where, with a *bissel* luck, he could shit in the eye of a captain."

"Your father told you this story?"

"And I'm trying to tell you, so listen, for chrissake. The dumb old man had hair in his ears and he didn't hear so good, and because he always kept his eyes on the ground he didn't see the guy."

"What guy?" Solomon asked, beginning to be caught up in Brindig's story.

"The Cossack captain on his horse. Because like I said, here comes the pogrom, here comes the Cossack snapping his whip at all the Jews. Zingo! Whap! The whip catches the old man across the face and he's got blood in his mouth. Then the whip's on his neck, his back, and snap-snap-snap across the kidneys. And that was the big mistake."

"What do you mean," Solomon asked, leaning forward on his desk. "Why was it a mistake?"

"Because," Brindig's voice rang, "the old man pissed his pants and the shame he felt gave him speed. Away he goes, up the street, across the fields, and just like a monkey, an old monkey, he climbs the tree from where he dreams he can fly. Up he goes. Up up up! And when he's standing at the tippytop, his pants wet with piss, blood like a river running through his teeth, he opens his arms like he's hugging the sky, kicks his feet, and whooooosh. The old man flies!"

"Fantastic!" Solomon said.

"But short," Brindig said. "Very, very short. Because the old man is not a sparrow in the sky. He's just a Jew with a dumb dream, and so splat is how he goes. He makes a big hole in the field and the Cossack bastard shoves him into it and rides away. That was the second mistake."

"Go on, go on," Solomon urged.

"This Cossack is even dumber than the Jew. He doesn't remember that a dead man has loose bowels. But in the *shtetl* they remember. They lift up the dead old man with hair in his ears and they look into the hole in the field and there in a puddle of shit is a diamond. Ain't that something, Solly? A Jew who flies through the air shitting diamonds? Whew!"

Brindig removed his handkerchief and patted his lips. Solomon frowned. "Is that it?" he asked. "What about you? I mean, saving your life and everything."

"Well," Brindig said, "one thing and another, it's that diamond which takes another dumb Jew, a little boychick, from Minsk to Pinsk, far away from the Cossacks, and into the streets of Wilkes-Barre, where he, too, makes certain that he's got a grade-A number-one go-to-the-head-of-the-class sweet-and-snappy sphincter!"

"Your father," Solomon said.

"Yeah, my old man." Brindig's voice was filled with pride. "He was quite a guy. Told a helluva story, huh?"

"Yes," Solomon answered quietly, "it's a helluva story."

"So." Brindig shook himself as if he were getting rid of any Cossacks who might have closed in, and he pointed to Manzinni's script. "Thursday. You'll fix this shit and give it to me on Thursday, right?"

Solomon nodded, his mind still on the story. He was pained by the tale of the poor Jew who dreamed of flying, but he feared that whatever words he used to Brindig, whatever response he offered, would sound like cheap sentiment. So he remained silent. How hard it is, he thought, to make ourselves accessible to each other. He heard Brindig cross the room, open the door, then pause.

"Hey, kid," Brindig said softly, "don't get your tit in a wringer." The door closed behind him.

For a long time after Brindig left, Solomon stared out the window, only dimly conscious of the clatter of typewriters in the hall, the shuffling tread of secretaries, the arrival and departure of men and women who had come to plead their cases with various executives of Trans-Global Films. He turned from the window and glanced at his bookcase, his gaze moving over the many manuscripts, which told tales of wonder and awe, of rage and pain, of complexity and dream, but none of them seemed as important as the mythic fable just recounted. He wasn't sure why Brindig had told him the story. Surely it had more to say than the monetary value of a sphincter-vised diamond. The image of the Jew lying in his puddle of shit was ignominious, but there had been a kind of nobility to his dream. And in the end, had he not been victorious? Had not Brindig's father escaped the Cossacks? Was not Brindig himself nourished by the legacy? The story, it seemed to Solomon, was an ancestral gift belonging to all those of the diaspora.

But not to me, Solomon concluded, nor to my father, for, as reasonable men, we chose to disconnect the past and live within the realities of our time, a time no longer threatened by tormentors. As hideous as the Holocaust had been it had, at least, pricked the conscience of men and the heat of bigotry had cooled. To hold on to the dissimilarity of men,

Solomon argued with Brindig, whom he visualized still standing before him, was to emphasize differences to a point of exaggeration and, therefore, to create a climate of distrust. Surely, such a condition would lead inevitably to a resurgence of bigotry. Following the course of his own logic, his fingers rapping the desk in emphasis, Solomon pointed out to the imagined Brindig that each man's obligation lay in assimilation.

Then why, Solomon asked himself uneasily, do I feel the seeds of accusation in Brindig's legend? I am not responsible for the past, nor will I accept the charge.

"Shit," he said.

Roughly, he pushed his chair away from the desk and began to circle the office, stooping swiftly here and there to retrieve those things Brindig had swept to the floor in his wild search for the diamond. He righted the overturned wastepaper basket, shoveled ash-smeared envelopes into it, slammed paper clips and staples onto the desk, not caring if their sharp points marred the glossy mahogany surface, and used the heel of his shoe to boot the loose cushion of the leather chair into its customary crevice. He saw that one of the framed hunting prints hung slightly askew and when he started to straighten it he had a desire to lift it clear of the wall and smash it so that he could hear the shattering of glass. Lifting it high over his head, he felt an imbecilic urge to roar like a lion. It was that impulse that saved the picture. The image of a jungle cat provoked another wish. Quickly, he rehung the picture.

He unlocked the armoire that stood against the wall. Suspended from a hook on the back of the armoire was a long, dirty canvas bag whose original purpose had been to hold the spinnaker of a sailboat. Solomon removed it. Carefully, he pulled a kite from it. Solomon unfurled it on his desk. It was made of black silk, and painted on the silk was the head of a golden lion, bold slashing strokes of vermillion outlining his dripping claws. A perfect circle had been cut into the center of the cloth to represent the animal's snarling mouth. When in the air, the animal's mouth opened and closed, and Solomon always pretended that he heard the lion roar.

From his desk, he removed a pouch of powdered glass and a pot of liquid glue. He dribbled glue along a length of his monofilament flying line, then sprinkled it with powdered glass, until it looked like a dangerous whip. That was Solomon's intention. Adroitly manipulated, the saber-sharp line could sever the line of another kite. Solomon was preparing for battle.

He fitted the kite into his canvas bag and hoisted the bag to his shoulder, grateful that soon he would be in the company of his friends Emilio and the Mouse, who never questioned why he wanted to roar like a lion.

Just before he left his office he glanced at the steel letter opener on his desk, then looked quickly away.

Jesus, he thought, I was ready.

John Luckey was in the elevator when Solomon entered. The scent of licorice was overpowering. Luckey's finger stabbed Solomon's shoulder.

"What's that thing you're carrying?" Luckey asked.

"A kite."

"What is it, a gift?"

"No."

Luckey winked at Solomon. "Sure it is. You're giving it to a client, right?"

"No."

"Yes, you are. You're giving it to a client. For his little boy. That's damn nice of you, Solomon. That kite, it must have set you back seven, eight bucks. More? Sure, more. Listen, put down thirteen seventy-five and I'll okay it."

The elevator reached the ground floor and the doors slid open.

"How'd you like an icicle up your ass?" Solomon asked the comptroller, and he walked out of the building.

17

Quietly, the old man and Jubal waded the stream. Keeping to the far side of the bank, pushing lightly through the surrounding ferns, they circled the apple orchard and then entered it, slipping easily among the crooked limbed trees. A small deerskin pouch hung low from a rope around Riordan's waist and as he moved, it thumped softly against his leg. A dark wet stain gradually spread across the leather of the pouch but the old man didn't seem aware of it. He motioned for the boy to be still. Hidden by the trees, they watched the farmhouse and the barn.

A vegetable garden was planted along one side of the barn, its produce mostly stripped, the remainder blackened by the October chill. A few shriveled zucchini lay on the earth. Bush peas, no longer bending under the weight of their pods, were scattered about. Green stalks of carrot heads lay flat on the ground. There was a flurry of movement at the corner of the barn and a small rabbit ran into the vegetable garden.

Jubal glanced quickly at his father. He knew better than to speak but he pointed toward a pocket in the old man's cloak where he knew Riordan carried his bola. The old man smiled but shook his head. He, too, thought of the delicacy of rabbit flesh but he wished to do nothing that might reveal his position.

The kitchen's screen door opened and Jabez Tuttle walked out of the house. He started for the barn. The rabbit stopped nibbling at the carrot greens and lifted his head, his nose quivering.

Jabez lifted a heavy stone in his path. Although the farmer was the man they had come to spy upon, Jubal was glad that the tall thin man had enough sense to try to kill the rabbit for his dinner. But Riordan was startled. The fact that Tuttle had bled his chicken had convinced him that the man was a Jew hiding behind the cloak of his pretended Catholicism. And Riordan knew that Jews shunned rabbits because the animal was without a cloven hoof. What game was this clever heretic playing? Perhaps, Riordan contemplated, he is trying to fool God. Riordan tensed as Jabez raised the stone in his hand and then hurled it. But Jabez threw the stone directly at the barn many feet from the rabbit. It was obvious that he meant only to scare away the animal. The rabbit leaped and flashed away. He had not leaped higher than Riordan's heart, for in the farmer's action was continuing proof of what the old man had concluded.

Tuttle walked to the barn and stepped through the door. After a moment the soft lowing of a cow could be heard from within the barn. Riordan tapped his son's shoulder and, bending low, they raced across the farmyard. They crouched under one window, slowly raising their heads to window level.

A cow, her head locked in an iron stanchion, stood quietly in the barn. Tuttle sat astride a three-legged stool, his head buried in the flank of the animal as he milked her. Her udders were full and the milk came easily, warmly foaming in a pail.

Riordan pulled at his son's shoulder and they retreated back to the orchard. Quietly, he instructed the boy to search the farmhouse while he, Riordan, maintained his vigil of the farmer.

"What am I looking for, Riordan?" the boy asked.

The old man tried not to be impatient but his fingers dug into Jubal's arm; he ignored the boy's gasp of pain. "Throw one small stone into a pool and do not the ripples spread?"

"Yeah, yeah," Jubal said, straining under Riordan's bear-trap grip.

"The tall man in the barn, the one who hides his Jew blood," Riordan whispered, "can he not have spread his venom like ripples in the water? Should he have colored the hunter with darkness, are we not obliged to give witness to the infamy? Look for signs of the soul's corruption, boy. For if we find them, should we not warn the hunter? Make him beware? Why else then do I carry these?" He tapped the wet leather pouch which hung from his waist. His fingers clamped harder on the boy's flesh. "Go!"

His eyes on the barn in case the farmer reemerged, Jubal ran to the Moons' farmhouse and quickly slipped through the kitchen door. He wished he understood more clearly what his father wanted, but he had not dared question further for fear of the old man's quick anger. A sign of the soul's corruption? For what telltale signs should he search? He was familiar with the smell of a tracked animal. Is that it? he wondered. Will there be a stink of fear in these rooms? Cautiously, he sniffed, but was aware only of the aroma of spices, bread, a faint hint of coffee. His gaze moved around the kitchen but he saw nothing that startled him. He walked into the living room and continued his search. It was a simple room unadorned by frills but cluttered nicely with soft cushions and woven rugs, and on one wall were many framed photographs. As he stepped toward the wall to examine them, Jubal noticed the television set. He paused and then moved to a window that looked out toward the barn. He saw that Riordan still crouched under the barn window, the old man's back to the house. Jubal wondered if he could chance turning on the television set for just a moment but he knew that that would be in defiance of his father and he lacked the courage for such an act. He started back to the wall of photographs but paused again when he noticed a jumble of cushions on the sofa. The pillows were of different sizes, but all were covered in Kendal's needlepoint. Most were of flowered design, a preponderance of English roses, but there was one that Kendal had copied from a Cluny design. Rabbits scampered on a field of green. In their midst was a prancing unicorn, and in the background was a golden castle. Propped against it was another cushion, and it was that which had arrested Jubal. The needlepoint, this time copied from a medieval tapestry, depicted a lonely figure of a haloed saint, his head bowed, an open book in his hand. The saint was done in quiet colors, but in one corner of the needlepoint panel was a pure white lily. In the opposite corner below the figure of the saint was the crimson stitching of a flame.

Why was a saint in a Jew's house? Was this what Riordan sought? Was the Jew pretending to be a member of the true faith?

The posture of the saint was so gentle that Jubal backed away from it, fearful that his closeness would diminish its sanctity. Slowly, he turned away from it to look upon the photographs on the wall. He recognized some of the people in the pictures. There was an old photograph of the woman he'd seen with the hunter in their red car. Dressed in a soft robe, she sat in a chair before a mirror. The mirror was ringed with brightly glowing bulbs and the glass reflected her image. Jubal had no way of recognizing that the picture had been taken in a theater's dressing room, but he admired the easy grace of the woman's body and the insouciant smile upon her face. He glanced to the left. He saw a photograph of a man bending over a piano, a brimmed fedora rakishly tilted over one eye, a cigarette dangling from the corner of his mouth. His head was cocked toward the camera and the eye not covered by his hat was half closed either in a wink or to avoid the smoke curling upwards. The man's face was wreathed in pleasure. Jubal squinted at it to make certain that it was the hunter at an earlier age. His eyes moved to the right. There was a photograph of another man. A small figure, his head covered by a strange high hat, he sat on the seat of a carriage. In one hand he held a stalk of celery. In the other he held the reins to a mule harnessed to his carriage. When Jubal examined the picture more closely he had the feeling that the man was only lightly perched, his body coiled in energy as if he were ready to spring from his seat. Feeding the animal from a leather bucket held in his massive hand was another man who smiled shyly at the mule.

Jubal walked further along the wall and saw many photographs of the same people, all in different and casual poses. He was amazed at how often those in the photographs were smiling or laughing. Still acutely conscious of the needlepointed saint who lay on the sofa behind him, Jubal turned, almost expecting that the saint would have raised his head and would now be staring at him in reproach as if to remind him that he was dallying at his mission. But when he turned to see if this was so his glance swept across another photograph that hung near the corner of the wall.

It was a snapshot of a very small girl seated on a pony. A man stood next to her. It was the hunter. The girl leaned from the pony as if she had just mounted or was preparing to dismount. The hunter's arms were raised in a circle around her waist and her hands were lowered to his neck, one on either side, her fingers just lightly touching. She was looking at the hunter, and her eyes, which Jubal thought were the largest, darkest eyes he'd ever seen, were so filled with love and trust that Jubal stared in awe. He looked at her hands circling the hunter's neck. They rested so lightly on his skin that Jubal could not be sure that flesh touched flesh; knew only that those hands were gestured in affection in a way that he had dreamed when he heard the songs of his harp.

He reached up and removed the photograph from the wall. He cracked it against the corner of a table. The framed glass splintered. Quickly, he pulled loose the shards and edged the photograph out from the frame. He placed it inside his shirt and returned to the window.

Riordan was gone.

Jubal froze. What should he do next? He remembered the pillow. Riordan would know. Jubal strode to the sofa, grabbed the cushion, and started for the kitchen. He heard a soft pounding. Quietly, he eased around the entrance door.

Riordan stood outside the screen door. The deerskin pouch was on the floor of the screened porch. It was empty. One of the two objects which had been in it had already been nailed to the top of the doorjamb. Riordan was nailing the other one across it. When he finished, he retrieved the pouch and stepped off the porch. He wiped his hands in the grass.

"Come," he ordered Jubal. His eyes glistened at the sight of the saint embroidered on the cushion in the boy's arms.

It was not difficult to follow Jabez Tuttle's trail. He had walked straight up the center of the dirt road that led to his mobile home, and it was obvious that he had carelessly carried a pail of milk. Drops of milk had slopped over the pail and Riordan and Jubal followed the spotted path.

There were no curtains in the high windows of the trailer. Riordan made a saddle of his hands and Jubal placed one foot in it. Riordan levered his hands upwards until the boy could just see through the window.

"His eyes is closed," Jubal whispered.

"Is he lying down, then?" There was a strange excitement in the old man's voice.

"Yeah."

"Mark you careful now, boyo," Riordan said, his voice trembling. "In what direction does he look?"

"I told you, his eyes is closed."

"In what direction does he look?" Riordan repeated urgently and Jubal heard the anger in the old man's tone.

"Can't look at nuthin', Riordan, his jaws near scratchin' the wall."

"Hail Mary, Mother of God," Riordan whispered. "He knows!"

It was not until they had returned to the hawthorn-hidden cave on the mountain that Jubal learned what the old man meant. They sat side by side at the stone table, candles flickering in the darkness of the afternoon, the cushion of the saint carefully stored on a shelf until it could be studied for further meaning, as Riordan opened his book of the *Alboraico*. Slowly, he turned the pages. He stopped when he found the passage for which he'd been searching and dipped a duck-quill pen into a bowl of red paint. He underlined the passage and shunted the book toward Jubal.

Jubal read: *And a Hebrew turns his face to the wall when death approaches.*

The boy stared at it, knowing now that Riordan had truly snared his prey. The tall thin man would die. Jubal felt a tremor move through his body. He turned to question Riordan but was unable to speak because he saw that his father's shoulders were shaking with mirth and that tears of laughter brimmed his eyes.

"What?" the startled boy asked. "What?"

"Don't you see, darlin'? All we need is a pearl."

"A pearl?" Jubal was bewildered. "What for?"

"You'll see," Riordan said, wiping tears from his eyes. "Oh, my, yes, you'll see!"

"Sumbitch done this," Ray Poole said, "he's got to be crazy!"

He and Sergeant Wilfred Callahan stood in a back pasture of the farmer's land. Lying on the grass in front of them were two dead Herefords. Although the land on which they lay was soaked in blood, neither of the cows had been butchered for their meat. Their bodies were intact but their jaws gaped grotesquely, for their jugular veins had been severed. Their tongues had been removed.

Callahan had been at police headquarters when Poole called. The investigation could have been given to any trooper, but Callahan had been preparing to return home to Derry, so he'd volunteered. He felt no need to explain that a girl named Darby lived on the high peaked road near Poole.

Staring at the neat cut of the jugular, Callahan said, "You in any kind of trouble, Ray? Anybody you know carry hard feelings?"

"Been here all my life," Poole said. "Ruffled some feathers, I 'spect, but ain't raised no fury so's you could notice. Well, oncet, mebbe."

"Once?"

"Country's changin', Wilfred. You know the stream come down from my trout pond?"

"Uh huh."

"Crosses a mowin' to the west. I let her lie fallow most times, but last summer I come down to put in some seed an', by God, if my fence warn't cut. Some damn fools been down to the stream. Left a considerable mess, I can tell you. Broken beer bottles an' little balls of that shiny aluminum paper, half chewed sandwich here an' there an' a whole shebang of them girlie magazines. Kind my boy, Andy, says shows the pink. Everywhere you looked was a little bitty trout. Warn't none of 'em but four or five inches, nuthin' to eat on 'em, just lyin' there, dead in the sun. You know what was on top of 'em?"

"No."

"Pair of torn damn panties. Seems to me them damn fools didn't know they was goin' to fuck or fish. Thing like that, it brought a fury to me but I didn't do nuthin'." Poole laughed at himself. "Hell, couldn't go around to all them tourist ladies here in the summer an' ask had they lost their drawers. I'd sure God like to have, but couldn't figure a proper way to put it."

Callahan laughed. "It'd be hard."

"You got yourself some time now?" Poole asked. "I ain't never posted my land. Thought about it oncet but figured it warn't neigh-borly. But it's time. It's sure an' hell time. Be obliged, you was to lend a hand. Andy, he's over to Bellows Falls. Leastwise, he says. Hard to keep track of that boy, got so much pussy on the mind. Well, we was all young. Don't much recollect it myself. Ain't felt real young since . . ." He stopped and Callahan knew that the farmer must be thinking about the pine tree that had crashed in the storm. Poole toed the rump of one of the dead cows. "Be obliged, you could help."

"Let's do it," Callahan said.

They returned to Poole's barn, where Ray rummaged around until he found a number of rectangular metal plates that warned trespassers that they would be prosecuted if they either hunted or fished on his land. Working together, they moved along the roadside bordering his land and hammered the signs to trees spaced roughly fifty feet apart. They labored in silence until they were close to the corner of Poole's property.

"Thing of it is," Ray said as he hammered one of the posting signs, "gonna be a lot badder'n this."

"How so, Ray?" Callahan asked.

"Come next month, it's deer time, that's how so. Use to be a man could go into the woods an' take his buck an' that was the end of it. Not now, no, sir. Damn fools from New York or Boston, they come high-tailin' it up here in them big fancy cars like they was on a African safari an' they just stick their guns outta the windows an' pump away at anythin' that moves. Don't know a buck from a backhoe, I swear. Last year, Curly Haines, he was ridin' his tractor, got his damn ear shot off. You think Curly looks like a deer?"

"I never caught the resemblance," Callahan said.

"Sold out, that's what Curly did, sold out. Course, that warn't 'cause he was ear shot." He snorted and removed a nail from his mouth. "Hell, way things are goin', man's better off with just one ear." He turned from the tree on which he was posting a sign and looked at Callahan. "You hear the mockin' birds sing? Close your eyes an' see can you hear any damn bluejays."

Callahan closed his eyes and listened for a song of birds, but all he was conscious of was a distant humming of a generator and the rhythmic thumping of a bulldozer's blade. He opened his eyes and scanned the sky.

A single crow glided overhead.

"Birds," Ray said. "They's thinnin' out, goin' toward the quiet. You hear that 'dozer?" Callahan nodded. "Land's full of 'em. Rippin' up the trees, pushin' fences down, diggin' foundations. Be a whole damn city up here 'fore you know it. That's why Curly got out. Him an' some others. Don't need cows no more. They got good damn money from the builders. Goddamn country's goin' to hell in a handbag."

Callahan listened for a moment to the distant sound of the bulldozer. "Seems a distance away."

"They're comin', Wilfred," Ray said. "Take my word for it, they're comin'. New people, they're gonna be the death of us."

"Well," Callahan said in an offhand manner, "you've got some new people up the road. They seem all right."

"The Moons, you mean. They mind their business way folks should. Don't see much hide nor hair of 'em. 'Cept Andy, cause he's got eyes for the girl. Weekenders mostly. A man can tolerate weekenders."

Callahan felt a twinge of disappointment. "That's all, just weekends?"

"Mostly."

"They ever run into trouble with trespassers? I mean, cut fences and things like that?"

"Don't know. Never said."

"Been reports of vandalism here and there."

"Wouldn't worry none. They got Jabez lookin' out."

"Well," Callahan said. "You never know."

A twinkle in Poole's eye, he looked slyly at Callahan. "You lookin' for trouble, Wilfred, or for passin' the time of day with a little filly?"

"Ray," Callahan said, "I do believe you're a dirty old man."

"I try."

As they talked they had moved steadily along the roadside, hammering their posting signs along the border of Poole's land. He took the last metal plate from Callahan's hand and drove in a nail.

"Here on up," Poole said, "land belongs to Moon. You might wish to tell 'em wouldn't do no harm they was to post it." He grinned at Callahan. "They ain't home, but a man could leave a note. Be the kind thing to do."

"Yes, sir," Callahan said, "be a kind thing." He started up the road toward the Moons' farmhouse. He paused and turned back to Poole. "What are you going to do about the cows?"

"Been freshly killed," Poole said. "Might's well butcher 'em. God, He tells us to be kind to dumb animals. Don't say nuthin' 'bout dead ones."

As Callahan proceeded up the road, he envied Poole his pragmatic theology. He wondered if his own disenchantment with the priesthood had led him consequentially into a practical way of life or whether law enforcement was just a substitute for another form of authority. He disliked exercising any arbitrary control over another man's life but he recognized the need for moral discipline. He tried to imagine what kind of man or men would have committed such an atrocity upon Poole's cows and whether it had been an act of wantonness or purpose. He could not conceive of its justification.

Callahan was a realist and accepted the fact that the rural areas of New England no longer represented a sanctuary from crime. But the nature of crimes perpetrated within these mountains related more to vandalism than violence. The hidden tensions of Vermont's taciturn men and women had sometimes exploded in rage but the occasions were rare, and members of the Bureau of Criminal Investigation, unlike many of their brotherhood on cosmopolitan streets, were still capable of empathy, of shock or disgust, when they encountered willful assault or rape or murder. This compassion, however, never hindered an investigation. They were skillful men who performed their duties with a deep sense of responsibility.

Regardless of his interest in Darby, Callahan truly felt that he had an official obligation to suggest to the Moons that they take normal precautions to dissuade any tentative trespassers. He felt even more strongly about this when he walked across their farmyard and saw that the front door of the house was slightly ajar. He suspected that neither the Moons nor Jabez Tuttle were on the premises and he knew that such a casual lack of security might tempt a passerby.

He knocked at the front door. There was no answer, so he eased it open further. He called out to see if anyone were home. No reply. Examining the door, he saw that it was the type which automatically locked when pulled shut. Callahan removed a small pad and a pen from his jacket pocket and, using his knee as a desk, wrote a note suggesting that the Moons would be wise to secure their house when they departed. He wondered if they had taken such precautions with the back door. He stepped into the house, feeling uncomfortably like an intruder, and started across the living room toward the kitchen. As he circled a table he saw a broken picture frame on the floor. It was surrounded by splinters of glass. He glanced around the room and saw that nothing else was in disarray, so was surprised that the Moons would leave any litter. He stooped, carefully picked up the shards of glass, and placed them on a magazine that rested on the table. He picked up the magazine so that he could discard the glass in a kitchen waste can. Again, he looked around the room, his gaze finally focusing on the wall of photographs. The wall was painted a light, soft beige but at the far end there was a slightly lighter square, its dimensions similar to the broken picture frame. It was obvious that that was where the picture had hung. It puzzled Callahan that the photograph had been removed, its frame and glass broken and left to lie on the floor. He laughed softly and reminded himself that the eccentricities of others did not justify an exploration of motives.

He carried the magazine into the kitchen and disposed of the glass. He shook his head when he saw that the kitchen door, too, had been left open. He returned to the living room, closed the front door, and left his note on the coffee table. He walked back into the kitchen, from where he would depart. As he stepped out onto the small screen porch and turned to pull the door closed, something wet dripped onto his head. He brushed a hand through his hair and reached for the door knob. His fingers glistened redly. Another drop fell on his head. He looked at the floorboards of the porch. A dark wet stain was spreading. He stepped back. He looked up.

Nailed to the doorjamb were the tongues of two cows. They were soft and slick with blood.

18

"Hoo ha," said the Mouse.
"*This* is a *knish*!"

The phaeton cab was drawn up on the north side of Central Park South, a few yards west of the Artist's Gate. Mouse, Solomon, and Emilio were crammed together on the front carriage seat, knishes in their laps. The knishes, wrapped in little squares of waxed paper, were very hot; when the men raised them to their lips and bit into them, little puffs of steam were released from the dough-wrapped mashed potato. The men chewed gingerly as the heat rushed into their mouths, and they juggled the hot delicacies in their fingers before returning them safely to their laps.

When Solomon departed the TransGlobal building he had walked down Lexington Avenue and picked up Emilio. Together, their kite bags over their shoulders, they had gone in search of the Mouse. Even though they planned to fly their kites earlier than anticipated, they knew the change of schedule would not bother Mouse. He was most amenable to pleasure. It was Emilio who, on spying the peddler's cart, had suggested they fill their stomachs before embarking on the afternoon's adventure.

Near them, an old man watched. He was a short, heavy-set man, his body looking even thicker because of the number of sweaters he wore. He wore old ski mittens whose ends had been cut off so that his fingers, permanently blackened from charcoal dust and greasy steam, protruded freely. His fingernails were short and split and filthy. His eyes were a wonder, huge popping orbs of black, so bright that they seemed to snap light at all things on which he focused. As he watched the Mouse, he stooped and, with a broken spatula, shuffled bits of burning charcoal into a heap that glowed in a pan in his peddler's cart. Little flags of flame leaped up between the iron bars of the grille and he pushed a half dozen kreplach into their heat. The kreplach were small pieces of baked dough filled with chopped meat and, along with the knishes, they were a specialty of the peddler's. Unlike others who hawked similar food, he was not content to offer a product that was simply baked. *His* knishes, *his* kreplach, were treated to a charcoal crisping.

"Hoo ha," repeated the Mouse, his jaws working furiously. "This is a knish!" He saluted the peddler, who watched him. And for each other's pleasure, they played the expected scene:

The Peddler (A BORED SHRUG):   *Es iz be'emes gor nit.*
(It's nothing really.)

The Mouse (SYMPATHETICALLY):   *Shver tsu machen a leben.*
(It's tough to make a living.)

The Peddler (SUCH MELAN-   *Folg mich a gang.*
   CHOLY):   (It's hardly worth the trouble.)

The Mouse (ALSO VERY SAD):   *Af luches, af tsu lehaches.*
(In spite of everything you do, it still comes out wrong.)

The Peddler (FROM THE HEART):   *Es gayt a raiech!*
(It stinks!)

The Mouse (TRYING TO HELP):   *Es vet zich alts oyzpressen.*
(It will all work out.)

The Peddler (ARE YOU KIDDING):   *Az a glick af mir!*
(I should have such luck!)

THE PEDDLER REACHES UP AND FLAPS HIS WRIST IN DISDAIN; HIS SHIRT CUFF PULLS AWAY FROM HIS WRIST. ON THE INSIDE OF HIS WRIST ARE A SERIES OF NUMBERS IMBEDDED IN THE FLESH. MOUSE IMMEDIATELY RECOGNIZES THEM AS THE STIGMATA OF A CONCENTRATION CAMP. AND THE MOOD OF THE SCENE CHANGES.

The Mouse (SOFTLY):   *Al kiddush ha-shem.*
(For the holiness of God.)

THE PEDDLER LOOKS LONG AT THE MOUSE; THEN ROUGHLY YANKS HIS CUFF DOWN TO HIDE THE NUMBERS.

The Mouse (GENTLY):   *A mentsh on glik iz a toyter mentsh, farshtast?*
(An unlucky person is a dead person, understand?)

THE PEDDLER CLOSES HIS EYES FOR A MINUTE. OPENS THEM. SLOWLY, HE SMILES.

The Peddler:	*Ich yog zich nit!* (I'm not in a hurry!)
The Mouse:	*Fun eir moyl in Gots oyern.* (From your mouth to God's ears.)
The Peddler:	*Alevei!* (It should be that way.)

THE TWO MEN SHAKE THEIR HEADS AT EACH OTHER AND CLUCK THEIR TONGUES. CONTENT WITH THE KNOWLEDGE THAT IT IS ANOTHER DAY AWAY FROM THE SMOKE OF TERRIBLE OVENS, THE PEDDLER WAVES HAPPILY TO THE MOUSE AND ROLLS HIS CART AWAY.

Although he didn't understand the content of the exchange, Solomon had paid close attention. He had seen the numbers on the peddler's wrist and it angered him to think of how little had been gained by the death of millions. But he was aware that what had appeared to be an initial despondency on the part of the peddler had been replaced with humor, and he envied the Mouse's ability to raise the spirits of men.

"He was in a camp, wasn't he?" he asked the Mouse.

"*Al kiddush ha-shem,*" Mouse repeated softly. He looked down at the bridle of his mule and stared at one of the attached metal disks. On it was embossed the name of one of Mouse's heroes: *Maimonides.* "In a little courtyard in Cordoba there's a stone statue of Moses Maimonides. Sometimes birds sit on it. Sometimes people leave a flower on his head. Sometimes the moon shines on it and makes the eyes alive. I've been told all this, but I've never seen it. I've never seen Moses Maimonides, *Rabbi Moshe Ben Maimon,* the greatest Jewish philosopher of them all. Do you want to know how great? We say of him, 'From Moses unto Moses there arose none like Moses.' That's how great. And once this great Rabbi said, 'If a Jew is murdered for no other reason except that he is a Jew, and, had he not been a Jew, he would have remained alive, then it may be said that he sacrificed his life *al kiddush ha-shem,* for the holiness of God.' " The Mouse raised his eyes from the little disk of Maimonides and looked toward the west, where the peddler, some distance away now, was pushing his cart. It was obvious that the Mouse was thinking about the awful numbers on the peddler's skin. And suddenly, as rapid as a rattler's strike, Mouse's hand reached inside his coat and whipped a short-bladed knife from a leather sheath on his belt. Striking backwards, between his legs, he plunged the knife into the wooden backboard below his carriage seat. Trembling with fury, he stabbed the board four or five times, the action so swift that both blade and hand were blurred. His anger expended, he pulled the knife free from the splintered wood and let it dangle in his hand as he pulled long breaths into his lungs.

Neither Solomon nor Emilio spoke. They were united by their shared memory of their first meeting with the Mouse. It was Sergeant Blum then, recently returned from the firefights of France, from the screech of tank treads, from the hedgerows, from the bleeding.

It had been a long and desperate war for the Mouse — years filled with the stench of decaying flesh and the screams of men. A furious anti-Fascist, he never questioned the validity of his cause, so he transgressed the unwritten law of the professional. He volunteered for any mission that came his way. He had no illusions about the sporting aspect of war. He came to kill. As lean as string, he twitched through rock-spined mountain traps and shot out the eyes of sentries. Icicles hanging from his eyelids, his feet pussed with sores, he was a winter soldier, an acrobat of death, walking a careful wire. He wept at the sight of dead men bobbing by, strapped to the wooden saddles of Italian mules. He snaked into pillboxes and pulled his dull black wire across German throats. He pissed on the rust and rubble of the ground. And each step he took brought him closer to the fearsome fact that energized him.

The pits of Belsen. At long last he stood on the lip of a fetid trench and stared at the twisted dead. The pale arms and legs and necks of Jews, maggot-bored and cracked at random joints, were crisscrossed in awkward angles as if the men and women and children had fallen from a high trapeze. Below the Mouse was a brittle mat of broken toes and black-gummed faces.

He was, at that moment, released forever from the anguish of his killing.

When the victory in Europe was bell-rung, Mouse had accumulated a plethora of combat points, so was one of the early men to return home. But the smell of cordite lingered on his skin and the sight of the broken dead was in his eyes and his anger was not swept away. He liked the feel of a blade in his hand and he knew he was a dangerous man. This knowledge pleased him, for it gave substance to his plan. He convinced himself that the only way he could release the residue of anger was through action. The Mouse knew where to find it. Throughout the four years of fighting, in foxhole or barrack, he had heard the drone of racial epithet. *Jew-boy. Kike. Sheeny.* He had chosen to ignore the slurs, or grin into the face of those who taunted him, preferring to focus his militancy on the more immediate target of German terror, but when that target was destroyed, the Mouse altered his course of action. Rather than accept an immediate discharge from the service, he requested prolonged duty. He knew that he would find his enemy within a gathering of unhappy men.

He petitioned for a cadre position on a training post. His task was to sharpen the fighting skills of men who would have no opportunity to fight. He perceived the absurdity of this assignment and relied on being surrounded by recent inductees who, impatient to participate in the blossoming peace, would question the sanity of his purpose. Daily, he would be confronted by frustrated men. It was the confrontation he sought. Deterred from their civilian future, these thwarted men would focus their anger on the Mouse and, if driven too far by him, explode in rooted bigotry.

Jew-boy.

Kike.

Sheeny.

The Mouse prayed for defamation. And honed his blade.

Because the majority of combat-hardened men had eagerly accepted early discharge, the permanent cadre at Mouse's post was lightly staffed and he was, therefore, assigned multiple duties. He drilled platoons, indoctrinated raw recruits into the intricacies of weapons, ran squads through obstacle courses, pitted man against man in close-combat training, explained the rituals of guard duty, and listened endlessly to the stumbling recitation of general orders. And during every minute of every hour he watched for some sign, some subtle tilt of head, some pointed finger, some gesture. Each day his fingers twitched more eagerly toward the handle of his blade, and he longed to hear a deprecation of his father's blood.

But the Mouse miscalculated and was caught in his own trap. He ignored the cardinal rule of a stalking man. He forgot to camouflage. He failed to recognize the projection of his own venom, and therefore was puzzled by the absence of slander. Although much later, in the years ahead, he would correctly diagnose his failure — and be gladdened by it — he did not, during that period on the post, understand why the men under his command stood silent in his presence. He was not aware that they considered him as hazardous as a stick of dynamite whose fuse was waiting to be lit. None dared to strike the match.

The war was over and the enlisted men serving Mouse were percentage players who recognized the foolishness of gambling with loaded dice. The word was whispered across the parade ground, in the target pits, and the mess hall, and as far away as the dry streets of Junction City.

The word was: *Don't fuck with the Mouse.*

Two young men paid no heed to the whispered warnings. They were Emilio Ho and Solomon Moon. Both in their teens, they had similar reasons for ignoring the implicit threat in any chance encounter with the Mouse. Each sincerely regretted that, due to his youthful age, he had been denied the opportunity to test himself in combat. The United States Army was not interested in accommodating their desire to measure themselves against other men. They were assigned to a baking school. After graduating they received their corporal's stripes and were posted to the kitchens of Fort Riley. As both were noncoms, they shared a small room at one end of the wooden barracks that housed recruits. Across from them, in another small room, was Sergeant Blum.

The three men liked each other immediately; their affection was sealed when they learned of each other's common interest in the martial arts. Emilio's interest in those arts was not based on any warlike instinct. He was simply a marvelously muscled man who had spent many hours at the Henry Street Gym in lower Manhattan working with weights, learning how to box, to wrestle, perfecting his balance on the leather horses, keeping supple on the rings. He flaunted neither strength nor agility but, like a good mechanic, tuned his machine. Like any good mechanic, he knew that the test of his machine was not in the preparation but in the run. The time had come to learn what his machine could do. On the other hand, Solomon's interest in things martial was not based on the potential physicality of events. He was not an envious young man, not jealous of the Mouse's combat experiences, but he yearned to participate in the perceptions of battle. He wanted terribly to know if he could have passed the bitter tests.

At first reluctant to reveal the bloody episodes of his recent past, the Mouse gradually succumbed to the questions of his friends. And in the slow recounting of his adventures he began to perceive the senselessness of his hatred. Night after night, Emilio and Solomon returned from their kitchen and brought to the bare wooden room secretly baked bagels and an offering of salami and a jug of steaming coffee laced liberally with sweet cream. The Mouse talked of torn flesh and eyeless men. He demonstrated the techniques of slaughter. Often, when the only sound in the barracks was the snoring of recruits, Mouse and Emilio and Solomon slipped outside and, under the Kansas moon, slammed each other to the cold ground. Their battles were without rancor and the intensity of simulated combat was generally vitiated by their honest concern for each other's welfare. There was, however, no attempt to avoid temporary bruises or cuts or sprains. Because of Mouse's experience and Emilio's brawn, one or the other was the usual victor; but once, after he had received an unintended but wicked blow to his kidney, Solomon spun toward Emilio and viciously lashed out with his boot. He caught Emilio on the knee and, grunting with pain, Emilio dropped. Solomon whirled, lowered his head, and charged into the Mouse. The velocity of Solomon's charge caught Mouse flatfooted; his breath exploded as Solomon's head rammed into his solar plexus and the Mouse crashed into the side of the wooden barracks. As Mouse's body slid to the ground, Solomon scooped a rock from the earth and raised it high over the Mouse's head. Frightened by the awful look on Solomon's face, Emilio ignored his pain. He dived at Solomon and the two men tumbled together on the ground, rolling over and over as Emilio clawed for the rock still held in Solomon's iron grip. As they struggled, Emilio heard the crunch of broken glass and knew that his weight on Solomon had crushed a discarded beer bottle beneath the other man's back. He thought of the wicked cutting edges of the glass and tried to hold Solomon still, but the smaller man twisted and turned and writhed wildly, so Emilio did what he had to do. He closed his massive fist and hooked Solomon hard on the mouth. He knocked his friend unconscious.

Emilio and the Mouse carried Solomon into the barracks latrine. They undressed him. The back of his shirt was shredded and the skin of his back was lacerated from the broken glass. They sat him in a shower and ran warm water and washed his wounds. As the water cascaded over his head, Solomon opened his eyes. He winced at the stinging water and when he tried to smile through his cracked and bleeding lips he winced again.

"Boy," he said. "Where'd he come from?"

"Who?" Mouse and Emilio asked simultaneously.

"The elephant," Solomon said. "The elephant who kicked me."

They put Solomon to bed, where he fell asleep immediately, his breathing as sweet and regular as a baby's. Emilio and Mouse sat together in the Mouse's little room and sipped from cold bottles of beer. After a long silence, Emilio spoke.

"He was going to kill you, Mouse," he said.

"No," Mouse said, "not me. He wasn't going to kill me. Something, but not me."

"Then what?" Emilio asked.

"I don't know," Mouse answered. He picked up the short-bladed knife he had carried through Europe, which was never far from him. He ran a finger along the sharp blade. "You and me, Em, we're lucky. We know who we are. I mean, what the hell, with you it's double, right?"

"I don't follow," Emilio said.

"With you, they can call you Chink or Wop, and either way it's a bull's-eye, right?"

"Oh, yeah. But who gives a shit?"

"I know. With me, it's Kike or Sheeny or whatever. What's the difference? — it all spells Jew. And whoever says it is very goddamn right. You bet your ass I'm a Jew. And that's the whole point. I *know* who I am. So do you. We got some kind of a shape to us. But Solomon . . ." He paused and took a long swallow of beer. "Solomon ever tell you about his grandfather?"

"No."

"He was a Sephardic Jew. From Seville. Rafael Fernandez Muñoz."

"I like that. That's a nice name."

"The shmucks at Ellis Island didn't understand it, so they called him Moon."

"What else?"

"What else what?"

"What else did Solomon tell you?"

"Nothing. That was it. I'm taking him through the obstacle course one day, yelling at him to keep his head down 'cause they're firing real ammo and out of the blue he winks at me and yells back, 'Rafael Fernandez Muñoz; Rafael Fernandez Muñoz!' Dumb son of a bitch almost got his head blown off. Then we're on our backs cutting through all that barbed wire and —"

"I hate that wire stuff."

"Yeah. And he tells me how the old man, his grandfather, came from Seville, and how he took the long dive out the window during the Depression, and all the time he's talking, those goddamn live rounds are zinging maybe a foot over his head. Crazy, huh?"

"The old man, Muñoz, he took his dive 'cause he was broke?"

Mouse swirled the last of his beer around the bottom of the bottle, then tilted it to his lips and drained it. "Solomon says he thinks it was the only way the old man could join the Gentiles." He wiped his mouth with the back of his hand then tossed the empty bottle into a waste bucket. He glanced down at the knife in his other hand. He hefted it for a moment and then carved a slice of air. "You know something, Em? I think one day our boy Solomon is gonna do something crazy."

"Like what?"

"Like carving a shape for himself." And he spun in a circle, thrusting and jabbing with the knife, puncturing the air, then flipped it end over end to where it stabbed deep into the wall.

"You wanna know something else, Mouse?"

"Yeah."

"We'd better be there."

Mouse looked at Emilio for a long time before he spoke. "Yeah," he said. He pulled the knife loose and then began attacking the wall in quick little thrusts. Emilio left and walked across the barracks to the room he shared with Solomon. Solomon's bed was empty. Emilio hurried to the latrine. He swung open the door. And stopped.

Solomon was alone in the latrine. He was naked. He stood with his back to the long row of mirrors. He was looking over his shoulder at his lacerated flesh. He was smiling. And other than the snoring of sleeping recruits, the only sound in the night was the muted and repeating thud of a knife in the Mouse's wall. Emilio realized that Solomon was listening to it, too. Quietly, Emilio closed the door and went to bed, knowing that neither he nor Solomon would ever forget the sound of that knife.

And now, sitting together on the carriage seat of the cab, they had heard it again. Emilio and Solomon saw that the Mouse's anger was subdued and that he had sheathed his knife. Still, he stared up the street toward the disappearing peddler.

"I think you cheered him up, Mouse," Solomon said, following the other man's gaze. "I really do."

"Maybe," Mouse said.

"What'd you say to him?" Solomon asked.

The Mouse shrugged. "Not much. What he wanted to hear. You know."

"What?" Solomon persisted.

"That he wasn't so bad off, that's all," the Mouse said. "That it could be worse."

"You gonna finish your knish?" Emilio asked Solomon.

"Wait a minute, Em," Solomon said. He turned back to Mouse. "What do you mean, 'it could be worse'? What could be worse?"

"It's getting cold," Emilio said, staring into Solomon's lap. "A cold knish is no good. Ain't that right, Mouse? A cold knish is no good?"

"No good for the knish or no good for the eater?" the Mouse asked.

"I never thought about that," Emilio said.

"Think about it," Mouse said and then looked at Solomon. *"A mentsh on glik iz a toyter mentsh."*

Emilio probed a finger into Solomon's knish. "It's like ice. It's very, very cold."

"Forget the knish, for God's sake," Solomon said as he swiveled in his seat toward the Mouse. "What'd you say?"

" '*A mentsh on glik iz a toyter mentsh.*' It's what I told the peddler. It means the same in any language. 'An unlucky person is a dead person.' So, with one thing and another, he's not so bad off, you understand?"

"Oh," Solomon said. "Yeah." He glanced over at Emilio who was chewing the last bit of the knish. "You ever hear that expression, Em?"

"I couldn't say," Emilio munched. "My mouth was full, you know?"

"Let's fly the kites," Solomon said.

The three men wiped the sticky residue of their knishes from their hands, and the Mouse gathered up the reins to his mule. He grimaced as his fingers closed on them.

"I don't think you got the right kind of bees, Mouse," Emilio said sympathetically. "Honest to God, you'd do better soaking your hands."

"Or maybe an indoor job," Solomon said.

"Yeah," said Emilio, "like in a steam room, you know?"

"I couldn't fold the towels," Mouse said.

"I never thought of that," Emilio said.

"Think about it," said the Mouse. Ignoring his stiff fingers, he tugged on the reins and the mule that thought he was a horse responded immediately. His steel-shod hooves pinging, the animal carved a graceful U turn and the phaeton rolled eastward through the ebb and flow of traffic.

The reins limp against its flanks, the mule slowed to a walk as it entered Central Park. Behind the animal's steady gait, the cab reached a curving section of the East Drive between the Mall and Overlook Rock.

"Why did he cover those numbers so quickly?" Solomon asked the Mouse.

The Mouse was startled and pulled up on the reins. The mule stopped. "What?"

"The peddler," Solomon said. "Why was he embarrassed?"

"Maybe," the Mouse said, "maybe 'cause he survived." He leaped down from the carriage seat and ducked into the body of the cab. From under the forward seat he pulled out his kite bag. "Let's do it," he said.

Under a threatening sky, the three men flew their kites. Solomon's lion sailed high, higher as he paid out line from his fishing reel. Emilio's kite was shaped like a dragon, its monstrous tail scaled in brilliant circles of dyed silk, each overlapping the other so that red bled into blue and yellow into green, turquoise and cobalt trembled against each other; when the dragon reached the height of Solomon's kite it looked like a serpent with rainbow veins. The Mouse flew a cylindrical kite made of rice paper dyed totally black; as it, too, rose to meet Solomon's kite, the black blurred against the gray sky and the rounded shape of the kite flattened, lost dimension, until it was hard to see what direction it flew. It satisfied the Mouse's intention, for each man wanted to deceive the other. Their mutual purpose was destruction.

Gently manipulating their flying lines, they moved their kites closer and closer, occasionally one outwitting the other by a sudden tug or twist or turn of his line. They searched for gusts of wind or unexpected currents so that they could maneuver into favorable positions preliminary to attack. The vagaries of the wind dictated the pace of combat. Each of the flyers attempted to pull his glass-encrusted flying line against his opponent's and thus sever a kite. It was a game which demanded both patience and skill. Lines would chafe against each other, scratch and graze, but it was necessary to avoid an entanglement that could lead to twisted or knotted lines devoid of friction.

The three strategists worked their kites in cunning circumvention. They foiled each other, outflanked each other, angled their kites in daring plunges and then swooped away. As the lion and the dragon and the barrel of black silk rose higher and higher so, too, did the men's spirits levitate. The concentration of battle erased the pain in the Mouse's arthritic fingers, Emilio's memory of the thudding knife, Solomon's image of the ugly numbers on a peddler's wrist.

The rain determined victory. The sun vanished under a blanket of cloud and a soft rain fell. The wide, flat surfaces of Emilio's and Solomon's kites withered in the drizzle and lost buoyancy. The Mouse quickly recognized his advantage. Firmly pulling his line taut so that the barrel kite rode in a vertical position, letting the rain drop harmlessly through the black cylinder, he plunged his kite toward Solomon's. Hampered by the waterlogged silk, Solomon could not escape. His kite was severed and flew free of its line.

Each man imagined the silent roar of the golden lion and they all hoped that he sailed toward some distant and hospitable jungle.

The game over, the three friends returned to the phaeton. The men felt fine. Solomon helped Emilio and the Mouse repack their kites; as they worked, they chatted about fighting kites, about technique and tactics, about the worthiness of bamboo struts and the shapes of umbrella silk. The very use of special nomenclature gave them as much pleasure as a fly fisherman's discussion of peacock feathers and the tiny size of hooks. As they stowed their kite bags in the body of the cab, the Mouse suddenly whistled.

"Holy cow," he exclaimed. "It's almost sundown!" He turned to his friends. "Listen, I do a thing on *Shabbis* or on a holiday. They wait for me."

"Who?" Solomon asked. "What do you have to do?"

The Mouse had already scrambled onto the carriage seat. He leaned down and reached under the seat and drew out a ram's horn. "I blow the *shofar*. I am the *Baal Tokea* of Forty-Seventh Street! Let's go!"

His excitement was contagious. For an instant Solomon thought about the film script on which he had to work but, looking at the Mouse's glowing face, he dismissed it and leaped up onto the carriage seat. Emilio grinned and joined them.

They raced through the park, Emilio and Solomon clutching the sides of the carriage seat as the cab rocked and swayed. Sitting between them, the Mouse urged on his mule and the little metal disks on the animal's bridle clicked and tinkled and the Indian feathers of his headdress bent under the rush of wind and rain. They left the park and galloped south on Fifth Avenue.

Traffic was at the mercy of the Mouse. Horns blared and men and women cried angrily from behind the wheels of their automobiles. The Mouse saw an opening between a laundry truck and a battered Jeep. The occupants of the Jeep were four young men identically dressed in checkered shirts, down-filled vests, and Australian bush hats. They shouted encouragement to the Mouse and the Jeep's driver slapped his gear into reverse and inched his vehicle backwards so that the Mouse would have room to sweep by.

"Take 'em!" Mouse shouted as he thrust the reins into Solomon's hands; and as they turned into Forty-Seventh Street and its rows of Jewish diamond merchants, Mouse lifted the ram's horn to his mouth. The long mournful bleat pierced the rain and Solomon saw dozens of men turn to wave. Most of them looked like the Jew who had fed his pigeon.

They wore black suits and coats and dark broad-brimmed hats and the beards and *payot* of Hasidim.

Why do you do that? Solomon wanted to shout. *Why do you hold on to the trappings of the past? Dress like the rest of us, for chrissake*, he silently admonished — then blinked, for he wasn't sure who the rest of us were. He stared at the line of diamond marts, at the splendid shops, the glittering displays behind their windows, the small cubbyholes where white-faced men huddled, loupes to their eyes as they examined precious stones.

My God, he thought suddenly, how many sphincters have been here!

Parked midway down the street was a charter bus; descending from the bus were women. One by one, they peeled off and marched determinedly toward various stores. They were all conservatively dressed in high-necked dresses, their arms covered in long sleeves, and they wore— *what*, Solomon asked himself, *they wore what?* He wheeled on the carriage seat.

"Mouse!" he shouted above the rain, which was drumming now, and above the wail of the ram's horn. "Wigs! They're all wearing wigs!"

"The Hasidim!" Mouse shouted back. "After marriage, they shave their heads and wear the *shaitel* and no man can uncover them."

Jesus, Solomon thought, one more archaic custom. "Why not?" he asked.

"It's against God's wish, of course," Mouse answered.

"But what are they doing here?" Emilio asked.

The Mouse laughed with joy. "They come here on *Shabbis* or like today, the first day of Sukkot — an occasion, believe me—and they make sure they get their men home before sundown. They're beautiful, aren't they? Aren't they beautiful?"

"They're beautiful," Emilio said.

Solomon said nothing. He watched, instead, as two men stepped out of one of the cubbyholes. The smaller man had a long piece of flannel draped over his shoulder and he held a small loupe to his eye. Even though the rain beat on his hat, he was examining a large diamond in the natural light of day. Next to him stood Ben Brindig.

Solomon gasped. He didn't want Brindig to see him, but there was no room to turn the mule away. He lowered his head, hoping that Brindig would not look up into the street. A young man in torn dungarees and dirty sneakers ran in front of the mule and it shied. Solomon hauled in the reins and settled the animal and when he looked again he saw that the young man in sneakers was moving swiftly toward Brindig. An elderly Hasidic woman, one of the women from the bus, had joined the jeweler with the loupe and was talking quickly to him. Solomon knew he must be the man Brindig had spoken about, Sidney Labowski, and she must be Labowski's wife. She was urging him to complete his business.

Once more, Mouse lifted the *shofar* to his lips and trumpeted the coming of sundown. As the notes floated over the mart, the young man in sneakers shoved a cheap pistol into Labowski's belly and grabbed the diamond from his hand. The jeweler's wife angrily stepped forward but the young man lashed out at her and his arm knocked off her wig.

The three men on the phaeton saw this and, after a frozen second, they leaped from their carriage seat and raced across the street toward the jeweler and his wife. As Solomon ran he saw a look of such disbelief and fury cross Brindig's face that he knew something terrible was going to happen.

Brindig lurched angrily toward the thief. The young man squeezed the trigger of his pistol. Brindig's face disappeared.

Men and women screamed and backed away and skidded on the slippery pavement. As the young man raced away from his killing, above the shouts and cries there came another sound. At first, Solomon thought it was the *shofar*, but then he saw that Mouse was pounding down the street, the horn in his hand as he pursued the thief. Emilio was behind him. Solomon sped after them and when he heard the sound again he realized it was the ululating wail of women, a sound of such unparalleled agony that he wished he were deaf.

And what he saw made him wish he were blind.

Labowski's wife, her shaved head naked under the rain, was weeping with shame. At the far end of the street, thirty, forty, even more Hasidic women surrounded the young man in his dirty sneakers and converged on him. Their mouths were closed now in toneless pain, their eyes dead. Silently, they tore the young man apart.

The Mouse and Emilio tried to push through them, but the women were knitted together in an unbreakable wall as they clawed at the young man, ripped at his flesh, convulsively slashed. Solomon saw them split the thief's nose and then snap the bone. He saw one woman rip the young man's ear off with her teeth then spit it back at him. Another woman drove her thumb into the thief's eye and it burst into scarlet foam. The screams of the young man were muffled under the women's sledging hands, under the terrible crush of their bodies. And then there were no more screams. There was no sound at all.

The women rose and stepped back, forming a circle around the dead young man who lay under the rain, the diamond still clutched in his hand.

Solomon turned and started back toward Brindig. The Mouse and Emilio followed him. The three men stood over the corpse which lay, faceless, in the gutter.

"*Al kiddush ha-shem*," the Mouse whispered.

"Yeah," Solomon said, his voice filled with bitterness. "For the holiness of God!"

THE
FIRST
ASSASSIN

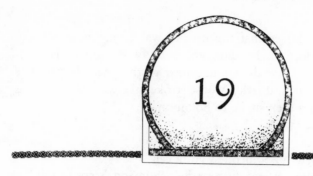

19

After they testified at the local precinct, police procedure necessitated a visit to the morgue where the bodies of Brindig and the thief had been delivered. There, in front of an assistant coroner, Solomon identified Brindig. No one stepped forth to do the same for the dead young man. A John Doe tag was tied to his toe and, unceremoniously, a morgue attendant wheeled him into a holding room. Solomon, Emilio, and the Mouse again gave statements of what they had witnessed. None could say with assurance which of the Hasidic wives had actually caused the death of the thief.

The men did not speak among themselves as they left the official building. Moving toward the curb of the dingy side street where the phaeton was parked, they passed Sidney Labowski and his wife, who once again wore her wig. Seeing the three men who had observed the witless act which had shamed her, the Hasidic woman turned quickly away. Keeping her face averted from them, she shuffled upstairs and into the building where she, too, would be required to recount the awful event.

Mouse left his friend and joined the jeweler. Quietly, the two men conversed in Yiddish. Solomon had a suddenly strange reaction. He wished he understood the language so that he could know if Mouse was as effective in offering his sympathy in this case as he had been with the peddler whose wrist was tattooed with numbers; and at the same time he wanted to urge both Mouse and Labowski to speak English, to give up a language symbolic of their separateness from other men.

Abruptly, Labowski and the Mouse moved toward each other. They embraced and kissed each other on the cheek and when they stepped apart, Solomon could see that the jeweler was crying as he wearily mounted the steps into the building where the two dead men lay.

Mouse rejoined his friends standing next to the phaeton cab. The rain had turned to a light drizzle. Mouse stroked the wet feathers of his mule's headdress and then spoke to Solomon.

"What about the family?" he asked.

"The what?"

"Mr. Brindig's family. Someone's gotta call."

"Of course," Solomon said distractedly. "Someone's got to call."

"It wouldn't be good," Mouse said softly, "she heard it from a cop, some stranger."

"No."

"You all right, Solomon?" Emilio asked gently. "I could call if you'd like. I could say —"

"No," Solomon said. "You didn't know him." He frowned. "I didn't either. I didn't know him either. It was so dumb, so goddamn dumb. The whole thing, so goddamn dumb." Absentmindedly, he put two fingers to his lips and whistled. "I've got to get a cab. I've got to go home. I've got to tell Kendal."

"It's awfully late, Solomon," Mouse said. "You won't find a cab down here. C'mon, we'll drive you to the station." He glanced at Emilio. "You drive, okay?"

"Sure." Emilio climbed up onto the carriage seat. He waited until Solomon and Mouse boarded the carriage, then picked up the reins. He clucked at the mule and the animal started forward.

Mouse and Solomon sat in the rear of the carriage. Solomon leaned forward and picked up something from the floor. It was a dime. He let it rest in the palm of one hand, bowing his head and studying it. Mouse watched Solomon. He was worried. Solomon's behavior reminded him of some of the men with whom he'd fought the war. These men, reacting to their initial exposure to violent death, had resorted to acts of abstract withdrawal. Some would smile for days and talk animatedly of tiny pleasures of their past, discoursing raptly on chocolate sodas and high school proms and jalopy carburetors tuned to perfection. Others would stare blankly at a blade of grass held in the hand, then weep uncontrollably when the wind blew it away. In most cases, a second incident of violence drove the absurdities from their minds and returned the men to the realities of the hour, but some men failed to recover from their introduction to carnage. These men forever whispered about the sweet taste of ices or walked in fields endlessly searching for a fresh blade of grass: a hopeless quest, for their eyes were blinded by blooded memory.

Along the dim streets of downtown, intermittent street lamps coned their lights over the heads of the carriage voyagers; each time they passed under these beams, Solomon raised his dime to let it flash in the light.

"God," Solomon said as he looked at the face on the dime, "he had style, didn't he?"

"Who?" asked the Mouse.

"Roosevelt. Franklin Delano Roosevelt. Christ, even the name. I mean, you put that in your mouth and you know you're chewing on something. Franklin Delano Roosevelt. Style, Mouse. You know who walked the streets then? Lucky Luciano in a pearl fedora. John Dillinger with the lady in red."

"They were shitty guys," Mouse said. He spoke quietly, not wanting to upset his friend.

"Sure," Solomon said, "but with style. You think those guys would have blown some little Jew apart?"

"Yeah."

"Uh-uh. There's no style to a thing like that. It's dumb. It's nothing. But now, today, why not?" Suddenly, Solomon hurled the dime into the street. "Ah, to hell with it."

"It doesn't take style to kill a man," Mouse said. "And that's a fact."

"The fact is," Solomon said angrily, "we live in a zoo and we're all so goddamn nearsighted we can't tell the animals from their keepers. Christ knows, we all smell alike."

"You think the smell was better yesterday, the day before yesterday, a hundred years ago?" Mouse asked. "You think it smelled so good when they burned the witches at Salem, and that every day the torchbearers said good morning to God? In the caves of Armenia when the Turks sliced the neck of a native, did the blood smell good? Was there perfume at Auschwitz? You think a man breathed deep in the ovens? For chrissake Solomon, use your head."

The voices of the two men had risen above the sound of the mule's hooves, and Emilio turned on his seat to look down into the body of the carriage. "You guys all right?"

"Just drive, okay?" Mouse called over his shoulder to Emilio.

"Whatever." Emilio shrugged and used the reins to tickle the mule's flanks. He was glad of the lateness of the hour, for there was little traffic and he could safely force the mule to a quickened pace. The sooner they reached Grand Central, the sooner Solomon could catch his train and see Kendal. Emilio was quite certain that only Kendal could offer the solace that Solomon sought. Below him, he heard the argument continue.

"I'm not talking about mass murder or the Holocaust," Solomon said hotly. "I'm talking about one poor single son of a bitch walking down the street afraid to turn the corner. Can't you understand that?"

"It's the same," Mouse said. "It's all the same. One guy holds the knife, another guy dies. But no matter where you walk, when you walk, how many streets you walk, there's always a corner and you gotta turn it. You, me, everybody — you gotta turn the corner, you gotta open the door, you gotta look on the other side. That's the privilege of being human."

"You think dying is a privilege?"

"No, goddamn it, living is a privilege! You can't control dying. It's a fact, a constant. We can't change it. We can't alter it. We can't stop it. We can only live with it. We can solemnize it with ritual, flower it with mystery, deodorize it with formaldehyde, but we can't outrun it. All you can do is live. Now. Here. With what you've got. With who you are. Your friend Brindig knew that. Oh, Jesus, he knew who he was!"

"You mean, a Jew, is that it? He knew he was a Jew. Well, goddamn it, if he hadn't been, maybe he wouldn't have died."

"We are all Jews!" Mouse's voice was like a trumpet. "Don't you understand that, Solomon? Everyone is a Jew!"

"Oh, sure, sure. 'If you prick us, do we not bleed? Poison us, do we not die?' "

"I'm not talking Shylock. I'm talking everybody is a Jew because everybody's in exile; everybody's wandering in his own wilderness, don't you see that? Brindig, the kid who killed him, that poor woman who stood there with a naked skull — they're all the same, we're all the same. We live with a terrible thing. We don't know if we're good! We ask ourselves, *Are we good? Are we moral? Is there virtue in us?* Those are terrible questions and we try to hide from them because the answers lie in the wilderness of ourselves. The questions exhaust us, Solomon. They're not safe, so we hide and say, Well, look, it's really not our problem, it's out of our hands, it's up to God, maybe, or fate. Jesus, what a terrible word! Fate. Think of what it means. Fate. It's like God is the judge who hands down a fixed sentence and no chance of pardon or even parole. But that's bullshit, Solomon, because what we do, what we are, rests in our own hands. That's the responsibility that wears you out, that drains you, that can kill you. And the terrible thing . . . no, the beautiful thing, the beautiful thing, is that it never ends. It doesn't make any difference you lived with the dinosaurs, or in the court of Louis fourteen, God forbid, or when Hitler danced or if the president's name is Franklin Milhouse Ronnie Shmuck — it never ends for us, it never goddamn ends. We are what we do, Solomon, and we can't escape that, even on the road to the Promised Land!"

"Listen to yourself, Mouse, you're blowing smoke. You say we have to live here, now, and then you yell about the Promised Land. For God's sake, what's the good of the promised land if it's always over the horizon, if it's always tomorrow?"

In his excitement, Mouse leaped up and stood in the jouncing carriage. "The Promised Land is now. The Promised Land is your heart, Solomon, your heart!"

Mouse tumbled and fell into Solomon's lap. He reached up and pulled Solomon's head down. "C'mere, shmuck!" he said. And he kissed Solomon.

"Hey," Emilio yelled, for he had been swiveling on the driver's seat as he kept one eye on the street ahead and the other eye on the passionate confrontation between his friends. "You guys better be careful."

"Careful?" Mouse grinned as he crawled out of Solomon's lap and returned to his own seat in the cab. "There's too much careful. We could drown in careful. Careful is the final bye-bye. Am I right, Solomon?"

"When you're right, you're right." Solomon smiled. He had been genuinely moved by Mouse's instinctive gesture of reconciliation, and he wished he were able to respond with equal spontaneity; but something held him back. What is it, he asked himself, what is the matter with me? Why can I not just reach out and crush this man in my arms and say, I love you, Mouse!

Because what the Mouse says frightens me, Solomon admitted to himself. Because if what he said is true, if we are what we do, then who am I? Kendal's husband? Darby's father? Brindig's toady? No, no longer that. The wood thrush fluttered in Solomon's mind, its wings weightless. But Solomon felt another weight; the steel letter opener in his hand. The knife he'd almost pushed into Brindig. My God, he thought, is that who I am?

"Listen, Mouse," he said urgently.

"Uh-huh."

But Solomon stopped. How do you explain to a friend that you wanted, really wanted, to kill a man . . . and that man's dead now? Mouse's previous words haunted Solomon. *We live with a terrible thing. We don't know if we're good. We ask ourselves, Are we good? Are we moral? Is there virtue in us? Those are terrible questions and we try to hide from them because the answers lie in the wilderness of ourselves.* Oh, Mouse, Solomon wanted to cry out, you are right. Each one of us lives in exile! Instead, he said:

"You smell like a radish."

"Hoo ha!" Mouse grinned. "You are what you eat."

Comradeship reestablished, both men leaned back in their seats. The mule clipclopped uptown. Solomon saw that Emilio had taken them up Third Avenue and soon they would be at the entrance to Grand Central. Small stores lined the avenue, but it was too late for most of the windows to be lighted. There was, however, one light burning behind the window of a camera store. The light illuminated an unusual display. Counting quickly, Solomon noted fifty photographs of a hand, its fingers relaxed and curling loosely inward.

Solomon was intrigued by the hands, and as the carriage rolled by the window, he craned around so that he might still observe the arrangement. Why fifty, he wondered, and all fifty the same? But were they? He squinted into the receding light. The fifty individual photographs were neatly arranged in five rows of ten photographs each. All were suspended within a wire framework, none receiving more prominence than the other. At first glance, when the carriage passed the window, Solomon had felt sure that the photos were absolutely identical. Now, peering from the back of the carriage, the configuration of the fingers seemed to vary slightly in the pictures. The fingers in the bottom row of prints looked as if they were straining to touch the palm of the hand, as if they were vibrating with an effort to press against their own flesh; but as the rows progressed upwards, the fingers seemed to lose their desire for this contact until, in the top row, the fingers had lost their tension and achieved a marvelous state of relaxation as if they recognized that whatever they had been holding or had been trying to touch was perishable and deserved release.

Solomon wished he knew whose hand it was and what it was that it had released. He looked at his own hand and saw that the fingers were clenched in empathetic reaction; suddenly he felt that if he could open and close his fingers at will he would be able to release the awful animal inside. It should be a simple act, almost one of reflex. But something stopped him. As he studied his hand he realized that he was picturing the hand of the thief whose fingers clutched the diamond. Had Brindig died with an open hand? Solomon couldn't remember. The carriage lurched abruptly as its wheels struck refuse in the street and, involuntarily, Solomon's fingers opened and he grabbed the door handle for support. What surprised him was an immediate sense of disloyalty. He felt somehow that Brindig would have wanted him to remain forever with his fingers clenched in a fist.

Morosely, he turned back to face the front of the carriage. He saw that Mouse sat quietly in his seat, his eyes closed, his body rocking gently to the rhythm of the cab. On the driver's seat, his back to Solomon, Emilio was singing softly to the mule. The men didn't speak until the carriage pulled up in front of the Lexington Avenue entrance to Grand Central Station. Solomon climbed down to the sidewalk.

"Thanks, Em," he said.

"You gonna be all right?" Emilio asked. "I could keep you company on the train, you want."

"I'm okay," Solomon said. "I'll see you both tomorrow."

"Listen, boychick," Mouse said, "get some sleep. Tomorrow you'll come in a little later. How could it hurt?"

"It couldn't hurt," they all said together and smiled at each other.

The station was dimly lighted and he hurried down the corridor toward the upper level information booth. He looked at the overhead clock and, seeing how late it was, understood why the station was so deserted. Then he realized that he'd missed the after-theater commuter's train. He faced an inordinate wait. He searched his pockets for change and walked to the bank of telephone booths across from the newsstand. He dialed his Westport number. The line was busy. Feeling he must have dialed a wrong number, for surely Kendal would not be on the phone at this late hour, he dialed again. The line was busy. He lit a cigarette, took two puffs, ground it beneath his heel, and dialed again. The line was busy. Who in God's name could Kendal be talking to? It must be the wrong number. He asked the operator to check. She reported there was no trouble on the line but before Solomon thought of asking her to break into Kendal's call she hung up.

He decided to call Brindig's wife. Regardless of the lateness of the hour, he knew that Mouse was right. She should not hear from a stranger about the murder of her husband.

Only once had he met Brindig's wife, Brenda. Solomon had been in Brindig's office at the studio. They had played their characteristic game.

Solomon had implored Brindig to extend the policy of TransGlobal in such a way that he, Solomon, could offer young novelists financial aid to assure the completion of their work, but when Brindig learned that the money expended would not buy a formal option he had resorted to his usual response.

"Hey, kid," he'd said, "don't get your tit in a wringer."

Unannounced, Brenda Brindig shimmered into the office. Shimmered was the operative word in Solomon's mind, for the woman was dressed in silvered slacks and blouse, the cloth so smooth and tight over her body that it looked like melted mercury. Her high-heeled opened sandals were also silvered, as was the paint on her toes. She wore silver lipstick and eyeshadow, and they emphasized the extraordinary suntan of her face. Her eyes were absolutely black as was her hair, cropped as short as a boy's.

"Listen, buster," she said to Brindig, her words rattling in fury, "you tap me again, it's over, fini, kaput. Capish?"

Brindig yawned. "Go away, sweetheart."

"I mean it, Ben. You take the goddamn bug off my telephone or I'll squeeze you dry!"

Brindig tugged at a hair in his nostril. "Say hello to Mr. Moon."

"Screw Mr. Moon." Her back to Solomon, she leaned so far over Brindig's desk that her blouse separated from her slacks and Solomon could see the thin hard muscles that flanked her spine and the top rise of her bronzed buttocks. With one hand she grabbed Brindig's jowls and shook them like a terrier would a weasel.

"Don't touch me 'less you want me, sweetheart," Brindig gurgled from his pinched jowls. He was totally unperturbed, grinning. Brenda relinquished her grip.

"Take me to lunch," she said.

"You got it," Brindig said. He nodded toward Solomon. "Now say hello to the nice man."

Brenda turned and looked at Solomon. Her hands resting on the desk behind her, she arched her back until Solomon thought that her hard little nipples would burst from the silvered cloth.

"Hello, nice man," she said.

"How do you do?" Solomon smiled and rose from his chair.

"You've got nice teeth," Brenda said. Solomon was aware that her voice had dropped almost a full octave, was now a husky purr. She opened her mouth wide and pointed to a rear molar. "Look at this, for chrissake, three times I've had it capped and it still breaks off. It's all jagged. Look at it."

"Yes," Solomon said.

"Feel it."

"I can see it." He heard Brindig chuckling.

"Feel it," Brenda said. "I'm not kidding." She took a step toward Solomon and lifted his hand. She guided his finger into her mouth. As he reluctantly touched the jagged molar, he felt Brenda's tongue slip wetly across his finger.

"How do you like them apples?" she asked, the words somewhat incoherent because of Solomon's finger in her mouth. Solomon saw that her huge, round black eyes gleamed with amusement. He wasn't sure if she meant how did he like her molar or how did he like her wet tongue, but he had an uneasy feeling that it was the latter. Solomon said nothing and withdrew his finger.

"C'mon, pussy," Brindig said. He cupped his hand around Brenda's right buttock and propelled her toward the door. "What do you want for lunch?"

"What do you think?" she said and made quick little biting noises as she left the office. Brindig turned in the doorway and winked at Solomon. "The best," he said. "I got the best." And then he, too, was gone.

As he sat in the stuffy telephone booth in Grand Central, Solomon wondered if Brenda's line was still tapped. He pulled his address book from his pocket, checked the number, and asked the operator to charge the call to his number, and to make it person-to-person. It was answered on the second ring.

"*Sí?*" It was a Mexican maid.

The operator explained to her that a Mr. Moon wished to speak to a Mrs. Brindig.

"She no wish, please," the maid said. "*No mas*, she say. *No mas telefone, por favor.*" The maid was crying.

Christ, Solomon thought, she knows. The police have called. "Please," he interrupted, "tell Mrs. Brindig it's important. Tell her —"

"Do you wish to speak to this party, sir?" the operator asked.

"— that I was with Mr. Brindig when —" Solomon continued.

"I'm sorry, sir," the operator said firmly, "but you cannot —"

"*Uno momento,*" the maid said. Solomon could hear the faint click of heels on a tile floor.

"Yes?" It was Brenda's voice. Clipped. Curt. Full of metal. The operator told her it was a person-to-person call. After a moment of silence Brenda said, "Yeah, all right, go ahead."

"Mrs. Brindig, this is Solomon Moon. Do you remember me?"

"No."

My goddamn finger was in your mouth, lady, Solomon wanted to shout. "We met in Ben's office."

"So?"

"I guess you've heard what —"

"The police called."

"I'm sorry. I'm really terribly, terribly sorry."

"I'll tell you something, Mr. Noon —"

"Moon."

"You're full of shit."

"What?" Solomon was nonplussed.

"You're full of shit. All of you are full of shit. You're not sorry. Nobody's sorry. Nobody liked Ben. Except me. So I'm the only one who's not full of shit. Do I make myself clear, Mr. Noon? This conversation is terminated."

"I was there," Solomon shouted, hoping she had not hung up. He heard her sharp intake of breath.

"I saw it happen," Solomon said. "I saw what Ben did. I wish I could explain, Mrs. Brindig. I mean, I don't think he thought about it, he just —"

"I know what happened."

"The police told you."

"My father told me."

"Your father?"

"Labowski. Sidney Labowski, the jeweler."

"Oh, my God, I didn't realize that —" Solomon paused as he remembered Brindig's look of outrage when the young hoodlum knocked off Mrs. Labowski's wig. Christ, Solomon thought, it was Brenda's mother. "Listen, Mrs. Brindig, if —"

"Brenda."

"— there's anything I can do —"

"Tell me, Mr. Noon, did you like Ben?"

Solomon saw the lighted windowfront and the display of fifty photographed hands and wondered if the clenched fingers were holding lies.

"No, Brenda," he said quietly, "I did not like Ben."

"Jesus," she said, "an honest man. Maybe you're not so full of shit after all. You want to help me, there is something you could do."

"What?"

"Bring Ben to me."

"I beg your pardon?" Surely he had heard incorrectly.

"My father's an old man and he's not well. And you can see the state my mama's in. I think it'd kill them to have to bring Ben back."

"Yes, sure," Solomon said, "I see that. I can understand that, but maybe the police —"

"They already told me. They don't need him." She laughed harshly. "I mean, what the hell are they going to do with him? Listen, Mr. Noon —"

"Moon."

"I wish to hell you'd stop correcting me."

"Sorry."

"I'm not asking for a big deal. You don't have to wrap him up and put him on your shoulder. My father's arranged the whole thing. He's going to have Ben cremated. It's what Ben wanted. He'll be in a little box. You can carry a little box, can't you?"

"Yes. Yes, of course. When exactly were you thinking of?"

"Tomorrow. No, day after tomorrow."

"What!"

"It has to be."

"God, I don't know."

"You really are full of shit, aren't you?"

"It's just I've got these things to do."

"What things?"

Solomon searched for *things*. "There's this script. *Shadow on the Grass*. Ben wants it fixed so that —"

"Ben wants it fixed?" Brenda's voice was incredulous. "*Ben* wants it fixed? What are you, crazy?"

"Oh. Yeah. Right." Solomon was silent. He gave up. "Okay. I'll be there."

"Bring your tennis stuff," Brenda said.

"What?"

"I'm sure you heard me."

"My tennis stuff?"

"Thank you, Mr. Noon." Brenda Brindig hung up.

"Moon," Solomon said to himself and, somewhat dazed, he replaced the telephone receiver. It must be the shock, he thought. How could a bereaved woman think of tennis after the murder of her husband? For just an instant, he had an insane vision of stepping off the airplane in his tennis shorts, a racket under one arm, an urn under the other. God, it's catching, he thought.

He called Westport; and still the line was busy. He wished he were home. Goddamn trains. Then he thought of Darby. She could drive him. He dialed her number. He hoped she had not turned off her phone as she sometimes did.

"Ummmmm?" She coughed softly and her voice was thick with sleep. "Hello?"

"I'm sorry to wake you, honey," Solomon said, "but —"

"Dad? What time is it?" Then she was instantly awake. "What's the matter — is something wrong? Is it Mom?"

"No, no, it's okay," Solomon said quickly. "I'm stuck downtown at Grand Central. You think you could drive me home? I know it's a helluva nuisance but —"

"Don't be silly. Of course I will."

"It's awful goddamn late but —"

"Dad, please. It's all right. Honest. Where'll I meet you?"

Solomon knew that it would be most convenient for her to take the West Side Highway and that it would take time for her to get her pickup out of the garage.

"I'll walk over to Fifth," he said. "I'll meet you in front of the library."

"Okay. I'll get there as fast as I can. Daddy?"

"Yeah?"

"This time of night, don't go wandering around, okay? I mean, the streets are full of crazies."

"Yeah," Solomon said, the image of Brindig's faceless corpse imprinted on his mind. "I know."

He left the station from the Vanderbilt Avenue exit and walked west on Forty-Fourth Street, pausing for a moment to stare into the windows of Brooks Brothers men's store. The expensive clothing was fashioned to please moderate men — men who would shun excessive behavior and who found comfort in restraint. Careful men, Solomon noted, like me. Suddenly, Solomon turned and headed for Forty-Second Street, where the night people roamed. He no longer wanted to be careful. Feeling a terrible need to test himself, wanting to learn if he had Ben Brindig's courage — senseless perhaps, but at least untainted by careful judgment — he kicked at refuse in the street, swore out loud, stared belligerently at the few men or women who passed him. He wanted to provoke a dangerous encounter. But like Mouse long ago in Fort Riley, he telegraphed his intention, and those who saw the strange, fierce fire in his eyes moved out of his path.

A young man, lithe and well dressed, drifted around the corner of Madison Avenue and moved in Solomon's direction. He moved gracefully, slipping into darkened doorways, then almost dancing out, his arms arched above his head, his body slowly twirling, studying his figure in the shop windows as if he were judging a secret ballet.

But he performed with no happiness. He looked forlorn, lost, aware of nothing but his own dark silhouette flashing across the windowpanes. He seemed, Solomon thought, to be looking for a friend behind the glass, hoping that some figure would reach through the glass and touch him and cry out, "Here! You belong here!"

He seemed an outcast from all things real; and Solomon understood.

For just a moment, Solomon stopped on the street and watched as the dancer moved closer. Then Solomon quickened his pace, started across the street, suddenly not wanting to intrude on the dancer's fantasy. His back was turned to him when he heard the muffled shout. Solomon whirled and saw two other men burst out of one of the darkened doorways and hurl themselves onto the young man, their fists slamming at him.

The rage in Solomon exploded. He raced toward the thrashing men and as he passed a parked car he reached out and snapped off the radio antenna. Slashing it in front of him, he charged into the men, snapping his steel whip across the backs and necks of the two attackers, lashing at their faces, ripping their skin, his wrath blinding him to their cries of pain, *the thing* within him roaring in his ears.

It ended as quickly as it began. The two attackers scrambled away and dashed up the street. The dancer rose from the pavement and staggered toward Solomon, but what he saw frightened him terribly and slowly he backed away and finally ran into the night.

Solomon's whole body was shaking, not purged of the explosive heat in his belly, unfulfilled, and he struck out blindly with the steel whip, not caring what he hit, needing only to strike something, anything. He lurched at a car in the street and raised the antenna and whipped it down, lashing faster and faster at the hood of the car, scourging the metal, ripping it, until the antenna broke in his hands and flew into the gutter. He leaned over the car, sweat stinging his eyes, gasping, unable to catch his breath, waiting for his body to stop trembling.

"Jesus," he whispered to himself. "Oh, Jesus!"

Finally he was still; but when at last he reached the library's steps he had to lean against one of the cold stone lions until Darby's truck pulled up.

As her father pulled himself into the cab of the truck, Darby saw that his eyes were downcast and that he was staring at his own hand, whose fingers were clenching and unclenching spastically. His face was filled with remorse.

"Dad," she said, "you look awful!"

"Well," he said hoarsely, "it hasn't been a good night."

As they drove up the West Side Highway, continued on the Henry Hudson Parkway, finally moving north along the Merritt, Solomon told his story. He spoke slowly and in great detail, allowing himself lapses of silence, during which he closed his eyes and leaned his head back against the seat and listened to the occasional clunk of a coin as Darby fed the toll booths. Darby asked no questions, did not once interrupt. She sensed his need to purge himself; and the horror of the event was accentuated by Solomon's lingering recitation. He remembered everything. He left out nothing. Minutely, he described the flannel cloth draped over Labowski's shoulder, the color of Mrs. Labowski's wig, the triumphant but melancholy sound of Mouse's *shofar*, the bright pink of Brindig's blood as it ran with rain into the street, the thin crack of the pistol, the ululating woman, two dead men.

He did not tell her about his encounter with the dancer. Darby wept so that she could not drive. They had entered Westport. She pulled into the deserted parking lot of the Red Barn Restaurant and turned off the ignition. She lowered her head to the steering wheel and sobbed. Solomon held her hand but said nothing. When at last her weeping had subsided, he talked very quietly.

"I don't know if Ben was a happy man. I don't know what he wanted in his life. But I think this, and I want you to understand it. I think he died for the wrong reason."

"He didn't die for the diamond, Daddy. You said so yourself. Mouse explained it."

"I know that."

"Then don't put him down. Can't you see that he couldn't bear to watch that woman shamed? What he did was part of him. Maybe it was foolish, or crazy. I don't know. But he did it because he had to."

"He did it," Solomon said, "because he felt Mrs. Labowski had been violated. It was what he'd been taught as a Jew. And that's sad. That's so goddamn sad."

"I don't understand you."

"Try. That's all I'm asking. I don't care if Ben was a Jew. What I'm —"

"You should. You should care."

"Darby, please, let me finish. The minute a man labels himself he becomes special. Not only to those around him but to himself. Countries do the same thing. They pride themselves on their borders, and the men who live within those borders invest themselves with a strange sense of . . . of sovereignty . . . some kind of divine attribute. It's as if the labels on the package were more important than the contents. If we go on like this, if we continue to label ourselves Jew or Catholic, black or white, Godfearing or atheist, the circles we draw around ourselves are going to grow tighter and tighter, and the more we'll be forced to arbitrarily defend these boundaries, these circles, these goddamned circles. It's what could happen to you, Darby, if you try to become something that you're not."

"I'm not trying," Darby said quietly. "I *am* a Jew."

"Goddamn it," Solomon exploded. "Don't you listen? A Jew is getting your head blown off. You want to become some kind of a fucking martyr, is that it?"

"No," Darby answered, her voice low and even. "But I'd be in good company, wouldn't I? I think, maybe, you die in good company only if you live the same way. I mean, you get what you give, don't you?"

"Ask Ben Brindig," Solomon said bitterly.

There was a long silence before Darby spoke again. "I think," she said tightly, "we'd better go home."

And that, said Solomon to himself, is that. The end of a perfect day. No, not quite. He still had to look into the eyes of a woman whose trust he'd violated. As Darby put the truck in gear and they drove home, Solomon flinched inwardly at the terrible tales he was about to tell his wife. He knew he had to inform her about Brindig's murder, and he felt that if he did not immediately reveal his foolish adultery, the secret would fester between them like a sore. He hoped terribly that she would understand, for if she did she might be able to explain it to him.

When they arrived at the house, Solomon was startled to see all the lights blazing. Kendal had obviously heard the truck for she threw open the front door and ran down the steps to meet them.

"Christ," she said to Solomon, "where have you been?"

"I'm sorry," Solomon said. "I tried to get home early, but —"

"God," Kendal interrupted, "I tried every bloody hotel you've ever stayed at. I called the office I tried Mouse and Emilio but I couldn't get anybody."

"It wasn't Dad's fault," Darby said quickly, and Solomon thought how much more gracious she is than I. Their dissension did not prevent her from being fair. "Something awful's happened, Mom."

Kendal stared at Darby and then at Solomon. "How could you know?" she asked in a trembling voice. "He said he couldn't reach you. That's why he called here. God, Solomon, what does it mean? Why would anyone do such an awful thing?"

Solomon was confused. Could she have heard about Brindig? Is that what she meant? "Ben?" he asked. "You mean Ben?"

"The tongues, damn it," she cried. "Those Christ-awful tongues!" But as she looked at Solomon, she realized that he didn't know what she was talking about. "Oh, Lord. Oh, dear Lord!" She could feel her body shaking and then Solomon's arms around her as he and Darby led her back to the house. When they reached the kitchen, Kendal seemed numb and unable to talk and Solomon sat with her in the corner alcove, unconsciously stroking her hair, and he asked Darby to heat some milk. Gradually, Kendal's shaking stopped. They all sat at the table, steaming cups of milk before them, and Solomon felt a wave of familial love, a binding such as he had not felt for a long, long time.

"Now take your time," he said quietly to Kendal. "I don't know what you mean by . . . by . . . tongues. Someone called you, is that right?"

"Callahan," Kendal said. "He's a policeman . . . or state trooper, or something."

"Callahan?" Darby sat up straight. "You mean Wilfred Callahan — Sergeant Wilfred Callahan — in Vermont?"

"Yes."

Solomon glanced at his daughter. "You know him?"

"I met him. He's a very nice guy. What'd he want, Mom?"

Kendal stared at the steam rising from her cup and shook her head slightly, frowned. "It doesn't make sense. It was a terrible thing to do."

"What, darling?" Solomon asked patiently. "What did someone do?" For a moment he was sorry he'd asked, for when Kendal raised her head there was an awful look in her eyes.

"Someone . . . someone . . ." she faltered. "Someone . . ." She looked as if she were about to be sick.

"Shhhhh," Solomon said. "Take it easy. Just take it easy.'

"Someone nailed tongues to our door. They did. They really did."

"Tongues!" Solomon stared at her. "You mean . . . real tongues?"

"They were very real, Solomon. Callahan said they were cut out of two cows that belonged to Ray Poole."

"God," Darby exclaimed. "That's sick!"

"Jesus!" Solomon was bewildered. "Why would anyone do that? What did Callahan say? Where was Tuttle? Did he talk to Tuttle?"

"He said that Jabez told him that he hadn't seen anybody around. He didn't hear anybody . . . doesn't know anything about it. Callahan wanted to know if we could think of anyone who'd do something like that . . . to us . . . to . . ." She turned and looked at her daughter and her eyes were fearful. "To Darby."

"To *Darby?*" Solomon was bewildered, his muscles tense, his pulse beating quickly. "What do you mean? What are you talking about?"

"Callahan said the picture on the end of the wall was missing. I told him it was Darby — when she was on the pony."

"It's got to be some kind of a freak," Solomon said, his voice too loud, his body suddenly chilled with the picture in his mind. "I mean, isn't that what Callahan thinks?"

"He doesn't know," Kendal answered. "He said he's never seen anything like this."

"I think Dad's right," Darby blurted out. "There's a whacked-out nut on every corner of the street. Look what happened to Mr. Brindig. He was just standing there and . . ." She paused and looked at her mother's tired face. "Oh, God, you don't know, do you? I'm sorry, I didn't mean to . . ."

"It's okay," Solomon said quietly. "It's okay."

This time, when he related the story of Brindig's death, he left out all the details, trying hard to be short and quick, eliminating the dreadful quality of the scene, censoring the grotesque, softening the shock as best he could. He knew that Kendal had had more than enough for one night; he knew that he would not be able to disclose his infidelity.

When he finished, Solomon held Kendal's hand, but when he pressed her fingers there was no response, and he saw that she was gazing abstractedly around the kitchen as if she were looking for some familiar object upon which to focus her sense of reality. Then her fingers spasmed in his palm and she rose from the table.

"I'm going to be sick," she said.

Darby followed her out of the kitchen and Solomon heard their footsteps retreat to the second floor. He put the milk cups and saucers in the sink, ran hot water over them, scrubbed them, dried them, put them away. He walked through the downstairs rooms, turning off all the lights, then moved onto the porch and sat in the glider and listened to the wind in the trees and wondered if there was a stranger walking through the woods of Vermont and who he was and what he wanted and why he would hammer such terrible objects to the door of his house.

And he wished suddenly that he'd been there.

His hand closed tightly on the arm of the glider and he squeezed until he could feel pain shoot through his fingers, then released his hand and raised it, pleased at how steady it was, and slowly curled his trigger finger into position. Holding his breath, sighting, his anger rising, he shot the stranger through the heart.

On his way to bed, Solomon passed Darby's open door.

"She's asleep," Darby said.

"Good." He hesitated, then continued. "May I come in?"

"Oh, Dad." She looked at him as if he should know better than to seek permission. She was dressed in a pair of his old pajamas, their folds engulfing her, making her seem tiny and vulnerable. She patted a place on the bed next to her and Solomon sat there.

"Your friend, Mouse," he began.

"Your friend, too."

"Yeah, my friend, too. He has an expression. 'Life,' he says, 'is not always pancakes and peachy pie.' He sure called it right today, didn't he?"

"He's usually right, isn't he?" Darby smiled.

"Well," Solomon said, "he bats pretty good. Not perfect, but good."

"I'd like to do that with you," Darby said.

"What?"

"Bat pretty good."

"What we talked about in the truck," Solomon said, "what I was trying to say is that I don't want you to get hurt. I wouldn't like that. I wouldn't like that a lot."

"I know, Dad."

"Can't you just let it alone? I know it's hard for you to believe this, but sometimes . . . sometimes it's just better to let things alone."

"But not me," Darby said gently. "I don't want to be left alone. I've been there. I've been there a long time. I'm the best there is at being alone and it's no good. It doesn't work. It's a lousy place to live."

"Oh, Jesus, Darby," Solomon whispered, "don't you think I know that?" He rose from the bed and walked out of the room and closed the door quietly behind him, feeling alienated from the world of his daughter, feeling terribly alone.

Kendal was asleep. She was frowning and her mouth twitched slightly as if she were talking to someone in an unpleasant dream. Carefully, not wanting to awaken her, Solomon slipped into bed beside her. Her body jerked and her hand trembled on the sheet and she mumbled. Solomon leaned closer. At first her words rattled incoherently in her throat but then Solomon heard: ". . . and deliver us from evil . . . is the kingdom . . ." The mumbling stopped. She was silent.

Easing away from her, Solomon lay back on the bed and stared at the window, watching the curtains move in the night wind, watching their amorphous shapes drift back and forth as if, he thought bitterly, they were waiting for a stranger to thrust them aside, a stranger with tongues in his hand. He wished the curtains were alive so that he could strangle them.

Gradually, exhausted by the day's events, he forced the tension from his body, closed his eyes, and accepted the analgesia of sleep.

But he dreamed.

Uncontrolled in a warp of time and place, the dream turned backwards. They invaded the piny woods, he and Kendal, and watched the moon rise and laughed and talked of hummingbirds and listened to an owl. They held hands.

They unpacked. The placement of porcelain was a taming act.

In his sleep, Solomon forced the dream forward, forged the climactic act. He and Kendal sat in an empty room of the farmhouse and waited to hear a stranger knock. They knew he was coming. Solomon anticipates a boom of knuckles and is certain that when the door is opened a phosphorescent gunman smelling of metal will enter. But there is no boom. There is only a timid scratching at the door. It swings open. The stranger is here. Cautiously, he shuffles into the room, an old man in a short-peaked cap. An old man with hair in his ears. The hem of his coarse blouse is shredded, its dark wool hanging in strips as if it had been neatly scissored by the lashes of a whip. The stranger's eyes are downcast and he brings no fragrance of metal into the dreamed room. He smells of steaming piss.

Solomon knows why. But he cannot move. He cannot wake. He cannot stop the dream.

His gaze still turned down, the stranger smiles and blood runs from between his teeth. He crooks his finger and beckons. Kendal and Solomon follow him upstairs, Solomon avoiding corners, into an imaginery room of white. There is one square of black within the room. It is the bed. They stand there, those three, side by side. Desire, unidentified with lust, fills the room with frankincense and myrrh, and Solomon reaches inward toward his sorrow, toward a wistful memory of his beginning, but he grasps nothing, touches nothing, feels only the fetid air that swirls around *the thing* within.

The dreamed moon, winding upwards in the night, cleaves a splendid passage to the bed. Now, Solomon prays, now in this luminous light savagery is dead. But a wind pulsates the windowpane and the stranger's dread reflection quivers. He lifts his hands toward the night, his thumbs as malevolent as thorns. He drifts toward the window, *through* the window, floats forward in the midnight air, and engulfed in the radiance of the moon, plunges to the limb of a pomegranate tree.

But there are no pomegranate trees in these woods, thinks Solomon. Startled, he turns to his wife. She laughs and touches him lightly and whispers him to be still. Her breath is sweet and Solomon knows he will not wholly die.

But does. Dies with the stranger in a pomegranate slide. Together, sparrows side by side, they plummet to the ground below the tree, two Jews shitting diamonds, burning their final passage in a blaze of white jewels.

And then, finally, come the words from his companion in the ground.

"We shall meet," says the blood-mouthed Jew. "We shall meet from time to time."

Rust rising in his throat, Solomon lies astounded in the recess of his grave.

And does not know if he is dreaming or awake.

20

Riordan knew that on the following day bulldozers would bury the waste that lay scattered in heaps on the dank ground of Down Derry's dump. There were things he needed, so he and Jubal crouched on the roadside along the ten-foot-high plank fence that enclosed the dump. A single pair of headlights moved toward them. The farm truck passed and the headlights did not reveal their position. The driver of the truck saw nothing but the curve of the road.

Riordan ran lightly to the padlocked gate. On various nights when he and Jubal had scavenged the dump he had noticed that the lock had been carelessly secured. It was not the case now. The gate was tightly closed. They would have to scale the wall. He motioned to his son and Jubal understood. The boy retreated from the fence then ran hard at it. His feet scrambled against the planking and almost ran up its height until he managed to grasp the top of the boards and pull himself over. He straddled the fence and leaned down. Riordan stretched and took the boy's hand. He levered himself up the fence. They both dropped to the other side.

Down Derry did not recycle its waste nor did the village have an assigned area for sanitary landfill. They resorted to an open dump where, once or twice a week, the town's bulldozers would dig deep pits and then scrape refuse into them. In between these burial sessions, the ground was littered with what the inhabitants of the village no longer considered useful or valuable. Riordan knew better.

Although the area of the dump covered several acres, its wooden enclosure contained the odor of discarded garbage mixed with the lingering acrid smell of burnt rubber. The air was redolent with decay. The ground was soggy with layers of wet newspapers and moldering scraps of cloth and the only sound in the dump was the scratching of rats.

Riordan had not informed Jubal of his purpose but had ordered the boy to search for certain specific things. Jubal hunted carefully, for he knew that he was expected to turn over mounds of debris; but he feared that as he dug into the dark heaps of garbage he would encounter broken glass that might cut his fingers so badly that he would be unable to strum his harp. When his father was not looking he resorted to kicking through the clutter rather than risk damage to his hands, but when he felt his father's eyes upon him he leaned quickly to the ground and dug his hands through whatever refuse lay before him. He hoped a rat would not bite him. At one point he struck something hard and cold. He pulled at it. When it came free from where it had been javelined, he saw that it was a long, rusted crowbar, its clawed end split and dulled from abuse. He held it up and whistled softly. Riordan turned and nodded with approval.

Riordan was on his hands and knees astride a mound of tin cans and plastic containers which had once held Clorox and fruit juices. The broken glass from whiskey and wine and beer bottles surrounded him. He dug into the mess but found nothing he wanted, so moved to another stinking little hill. He was about to abandon that area, too, when his gaze fell upon an oblong metal box whose hasp was broken. It was a tool box, its hinged shelves sprung, their compartments dented out of shape. Inside the box were broken tools: a hammer with half a head, saw blades that were almost toothless, screwdrivers whose metal ends were rounded into worthlessness, a chisel. Riordan examined the chisel. The thick hickory handle was split, but he knew that it could be re-united if carefully wrapped with tape or finely wound string. The cutting edge of the tool was cracked unevenly. Sledged against stone, the blade would make uneven cuts, but the job for which Riordan wanted it did not call for pure precision. He pocketed the chisel.

Jubal walked quietly across the rubble, startled once when a rat ran between his legs, and informed his father that he had discovered discarded rope in one corner of the dump. Riordan hurried to it. It was half buried under fishheads and coffee grounds and the parings from rotten vegetables; the rope was crusted with oil and slime, and many of the strands were shredded.

The old man pulled it loose. It was many feet long and he saw that it too could be repaired. He coiled it swiftly into loops and hung the circles from his shoulder.

Having found what they wanted, Riordan and Jubal started back across the dump toward the board fence. Suddenly, the old man stopped, peering intently toward a plastic garbage bag. Its sides were split, and bulging from the opening were an old shoe and some crumpled cloth. Riordan moved to it and further split the sack. It was filled with a woman's discarded clothing: stained blouses, a torn skirt, frayed scarves, an old overcoat holed by moths. Among the odds and ends was a black velveteen purse appropriate for evening wear. The cloth was slit and had lost its sheen, but threaded on both sides of the bag, in a matching design, were little flowers of false pearls.

Softly, Riordan laughed. He picked up the purse and tore a single pearl from its cloth. His shoulders shaking with mirth, he rubbed it clean, placed it in one pocket of his cloak. He beckoned the boy to follow him, and they left the dump as they had entered it.

Back in their mountain cave, Jubal and Riordan repaired the rope and the handle of the chisel. While they worked the old man softly sang Gregorian chants, stopping occasionally to chuckle as he touched the pocket in which he kept the pearl. Jubal wanted to inquire about the purpose of the pearl, but he knew that if his father wished him to know he would tell. Since the old man did not speak, Jubal contented himself by secretly touching that which gave him pleasure — the photograph of the girl hidden beneath his shirt. When at last the rope and the chisel were in good order, Riordan asked the boy to come outside and bring the crowbar he'd found in the dump.

They stood in the clearing outside the cave. Riordan's gaze swept the ground, lingering over irregular slabs of rock, most of which were partially covered with moss or half-hidden under brush. He moved to one of them and crouched alongside it. Using a thick staff of wood, he scraped along one side of the rock. In a few minutes he had removed enough loose dirt to reveal the contour of the rock. It was more than an inch thick, jagged along the edge, and most of its surface was heavily covered with vegetation. The old man studied it and then nodded with satisfaction. He showed Jubal how to use the crowbar to pry the rock loose and helped the boy by levering it with his staff of wood.

They worked all night, prying loose great slabs of rock and stacking them under a huge maple tree whose lower branches spread some distance over the clearing. It was exhausting work but Riordan never suggested that they stop for rest. He satisfied himself, and made Jubal do the same, by lying on his belly and lowering his head into the stream, drinking deeply of the cold water. They both munched hazelnuts they found scattered on the ground. Riordan crushed their shells between the heels of his hands.

When they finished, Riordan allowed Jubal to rest by the stream. The boy soaked his hands and listened to the night wind. Riordan entered the cave then emerged with the stone chisel and a wooden mallet, the newly repaired rope coiled again over his shoulder. He moved to the stone stack. Grunting with the effort, he slid the heavy top slab from the pile and laid it flat on the ground. He uncoiled one end of the rope and dangled a length against the thickness of the stone. With his chisel he drew vertical lines on either side of the rope, measuring its width against the stone. He hunkered next to the stone, shuffled around it and marked the width of the rope on each of the four sides. He sat down, legs folded like Buddha, and, using the mallet as a hammer, started to carve niches in the measured markings. His chisel pinged against the stone slab, ringing cleanly in the mountain air. When he was through with the first stone slab he started on the second. Stone by stone, his chisel rang. He never rested until he finished carving the rope-width niches into each of the four sides of every stone slab. Then he smoothed the channels with a piece of granite. He greased each of them with bear fat. He tested the fit of the rope into each niche. It fit perfectly. Running the rope across the length and width of one slab, using the greased niches as anchoring channels, he tied it so that a slip knot rested on the top of one flat side, the long length of rope running free above it. He tossed the free end of the rope over a strong branch of the maple. Slowly, he pulled on it. His back bent with strain but the slab rose in the air, and when it dangled some ten feet in the air he used a nearby stump to tie off the rope end he held in his hands.

Riordan moved under the dangerously swaying stone slab and, occasionally glancing up to be sure that he remained centered under it, he used his beaver-toothed knife to etch into the soft ground an outline of a man lying beneath the suspended stone. When he finished, he held up a tall branch. One end touched the hanging stone slab, the other end reached to the chest of the earth-drawn figure. Riordan returned to the stump and freed the rope. Bracing himself against the weight, he slowly lowered the massive stone.

Riordan turned to Jubal who, fascinated by the actions of his father, had not moved from the bank of the stream.

"Peine forte et dure," Riordan said. "We will press truth from the Jew."

The old man began to sing.

21

Unrefreshed by his nightmared sleep, Solomon awakened to the sound of a bell. Unsure whether he was still dreaming, he remained still. The bell continued. It was the telephone. Gritty-eyed, he removed the pillow from his head and turned toward Kendal. She was gone. The harsh jangling of the phone cleared his mind and recalled the events of yesterday. Reluctantly, he lifted the receiver.

"Yeah?"

"Solomon, it's Mouse."

"Oh. Yeah."

"You get any sleep?"

"I don't know. I guess so."

"Last night," Mouse asked, "you get hold of Mrs. Brindig?"

"Yeah."

"You know then, huh?"

"Know what?"

"The thing she wants."

Solomon recalled his strange conversation with Brenda Brindig. "Sure," he said, "she wants to play tennis."

"What?"

"Nothing."

"You okay?" the Mouse asked.

"Terrific," Solomon said.

"Mr. Labowski called me. We arranged where he'd leave it so you can pick it up."

"Leave it?"

"You know," Mouse said, "what you got to take out to Los Angeles."

"Oh, Jesus," Solomon said.

"They're going to cremate the body later today. I told Mr. Labowski he could leave the urn at Em's this evening. I couldn't figure any other place. That okay, Solomon?"

"God," Solomon said, "at a deli?"

"Yeah, I know. I just couldn't figure."

"Yeah."

"So you'll be in later, right?"

"Okay. Right."

"You feeling any better? How'd Kendal take it?"

"I'll see you later, Mouse."

"Yeah. *Zei gezunt.*" He hung up.

Zei gezunt. What the hell did that mean? Solomon stared at the ceiling. He could not erase the picture of Brindig's faceless head in the gutter. The abruptness of death was startling and made Solomon terribly conscious of the finiteness of a man's life. From downstairs he heard the soft chimes of the grandfather clock and, lying in the empty bed, he felt as if the ticking of his own life's clock were growing fainter and fainter. He glanced around the room, almost expecting to see that his own ashes had collected like dust on the polished furniture. One quick swipe with a cloth and he would be gone.

His gaze caught the table clock. Surprised at the lateness of the hour, he rose quickly and entered the bathroom. The thought of following his usual routine of pushups and bath displeased him. He would, he decided, no longer be a victim of his own dull patterns, including the pattern of mediocrity in his professional life. He wondered if his thoughts of rebellion would please Brindig. He thought so. He hoped so. Startled somewhat by the train of his thoughts, he realized that he wanted to please the dead man, the man of commitments, but that he was tired of trying to please anyone else.

As he shaved he peered out the bathroom window. He saw Kendal and Darby, both in bathrobes, sitting on lawn chairs by the pool, drinking from mugs of coffee. They were deep in conversation. Looking down at them, Solomon had the novel sensation that they were visitors who had dropped by unannounced but who, in the interest of his privacy, had elected to remain remote, content to comment on the garden, the weather, the color of the sky. Objectively, he noted the intensity of Darby's pose. She seemed marvelously balanced on her chair as if, at any moment, she could bounce with impetuous flair. Not so objectively, he saw how lovely Kendal looked and with what easy grace she gestured.

So different from Rena Nussbaum's hard, staccato moves.

Shit.

He brushed his teeth, combed his hair, dressed, went down to the kitchen. He poured a mug of coffee and went outside onto the lawn. When he joined his wife and daughter he saw that a small transistor radio rested at Darby's feet, low, soft music coming from it. Kendal saw his glance.

"I called John Luckey and told him you'd be sleeping late today," Kendal said.

"Thanks." Solomon looked at the radio.

"I thought maybe there'd be something on the news about . . ."

"Ben," Solomon said.

"Yes."

"Was there?"

"Just a mention. Nothing much. They still haven't identified the young man."

"I guess it doesn't much matter now, does it?"

"No. No, I guess not."

Solomon smiled at his daughter. "How are you, kiddo?"

"Okay, Dad."

"Would you do me a favor?"

"Sure."

"I'd like to talk to your mother."

"Oh. Okay. I've got to get dressed anyway." She rose and started toward the house, paused, then turned back. "Hey, Dad, did you see Rena yesterday?"

Solomon looked quickly at Kendal, then looked away. Kendal saw the look. She leaned down from her chair and began to pick crabgrass from the lawn.

"Yeah," Solomon said, his eyes on his coffee mug. "Yeah, I saw Rena."

"Who's Rena?" Kendal asked, searching for more of the offending crabgrass.

"You know, Mom," Darby answered. "The woman who's producing our show. I told you about her. She's terrific. I did kind of a sneaky thing. I asked Daddy to have lunch with her so they could talk about a cable deal." She turned to Solomon. "Did you see the Giacomettis? Aren't they incredible?"

"You go to the museum for lunch?" Kendal asked.

"Rena has them," Darby said. "She collects them."

"Oh." Kendal tugged harder at the crabgrass.

"I'll see you later," Darby said and ran up to the house.

Kendal stopped picking at the grass and leaned back in her chair and looked at Solomon. She was surprised that he'd dressed in a gray tweed sports jacket, gray flannels, a black-checked gingham shirt, tassled black mocassins.

"You look nice," she said. "You going to the office that way?"

"No. I have to go to Los Angeles."

"Oh?"

Solomon told her about Brenda's request. About the urn. Not about the tennis stuff.

"Were they good together, Solomon? Were they happy?"

"Yes. I think so."

"It's going to be awful for her," Kendal said. "Being alone now."

Solomon took a deep breath, then sat on the grass next to Kendal's chair.

"Last night," he said, "in your sleep, I heard you praying."

"Was I? I don't remember."

"Do you do that a lot? I mean, more than I know?"

"I don't know. I guess so. I don't really think much about it." She stared again at the crabgrass. "Habit, I suppose. I mean, when we're in trouble we all do things that . . . I don't know . . . we all do things."

"Yeah," Solomon said. "We all do things. I did something. Yesterday." In what appeared to be an involuntary motion, Kendal glanced toward the outdoor shower she had attached to the barn. Solomon felt as if his whole body winced. "What I did —"

"Solomon," Kendal said quietly, "you don't have to tell me."

"I guess I already did," he said.

She nodded. "Yesterday was not a good day for us."

There was a long silence between them, broken, finally, by static on the little transistor radio. Solomon twirled the dial until he heard music. It was a broadcast of hard rock. He dialed again until he heard the sound of a piano and the melody was clear.

"Basie?" Kendal asked.

"Uh-uh. Price. Sammy Price. Used to play with Bechet. Christ, wasn't he fine?"

"He was fine," Kendal said. She closed her eyes and listened to the soft piano blues and she felt that she was back in Solomon's Greenwich

Village apartment on the night they'd first made love and, as if Solomon were reading Bechet's words, she heard his voice. *The music, it's that road. There's good things alongside it, and there's miseries. But the music itself, the road itself, there's no stopping that. It goes on all the time.* She opened her eyes and looked at Solomon. He was watching her and she knew that he, too, was thinking of that night.

"We don't hear it anymore, do we?" he asked quietly.

"No," she said.

"We got off that road."

"How does that happen?" Kendal asked. "Was it my fault?"

"Yours, mine, I don't know," he answered. "There are an awful lot of roads people take."

"How do you mean?"

Solomon was silent for a moment, searching for a way to explain his thoughts. He placed his empty coffee mug on the ground and took Kendal's hand. "Roads," he said, "they're just journeys, aren't they? — just journeys toward something, away from something. I think you, me, all of us — we're always on some kind of journey. We're never off the roads and they lead to — to what? — to foreign countries, I guess. I mean the countries inside you, the alien places. And each time we move down one of those roads we see a different landscape. Behind that landscape is a mystery. Does that make any sense?"

"What kind of a mystery?" Kendal asked.

"I don't know," Solomon smiled. "If I did, it wouldn't be a mystery, would it?"

"What about us?" Kendal asked softly. "Are we in the same foreign country? Are we on the same road?"

"I think," he said, "we want different things."

"Oh, Solomon, that's not true!"

"I don't know where it came from," Solomon said slowly. "Your father, I guess, or Upper Chine."

"Say what you mean, Solomon." Kendal withdrew her hand from his. It was an unconscious and self-protective gesture — as if in order to receive his criticism she needed physical isolation.

"Maybe it was the Church of England," he continued, thinking of her nighttime prayer. "Christ, I don't know, maybe you're born with it."

"I don't know what it is," Kendal said tartly, "but you make it sound like some awful disease."

"Well," Solomon said, "I guess it is, in a way. I mean people who have it, people like you, spread it around. It's contagious."

"Are you going to tell me what it is, or do I have to guess?" Kendal knew her voice was angry. She didn't care.

"Don't get sore," Solomon said.

"I'm not!"

"All right," Solomon said. "What you have, what's part of you, the thing that makes you tick, the thing you want to give everyone else, is this need, this awful goddamn need to fulfill yourself, to what you call 'live up to one's capacity.' "

"And?" Kendal asked.

Solomon stared at Kendal. He frowned. "And nothing. That's it."

"That's *it*?"

"That's it."

She started to say something. She stopped. She looked at him with disbelief. "I don't believe this."

"Believe it."

"Solomon, are you saying that you resent that? You resent my wanting to . . . to . . . use whatever I have as best I can?"

"No, I'm not saying that. I am saying that what you do, what you want, what you believe, is fine for you. It works for you. Great. No argument. But that doesn't mean it has to work for anyone else. Can't you understand that?"

"Listen to yourself!" Kendal hunched closer to Solomon. "You don't mean that. You don't approve of people wasting themselves anymore than I do."

" 'Waste' is your word, Kendal, not mine."

"But we're all alike. We're all in the same boat. We all have this . . . this obligation . . . this need to do something that has purpose. God, I didn't invent this, Solomon. I mean, everybody ought to contribute to —"

"Calvinistic bullshit."

"Oh, come on, don't be simplistic."

"Would I be more profound if I agreed with you?"

"In a minute you're going to give me all that Existential blah-blah-blah."

"Jesus," Solomon snapped. "Why do you do that?" He snapped off the radio. "Why do you always have to label everything?"

"I don't *always* do anything!"

"Listen to me," Solomon said. "I don't want us to fight. I really don't. I just want you to understand something. I don't know where I am. Or how I got there. Or why. I only know it's the wrong place.

What I've done before, what I'm doing now, it doesn't mean a damn thing to me. Not a damn thing."

"May I say something?" Kendal asked.

"Sure."

"The plays you produced, aren't you proud of them?"

"May I say something?" Solomon smiled.

"Sure."

"Would it have made any difference if they'd never been seen?"

"That's not the point. They had something to say, something very special."

"You didn't really answer the question, did you? Want to try again? What's special about what I'm doing now?"

"You mean TransGlobal?"

"I mean TransGlobal."

"My God, Solomon, you're one of the few people there who doesn't want to do crap. And that's important. That's very goddamn important."

"To whom?"

"To you."

"You're wrong. You've got it backwards," Solomon said. "It's important to you. It makes you think I'm contributing. Participating. Using myself. And that pleases you, doesn't it? That pleases you a great deal."

"Oh, Christ, we're going around in circles. Don't you think we're going around in circles?"

"I think," Solomon said very quietly, "that I am tired of pleasing people."

He lifted his hand and studied it as if it belonged to a stranger. He curled his fingers into the configuration he'd seen behind the photographer's window, and when he let his fingers unfold he felt excited, for he thought he understood what the photographed hands had released. They had let go of the outer shell of self. They had freed themselves of the soul's deceit. And now it was his turn. It was as if his own fingers had reached inside his belly and pulled loose the soft tissue of compromises, scraped away the false adjustments of his life, tore loose his endless accommodations, and made room in the newly hollowed chamber for something else. He knew what it was. He felt it. But this time there was a difference. *The thing*, the animal within, stirred, stretched, moved its hundred legs, but now its claws were rounded, its jaws closed, its breath sweet. Slowly, a gentle reminder of its elusive shape, *the thing* swelled, pressed, pushed through the arterial map of Solomon's body until he heard the dark drumbeat of his heart. For a moment, his eyes blurred and, in kaleidoscopic vision, he saw frozen images, each seemingly embossed on a tiny bit of colored glass. Pomegranates were black. The dreamed Jew red. Brindig died in green. Purple tongues hung from the farmhouse. The little pieces of glass rotated, lost their symmetry, fell one against the other, shattered silently, re-formed into a terrible rainbow which pierced the corneas of Solomon's eyes. He tasted blood.

When he heard a raucous cry he had a terrible feeling that he'd screamed out loud but then he saw two mallard ducks burst from below the weeping willow tree, skim the surface of the pool, only inches from the water, then climb higher and finally vanish in the sky.

"They come back every year," Kendal said quietly.

"I wonder why?"

"It's home," Kendal said.

"Yeah."

Each knew what the other was thinking. The ducks felt more at home than either of them. Solomon rose, dusted his trousers, flicking grass from them, and put his hand lightly on Kendal's shoulder. She covered it with hers. But they did not look at each other.

"I don't know how long I'll be gone," Solomon said. "I'll be at the Beverly Hills Hotel."

"All right."

"I'll call you."

"All right." Kendal bit her lip. She didn't feel that she could keep talking. "Do you want me to take you to the station?"

"I'll get a cab. Thanks."

"All right."

"Kendal . . ." Solomon stopped. For a moment, their joined hands clung tightly to each other, then, as if by mutual consent, slipped slowly apart.

"I know," Kendal said.

When Solomon walked back to the house he saw Darby standing behind the window of the kitchen, watching him and Kendal. He lifted a finger in a small acknowledgment of her presence. She returned the simple gesture. She was still in her bathrobe and Solomon had no doubt that she had watched him and Kendal, had heard their voices lifted in anger. He wished he had a special formula to erase her loneliness. But he didn't.

Darby stayed at the window, watching her mother, who sat, still and rigid, at the pool. She heard a cab drive up and then saw Solomon cross by the barn. He carried a small bag and a tennis racket. She hoped that he would return to the lawn and kiss Kendal, hold her for a moment, but he got into the cab and drove away. Darby stepped out onto the kitchen porch, trying to think of something, anything, that would bring some comfort to her mother.

"Hey, Mom," she called, "we're going to need some beer and eggs and a couple of teabags."

"What a ghastly combination," Kendal said as she walked across the lawn and into the kitchen, wanting not to impose her unhappiness on her daughter.

"Not for a rinse and facial," Darby said firmly. "It's the best."

"You going to have a facial?"

"*We* are going to have a facial." Darby turned on the kettle. She threw open the refrigerator door.

"Maybe later, darling," Kendal said.

"Now," Darby ordered. "Here." She pulled a carton of eggs from the refrigerator and gave them to Kendal. "Separate 'em and save the yolks." As Kendal did what she was told, Darby uncapped two bottles of beer. She took a quick swig from one of them and grinned at her mother. "Don't need all of it, right?" The kettle was boiling now and Darby placed two teabags in a cup and covered them with boiling water. After a moment, she fished out the bags with a spoon and put them on a plate. Carrying the plate and the two bottles of beer, she started out of the kitchen. "Let's go." Kendal followed, a saucer of eggyolks in her hands.

They both took long steamy showers, each rinsing her hair in beer to give it body, wrapped themselves in thick terrycloth robes, and stood side by side in front of the bathroom mirror and applied coats of fresh eggyolk to their faces. Side by side still, they lay on their backs on Solomon's and Kendal's four-poster bed and promised not to make each other laugh as they waited for the yolks to harden. The promise was more difficult for Darby, because she had given her mother the two used teabags to place over her eyes in order to remove any vestige of puffiness, and the combination of hardening eggyolk and wet teabags presented a grotesque mask. Neither dared talk for fear that she would crack the stiffening facade.

When at last the eggyolk had lost its elasticity and solidified over their features, drawing their skins into pleasantly unfamiliar tautness, they both proceeded to execute a series of facial isometrics which slowly fissured the masks into a dozen diminutive cracks and little blisters of dried yolk.

Mother and daughter returned to the bathroom and stood in front of the mirror. They immediately broke into laughter and a fine ocher dust from the crumbling eggyolk fell into the bathroom sink.

"I've missed you," Kendal said. "I have missed you a great deal. We don't see each other enough, do you know that?"

"Yes," Darby said, "I know that."

Kendal held out her arms. Darby stepped into their circle and they held each other in a warm embrace, their cheeks touching.

"God," Darby said, "we smell like omelets."

They took turns splashing cold water on their faces to remove the sticky masks. They pulled towels from a rack and sat on the edge of the bathtub, rubbing their faces vigorously, enjoying the tingling rush of blood to their skins. But, gradually, the vigor of Kendal's towelling dissipated and she finally stopped, letting the towel dangle uselessly between her knees. Darby put her arm lightly around her mother's shoulders and spoke gently.

"You want to talk, Mom? I'm a good listener. I really am."

"You heard us, didn't you?"

"Yeah. It's funny. I don't ever remember you and Daddy fighting. I'm not sure that's good. I mean, sometimes it's a good thing to just let it out, to blow off steam."

"Maybe."

"Do you think he's gone away, is that it?"

"I think he's been away, darling," Kendal said quietly, "but I don't know where."

"You mean, in his head?"

"Yes. Does that make sense?"

"Sure it does. We all do that, don't we? Take little journeys by ourselves?"

Kendal studied her daughter, then reached out and took her hand. "How do you know that?"

"Because I do it, and I don't really think I'm different from anybody else."

"And where do you go on these — these journeys?"

"Well, that's the tricky thing, isn't it?" She interlaced her fingers with Kendal's and stared at their clasped hands. "Sometimes, I think that when I travel in my head I'm looking for some special destination and other times I think I'm just looking for someone to travel with, some friend I haven't met, someone, maybe, to whom I belong. That's not very clear, is it?"

"Don't you feel part of us?" Kendal asked. "Part of your father, part of me?"

"Yes. But separate, too. I don't mean that in a bad way; it's just a fact, just something you live with. I guess everybody's separate from everybody else. Haven't you ever felt that way?"

"I didn't use to," Kendal said. "You don't think of being separate from the man you marry or the family you raise. You take it for granted that you're all part of one thing. Perhaps that's a mistake. I'm not sure. I don't feel very wise these days."

"I think the mistake," Darby said gravely, "would be to blame yourself for whatever's going on with Daddy. I know you love him, but you can't protect him. You can't protect anybody. No one can."

"Is that what you think I do, protect him?"

"Well, in a way. In the same way you protected me when I was a kid."

"What do you mean?"

"You tried to make everything safe. Daddy did, too. I don't think you knew it, or meant it that way, but it's what you did. God, I don't know how to explain it."

"Try," Kendal said.

Darby paused for a long moment as she concentrated her thoughts. "Do you remember what you used to call white bread?"

"Yes." Kendal smiled. "Thumbprint bread."

"Do you remember why?"

"Because it was so spongy that when you picked it up, when your fingers pressed into it, your thumb print would remain."

"Right," Darby said. "Well, I think you were afraid that I was made of white bread and that if you — you or Daddy — pressed too hard, put your prints on me, they'd never come out. Do you understand what I mean?"

"That's terrible."

"I know," Darby said. "You have to spend an awfully long time looking for yourself. And while you're looking, you get angry. You don't even know why, but it's there, and so you do dumb things . . . crazy things . . . things that aren't so good."

"You're talking about your father, aren't you?"

"Yeah, Mom, I'm talking about my father." Darby held tighter to her mother's hand and when she continued, there was an edge of fear in her voice. "I think," she said, "that he can do things that aren't so good."

22

There was only one thing Solomon wanted at his office: Manzinni's script of *Shadow on the Grass*. After he tucked it into his suitcase, he told Priscilla where she could reach him in Los Angeles, asked her to cancel any appointments, then left TransGlobal Films.

He knew that Mouse would arrive at Emilio's delicatessen at the end of the day and he had a question for his friend. But before that he wanted, once more, to walk the street of diamond merchants. He was drawn to the place. He spent the afternoon on Forty-Seventh Street, peering into the windows at rows of jewelry, much of it studded with tiny diamonds, and then lifting his gaze to study the faces of Jewish sellers, their white skin accentuated by their dark coloring and as he watched them bartering with customers, chattering among themselves, he was terribly conscious of their open camaraderie. And he was jealous of it.

When, at last, the sun paled and there was a chill on the street, he walked to the deli. A young Puerto Rican girl was behind the counter, moving quickly at her chores: slicing ham and turkey and pastrami, plucking pickles from a jar, wrapping, serving customers.

"Is Em here?" Solomon inquired. She nodded, too busy to talk, and motioned toward the back room. Solomon threaded his way through the customers and entered the back room.

It was too early for the evening crowd. Mouse and Emilio sat in a booth. On the booth's table was a bowl of ice in which Mouse's hands were submerged. A jar of buzzing bees was in front of Emilio. Solomon slid into the booth.

"And?" the Mouse asked. "What's new on the Rialto?"

"I got tongues on my door," Solomon said. He related Callahan's call and told them what had happened at the house in Vermont. During his recitation, he helped Emilio place the live bees on Mouse's knuckles and then remove the spiraling stingers, so when Mouse interjected a muttered "oh" or "ah" Solomon was not certain if the reaction was to pain or to his story.

Mouse flexed his fingers. "It doesn't make any sense," he said. "It's crazy. What'd this Callahan think?"

"I don't know," Solomon said. "Probably what I think. Another goddamn crazy."

"Solomon," Emilio said, his voice tinged with worry. "This picture of Darby. Why would a guy take that?"

"God, I don't know, Em. I wish I did. I wish I knew what the hell was going on. I wish I'd seen the son of a bitch so I could have . . ." He jerked roughly with the tweezers and heard Mouse's sharp intake of breath. "Sorry, Mouse." He laid down the tweezers he'd used to pull the stinger. "Listen, what does *zei gezunt* mean?"

"A guy says it," Mouse explained, "he usually means 'be well.' But it also means 'so long.' "

Solomon nodded. "I want to ask you something."

"Go," the Mouse said.

Solomon spoke carefully. "If you'd been in the house when this, this son of a bitch, broke in, what would you have done?"

"What do you mean?"

"Just that."

"Well, I'm not sure. I mean, I'd probably've been scared to death."

"Not you."

"Yeah, me. Any luck, maybe I could have reached the cops. This Callahan." Mouse looked curiously at Solomon. "Why?"

"Oh, I don't know," Solomon said. "I just wondered."

"Bullshit," Mouse said, and then repeated his question. "Why?"

"Because," Solomon said quietly, "I think I would have killed him."

"What are you, crazy?" Emilio stared at him.

Mouse sighed. "That's no good, Solomon. That's no good at all. That's lousy."

"Maybe," Solomon said.

"I'm telling you," Mouse said sternly. "It's lousy. Killing a guy is lousy."

"Maybe," Solomon repeated, his tone noncommittal.

"Shit," Mouse said.

There was a long and awkward silence in the booth, broken finally by Emilio. "You guys want some brisket? I made this great brisket of beef. I can grate some fresh horseradish, an —"

"Labowski bring the urn?" Solomon asked.

"Em asked you, you want some brisket?" Mouse said.

"No, Em, thanks," Solomon said.

"It's on the piano," Emilio said.

"The brisket?" Solomon asked, his eyes widening.

Emilio laughed. "No, dummy, I got the ashes on the piano. You know, Brindig's."

Solomon turned on his seat and looked toward the far end of the room. The battered upright piano he'd played so many years ago still stood against the wall. On top of it was a small box covered in plain brown wrapping paper. Solomon stared at it. Its smallness seemed obscene. There was no way it could hold a man's life. Or death.

"You got any Johnny Walker Black, Em?" Solomon asked.

"Sure." Emilio stood up, squeezed past Solomon, and crossed the room to the free-standing English pub bar.

Mouse stared at Solomon, and when he spoke his voice was angry. "You think Kendal'd like it, you killed someone? Or Darby?"

Solomon didn't answer. He rose and joined Emilio. A bottle of scotch and three shotglasses were on the bar. Emilio filled the glasses. "Mouse?" he called across the room. Mouse shook his head and remained in his seat. Emilio and Solomon raised their glasses.

"To Mr. Brindig," Emilio said.

"Yeah," Solomon said.

Both men downed their drinks. Solomon poured himself another and walked over to the piano. He stared at the boxed urn. He pulled out the piano bench. He sat down. He blew into his fingers.

"That's nice," Emilio said. "Just like the pros."

"I was a pro," Solomon said. "I am a pro." He leaned over the keys and thumbnailed two octaves.

"It's lousy," Mouse said. "It's lousy to kill a guy."

"Leave it alone," Solomon said. He began to play a slow, easy blues. The melody haunted the room.

"Shit," Mouse said.

"Zei gezunt," Solomon said.

He didn't know if he meant "be well" or "so long."

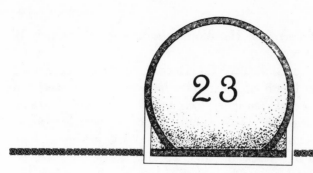

23

Curled on the stone dust of the cave's floor, Jubal slept, his arms embracing the Irish harp, which he had played long into the evening.

Riordan listened to the rain stinging the ground outside and watched the candle's flickering flame, its light filling him with holy thought. His fingers moved inside the buckskin coat, touching the names of the apostles. In this way he silently conversed with those whom he believed to be his ancestors. He conceived of them all as his fathers to whom he owed familial allegiance and for whom he would soon scourge the land of a heretic. He assured his fathers that he felt no pride in his actions; rather, he was suffused with pity and love for the man who had wrongfully bled his chickens and who had masked himself by sinful genuflections before a God in whom he did not truly believe. The old man cocked his head as he listened to the response from Peter and Andrew and James.

They told him that what he planned was not complete. They told him that any who had given refuge to the sinner dwelled in a house of disorder and that they must receive the charity of alarm. At first, Riordan was puzzled by this declaration. Had he not hammered tongues over the hunter's door? In an attempt to attune himself more closely to the vibrations of their voices, his fingers moved again over the names of the apostles. When he touched the rough cloth in which was sewn the name of Saint Matthias, who had been chosen by lot to fill the place of Judas, the truth of the words came to him.

The charity of alarm. How simple. How just. Riordan understood that the saints were telling him that for those who live in disorderly houses the warnings *must never cease.* He, Riordan, must forever be God's instrument of foreboding.

The old man surveyed the cave, his glance coming to rest on a stone shelf where Brother Death sat. Next to the bird were long rectangles of birchbark, all stripped of their inner fibers and all neatly stacked one on top of the other. Riordan rose, removed one of the flexible strips of bark, and returned to the table. He placed the bark in front of him, dipped a quill pen into black ink, and, working slowly, he inked his warning on the smooth side of the bark. Finished, he rolled the bark like a parchment and left it on the table. He looked once more at his son and saw that he slept deeply. Riordan walked through the cave gloom, through the low tunnel, and out into the evening.

Although chilled by the heavy rain, he undressed. He stepped into the mountain creek and submerged himself. Underwater, his eyes remained open; the ebb and flow of current nicely distorted his view. It was what he sought. For beneath his sanctuary stream, his arms undulating like the fins of passing fish, the stained-glass windows of weed and plankton drifting before his eyes, the old man best remembered his whoring mother and the legacy she had bequeathed him: duty to the Father of Fathers.

Invigorated by his holy bath, he returned to the cave and awakened his son.

Jubal blinked and saw an image of the tall, thin farmer who had bled his chicken. He rose quickly from the stone dust and listened to the old man's instructions. From various shelves and corners of the cave, he gathered those things his father wished.

Together, the old man and his son constructed two rude wooden crosses, the vertical poles split at the top ends. They inserted two squares of birchbark, which were encrusted with paraffin and salt, into the split ends of the poles. Riordan lit the bark in Jubal's pole and as the paraffin burst into bright green fire Riordan and Jubal crossed themselves.

"For the Father and the Son and the Holy Ghost," they said.

As they walked across the cave, their shadows darkening the niches of apostles, Riordan whistled softly.

Brother Death flew to his shoulder.

Their faces green under the burning paraffin and salt, the old man and his son slipped out of the cave. Riordan forced the end of his pole into the soft ground beneath the hanging slabs of stone. The pole punctured the heart of the figure of the man he'd drawn on the earth. The salt-fed flares licked green around the pole that Jubal carried, and Riordan moaned, for what he saw was not a simple cross of elm and hickory. He saw the Cross of the Holy Office. He would burn the other one tomorrow when he and the boy bore it toward a distant farm.

And toward the wrath to come.

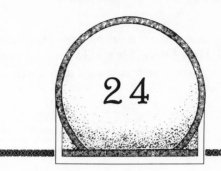

2 4

Solomon flew Eastern Airlines Flight 225 from Kennedy at 10:15 P.M. and arrived in Los Angeles at 1:10 the next morning. The normally busy airport was uncrowded and Solomon had no difficulty finding a taxi to take him to the Beverly Hills Hotel. Leaving the San Diego Freeway, the cab driver cut through a passageway between the Hilton Hotel and Robinson's store and entered the quiet residential streets of Beverly Hills. As always, Solomon found it difficult to understand why million-dollar homes were squeezed together, cheek-by-jowl, as if the builders had been tormented by the possibility of spatial freedom for the homes' inhabitants. The plantings outside these homes were so meticulously groomed that trees and bushes and flower gardens looked as if they were cardboard cutouts that had recently popped out of children's books. Only the gentle wind movement of their leaves made the foliage believable.

The Beverly Hills Hotel lobby was deserted. A sleepy nightclerk checked in Solomon who declined the services of a bellboy. He found his own way down the long carpeted corridor on the ground floor. As he turned the corner toward his room, a door closed further down the hall. Before it snapped shut, Solomon caught sight of a bearded man. It startled him. The man looked like his dreamed Jew. But the whiff of marijuana smoke drifting from the room dispelled the vision and made mystery mundane.

The window in Solomon's room faced a small garden. He opened the window and breathed in the scent of jasmine. He felt far removed from the turmoil of Manhattan's streets and the tongued door of a farmhouse, but as he prepared for sleep the vision of the bearded man returned and words echoed in his mind.

We shall meet from time to time.

Solomon settled into bed and turned off his light. In the darkness, unable to see but terribly aware of the small box he'd placed on the desk, the box which held Brindig's ashes, he pondered the meaning of the words. He felt quite certain that the bearded Jew with whom he'd dream-dived toward the pomegranate tree had not lied. What surprised Solomon was the strange sense of excitement he felt as he contemplated such a meeting. Puzzled, he fell asleep. He was too weary to dream.

The next morning, with Manzinni's script, *Shadow on the Grass,* lying on the table before him, Solomon breakfasted alone in the Polo Lounge. It was a quiet but cheerful room whose tables were constantly occupied by studio executives and producers and directors and agents and writers and actors and tax-shelter wizards who had come together to share their fantasies, to turn a dollar, to discover who was doing what to whom under the guise of creativity. Within this sunlit dining area could be heard the scratching of pens as contractual clauses were initialed, whispers of indignation as these same clauses were explained, the hurried turn of slick pages as *Daily Variety* and the *Hollywood Reporter* were thumbed for grosses registered or lies accepted, the belly growls of an ulcered stomach.

Seated near Solomon were a writer and a film producer. Although he did not know them personally, Solomon recognized them both. The writer was from New York, the producer was a major figure in Hollywood. As he sipped from his large glass of fresh orange juice, wonderfully thick with pulp, Solomon watched them. He knew the game they played. It was a familiar ritual. Solomon had no doubt that they were meeting to discuss how to dramatize a novel the writer had recently published. Solomon nodded with inner satisfaction as he caught snatches of their conversation but he maintained a solemn expression so that his eavesdropping would not be revealed.

The writer and producer exchanged the requisite endearments of such a meeting, each assuring the other that the collaboration of their respective talents would result in a motion picture of exquisite importance, rare insight, and the sweet cacophony of clinking coins. Solomon heard words and phrases which were commonly favored in such conferences: *objectify* and *externalize the interior motives of the piece* and *we'll go to the moon with this baby* and other colorful inanities. Solomon was buttering his rye toast when he realized that the producer was so thrilled at the writer's swift acclimatization of the meeting's jargon that he, forthwith, offered the writer a firm deal. There was a mutual grasp of hands. The producer winked at a waiter who, cognizant of the rules of the game, immediately whisked away the half-empty glasses of orange juice and returned with iced goblets of fresh juice and a chilled bottle of champagne, with which he topped the glasses into a frothing wine-and-citrus concoction known as a Bellini. After many ceremonial sips, the producer and writer sealed their new liaison by acknowledging that a "creative collaboration" would more likely come to fruition if both parties concerned openly revealed their strengths, their frailties, their fears, and their dreams.

Solomon finished his second cup of coffee as he listened to both men pretend to open up their hearts. They did not really do so, for, as Solomon knew, the producer and writer were fully aware that honest disclosure could guide one or the other toward emotional blackmail.

Poor bastard, Solomon thought as he watched the writer; for Solomon was acutely conscious that the producer's verbal caresses had carefully avoided one irrefutable factor.

Solomon glanced at Manzinni's script. He beckoned to a waiter, asked for a pencil and piece of paper. The waiter obliged. Solomon scribbled swiftly. *Beware the cutoff.* He folded the note, and asked the waiter to deliver it to the writer.

The producer and writer rose from their table, swearing fidelity to their mutual future, and hugged. The embrace was interrupted by the arrival of Solomon's note. As the writer unfolded it, Solomon rose, bowed to him, and left the lounge.

He was climbing into his rented Volkswagen outside of the hotel when he saw the producer and writer emerge and start down the long awning-covered path to the parking area. The writer's face was grim. The producer, his hands clawing at the writer's arm, was imploring him to listen to reason. The writer was not receptive. Solomon honked his horn. *Da da da dum!* The writer glanced his way and Solomon held up his fingers in a V for victory before slapping the car into gear.

The precipitous twists and turns of Coldwater Canyon presented a challenge to Solomon and he welcomed it, purposely driving too quickly, skidding around steep curves, gunning the engine on short straightaways, assuming an adversary attitude to other vehicles, declaring war on safety.

Entering the valley, he turned on Ventura Boulevard, its tawdriness pleasing, for it reminded him of the Post Road in Connecticut. The

street was lined with unpretentious establishments: small gyms popu-
lated by citizens seeking the fountain of youth, a dozen sushi bars, adult
motels featuring pornographic films, photo-copying services where
thousands of pages were daily Xeroxed for writers aspiring to feed the
hungry mouths of film production, escrow companies, branch banks,
boutiques whose life expectancies were disastrously short. The boulevard was the antithesis of Beverly Hills chic. It radiated a kind of hungry
energy, a clawing ambition which, Solomon thought, the dwellers of its
more affluent neighborhoods pretended to deny.

The morning traffic was heavy and Solomon could only drive slowly
with its flow. The traffic snarled and Solomon braked easily to a halt. he
looked casually toward the sidewalk. Ahead of him was a bus stop. A
boy sat on a bench.

The boy was beautiful. He was about fourteen years old, with huge
violet eyes and long golden hair in a pageboy cut. His skin was beach-
bronzed, so shiny that it looked oiled. He wore a short-sleeved green-
satin shirt and the drawstring-tied white muslin trousers of a Mexican
peasant. He was barefoot. Hanging from a braided strap on his shoulder
was an Indian bead bag. He saw Solomon looking at him and he smiled,
tilting his head back and opening his mouth as if he were trying to catch
rain. It made Solomon acutely uncomfortable; he tried to avoid looking
at the boy but he couldn't. He had never seen a crueler face.

Solomon heard a horn, and a powder blue Mercedes convertible
eased past his car and slid to the curb near the boy. The driver was a
rotund man with an ill-fitting toupee. He leaned across the front seat,
pushed open the passenger door, and nodded once. The boy rose immediately from the bench, walked to the curb, and spoke to the man. Solomon could not hear the words. The man frowned and shook his head
but the boy slid into the car and edged along the leather seat until he was
very close to the driver. Slowly, he raised one golden arm and traced his
fingers across the man's cheek. It wasn't until then that Solomon noticed the boy's fingernails. They were long and curved and painted
green, and were sharpened into terrible points. When the boy removed
his hand, the toupeed man's cheek was bisected by a tiny trail of blood.
The man reached down toward the boy's crotch.

The traffic flow resumed and Solomon accelerated swiftly, needing to
put distance between himself and whoring.

Solomon parked in the visitor's lot at TransGlobal Films. At the reception desk of the production offices he identified himself. He took the
elevator to Wilton Forest's penthouse suite. Wilton's secretary, al-

though surprised by his visit, greeted him pleasantly. Mr. Forest would be happy to see him.

Forest sat behind his marble desk. He was staring at the faceless painting on the wall.

"Once upon a time," Solomon said.

"Ah," Forest said. "Good. I like your stories."

"There was a man," Solomon said as he settled himself comfortably into the soft cushions of the sofa, "who sold his shadow, his soul, to the Devil." Manzinni's script in his lap, Solomon told the story of *Shadow on the Grass*. Throughout the recitation, Forest's eyes remained on the faceless painting; not once did his expression alter. "Well," Solomon said when he finished, "that's it. Do you like it?"

"Do I like it?" Wilton Forest addressed the question to himself rather than to Solomon. "Do I like it?" He swiveled his chair away from the painting and looked at Solomon for the first time. "A sort of parable, would you say? An allegory?"

"I suppose," Solomon said. "But the point is, do you like it?"

"No, Solomon," Forest said. "That is not the point. That is never the point. The point is what you wish to accomplish with the story and whether such a wish is practical."

"Don't you have an opinion of the story?"

"Why?" Forest asked politely. "Are you lacking one?"

Solomon felt a tiny scratching claw within him and he breathed in deeply to calm the familiar animal. He was surprised at the fragrance he inhaled. "You've changed your cologne," he said to Forest.

"Yes," Wilton said. "It's the musk of carnations. A more earthy scent. And do you see anything else? Any other change?"

Solomon glanced slowly around the room. The ferns were gone. They had been replaced by dozens of succulents, the fleshy-stemmed plants, leafless, spiny, and unflowered. The soft garden of previous times had given way to a severe landscape and Solomon saw now that tiny lights had been installed at the base of each plant so that each succulent threw its small but grotesque shadow on a wall. The office no longer projected an ambience of hospitality. It looked like a cold and dangerous desert.

"When did you do this?" Solomon asked. "Why?"

"My people worked all day, all night," Forest replied. "It seemed a fitting memorial to Ben."

"I don't understand."

"Don't you?" Forest's gaze moved across the abundance of harsh plants. "To the casual eye, the plants look different, one from the other. Stonecrop is dissimilar to agave, houseleek bears little resemblance to the yucca. They are not unlike men and women, each of us shaped in our own form."

"I see," Solomon said, remembering Forest's great concern with the individuality of things. "You're moved by the . . . by the originality of each."

"No," Forest said. "I am moved by the sameness of each. The common denominator among them. The common denominator among us all. The thing which, regardless of our shapes, we share."

"And what is that?"

"Death," said Forest.

Solomon was surprised at the turn of the conversation. He knew Forest to be a sensitive man, but he had never thought him to be of a brooding nature. He wanted very much to return to the topic of Manzinni's script, but as he looked at the cactus shadows on the wall he wondered if Forest were not, after all, referring metaphorically to the story. He waited for the older man to continue.

"I do not think God was kind to take Ben that way," Forest said. "Was he prepared? Would you say that Ben was ready to leave?"

The picture of Brindig instinctively stepping forward to redress the violation of a Hasidic woman flashed in Solomon's mind. "I don't think he was frightened."

"Nonsense," Forest said. "We're all frightened." He swung around in his chair and stared once more at the faceless portrait of the woman. "We need more time. We must have more time. One is dead for so long a time." He turned and motioned toward the potted plant on a table next to Solomon's sofa. "The cacti know that. They have learned. Feel their leaves."

Solomon recognized that Forest's request was not casual. He reached out and ran a finger over a cactus leaf.

"Can you feel the waxy substance?" Wilton asked.

"Yes."

"It minimizes the evaporation from their inner tissues. It allows them to store water for a long period of time. It allows them to live. They do not die, Solomon, before their time. We would do well to follow such an example."

Solomon spoke carefully. "I don't think, Wilton, that we can control that."

"But we can be prepared."

"Perhaps. I'm not sure."

Forest looked at the portrait on the wall. "Have you ever wondered about that faceless portrait? Yes, of course you have. All who come to this office wonder. It is a painting of my wife."

Solomon was startled. He could not imagine wanting a faceless portrait of Kendal.

"There are not many men who really love their wives, Solomon," Forest continued. "They are fond of them. They might even admire them. But over the years, they get used to them. They take them for granted. They no longer see them. They are faceless, don't you see." He withdrew the neatly folded handkerchief from his breast pocket and sniffed it, breathing in the dark fragrance of carnations. Wilton's concentration was so total that Solomon felt that the chairman of Trans-Global was sustaining himself by the act. Solomon thought that perhaps the flower's scent reminded Forest of the earth to which men return. Forest replaced the handkerchief and continued. "In my home there is a portrait of me in Sarah's bedroom. It, too, is faceless. We are forever reminded of each other. And we are warned. We are warned about what we will confront when the other passes. Inevitably, the time will come when one of us passes and the other will be forced to re-create the features of the one he or she has loved most deeply. And so we prepare for it. Now. It is a responsibility we cannot shun." He lowered his head and sniffed again at his handkerchief. When he looked up, his eyes were moist. "There are other responsibilities, Solomon, and it is time to assume them. This company has not fulfilled its obligation. We have not used our facilities in the highest fashion. I mean to correct that. With your help, of course. It is the least we can do for Ben."

"Wilton, I don't mean any disrespect," Solomon said, "but Ben Brindig was not, uh, overly concerned with high purpose. Regardless of the manner in which he died."

"Exactly!" Forest spoke triumphantly. "And, therefore, he was not prepared for that final journey. We need not let that happen to others. We must not let that happen. Solomon, *you* will not let that happen!"

Solomon was startled at Forest's vehemence. "I don't think there's much I can do about it."

"You're wrong. There's a great deal." Forest rose from behind the desk and walked to a wall of windows that overlooked the studio. He stared down at all he controlled. "Am I correct, Solomon, that there have been times over the last years when you have been unhappy with what our company produced?"

"You once told me that you don't like liars, Wilton."

"That is correct."

"Then unhappy is not an accurate word. What this company produces disgusts me."

"Then change it."

"I beg your pardon?"

"Change it. I am offering you a chance to change it. Don't misunderstand me. I do not think you can replace Ben. There is something else I have in mind. I want you to produce a series of special films. We'll place them on television first and then, combining them, release one or two features abroad. Are you interested?"

"I'm interested in *Shadow on the Grass.*"

Forest ignored the statement. "The young man who killed Ben — do you think he was prepared to die?"

"Christ, Wilton, I don't think the son of a bitch thought about it."

"Please don't be profane, Solomon. Of course he was not prepared to die. Nor are thousands of others. Do you see what I'm getting at?"

In his mind's eye, Solomon saw birds flying into the sun, dying well, their journey from beginning to end complete. He could not answer Wilton Forest.

"Solomon," the older man continued, "there may be millions who have no sense of their spirituality, no sense of what their history has offered them. Can you understand that?"

Oh, Jesus, Solomon wanted to say, *don't push me into this. Leave me alone.* But he could not speak, for he was listening to another voice.

We shall meet from time to time.

As Solomon stared at the cactus plant on the table, the dreamed Jew stepped from behind the shadows on the wall. Solomon stiffened.

"Are you listening to me, Solomon?" Forest persisted. "I said there must be a great number of people who do not have a sense of their own religious history."

The dreamed Jew smiled. Solomon looked away.

"I want you to research the great religions of the world," Forest continued. "All of them. Catholicism. Buddhism. Judaism. Hinduism. The Protestants. Islam. All of them, Solomon. Then tell their stories, expose the teachings, the wisdom, the solace offered one who participates, who believes. I am not interested in superficial pap. I want no part of what this industry has done before — no sprawling Technicolor epic that reduces the complexities of these stories to romantic and sentimental nonsense. I think you should tell a story. That's the first thing. The story of an ordinary family. A simple man and his wife, his child. How are they affected by one of these great religions? Were they believers? Did they reject it? Why? What are the consequences of acceptance or rejection? There are so many questions, Solomon, so many thousands of questions! Let us look for the answers! Let us prepare people, Solomon! Let us prepare ourselves!"

Exhausted, Wilton Forest turned from his window and retraced his steps across the office. He sat behind his desk, both hands palm-down on the marble, as if he wished the stone to cool him. Forest's breathing was so labored that Solomon feared he was hyperventilating. He started to rise from the sofa so that he might comfort the older man, but Forest closed his eyes and leaned his head against the back of his chair and his breathing slowed to normal. Solomon settled back in his sofa. Forest withdrew his handkerchief and unfolded it. He lay the silk square over his face. A small section of it moved in and out of his mouth as he breathed through open lips.

"Death is so very long," Forest whispered, his voice muffled beneath the handkerchief. "So very, very long."

Solomon sat silent. He recognized that Forest's deep disturbance was not a pose. He had no wish to offer cheap formulas to alleviate the older man's fear of dying. Like most men of middle age, Solomon had awakened on a number of midnights and, eyes wide to the dark, had tried to imagine death. He had held his breath, blanked his vision, deafened himself to sound, dwelled within his melting bones, and embraced the void. At such dark moments he had felt a terrible regret that one day he would enter emptiness but, because all these things — the holding of his breath, the blanking of his vision — were superficial impositions, he had acknowledged that death was still unknown. He had felt sorrow rather than fear.

Wilton Forest removed his handkerchief and leaned forward in his chair. He smiled sadly at Solomon. "There are not many men," he said, "who have seen me naked. Such uncovering imposes a responsibility on the viewer, and thus it is unfair. I apologize."

"There's no need to," Solomon said.

"Will you accept this assignment?"

Under half-lowered eyelids, Solomon searched discreetly for the Jew. Where was he hiding?

"I think you should know, Wilton," Solomon said, "that I came here today with an ultimatum. Either we make *Shadow on the Grass* exactly as it's written or I'll resign."

"Surely, you're not serious!"

"Yes. I am serious."

"Solomon, I hardly consider you naïve. You must be aware that a picture of that nature could be made only at considerable risk."

"I'm aware of the risk."

"TransGlobal was not built on foolish gambles. You're being difficult. That's not like you."

"Isn't it?" Solomon asked.

"Just who do you think this picture will please?"

"Me," Solomon said. "It will please me."

In silence, the two men stared at each other. Forest lifted his gaze to the portrait of his faceless wife as if seeking some words of advice. He looked again at Solomon.

"You've changed," he said.

"Perhaps," Solomon said.

"You want to bargain your project for mine, is that it?"

"I'm not bargaining," Solomon said.

"Nor I," said Forest. "Can you afford to leave the company?"

"Can you afford to have me leave the company?" Solomon asked quietly. He wished Brindig could hear him, and Manzinni. He felt unafraid of failure.

"Let us think about it," Forest said, swiveling his chair toward the window, turning his back on Solomon.

"Let's do that, Wilton," Solomon said, and left the office. He saw no trace of the dreamed Jew.

When Solomon returned to the Beverly Hills Hotel, the desk clerk informed him that a message had been delivered. Solomon took the sealed envelope to his room. He opened it. The message was from Brenda Brindig. She requested his presence at her home at exactly five o'clock in the afternoon. Solomon remembered that five o'clock was the time when a fighting bull met his final hour. Brenda's postscript, heavily underlined, reminded Solomon to dress in his tennis whites.

He pulled the draperies across the window, shutting out the sunlight. He notified the front desk to call him at four o'clock, then undressed to his shorts. He lay on the bed, closed his eyes. He slept peacefully. The telephone awakened him. It was the front desk telling him it was four o'clock. Solomon smiled. He had succeeded in what he'd set out to do. He'd spent the day pleasing no one.

At four-thirty, dressed in his tennis whites, he picked up his racket and the boxed urn and left his room. North Canon Drive was so near the hotel that Solomon decided to walk. He reached Brindig's home only a few minutes after five. A number of expensive cars were drawn up in the circular driveway.

The Mexican housekeeper opened the door. She did not look happy as she stared disapprovingly at his attire. Solomon introduced himself, walking in. She nodded curtly and, in halting English, mumbled something about the rear of the house. Before Solomon could inquire further, she stomped out of the room and swung through the kitchen door. Solomon was left alone. Although he heard the faint sound of voices, he saw no one. He looked around the living room. It was furnished in decorator style, everything muted, shape and color blending together, spotless and ordered. There was no feeling that the room was ever used. A large archway led to an informal sunroom furnished entirely in white wicker and brightly colored cushions. At the far end of the room, French doors were slightly ajar. A formal garden was planted just outside. As Solomon was trying to decide where to place the urn, he saw a woman enter the garden. It was Brenda Brindig. She was dressed for tennis, her short skirt swinging jauntily and revealing the lower curves of her buttocks. Her armless cotton shirt exaggerated the contour of her breasts and was as bright red as her lip gloss and nail polish. She did not look like a grieving widow. She rounded a carefully clipped hydrangea bush and saw Solomon. She hurried into the house.

"Where've you been?" she snapped. "We're waiting."

"It's just after five." Instinctively, Solomon started to apologize, then heard himself, stopped.

She pulled the box from his hands and ripped it open, indiscriminately throwing scraps of paper onto the wicker stools and tables. Once it was exposed, she held the plain metal urn in her hands and stared at it. "How do I know it's him?" she asked.

"Mrs. Brindig—" Solomon began.

"Brenda," she said.

"Brenda, Mr. Labowski delivered this. I don't think there could be any mistake."

"With my luck, who knows?" she asked tartly. "C'mon, let's go." Abruptly, she wheeled around. Solomon followed her out of the sunroom and through the garden. The voices he'd heard before were louder, and when Brenda led him to the tennis court he saw that half a dozen men and women were gathered in a redwood gazebo next to the court. All of them were dressed for tennis. He recognized only one man:

Harry West, the actor for whom Ben Brindig had demanded rewrites on *Shadow on the Grass*, the actor without whom Ben had announced the picture would surely go down the toilet. He was an exceptionally good-looking man, tall and bronzed and muscular, his ruggedness enhanced by a rolled red-and-blue bandanna he wore as a sweatband around his head. The voices stopped as Brenda approached the gazebo.

"All right, people," she said, "he's here." For a moment, Solomon thought she meant to introduce him but then realized that the *he* to whom she referred was the urn Brenda now held high in her hands. "Ben Brindig is here!" Her voice rang. The guests stood up. One man removed his visored cap.

"Harry," Brenda said, "you know what to do."

"Uh-huh." Harry West touched a finger respectfully to his sweatband, then moved to the far end of the court. A wide broom leaned against the fence. Harry took it and positioned himself at the center of the service line. Solomon now saw that, unlike almost all the tennis courts in Los Angeles, this one was not paved with asphalt. It was a red clay court with a dry, powdery surface. Brenda opened the urn and placed the metal lid on one of the gazebo benches. She walked to the center of the court and stood at the net on the same side where Harry waited with his broom. She turned to her guests and her voice lifted in declaration.

"Ben Brindig was my fella! He was a prince! A gem! Ben Brindig was a giver. Believe me, a giver! He didn't know about selfish. All the years we're together, all he wanted was to please me. And now it's my turn. It's my turn to please him. And your turn. Together we will remember him the way he wanted." She angled her body toward the house and shouted. "Maria! Maria, now! Now!"

Solomon and the other guests turned toward the house and saw the housekeeper. She carried a silver tray. As she came closer, Solomon could see that on the tray were peeled hard-boiled eggs. Not looking at anyone, Maria placed the tray on the gazebo table and left hurriedly.

"Pick them up!" Brenda's voice was a command. Solomon and each of the others lifted an egg from the tray. "In the middle of death," Brenda continued, "this egg is a symbol of life. Life! The thing Ben had so much of! And this — " She paused and in one swift motion tore the front of her bright red shirt. One breast was exposed. It did not look unlike the hard-boiled egg. "This," she said as she pointed to the rip in her clothing, "is *Keriah*, a rending of the garment, which is a sign of grief. Can you see what is left of a man? A torn piece of cloth and a hard-boiled egg! But not Ben. He was more than that. Much more. He was a prince! A gem! And so we're going to do what he asked. We're going to do what he told me." She paused, dramatically threw her arms wide, the urn trembling in one hand, and she implored them.

"Listen to the command of a prince," she called out. "Listen to his words." And in an exact and eerie duplicate of Ben's tone, she shouted, "Don't get your tit in a wringer, kid, just play on my bones!"

Quickly, she started up the center of the court and as she did so she tipped the urn at an angle so that Ben Brindig's ashes spilled in a straight line bisecting the middle of the court. By the time she reached Harry West the urn was empty.

Solomon gasped. He was appalled at the irreverence of her action, the seeming profanation of a man who had sacrificed his life for God.

"Go, Harry, go!" Brenda screamed; an Harry began to sweep the ashes evenly over the court, mixing them uniformly with the red clay dust. "Eat! Eat for his life!" Brenda shouted at the guests and, mesmerized by her passion, each of them raised a hard-boiled egg to his mouth and began to eat.

Afraid that he would choke, Solomon held the egg to his lips but could not bite into it. He wanted to run but he didn't move. He wanted to cry out but he remained silent. He felt the raging *thing* inside him and he welcomed it, but as it grew and swelled in his belly he knew his rage was rudderless and that he was unqualified to scream in protest, for he stood outside of all community; he had nothing genuine to contribute, no gesture to make, no words to speak that would truly honor Ben Brindig — for he, Solomon, was crippled by his lack of connection to the dead Jew.

To all Jews!

Anguished, he stared in horror as Harry West continued his sweeping and the other guests dutifully chewed their eggs. Brenda ran from the court and disappeared in the garden. As soon as she was out of sight the guests lowered their eggs and put the remaining pieces on the silver tray. Harry stopped sweeping. He looked at the others.

"I think you should play," he said. "It's what she wants."

The man who had removed his visored cap nodded solemnly. "For Ben," he said and opened a fresh can of tennis balls. He walked onto the court. He walked gingerly, not looking down. After a moment, another man and two women joined him. They kept their gaze straight ahead.

"First one in?" The visor-capped man prepared to serve.

25

Callahan turned up the collar of his slicker and stepped out of the car. He ran across the farmyard. The driving rain plastered his hair to his head, and he could feel the squelch of mud underfoot. He tried the front door of the farmhouse. It was locked. Good. Tuttle had remembered. He ran around to the rear of the house, stomped his muddy boots against the stone door step, and entered the screened porch. He tried the rear door. It, too, was locked. When he returned to the farmyard, he decided it wasn't necessary to check the windows. Only a damn fool would choose a day like this to break into a house. Not that the world wasn't filled with damn fools. He ran back to his car.

He had left the ignition on, and the wipers were fanning briskly across the front window. Autumn had come with a vengeance, he thought, as he watched the tree limbs whipped by the morning's rain and wind. He opened a thermos of coffee he'd rested on the passenger seat. Fragrant steam rose from the thermos and he didn't bother to pour the coffee into a cup, rather tilting the thermos directly to his lips. The coffee was laced liberally with sugar and heavy cream and as he drank it he was amused at his own self-indulgence. The hot sweetness pleased him and he sighed with content. He turned on the heater of his car and rescrewed the top of the thermos. He shifted into low gear and started out of the farmyard. The car skidded for an instant, the tires spinning over mud, but then found traction and surged slowly forward. As he drove toward the road to Tuttle's mobile home, he glanced into the rearview mirror. Behind him, the Moons' farmhouse looked safe and comfortable, needing only smoke to rise from its chimney to lend final credibility to its snugness. The sight reassured him. The earlier strange occurrence at the house had truly perplexed him. He had twice since checked the house. There had been no further signs of violation. Perhaps, after all, it had been an incidental ugliness, senseless and without design. When speaking with Mrs. Moon he had implied that such might be the case. He had not wanted to panic her with a gratuitous and gruesome description of the cows' tongues. As he turned the corner of the drive, he looked back once more. He wondered in which room Darby slept.

The road to Tuttle's was slippery with mud and he drove slowly. He had no need to hurry. He wanted only to satisfy himself that the caretaker was on the premises. When he reached the mobile home, he saw that a light burned within and that smoke curled from its metal stovepipe. There was little doubt that Tuttle was home. Callahan backed into tractor ruts on pastureland opposite the trailer, then swung onto the road. Keeping the volume low, he turned on the radio and listened to the morning's police reports. They were mostly of a vehicular nature. The roads in southern Vermont were rain slicked and the reportage of accidents was constant. Although most of them were minor, Callahan did not envy the troopers on the road. He switched the station to a commercial channel. Willie Nelson was singing "September Song." *And the autumn weather turns the leaves to flame . . . and I haven't got time for the waiting game.* Callahan thought the music perfectly attuned to the melancholy rain. As he drove away, humming softly to himself, he wished Darby were sitting next to him.

He remembered with absolute clarity the sexuality projected between them, unspoken, guileless, silently acknowledged, as she asked him if he knew the legend of the waxing moon. He had not. Then.

After her departure, he had returned to his house and perused his extensive collection of books. The bulk of his library related to things theological. Among the histories and philosophies and learned dissertations were simpler volumes dealing with folktales and myths and superstitions of various religions. It had not taken him long to discover the legend of the waxing moon. Ancient Hebrew scholars had advised cohabitation under the waxing moon, such lighted intercourse, they suggested, assuring the issue of a benevolent child. He had closed the book and walked to his window and looked at the sky. The moon was on the rise. In a few days, a week at most, it would be full. He wondered when Darby would next arrive.

Now, driving through the stinging rain, he hoped it would be soon.

· · ·

Jabez Tuttle sat in his Sears reclining chair, barefoot, dressed only in his stained overalls, munching saltines and sipping from a can of condensed milk as he watched a late-morning soap opera. Earlier, he had heard Callahan's car. He'd edged open the curtain on his window, standing so that he could see but not be seen. He had no wish to be interrupted in his morning viewing and was pleased to see Callahan drive away. He turned off his lights so that no one might be tempted to visit. The only illumination in his mobile home now came from the television screen. The sound of rain on the roof was a metallic tattoo that seemed to heighten the drama played on the small screen. Outside, the sky was dark with storm and that, too, added to the ambience of crisis projected from the television. A handsome young actor faced an elderly man who was angrily accusing him of embezzlement. The young man protested vigorously, pleading innocence, bolstering his argument with a demand for apology.

"By Jesus," Tuttle admonished the elderly man on the screen, "don't pay no nevermind to what he's tellin' you. He's lyin'. Just as plain as the nose on your face, that sumbitch's lyin'!" To emphasize his point, Tuttle lifted one buttock and farted. He sniffed at his own gas. He thought maybe he'd better eat something that would clear him out. The stewed rhubarb in his refrigerator would do nicely. He rose from the chair and, eyes riveted to the screen, slowly backed across the room toward the refrigerator. Fumbling behind him, he found the handle and pulled open the door.

On the television screen, the voices of anger rose stridently and the young man's hand dipped into his pocket.

"Watch him!" Tuttle shouted. "He's like to got hisself a knife!"

But the young man removed a package of cigarettes and so Tuttle thought it would be safe to turn and remove the dish of rhubarb. He quickly plucked it from the refrigerator. As he turned back toward the television screen, his gaze swept past the windows in the side of his trailer. He thought he saw a flash of green fire in the distance but he didn't give it much attention, as his interest was entirely focused on the drama he feared he might miss. He settled himself again in his reclining chair and slurped from the dish, not bothering with a spoon, just tilting the shallow bowl to his lips and letting the wet rhubarb and its juices slip into his mouth as he watched the two actors confront each other. But before the dispute could reach its climax, the drama was interrupted by a commercial. Rhubarb juice dripped from Tuttle's chin and ran down his chest behind the billowed overalls. The fluid trickled across the white scar, and Tuttle thumbed it away as he watched the commercial. It was an advertisement for pantyhose; a young girl was extolling the virtues of elasticity as she danced prettily and showed her long legs. Her skirts swirled high on her thighs and Tuttle was momentarily reminded of his youthful fumblings.

"Yeah," he mumbled, "coulda done you good!"

As he winked at the girl on the screen, the door to his mobile home was pushed open and Jubal stepped across the threshold, the burning green cross of the Holy Office thrust before him.

"Hey!" Tuttle said. He was so startled by the apparition that he didn't attempt to rise from his chair. When he saw Riordan Flynn enter, his white beard dripping rain, Tuttle's mouth opened wide, strings of rhubarb hanging from his lips. The look on Riordan's face frightened Tuttle and he dropped his dish of rhubarb and rose from the chair. He stepped toward a pump-action twelve-gauge shotgun that hung on the wall, but even as he moved he heard the old man's words.

"We've come with wings of love, Jew," said Riordan softly, and then he whistled.

The black crow flew from Riordan's shoulder and, in a frenzy of wings, burst toward Tuttle. Tuttle stumbled backwards and raised his arms, but the bird's flapping wings beat around his head and Brother Death's beak raked his face. Tuttle crashed into the television set. He heard the glass break.

"Goddamn!" He swung wildly at the bird but the crow darted through his arms and Tuttle felt the bird's beak slash his neck, and then the awful black wings raked his eyes and he couldn't control his tears. Sobbing, he started to crawl toward the shotgun wall. Tuttle saw Riordan standing in the center of the room but the old man's image was cobwebbed by the blood running from Tuttle's eyelids. He could only faintly perceive that Riordan's arm was moving in swift circles, and Tuttle could not understand the high whistling sound that seemed to emanate from that arm. The whistling grew louder and higher, shriller, and then what looked to Tuttle like a fistful of snakes flew through the air and a terrible thing wrapped around his neck and choked him. His fingers clawed at his throat but he couldn't pull any air into his lungs and the scarlet vision of his own blood turned black. As he fainted, he heard the sweet laughter from the boy who carried the burning green cross.

When he regained consciousness, Tuttle had the crazy thought that he was being punished for his early years of deer-poaching. His throat hurt so that he was sure he'd been shot in the neck, and his hands and feet were bound in leather thongs. He was draped over the back of his reclining chair, his head down into the cushion, his feet dangling toward the floor. He knew he looked like the deer he had curved so often over the front fender of his truck. Then he remembered the old man and the boy and even in his pain-flogged mind he knew that what they had done to him had little to do with the slaughter of a deer. The room was silent. There was no sound from the television set. But Tuttle felt the presence of the two invaders. He kept his eyes shut as he tried to reason why they had attacked him.

"Nuthin'," he said aloud, "I ain't got nuthin'."

"No," said Riordan, "you are empty."

Tuttle opened his eyes. He hadn't meant to speak out loud but now there was little reason to feign unconsciousness. In his awkward position it was difficult to raise his head but he turned it to the left. All he could see was the arm of his reclining chair. He felt a pair of hands close around his shoulders; he was lifted easily from the chair and set on his feet. The hands turned him and he stared into the face of the boy. It was at that moment that Tuttle became truly terrified. The boy's hands, which still rested on Tuttle's shoulders, were gentle and the boy was smiling, but his eyes shone with such excitement that they looked like two chips of black ice on a January road. Only once before had Tuttle seen such eyes. It was when a bobcat had attacked the carcass of a bear.

"Please!" Tuttle whimpered.

The boy removed a knife from under his bark vest.

"Oh, Jesus," Tuttle said. "No!"

"Easy," Riordan Flynn said. "Easy, now."

The boy cut the leather thongs from Tuttle's hands and feet. Tuttle did not try to move. He was limp with fear. He glanced at the old man who stood in the doorway, the terrible black crow on his shoulder. Behind him, stuck into the wet ground outside the trailer, was the burning green cross. It sizzled slightly in the rain.

"I wouldn't tell nobody," Tuttle pleaded softly to the old man. "You can take anythin', you take it all, it's okay. I swear to you, I wouldn't tell nary a soul!"

"I know," Riordan said. "I believe you."

"You can clean me out," Tuttle continued quickly, encouraged by Riordan's tone. "I'll help you. I mean it truly, I'll help you."

"I want you to help us," Riordan said.

"Sure, sure." Tuttle was beginning to regain hope. "Just tell me, is all. What do you want? Just tell me!"

Riordan looked at Jubal who stood quietly, the knife still in his hands. "What do we want, darlin'?" Riordan asked.

"To let the light in, that's what we want. To let the light in!"

"Yes," Riordan nodded. "To let the light in."

"Huh? What?" Tuttle looked quickly back and forth between the boy and the old man who seemed so reasonable. "To what? I don't get it. I don't understand what you're tellin' me. I'll do whatever it is, but I just don't understand, is all. You got to tell me plain!"

"Yes," Riordan said. He nodded to the boy.

Jubal used his knife to slice through the shoulder straps of Tuttle's overalls. The overalls fell to Tuttle's bare feet. He was naked. Riordan stared at Tuttle's penis.

" 'And God said unto Abraham,' " the old man said, " 'thou shalt keep my covenant therefore, thou, and thy seed after thee in their generations; Every man child among you shall be circumcised.' "

Bewildered, Tuttle looked down at himself. He was not a prudish man but the attention to his penis embarrassed him terribly. He started to cover himself with his hands but Jubal's knife flicked out and the point caught the palm of Tuttle's hand. He pulled it back sharply.

"It is foolish to hide, Jew," Riordan said.

"It's just a dong!" Tuttle cried out, still staring at himself. "Ain't no different'n yours. It was the army done the cuttin'. I got me an infection onct an' them army doctors cut 'fore I could . . ." He shook his head with the remembrance. "Jesus, hurt like hell, but . . ."

"Your shame is not that you are circumcised," Riordan said quietly. "It's in the hiding, can you not see that?"

The fact that the old man still addressed him calmly relieved Tuttle of some apprehension, and his embarrassment turned to anger. "I can't see a goddamn thing!"

"No," Riordan said in a voice dulled by sorrow, "of course not. For you have swallowed the darkness." Slowly, he opened his bark vest and reached inside the folds of his great buckskin coat. He pulled loose the long thorn whip he wore around his waist. He held it lightly in one hand and let its length coil onto the linoleum floor of the trailer. A look of beatific joy crossed his face. He nodded at Jubal, and the boy sang.

"De la crudel morte de Cristo / ogn' om pianga amaramente / Quando Juderi Cristi piliaro / d'ogni parte lo circondaro / le sue mane strecto legaro / com ladro villamente."

With the knife he held in one hand, Jubal crossed himself, and continued his chant.

"A la colonna fu spoliato / per tutto 'l corpo flagellato / d'ogne parte fo 'nsanguinato / commo falso amaramente."

Riordan smiled at Tuttle and lashed out with the whip. It sliced across Tuttle's chest, and a thin rivulet of blood burst the flesh. Tuttle felt he had been stung by a hundred bees and he screamed. But before the sound was completed in his mouth he felt the whip rip skin from his neck and he fell backwards, entangled in his overalls, which heaped around his feet. He struggled onto hands and knees and again the lash snapped and the terrible thorns bit into his thin buttocks. He sobbed openly and crawled forward, his feet released now from the overalls. The lash again ribboned his buttocks, and pain made him urinate. Still on his hands and knees, he lurched through the open door and the sour smell of his piss mingled with the warm damp odors of the rain-drenched earth. The storm's intensity had increased. The sky was black, intermittently shredded by pale gold lightning, followed by the boom of thunder. Driven like some dumb animal under the stinging lash rising and falling against his flesh, Tuttle crawled toward the road, and all he could think of, all he heard, was the dirge of blacks during that time long ago when he did his time on the prison farm in Texas.

"Oh Lord, I'm hurtin' all over. Oh Lord, I need a doctor. Oh Lord, my body's achin'. Oh Lord!"

It was a medieval procession. Carrying the burning green cross, Jubal led the way down the road toward the Moons' farmhouse. Behind him, Tuttle crawled and sobbed. At the rear, Riordan walked slowly, his eyes brighter than the flame of the cross, his thorny whip cracking sharper than the lightning that split the sky.

As they moved down the road, past dead fiddleheads and hidden butterflies, past tall grasses bent in nature's genuflection, Riordan called to the heretic who crawled before him. The old man beseeched the bleeding farmer to erase the darkness of his soul and to fill himself with the testimony of beauty. His voice overriding the cannonade of thunder, Riordan implored Tuttle to follow the path of Augustine, who, knowing that man is corrupt and helpless, chose to dwell in the City of God where all can embrace the testimony of beauty.

" 'For the Lord is the first author of beauty,' " roared Riordan, exactly quoting Augustine, "and if you do not believe this, 'ask the loveliness of the earth, ask the loveliness of the sea, ask the loveliness of the sky! Ask the sun making the day light with its beams, ask the moon tempering the darkness of the night that follows, ask the living things which move in the waters, which tarry on the land, which fly in the air; ask the souls that are hidden, the bodies that are perceptive, the visible things which must be governed, the invisible things which govern!' "

Riordan was weeping as profoundly as the skies as he bellowed his final proclamation. " 'Ask all these things and they will answer thee, Lo, see we are lovely. And their loveliness is their confession!' "

When the parade of three men reached Solomon Moon's farmhouse, Riordan ceased using his lash. Tuttle sprawled flat on the soaked ground, not caring that with the air he so desperately sucked into his lungs came other things, mud and dunged straw. Whimpering, he ate the earth. He blinked bloody sweat from his eyes and saw the old man move close to Jubal, but he could not hear what was said, as thunder was the only distinguishable voice. He saw Jubal nod several times and, as the old man disappeared around the back of the house, the boy planted the green-burning cross in the soggy ground. By the time the stake had been driven deep, Riordan had returned and now, in between the claps of thunder, Tuttle heard the old man's voice, for it was lifted in fury.

"He has removed the tongues!" Riordan's voice trembled under the rain. And then, in a gesture so swift and deadly he could have been drawing a sword, he pulled the rolled parchment from his cloak. Leaning down, he placed the rectangle of bark on the ground and drove his knife through it. He snapped a thin branch from a nearby tree and broke it into short pieces. Swiftly, he whittled one into a peg. He moved to the front door of the farmhouse. With the heel of his hand he hammered his knife into the soft wood over the frame. He rammed home the peg that held the bark. When he saw that his scrolled warning dangled securely over the door, Riordan turned back to the farmyard. He gestured angrily to Jubal. Instantly, the boy turned and entered the barn.

Riordan raised his thorn whip over Tuttle's head and pointed toward the woods. Tuttle understood immediately. He pushed himself up onto his hands and knees and, like a broken beast of burden, moved in the direction his master had indicated.

As they entered the woods, Riordan resumed his Gregorian chant, which told how the Jews had taken Christ and stripped Him naked and beaten Him until every part of His body bled bitterly as if He were false.

Jubal studied the barn, its interior faintly illuminated by the flames of the burning cross. Running lengthwise down the center of the cement floor were two dozen stanchion bars, empty save for one Holstein cow. In front of the cow was a feeding trough partially filled with hay. Behind the animal, running the length of the barn, parallel to the trough, was a cement gutter into which an animal could defecate and which easily could be hosed clean. The gutter behind the Holstein was filled with fresh cow flop.

Jubal peered into the shadows of the barn and saw various tools hung on one wall. Underneath the tools was a wheelbarrow. He started toward the tools but paused as he passed the cow. He saw that her udders were swollen with milk and he heard the moan as she twisted her head within the stanchion bars.

"Well, now," he spoke softly to the animal, "you think I come to strip you down, doncha?" He stepped close to the cow and ran his hand along her flank and the animal bawled. "Yeah, that's what you think, all right." He knew the swollen udders pained the cow and he felt sorry for her; he felt a growing anger at the tall, thin farmer who had neglected the animal. He leaned down and put his lips against the cow's ear. "Jew didn't do you, did he? Don't you worry none, we gonna take care of you. Yeah, you an' him both."

He squatted next to the cow and buried his head into her flank and tenderly stripped milk from her teats. He let the milk run freely onto the cement floor. Once, before he depleted the animal of her supply, he bent lower and pointed one of her teats toward his mouth and drank of her warm sweet milk. He wished he could stay this way forever, not moving, just hunkered up, the fragrance of steaming dung drifting around him, warm milk in his mouth. But he knew he couldn't.

When Jubal finished and the Holstein was quiet, he took a shovel from the wall and began to fill the wheelbarrow with the fresh cow flop. He wheeled the load out of the barn. The rain was lighter now, and the salted ribbons of wax that threaded the wooden cross burned brighter. Jubal rolled his load of dung toward the Moons' farmhouse. He stopped at the kitchen door. He took the spade, whose blade was buried in the dung, and crashed it through the window in the kitchen door. He reached inside and turned the latch. He opened the door and rolled the wheelbarrow inside. He set to work.

It was some time before Jubal waded the stream and climbed high into the mountains. As he approached the cave he heard a high, undulating moan, and he thought that the old man must be blowing his cow's horn in celebration of the night, but as he stepped into the clearing in the woods he saw that he was wrong. The sound came from Tuttle.

The farmer lay on his back, his arms outstretched, his wrists rawhide-pegged to the ground, his legs crossed at the ankles, crucified to the earth. Blood trickled from his mouth. His eyes were wide with pain. A great stone slab rested heavily on his chest.

Riordan, the thick hemp rope in his hands, was slowly lowering another stone and as its terrible weight inched closer to the body of the tall thin man, Riordan lifted his voice in the words of the warning which Jubal had seen on the bark.

"Thou art in trouble today," sang Riordan, *"and I too; another is in trouble tomorrow, I too; after this generation other descendants who succeed your descendants are in trouble; I am in trouble down to the end of the world!"*

And then the old man howled.

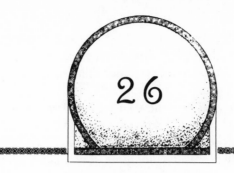

26

Depressed by not hearing from Solomon for two days, Kendal wandered through the house, dusting tables that were without dust, waxing already burnished wood, straightening a chair here, replacing a lamp there, searching for loose threads on upholstery that was without blemish, flipping pages of a cookbook for exotic recipes that could be prepared (for whom? she wondered) and frozen but whose ingredients she knew she was without, munching a stalk of celery, and generally pretending to set her house in order. These capricious actions relieved her not at all, for she knew that her house was in order and, as she glanced around at the accumulation of years, she admitted that she didn't really give a damn one way or another.

"It's not your house, twit," she said aloud, "it's your life."

Plucking a pear from a fruit bowl, polishing it on her sleeve, she walked from room to room, never lingering in any one of them, just standing in the doorways, her glance sweeping over objets d'art and bric-a-brac, a framed print, a silver bowl, a weaving: mementos of moments shared with Solomon or Darby. Normally, the sight of these things triggered a warm remembrance, a sense of family continuity, but as she studied them now she felt resentful toward them. She felt that in the acquisition of her collection she had been robbed of energy best suited for another purpose.

She moved into her bedroom and propped herself against the pillows of the four-poster bed. Through narrowed lids, she peeked through the lace pattern of the canopy. The lace was delicately embroidered in swirling circles and its edges hung just below the canopy frame. Fine silk tassels bordered the lace; they stirred slightly, driven by air flowing gently from a hot-air vent in one wall. Kendal had turned up the thermostat to ward off the chill of the evening's incessant rain. The tiny, constant rhythm of the tassels made her think of frail Chinese dancers and she tried to imagine the plucking of a lute.

She bit into her pear and the cold juices refreshed her mouth, ran sweetly down her throat, and reminded her of the many times she and Solomon had picnicked on fruit, a round of brie, a chilled chablis. She looked at a wall where a watercolor hung. It was a lovely rendition of La Colombe d'Or, the inn at St. Paul de Vence, perched high in the hills of Provence.

The summer before Darby was born, Kendal had been hired to play a featured role in an English film. It was a melodrama to be shot in and around St. Tropez. Her excitement about the opportunity was shared by Solomon. The film was a tidy story of suspense and passion. Of equal importance was the chance to explore southern France. To make matters complete, the owner of a harbor café, learning of Solomon's skills, hired him to play nightly piano. During the days when Kendal's presence was not required on the set, she and Solomon roamed the hills and villages of Provence, and each night Kendal sat at a small table overlooking the sea and as she listened to Solomon's piano, she watched the parading revelry at harborside. Kendal's job meant going early to bed, so she rarely heard Solomon come home. But in the mornings they would sit together in bed, drink dark French-roast coffee, eat buttered croissants, and make love. It was a month of enchantment for the Moons.

Looking at the watercolor of St. Paul de Vence, Kendal remembered their final lunch at La Colombe d'Or. As they lingered over a last wine, the bells of the Angelus tolled. Lovely white doves, which seemed to perch on all the balconies and parapets of the inn, rose as one and flew into the sun, their wings turning golden.

"Why don't we stay?" Solomon asked.

"I've an early call tomorrow," Kendal said.

"I don't mean stay tonight. I mean, stay. Just stay."

"What a lovely thought," Kendal said. "You'll be the Beethoven of the docks and I'll bake croissants. Thousands and thousands of croissants."

"Do you like baking?"

"I hate baking."

"Then do nothing."

"I don't know how to do nothing."

"I know," Solomon said. "I'll teach you."

· "You're serious."

"Yes."

"C'mon, love," she said, rising from the table, wanting suddenly not to take him seriously. "It's late."

"Yeah," he said, "it's late."

The taste of pear was no longer sweet in Kendal's mouth. She wrapped it in a Kleenex and put it on the bedside table. She stared at the watercolor of La Colombe d'Or. She'd purchased it from a local artist in Provence and given it to Solomon as a gift. He rarely looked at it. He'd thanked her but he rarely looked at it. Kendal had thought that perhaps he did not like the angle from which it had been painted or that he'd been disappointed that the artist had failed to include white doves flying toward the sun. But now she was not sure. Perhaps it reminded him of what he'd wanted and could not have. His response, Kendal realized, was similar to when he beheld a piano. He might look at it, touch it, but, always, he would walk away.

Listening to the rain, Kendal pondered over these avoidances. Had she been the catalyst for his withdrawals? Had she pushed him toward obligations he'd wished to shun? But no, she told herself, without fuss he had accepted responsibility.

Except, perhaps, in his relationship with Darby. But whose fault was that? Had Solomon wanted a child? He'd never said. Kendal was not unaware that in their mutual attempt to lead a child toward independence, she and Solomon had erred on the side of leniency and had not provided Darby an emotional touchstone to which she could refer her actions. Solomon had played the role of father much as an actor assumes his part. Remembering Solomon's accusation, Kendal felt remorse tinged with guilt as she acknowledged to herself that his role-playing might have been one more attempt to *live up to his capacity*, the ethic she realized by which she had been raised and to which she still adhered. Was it wrong to foster such a principle? Was it wrong to encourage excellence? Or was that what she had done? She had wanted Solomon to use his skill and talent in ways that would enrich his life. No, she said silently, that is only half true. Solomon's statement was the other half. I wanted his talent to enrich both of our lives. The thought disturbed her.

She squinted at the watercolor as if she would find an answer to her confusion hidden behind the walls of the painted inn. There had been such delight in their lives when they were in France. And other times. Many other times. During all those years in the theater, whether she was playing New York or London or touring across the country, Solomon had found ways to join her. The length of his visits were incidental. A weekend was as good as a month. They played time like an accordion, folding it in and out while they danced to its tune. They laughed and made love and sang ribald songs, ran hand in hand down midnight streets, and talked, incessantly talked. There was no limit to their enthusiasm.

Suddenly, Kendal tensed. There was a common circumstance that linked those memorable occasions. She had been working. She had been living up to *her* capacity. Was that it? Was it that simple? Had she so missed her career that she had deviously encouraged Solomon so that she might at least walk on the perimeter of his life?

"Shit," she muttered to a Solomon whom she imagined stood at the foot of the bed. "Then why didn't you say something, do something?"

And the imagined Solomon packed his suitcase and left.

He had done something.

From downstairs Kendal heard the Westminster chimes of the grandfather clock. Once again she thought of the Angelus bells of St. Paul de Vence and she wished she knew if Solomon had been correct.

"Yeah," he'd said, "it's late."

Perhaps, she thought, it is too late.

She left the bed and crossed the room. She opened the window. She smelled the rain and wished she and Solomon were walking in it. She held out her hand and let the rain fall into her palm and thought about calling Solomon, but when she withdrew her hand, touched the palm with her mouth, moistening her lips with the water, it tasted cold and sweet, reminding her of her solitary childhood journeys through Windsor Park, and suddenly she yearned for solitude, for a time truly alone, for a place where, like a small girl again, she might amble in the silent woods and hear no voices, not even her own.

She whirled from the window. She pulled a small suitcase from under the bed. She began to pack. She knew where to find a silent woods.

Vermont.

27

When he left the tennis court, Solomon returned to his hotel and ordered a bottle of Johnny Walker Black but drank none of it. *The thing* inside him left no room for alcohol. He dialed the operator and placed a call to Kendal, then canceled it. He didn't feel he could explain to Kendal, a product of the Church of England, how ugly the memorial to a dead Jew had been; nor could he define the rage within him. He checked his watch, wondering if he could reach the Mouse, then placed a call to Emilio's deli. The line was busy for a long time, but finally Solomon made contact.

"Emilio here. The whitefish is terrific!"

Solomon felt a rush of love at the sound of his friend's cheerful voice and wished he could reach across the continent and hug him.

"It's Solomon."

"Hey! Where are you? I'm not kiddin', the whitefish is terrific."

"I'm still in L.A."

"Oh. Yeah. Listen, how'd it go? You get through it okay? I mean, Mrs. Brindig and everything."

"It was terrible, Em. It was really terrible."

"Gee, I'm sorry, Solomon."

Solomon heard the clink of silver, the rattle of plates, the voices of waiters in the background, and he knew that the deli must be packed. "Are you busy, Em?"

There was only a slight pause before Emilio answered. "No, not what you'd call real busy. A little off tonight, ya know?"

Oh, you lovely liar, Solomon thought. You know, don't you? You know I want to talk. Solomon took advantage of it. He spilled out the story. He couldn't stop talking. He made every detail vivid. He was aware that occasionally the sounds of the restaurant diminished and he knew that Em must have covered the telephone with his hand as he issued orders to the waiters, welcomed new customers, said good night to old ones, checked supplies of beer and beans, corned beef and seeded rolls, and never once indicated to Solomon that he had any interest other than the tale Solomon told. When, finally, Solomon had recounted everything he remembered, Emilio spoke.

"Listen," he said gently, "come home."

"Yeah."

"When?"

"Maybe tonight. Maybe I can get a late flight."

"No. Tomorrow. Get some sleep tonight. You can leave tomorrow."

"I think there's a late —"

"Solomon, please," Emilio said quietly. "I know what I'm talkin' about. Do what I tell you, okay?"

"Yes, Em, whatever you want." Solomon meant it. "Listen, is Mouse there?"

"Tomorrow night I got this thing with the Mouse. You'll meet us in front of the store. You'll come with us."

Solomon remembered Mouse's anger at the deli. "I don't want to interfere, Em. I mean if you and Mouse planned —"

"Jesus." It was said so softly that Solomon hardly heard the word. "I'm gonna pretend I didn't hear you, Solomon. I just didn't hear you."

"I'll see you at the store," Solomon said.

"Right," Emilio said. "And listen. What Mrs. Brindig did . . . don't put her down too quick, all right? I mean, some people . . . some people . . . they just don't know how to cry. You understand what I'm sayin'?"

"Sure, Em, sure."

The following morning he took a plane to Kennedy airport and arrived early in the evening. He tried to phone Kendal but there was no answer. He remembered there was a British comedy playing at the local movie theater. He hoped she'd gone and was enjoying herself.

After giving a cab driver the address of Emilio's deli he asked to be taken on a roundabout route. The driver, pleased at a larger fare, was glad to accommodate and drove by the photographic store which, in the window, had the display of hands. Solomon did not ask him to stop. He was content to note that the fingers of that final photographed hand were still in graceful repose.

The taxi pulled up at the delicatessen. Both Em and the Mouse were waiting. They were conversing quietly as they took turns stroking the mule's nose. As Mouse greeted Solomon, Em climbed onto the driver's seat. Solomon understood that it was a tactful act.

"Em told me," Mouse said as he hugged Solomon. He took the tennis racket and suitcase from Solomon and tossed them into the carriage. For just a moment, he stared at the racket. "Some game, huh?" Solomon just shook his head. "I had this buddy," Mouse continued quietly, "a helluva guy. Gone through the whole thing — Africa, Italy, Germany. Not a scratch. A goddamn miracle kid. One night he's taking a dump in a slit trench and bam! Fucking mortar got him. Only thing left was his legs, his pants down around his knees. You know what I did?" Again, Solomon just shook his head, and the Mouse continued. "I go to the medics and I get a pocketful of these little laxative pills and I took 'em. I mean, all of 'em. Every goddamn one of 'em. I shit for two days straight. I couldn't stop. What I'm saying, Solomon, there's a whole lot of crazy ways to say good-bye. Go figure."

Together, they climbed into the phaeton. Em clucked at the mule and they started downtown.

"Where are we going?" Solomon asked.

"You'll like it," Mouse said. "Trust me."

They rode downtown in companionable silence and from the route they took Solomon knew that Mouse was going to stable his mule. Solomon had traveled this way before with Mouse, but he realized that he had not done so for a long time. They reached lower Manhattan and the carriage passed a range of commercial buildings, most of which still retained their nineteenth-century cast-iron decorations. Observing the neighborhood through which they passed, Solomon felt a twinge of envy, for what he saw represented passion rather than mediocrity. What had once been an area of warehouses and commerce now housed hundreds of the city's artists: painters, sculptors, musicians, photographers, dancers, potters. Tucked among the squat buildings of soot-grimed brick were smaller shops, gaily decorated, and through whose windows could be seen the results of artistic effort. There were marble statues and steel birds soaring, weavings of Indian hues, an abstract seascape in which wind and wave were joined, a vase in the form of a pheasant, its ruffled wings a rainbow of handblown glass. There were blocks of granite polished into strange shapes by their creators, and portraits in oil so thickly daubed that the features of those who had posed bulged from the canvas, and watercolors so delicate and pale that any who viewed might believe the artist had painted a sigh.

The carriage moved east, past Peretz Square, and then turned south. Small shops lined both sides of the street: a barbershop, bakeries, a kosher cafeteria, pawnshops, delicatessens, a bookstore, a specialty shop for children, a hardware mart whose neon lights blinked its wares, a Chinese restaurant. All these stores were on street level and crowned by tenements. Most of the buildings were only four or five or six stories tall, and all were fitted with rusted fire escapes zigzagging down the front facade.

What astonished Solomon was what stood on the landings of the various fire escapes.

Crude booths had been erected. Each one was similar to the one Solomon had seen on the rooftop in Harlem where the elderly Jew had fed his pigeon. The back wall of each booth was the facade of the tenement, and jutting at right angles from the walls were two more walls made of cardboard or canvas sheeting or stacks of orange crates. The roofs of the makeshift stalls were made from strips of wood or bamboo reeds or boughs of evergreen, but none of the material was so dense as to restrict the passage of sun or rain or the sight of the stars above. Either one side or the front of each booth was open to the street, and through this opening Solomon could see that the booths were festooned with fruit and nuts, and that hanging on the interior walls were plaques and tapestries and paintings, all these things illuminated by lanterns that glowed warmly within the walls. Tables were crowded in the center of the booths and there were chairs or stools or benches around the tables. Men, women, and children sat around the tables, all of which seemed abundantly laden with food and wine, and as those inside ate and drank, their talk and laughter swelled, seemed to bulge the poor walls, drifted across the twisted fire escapes and into the street, and all the sound was jubilant. Solomon gaped.

"It's beautiful, isn't it?" Mouse asked.

Numbly, Solomon nodded. Never had he witnessed such a community of joy.

Before he could express his awe, Solomon heard Emilio cluck sharply, and the mule pulled the phaeton cab around a corner into a long alley. Until now, the wooden carriage wheels had rolled quite smoothly along the city's slick streets, but when they turned into the alley Solomon was immediately aware of a bumpy passage, and he knew they were approaching the stable. Although he was familiar with the jouncing passage, he had never been here at night and he found the landscape exciting. The sight of the gaily lighted booths had awakened a new curiosity.

He looked down and saw that they were traveling over old cobblestones, which glistened darkly from an earlier rain. The light on the stones flickered and seemed strangely yellow. Solomon glanced up and saw that the narrow alley was illuminated by antique gas lamps, their flames hissing softly within globes of finely etched glass. The cobblestones and gaslights projected a sense of Edwardian grace, but that was quickly dispelled when Solomon saw that the gutters on either side of the alley were littered with broken glass, scraps of metal, bits of browned apple cores, used condoms. The low buildings that flanked the alley were boarded up and scarred by graffiti. Most of these buildings had unusually wide double doors which, if unsealed, would swing directly onto the alley. Although not redolent, there was a noticeable scent in the air. It was not unpleasant and Solomon knew its source. These buildings were stables, which had been used by peddlers of long ago who had hawked ice and coal from horse-drawn wagons.

Emilio dropped the reins and the mule proceeded on his own. The animal slowed and came to a halt at the end of the alley. Although the building where the mule had stopped was similar to the others, squat and double-doored, the resemblance ended there. The doors were not sealed. They were carefully locked with straps of black wrought iron from which hung a padlock. There was no graffiti on the building. It was painted barn red. Outside, on a narrow strip of ground, roses were planted. Although no flowers blossomed, green leaves still clung to their stalks.

Emilio leaped off his carriage seat. He started for the stable, but just as he reached it, he swerved into another alley. Solomon was surprised. He'd never noticed the alley before. As Emilio disappeared, Mouse climbed out of the cab and moved to his mule. Solomon followed. Together, they unhitched the animal. Mouse leaned down and plucked leaves from a bush. He cupped them in his hands, and fed them to the mule.

"The thing is," he said to Solomon, "he's very particular. We tried all kinds, but all he'll eat is Mr. Lincoln."

"That's funny," Solomon said, hearing the familiar name of the rose, "that's what Kendal grows."

"Nu?" asked the Mouse. "So where do you think it came from?"

"Kendal gave you that?"

"No, Darby." As the mule munched contentedly, Mouse ran a hand over the animal's neck and then looked at his fingers. He shook his head. "Hoo ha," he said. "I knew it. The *gonif* who sold me the paint, he swore it was waterproof. So what's this?" He held his hand under a gas lamp. His palm was streaked with the paint he'd used to make his mule believe he was a pinto pony. "C'mon, horsie, we'll take you in to dry."

Mouse unlocked the stable, and he and Solomon led the mule through the doorway. Mouse turned on a light, revealing four box stalls in the small stable. All were empty, but the floor of one of them was covered with soft blankets, and a bale of hay stood in the corner. The mule moved directly toward the stall. He nosed up the restraining bar and moved into the stall. He turned so that he faced the front, slowly bent his legs, and lowered himself onto the blankets. His head was some four feet from the bale of hay. He looked at it. He brayed. He swung his head toward the Mouse. The animal looked wistful.

"Oh, boy," said Mouse, "he knows about the paint. He's gonna make me pay. 'Lookit me,' he says, 'lookit what you done. One more storm, I'm a has-been. I'm a horse who wasn't there. So feed me, feed me before I fade away.' I'll tell you something, Solomon. This horse, he's got *chutzpah!*"

Mouse walked into the stall and pulled handfuls of hay from the bale. He scattered it in front of the animal. The mule's head dipped and his lips pulled back to reveal his huge yellow teeth.

"I think he's laughing," Solomon said.

"He keeps it up, I'm gonna let him know about this delicacy I got in mind."

"What's that?"

"Muleburger," the Mouse said. He stepped out of the stall and started for the door. He turned and looked back at the mule. "I didn't mean it." He moved out of the stable and Solomon followed. Mouse relocked the door. Solomon remembered the lamp Mouse had turned on.

"You going to leave the light on?" he asked.

"You like to eat in the dark?" Mouse asked.

Mouse led Solomon down the alley where Emilio had disappeared. It was a passage to another cobblestone street parallel to the stable's alley. At the far end of it was a building. It was exceptionally narrow, no more than twenty feet wide, and faced with yellow brick, which was chipped and peeling and which appeared, even in the dull gaslight glow, to be blackened by fire scar. The building was gently domed, and crested with an iron Star of David. Solomon realized that it must have been a synagogue, but he could not believe that it still served that purpose, for the central entrance at the top of a flight of stone steps was entirely sealed with brick. The synagogue was three stories high. The door was shaped like a keyhole, reflecting a Moorish tradition. The two small windows on the first floor and the two corresponding windows on the second floor were also keyhole-shaped; they, too, were sealed with brick. Set high into the front wall of the third story was a round stained-glass window. Only a few panes remained, unshattered. At street level, below the central entrance, was a heavy wooden door, which appeared to lead to the basement of the building. A thin strip of weeds separated the synagogue from the alley. At the far end of this pathetic garden, at the left-hand corner of the synagogue, was a chain-link fence that led to another narrow alley. The right-hand wall of the building was joined to its neighbor, a mean structure identified by a garish hand-painted sign: Omega Exterminators.

Solomon could not imagine what a seemingly abandoned synagogue was doing in the midst of stables. He and Mouse stepped across the strip of weeds and walked down three steps to a basement door. When Mouse pushed open the door, Solomon was surprised at its weight and saw that it was made of heavy oak panels. The oak was strangely pitted with little scoops of charred wood. Solomon ran a finger across the indentations and glanced questioningly at Mouse.

"Cherry bombs," Mouse said.

"Sons of bitches," Solomon snapped, then was startled by his own quick reaction. It was more than vandalism he cursed. He felt personally attacked. It was not the profanity that surprised him, it was the intensity of his reaction. He wished he stood before those who had scarred the synagogue, the whip antenna in his hand.

The basement was in total contrast to the exterior of the synagogue. It was as white and clean as a cube of snow. The floor was covered with wide pine planking, the wood almost colorless from bleach. The walls had been stripped of old horsehair plaster to reveal their original brick, which was freshly whitewashed. The exposed joists of the ceiling, which were hand hewn, had been sanded smooth and painted as white as the walls. In the center of the room were six benches, neatly placed one behind the other, made of wooden slats on iron legs. Solomon realized that they were park benches. Resting on the seat of each bench were two prayer books, some closed, others opened at random. They were not new. They were bound in leather that was stained and cracked, and many of their pages were loose or torn. In one corner of the basement, near a short flight of stairs which rose to a door Solomon assumed led to the synagogue's main floor, was a long cobbler's bench with a low milking stool set in front. In the small compartments that had once been used for tacks and needles were quill pens made from the clean feathers of a fowl, and small, open bottles of black ink. Where strips of soling leather once rested, there were now rolls of parchment hide. One of these hides was stretched flat on the working surface of the bench. Inscribed meticulously in black ink on the parchment hide were sentences of Hebrew words. The last sentence was incomplete.

Solomon wanted to ask Mouse what the words meant, what truth they might convey, what solace was implied, but, turning slowly to survey the room, he saw something unexpected. On one white wall was a small black square, a vivid contrast to the rest of the room. He had seen it before. Where? Of course! In his dream of the blood-mouthed Jew. The black square had been a bed in the white room where he and Kendal and the Jew stood moments before the Jew dived toward the pomegranate tree. But there was something else, something not of a dream. The secret photograph! The black-and-white print of his grandfather who, in his dark suit and white shirt, stood in a square of sunlit field.

"What is that?" he asked Mouse. When he spoke he saw the white vapor of his breath, and for the first time was aware of the deep chill in the synagogue.

"Tradition," Mouse answered. "A reminder."

"Of what?"

"The destruction of our temples. The black days of our lives."

"Listen," Solomon asked, "where are we? What is this place?"

"The *bes medrash*. A house of study."

"Did you do all this? Clean it up, paint it?"

"Who else?"

"It must have been a helluva job."

"Tell the truth, I had help."

"Em?"

"I had help," Mouse repeated. He climbed the small stairway in the corner and opened the door that led upstairs. "Come."

When Solomon stepped into the upstairs room his foot was engulfed in sawdust. He was in a room of rubble. The brick-lined walls were crumbling, their fine redstone dust clinging to everything and mixed so thoroughly with the sawdust underfoot that it looked as if dried blood had been sifted through a sieve. Old wooden pews that might have been rescued from abandoned railroad stations were placed haphazardly around the room, their oak veneer pitted and scarred. Scattered among them were antique ceramic spittoons. The synagogue was gutted, but through a network of remaining joists Solomon saw a domed ceiling of embossed sheet metal. Although in spots the metal was buckled and rusted, squares of faded paint were still visible. They were signs of the zodiac. The shattered stained-glass window in the front of the building just below the dome still held two panes. Their designs were in the shapes of flower petals. Solomon's gaze moved down from the window to the floor, which was spattered with pigeon droppings and chunks of crumbling plaster. Across from each other, on the facing long walls, were two narrow balconies. The balconies were in shadow. In the center of the synagogue was a *bimah*, a raised reader's platform, whose four corners were ornamented with unlit gaslamps enclosed in Victorian glass shades. At the rear of the synagogue a *ner tamid*, the eternal light, was suspended by a long iron chain from the tin ceiling. The lamp, a huge copper globe, hung over an unadorned Ark whose doors hung loosely from broken hinges. Emilio stood on a stepladder underneath the lamp, filling it with olive oil from a can.

Solomon turned in a small circle as he observed all these things. He saw that Mouse stood at a curving stairway that led up to one of the balconies. Mouse was watching him.

"What do you think?" asked Mouse.

"Who owns this place?" Solomon asked.

"I do," said the Mouse.

"You plan to live a long time?"

"Why?"

" 'Cause it's going to take a hundred and two years to fix it up."

"Yeah," Emilio said as he climbed down the ladder, "that's what the city said when Mouse here give 'em the nod."

"Mouse what?" Solomon asked.

"Give 'em the nod," Emilio repeated. "You know, like in the movies, one guy nods, another guy tips his hat, a lady maybe scratches. Mouse, he uses the nod. It's like a class act, ya know?"

"Sometimes," Solomon said as he stared at Emilio, "I find you a tad enigmatic."

Mouse laughed. "He's talking about the auction. Em went with me."

"You wouldn't like to start from go, would you?" asked Solomon.

"Sure." And Mouse explained.

The synagogue, built in the nineteenth century, had for many years served as the house of study and worship for hundreds of Jews who had immigrated to the Lower East Side. But as time passed, the neighborhood changed and with it the needs of its people. What had been primarily a residential area of poor tenements gave way to commercial property. Families moved and were no longer attracted by the proximity of the *shul* to their homes; these same families benefited from the growing commerce. No longer penurious, they sought the more affluent ambience of grander temples in which to worship. It was not necessarily a conscious choice but one that reflected a desire to lift themselves from mean and humble streets. Prosperity needed a face. It was not long before the tiny synagogue in the alley had a difficult time attracting a *minyan*, the minimum number of ten male Jews required for religious services. The neighborhood worsened and became the playing ground for bullies who perfected the art of vandalism and arson. They turned the synagogue into a rat-infested shell. The few men and women who thought of it as their own were elderly and without means to assume the responsibility of maintenance and so they turned it over to the city.

One morning, many months ago, leading his mule out of the stable, Mouse had seen a newly printed sign on the door of the synagogue. It was an announcement that the city had no practical purpose for the synagogue and that the building would be auctioned. Should no acceptable bid be forthcoming, a court order for demolition was pending. Mouse's nod bought the *shul* for an absurdly low price.

At the conclusion of this discourse there was a flash of motion on the floor and Solomon saw a rat dart across the mound of pigeon droppings then disappear through the hole in the brick wall. Mouse smiled and shook his head.

"That's a dumb rat," he said. "That is really a very dumb rat. He could sit here nice and quiet, minding his own business, thinking maybe a little about Moses, contemplating the prophets perhaps, and what does he do? He runs next door to the exterminator, where, if you follow me, he faces a very limited future." Mouse paused, a contemplative look on his face, then shrugged. "On the other hand, who doesn't?"

"I don't," said a bright voice from above. "Like Methuselah, I shall live nine hundred and sixty-nine years."

Slowly, a figure rose from behind the brass railing of the balcony and Darby Moon looked down. The flickering light of the *ner tamid* struck the tin ceiling and bounced back to illuminate her. Solomon held his breath. He had never seen her look quite so beautiful. Looking at her, he knew it wasn't the lamplight that made her so radiant. She glowed from inside as if a fire burned. Oh, how marvelous, he thought, to own that fire!

She stared at him for a long moment, pain moving across her eyes, then spoke quietly.

"You look so tired, Dad."

Quickly, she crossed the balcony and descended to the floor of the synagogue and swept Solomon into her arms.

"I love you," she said.

Solomon drew his daughter to him, and it startled him to realize how long it had been since he'd held Darby in his arms, since he had smelled the fragrance of her hair, since he had recognized, truly recognized, the flesh of his own flesh; and he wanted terribly to share her world with her, her new world bounded by the walls of the synagogue, the world in which peasants flew like sparrows and men like Brindig were not afraid to die in the gutter, the world which offered community to Jews.

But he didn't know how. It was *their* world and he was an alien who had stepped inside it.

Confused by his own inability to accept what attracted him, he released Darby and moved slightly away from her and the Mouse, not wanting to betray their own communion. To cover his retreat he asked the Mouse to tell Darby about the tennis memorial.

Emilio disappeared down the stairway to the basement. Mouse and Darby sat together on the floor in the red sawdust looking, Solomon thought, like children playing in a sandbox. Solomon moved further away, roaming around the synagogue, shuffling through the sawdust, here and there touching an exposed wall stud, stopping occasionally to stare at some spot on a crumbling brick wall as if it held a special meaning, pausing for a moment to run his hand over the black square on the wall and instantly recalling his anger at the disappearance of his grandfather's photograph, moving on to the raised reader's platform, circling it carefully, then climbing its stairs to face the Ark, whose doors he swung back and forth while he listened to the squeak of broken hinges, whose sound echoed the rasping throat of the man he'd attacked on Forty-Second Street. His hands trembling, he closed the doors of the Ark, descended the *bimah*, and backed across the synagogue until he felt the squish of pigeon shit under his shoes. He was still staring at the Ark when he felt his daughter's hand on his arm.

"It's hard to say good-bye to people," Darby said, her voice low and gentle. "What Mrs. Brindig did, I guess it was the only way she knew how. I'm glad you came here, Daddy. It's a good place to say good-bye."

"Or, hello," Solomon said softly. "It's a good place to say hello." From the gentle pressure of her fingers he knew that Darby understood his overture. "It's you, isn't?" he asked quietly. "You're the one who's helping Mouse." He drew a circle in the air, describing the synagogue. "Here, I mean."

"Yes."

"Do you believe in God, Darby?"

"I don't know. Sometimes."

For the first time since she'd moved to him, Solomon turned and looked at her. "I like you," he said. "I like you very much."

As she smiled at him, they heard Emilio, who stood on the landing of the basement steps.

"Okay, guys," he called. "It's ready!"

Not knowing what was ready, but anxious to find out, Solomon followed the others to the basement. At the far end of the white room was a door, so low that they all had to bend as they passed through its archway and into the small courtyard at the rear of the synagogue.

As Solomon stepped through the doorway he saw that a booth, similar to the ones he'd seen earlier, had been erected on the rude square of ground and that it, too, was decorated with fruit and stalks of corn through whose separated layers he could see the dark and now rainless sky. On the back wall, taped to the synagogue brick, were seven small portraits, and printed in chalk underneath each one was a name. The practical furnishing of the booth was made entirely of orange crates. Four had been pushed together to form a makeshift table. Other crates flanked the sides of the table and there was one at each end. These crates served as benches. A beautiful lace shawl was draped as a tablecloth over the center crates, its fringed fingers lightly brushing the bare ground beneath. Solomon thought there was something familiar about the shawl, about the intricate weaving of its lace, about the delicacy of its fringe, about its rich cream color. He looked more closely. It was the shawl he had purchased many years ago for Kendal and which, she in turn, had given Darby as a coveted graduation gift. Tiny drops of soft white wax had splattered the center of the lace — drippings from the candlestick in the center of the table. It was a *menorah*, the flames burning brightly from candles in its eight branches and from the ninth candle placed in the central holder. On either side of the *menorah* were jugs of wine. Gaily painted ceramic dishes were placed all around the table. Each was filled to overflowing. There were dishes of gefiltefish, pickled herring, smoked whitefish, borscht, Bermuda onions, black bread, horseradish, red and green relishes, sliced pot roast, cold cabbage, salads of cabbage and peppers and carrots, pickled beans, roasted chickens, blini and sour cream, shelled almonds, mustard greens and leeks, lentils, radishes, jellies of blackberry and guava and mint, thick slices of luscious melons, their pink and yellow and green flesh glistening in the candle glow. Solomon was overwhelmed at the richness of the banquet. But in his mind's eye he saw two men who had died with their faces in the gutter and he felt that perhaps the feast he beheld was inopportune.

As if reading Solomon's mind, the Mouse spoke quietly. "We are taught that death is not an end, only a door through which a man enters into the world of truth." And then, stepping into the festive booth, he said a short prayer in Hebrew.

Darby move to the doorway of the booth. As she entered, she started to repeat the Mouse's prayer. She stopped suddenly and turned to look at her father. "It's a prayer. You say it when you enter the *sukkah*, the booth, and when you leave it. Will you say it with me? In English?"

"I think," Solomon answered, "that I would feel foolish."

"No, I won't let you feel foolish." And she began the prayer. " 'May it be Thy will that the Divine presence dwell among us . . .' " She paused. She smiled at Solomon and her voice was gentle. "It's simple, Daddy, it's really very simple." As she repeated the opening of the prayer, she nodded encouragement to him. " 'May it be Thy will that the Divine presence dwell among us . . .' "

" 'May it be Thy will,' " Solomon said hesitantly, " 'that the Divine presence dwell among us . . .' "

" 'And spread over us the tabernacle of peace by virtue of our observance of the mitzvah of *sukkah*.' "

" 'And spread over us the tabernacle of peace by virtue of the . . . the . . .' " Solomon was lost.

"Mitzvah," Darby prompted.

"In the Torah," Mouse said, "there are over six hundred mitzvahs. It means an obligation, a moral or religious obligation. The dos and don'ts, you might say."

"Mitzvah," Solomon said. "Mitzvah. Did I say it right? Did it sound good?"

"It sounded good," Mouse smiled.

"I wonder," Solomon said softly, "I wonder if you'd say the whole thing again, only in . . . Hebrew."

Together, Mouse and Darby repeated the prayer in Hebrew. Shyly, carefully enunciating the alien prayer, Solomon repeated it after them. When he completed the prayer, he blushed.

"Oh, Daddy," Darby said, "I love you!"

When Mouse and Emilio broke into applause, Solomon felt as if a tidal wave were rolling over him, threatening to drown him in a growing excitement.

Wanting suddenly to know more, much more, about this booth, his eyes swept the area, observing the banquet and the seven portraits taped to the wall, and, for the first time, he saw that leaning in one corner of the booth were branches — one from a palm tree, two from a willow — with three twigs of myrtle nesting among them. On the floor beside these leafy boughs, half hidden by their foliage, was an exquisite oval box of beaten silver, an almost imperceptible horizontal crack indicating that the top was removable. A silver nipple protruded from one end. The contour of the box resembled a lemon, the nipple its stem. Solomon felt as if he'd stumbled into the museum of a foreign city. He urgently required the services of a guide.

"Who are they?" he asked, his finger stabbing toward the taped photographs. Without waiting for an answer, he stepped across the earthen floor of the booth and ran his hands down the length of the willow branches and realized that all the branches were tied together in a woodsy bouquet. "What are these for? This box, this silver box, is there something in it? Does it mean something? What do you do with it? Who made it?"

"Whoa! Whoa!" Mouse cried. "Say, listen, you can't be a rabbi in one night!"

"I'm hungry," Emilio said.

"All right, all right, we'll eat," Mouse said. "We'll eat, we'll drink, we'll laugh a little and then a little more, Solomon, because that, too, is a mitzvah, for the Lord commanded that we rejoice in the Festival of Booths."

"The Festival of Booths?" Solomon asked.

"Sit," Mouse ordered, "and listen."

They sat on the orange crates. When they had all made themselves comfortable around the lace-covered table, Mouse lifted one of the jugs and poured wine for the others and himself. Then he filled another goblet and placed it at the end of the table and called out in a ringing voice. "Enter, enter, exalted holy ghosts. Come guests, high and holy. Come our fathers, high and holy. Come Abraham, Isaac, Jacob, Joseph, Moses, Aaron, and David!" He turned and faced the taped portraits on the wall and raised his glass. "Welcome!"

Mouse drank deeply of his wine then turned to Solomon. "Abraham, the father of what we are, who we are, was a very cordial fellow, and he would walk the mountains and the desert searching for those who had less than he, and he would welcome them to share in whatever food or drink he could provide. This custom is called *ushpizin;* we continue it because it reminds us of those who came before us and those who will come after us. But the interesting thing, Solomon, the best thing, is that the Feast of the Tabernacles, the Festival of Booths, is for all people. You see, Zechariah prophesied, 'It shall come to pass that every one that is left of all nations that came up against Jerusalem shall go up from year to year to worship the King, the Lord of Hosts, and to keep the Feast of Booths.' What he was saying was that all the world will come under the shadow of the *sukkah* — which, put another way, is the protection of God's kindness. A great rabbi once said, 'whoever abides under the shadow of faith acquires freedom for himself and his descendants in perpetuity.' Now *that* is something to think about!"

Yes, Solomon said to himself, that is certainly something to think about. Could he, too, find freedom under the shadow of the *sukkah?* Would that quiet the scratching animal in his belly? The question disturbed him, for he wasn't ready to relinquish the presence of *the thing*. Somehow, that unfocused rage had given him the strength to divorce himself from unwelcomed accommodation. He was reluctant to turn backwards to passivity.

Mouse lifted his cup and looked at the others. "Darby, did you study the words of *kiddush?*"

Nodding eagerly, Darby closed her eyes, and Solomon saw that her lips silently formed words as if she were making sure of their exactness, then she opened her eyes and lifted her cup.

"'Praised art thou,'" Darby said, "'O King, King of the universe, who created the fruit of the wine.'"

"'Blessed art Thou, O Lord our King of the universe,'" Mouse responded, "'Who has kept us alive and sustained us and enabled us to reach this season.'"

Not all of us, Solomon thought, not all of us have reached this season, not Ben Brindig. He hid his hands under the table, for they were trembling again at what else he was thinking. For if he'd had his way, the stranger who'd hammered tongues to his door and stolen the picture of his daughter would reach no further season.

"Now?" Emilio asked. "Do we drink now?"

"What we celebrate here," Mouse said to Solomon, "is like the Pilgrims' Thanksgiving, a season to rejoice in the harvesting of our fields and in the harvesting of our souls."

Solomon thought of Kendal praying in the night and suddenly wished she were here, that they were sitting together in this strange little booth, touching, sharing some experience of discovery, closing the distance between them.

"It recalls those long years of wandering in the wilderness when we lived in little booths under the sky," Mouse continued, then turned to Emilio. "Would you like to hang the pomegranate?"

"Oh, yeah!" Emilio said. He lifted the polished fruit from the table where Mouse had placed it, rose from the orange crate, and stood under the cornstalked ceiling. He was tall enough to easily reach the threads of string hanging from the roof. As Emilio tied the pomegranate, Solomon thought how much he looked like an excited little boy decorating his first Christmas tree, and the excitement was infectious. A sense of ritual permeated the booth, warmed it. Solomon heard Darby laugh and when he glanced quickly at her he saw that she was leaning far forward on the table, her eyes so filled with delight as she watched Emilio that she might have been a child observing a magician's rare and wondrous trick.

"Tell me more, Mouse," Solomon urged. "Tell me everything!"

Elaborating in detail, Mouse explained the wonders of the Feast of Booths. He said the Torah, the first five books of the Bible, tells us that the Lord spoke to Moses and told him that on the fifteenth day of the seventh month there must be a Festival of Booths to the Lord for seven days, for the harvest would have been reaped then and it would be a time for all to dwell within the booth and rejoice and remember the past.

A rabbi has said, Mouse continued, that when the Jews made their first diaspora God put seven clouds over their heads to protect them, the *clouds of glory,* so now when we eat and drink and tell stories during the seven days within the booth, it is to show that we are living in the shadow of faith. That explains why the things the booth are made of have no inherent strength. What *is* strong is the spirit within the walls.

Emilio had finished tying his pomegranate and returned to the table but Mouse was on his feet now, moving quickly around the booth, touching the walls and ceiling and fruit and hanging nuts and the bamboo curtains, and then running his hands over the branches tied in the corner as he sang the history and necessities of each.

He touched the cornstalk roof, the *sekhakh,* he called it, and told how it must be made from that which grows in the ground and that it must be cut down, and that when the *sekhakh* is laid across the top of the walls it must not be so dense as to prevent rain from falling on those below, and that it would be considered even finer if those who dwelled in the booth could see the night sky and maybe the moon. He gestured toward the hanging pomegranate and the baskets of nuts and bunches of grapes, and he said that such adornment was told of in the Talmud, the elaborate literary work which contains the Jewish code of laws and the discussions held by learned men about the meaning of those laws.

Solomon's head was spinning with new knowledge, and he was glad that the Mouse had to pause in his recitation and drink deeply from his goblet of wine; and yet he, Solomon, almost resented the momentary hiatus, because the things he was hearing awakened in him that comfort all men feel, the mysterious comfort of myth.

"And the most beautiful of all things," Mouse said, the dark red wine glistening his lips, "are the Four Species."

He crouched in the corner of the booth and raised the branches. Calling on Solomon to pay close attention, Mouse displayed the branches one by one. He noted that each was separate, but that the *lulav,* for so he called the collection, was to be considered as a whole for their totality is not unlike the Jews, the deficiencies of one redressed by the excellence of the others.

Then Mouse demonstrated how the *lulav* is held in the hand and pointed three times toward the east, toward Jerusalem, then three times toward the south, the west, the north. While pointed the branches must be waved and the holder of the *lulav* recites from the Book of Chronicles.

" 'Then shall the trees of the forest sing for joy before the Lord, for He is come to judge the earth,' " sang the Mouse. "And that is followed by a verse of the Psalms: 'O give thanks to the Lord, for He . . .' "

The Mouse stopped. He leaned the *lulav* against a wall. His gaze had fallen on the little oval silver box resting on the floor in the corner. Arrested in the middle of his verse, his mouth was open. Solomon thought Mouse's jaw had locked, but then the Mouse slowly closed his mouth and in the silence of the booth they all heard him swallow. But he didn't remove his gaze from the silver box. He opened it so carefully he might have been defusing a bomb.

Solomon glanced at Darby and Emilio. They sat side by side on their orange crates, their shoulders touching, his massive hand over hers, and they wore the grins of conspirators.

Mouse rose from the corner. He carried the silver box to the table and sat down. He placed the open box near the center of the table, where the glow from the *menorah* candles bathed it in fire. Cradled inside the box was an object wrapped in linen. His fingers trembling, Mouse unfolded the soft linen. It held a pale-yellow fruit which, although larger and with a thicker rind, resembled a lemon. It was a citron.

"Oh, Darby," Mouse whispered. "Oh, Darby!"

"It's a gift," Darby said. "I found it in an antique store. But Emilio got the citron."

"Never," said the Mouse, "never have I seen such a beautiful *etrog* box. Never."

"I know this guy in Florida, ya know," Emilio said. "I told him the fruit had to be perfect. I told him he finds a perfect one, he should send it to me. Is it perfect?"

"It's perfect," Mouse said. He turned the fruit over in his hands, caressing it like the breast of a woman. "Not a bulge, not a scar. Perfect!"

Mouse made little clucking sounds of delight, then turned to Solomon to explain his joy. He told him that the *etrog* was the most important part of the Four Species, and that there were special requirements, particular qualities that must be inherent in the fruit. It needed to be examined as carefully as a jewel, for it must be flawless to serve its purpose. There must be no split in the rind, no holes, and the fruit had to be lush and full of juice. He told of how over the centuries there have been certain wise men who were honored for their discerning eye, their ability to judge an *etrog*. And others were honored for their exquisite craftsmanship displayed in the boxes they made to hold the *etrog*. Most important of all, the *etrog* must not be borrowed by those who wished to use it in their rituals; it must be owned by he who holds it or must be a gift to the synagogue in which it will be used, and if the latter is the case, why then, all should contribute to its purchase and in that way all will own it collectively, and when they hold it in their hands together with the *lulav*, and wave the branches toward Jerusalem, they will all be richer in their hearts and in their spirit, even unto, the Mouse continued, falling unconsciously into the rhetoric of the Torah, even unto the Seventh Day of the Willow.

"The Seventh Day of the Willow?" Solomon asked quietly. He was struck by the beauty of the phrase.

"In the Talmud," Mouse explained, "it is called *yom hashevi'i shel aravah*, the Hoshana Rabba, which is the seventh day of Sukkot, and it is said that on that day man's fate is sealed. It is the final judgment from God. In order to make it sweet a man often spends that day eating honey, and he spends the night reading from the Book of Deuteronomy."

"Tell about the shadow," Darby said.

"And then can we eat?" Emilio asked. "I mean, gee whiz."

Mouse laughed and the sound covered the faint, distant ringing of a telephone. "Say, listen," he said, "I'm talking too much. It's a terrible thing to let such gefiltefish spoil. And look at that cabbage. Hoo ha, so crisp it could stand and salute. So, enough, enough, let's get to the belly."

"After the shadow," Darby said. "Mouse, I love the story about the shadow. It's scary."

An uneasy look crossed Mouse's face. "It's just a legend, a folktale, a once-upon-a-time kind of thing."

"Please," Darby persisted.

"A long time ago," Mouse spoke slowly, "some people — not many you understand, just some; maybe only one man, who knows? — swore a certain thing. He said that if a man did not see the shadow of his head on the night of the Seventh Day of the Willow, why then, then . . ." He paused.

"Then?" Solomon asked, intrigued by Mouse's obvious reluctance. "Then?"

"If he did not see the shadow of his head," Mouse repeated, "he would meet death within the year."

In the silence that followed, they all heard the ringing of the telephone, but because they had been affected by the foreboding nature of the legend just recounted no one moved. The telephone rang again.

"It's in the basement," Emilio said.

Solomon was surprised. "You have a telephone here?"

Mouse nodded. "The basement wall connects to the exterminator next door. He let us break through — temporarily, you understand — and tap it. A very nice man."

"Don't you think we should answer it?" Darby asked. But she made no move to rise.

"It's probably for the rat man," Emilio said.

"Yes," the Mouse said. "The rat man."

The telephone was insistent. Solomon looked around the table and saw that none of the others had budged. They all appeared as if they had been mesmerized by the legend of shadowless heads.

"Hey, c'mon," he said, "you've got to be kidding. You're like kids at the campfire, telling ghost stories."

No one said anything. Solomon rose from his orange crate and walked out of the booth. He ducked through the low doorway and entered the basement, struck once more at the whiteness of the room. He looked toward the wall that adjoined the exterminator's. Near the corner, several bricks had been removed. A wire ran through the aperture. At the end of the wire, on the floor, was a telephone. Solomon crossed the floor, crouched down, and lifted the telephone receiver.

"Hello?"

"Is this 555-3687?" a man inquired.

"You looking for the exterminator?" Solomon asked.

There was a pause. "No, sir," the man answered politely. "No, sir, I'm not looking for the exterminator. We're trying to locate a Miss Darby Moon."

Solomon was struck by the gentleness of the man's tone, but he wondered who in hell would know that Darby was spending the evening in an abandoned synagogue.

"Why do you want Darby Moon?"

"May I ask with whom I'm talking, sir?" the man spoke with old-fashioned formality.

"This is Darby's father. This is Solomon Moon."

"Oh. Oh, I see." It was obvious to Solomon that the man had turned his head away from the telephone and was mumbling indistinctly to someone else. Solomon could not make out the words and it irritated him.

"Listen," Solomon said impatiently, "what do you want? Are you still there?"

"Yes," the man said. "I'm still here. Mr. Moon, I'm sorry to have to call you like this."

"Who is this, for chrissake?"

"This is Sergeant Wilfred Callahan, Mr. Moon," the man said. "From the Vermont State Police."

28

L ook!" Darby cried.

Solomon squinted through the window of her pickup truck. It had taken hours to drive to Vermont and his eyes were tired from staring into the night. Darby had taken the back road, so they would pass Tuttle's trailer before reaching their own farmhouse; Solomon saw that the woods far ahead seemed to be on fire. A dull, red glow swept among the lower branches of pine and birch. But there was something strange about the fire. Its flames swept in a horizontal pattern round and round the woods, the visual rhythm ceaseless.

Darby pressed the accelerator to the floor of the truck and they careered up the road, jouncing over potholes filled with rainwater, swerving around rocks dislodged from the road banks, skidding dangerously close to the deep ditches that flanked the country road. As they rounded the corner which marked the boundary of Solomon's farm, Darby braked hard, for they saw what they had believed to be a fire. A green-and-gold Plymouth Fury with the markings of the Vermont State Police was parked outside of Jabez Tuttle's mobile home. The car's emergency red light revolved on the roof, its bright beam circling the surrounding trees.

"Stay here!" Solomon barked at Darby. He leaped out of the truck and ran across the soggy ground to the mobile home. The door was open. Solomon rushed in. The trailer was empty. Solomon saw the broken television screen and its glass shards scattered on the floor. Mixed with the shards were what appeared to be the torn feathers of a bird.

Solomon's gaze swept the floor and he saw that dried drops of blood led past the reclining chair and out the door. He leaned down to study the mixture of glass and feathers. During his phone call, Callahan had informed Solomon that the farmhouse had been defiled with animal shit. Kendal had discovered it. But nothing had been said about what had happened in Tuttle's trailer. Solomon reached toward one of the feathers on the floor.

"Hold it, buddy!" A voice behind Solomon was tight with command. Without thinking, Solomon lifted the feather. "I said, hold it, goddamn it!" Solomon froze. "Now turn your ass, mister." The man banged out the words.

Still crouched, Solomon pivoted on his heels and stared toward the open door. A .357 Magnum was leveled at him. It was held in the hand of a uniformed Vermont State Trooper. He was a young man, well over six feet tall, with enormous shoulders, his uniform skin-tight and immaculate. Underneath the trooper's broad brimmed hat Solomon could see blond sideburns, short and clipped, and a face burned by weather. Standing slightly to the side and in front of the trooper was Darby.

"He was in the woods, Daddy," Darby said, unable to restrain a nervous giggle.

"Is that funny?" the trooper asked without humor. "Does that make you laugh, lady?"

"No, sir," Darby said. But she had to bite her lips.

"Good," said the trooper. " 'Cause I don't think there's much to laugh about. Not here. Not tonight." He looked hard at Solomon. "You. What are you messing around here for?"

"Well," Solomon started to rise to his feet.

"Did I ask you to get up?" the trooper asked sharply. Solomon stopped moving. The .357 waved slightly at Darby. "Why don't you join that feller? Just sit down nice and quiet." Darby moved away from the trooper and sat down on the floor next to Solomon. Solomon lowered himself to join her. He looked at the black feather he still held in his hand.

"You want this?" he asked the trooper. The trooper didn't answer, just stared at him. It made Solomon nervous. "It's a feather," Solomon said rather inanely.

"Is that so?" the trooper asked quietly.

"Could you put that gun away?" Darby asked the trooper.

"What are you people doing here?" the trooper asked.

"My name is Moon," Solomon said. "Solomon Moon. This is my daughter. We own this farm. We were —"

"You have any identification?" the trooper asked.

"Can I reach into my pocket?" Solomon wanted to know.

"What?"

"Can I reach into my pocket? In the movies if you reach into your pocket it makes the cop very nervous." Solomon's eyes were on the huge .357. "I don't want to get you nervous."

"Oh, man." The trooper shook his head sadly. "Reach into your pocket."

Solomon reached into his pocket and withdrew his wallet. He opened it so that it revealed his driver's license.

"Put in on the floor, Daddy," Darby said, "and push it toward him with your foot. Slowly."

"You think he's nervous, too, don't you?" Solomon asked his daughter.

"I think it's a possibility," Darby said.

Solomon placed the wallet on the floor in front of him and then gingerly eased it over to the trooper. The trooper retrieved it. He studied Solomon's license. He studied Solomon. He studied Darby. He holstered his .357. He tapped the license with his fingernail.

"Okay, sir," the trooper said. "This looks good. This looks fine. This looks A-okay. You can get up now, sir. Sorry I had to hassle you."

Solomon and Darby rose from the floor and brushed glass and feathers from their clothes.

"Is my wife all right?" Solomon asked the trooper.

"How would you be," the trooper answered, "if you'd walked into a room full of shit? Oh, sorry, miss. I'm very sorry."

"Can we go now?" Darby asked.

"Sure. Only I'd appreciate it if you'd try to walk in a straight line."

Solomon blinked. He turned to Darby. "Have I missed something?"

"All we had," Darby said tartly to the trooper, "was some Mogen David, and that was hours ago." The trooper stared blankly at her. "You know what Mogen David is?"

"No, ma'am."

"I didn't think so. Wine. It's wine. Why do you want us to walk in a straight line? Is it some kind of a test?"

"Oh, no, ma'am. I mean when you go back to your truck, if you could just stay in a single line it would help not to mess up the footprints we've got outside. The BCI'll want to make casts of 'em."

"The BCI?" Solomon asked.

"The Bureau of Criminal Investigation, sir."

The name of the agency filled Solomon with sudden apprehension.

He stared at the tiny drops of dried blood on the floor and then, without another word, he turned and walked out of the mobile home. Darby followed. Behind them, the lights from the trailer cast a sheen onto the soggy ground and both Solomon and Darby now noticed the deep impressions left in the ground, hardening in the night's cold air. They saw, also, that Solomon's own footprints leading from the truck to the house had smeared many of the earlier impressions and falsified their shapes. They skirted the indentations and returned to the pickup.

The farmhouse was ablaze with light. Parked outside was Solomon's red Mustang. Nearby was a large six-wheeled truck and a black four-door Plymouth Volare. The rear doors of the truck were open and the lights within revealed that the interior of the truck was appointed like a scientific laboratory, complete with shiny steel sinks, small refrigerators, chests of medical equipment, and a sophisticated microscope attached to a long shelflike table. A small elderly man who sported a walrus mustache as if to defy his totally bald head stood in front of one of the sinks. Squinting against the smoke curling upwards from the cigarette that seemed glued to the center of his mouth, he was mixing something in a metal pan. He ignored the ashes that fell into the mixture. He turned at the sound of Darby's pickup. He lifted the pan out of the sink and moved to the open doorway of his truck. As Solomon and Darby started across the ground toward the farmhouse, the man called out to them.

"Watch where you walk, woncha?" It was a weary request, spoken as if the man knew it would be ignored.

Already alerted by the trooper in Tuttle's home, Solomon and Darby were quick to see that circles of string surrounded a half-dozen impressions in the mud outside the house, and they made certain not to tramp across them.

As they walked into the farmhouse, Solomon and Darby were overwhelmed by the odor of excrement, and what they saw shocked them. Smeared on every wall of the living room were crisscrossed paths of cowshit. Mounds of dung were heaped on the sofa and on the upholstered chairs. Trails of it laced across the floor, darkly staining the polished pine boards. Her face covered by a red bandanna, Kendal was shoveling dung from the floor and tossing it into a wheelbarrow. Above the cloth mask, her eyes were glazed with anger. In one corner of the room, a man stood in front of the copper dry sink the Moons used for a bar. Resting on top of the bottles was a small rectangle of birchbark. The man's eyes were riveted on it, his concentration as total as a cone of light, though his angular body looked as loose as a puppet's. From his closely cropped gray hair and his deeply seamed profile Solomon judged him to be about forty. He was dressed in a light-gray flannel suit and an even lighter-gray shirt; a gray tie was knotted neatly at his throat. He wore gray suede shoes with crepe rubber soles. A gray handkerchief poked out of the breast pocket of his jacket.

"Oh, Mom!" Darby cried and Kendal wheeled at the sound. She whipped the bandanna from her face and moved quickly to her daughter, embracing her tightly. Solomon marveled at how, standing in the middle of filth and despair, flakes of dried dung clinging to her shirt, it was Kendal who proffered consolation. Over Darby's shoulder, Kendal's eyes met his. She smiled grimly.

"Welcome to the House of Usher," she said.

Solomon was speechless. He didn't know what to say to her. He knew that she, too, felt the tension between them, the dissension of their last departure.

The gray man at the bar turned, stepped toward Solomon, and put out his hand. "Evening," he said, his voice low and rumbling and holding in it the sound of disappearing thunder when the sky lightens and there is promise of the sun. "I'm Sergeant Callahan."

"Hello, Wilfred," Darby said.

"Darby," Callahan said.

The gray man smiled at her and Solomon was aware that they looked at each other with more than a little interest. How well did she know him?

"What in God's name went on here?" Solomon asked, speaking slowly because he feared that he might gag at the awful smell.

"Might be better if we talked outside," Callahan said. "I suspect your wife could use a touch of cold air. I know I can." He smiled at Kendal, picked up the rectangle of birchbark, and led them out of the farmhouse.

The headlights from the laboratory truck spilled over a figure hunched over the ground within one of the circles of string. It was the little man with the walrus mustache. His metal pan lay on the ground, filled with wet plaster of Paris, and Solomon saw that he was making a cast of a partial footprint. As the group passed him, Callahan spoke.

"What do you think, Charles?"

"I ain't paid to think, Wilfred. I'm paid to play in the mud."

"That's a fact and then some," Callahan said. He looked toward the apple orchard and, veering in that direction, spoke to the Moons. "Might be a good place to sit if you don't mind the cold."

Kendal said she welcomed it.

Solomon was about to suggest that they sit in one of the cars but then realized that the wind was blowing in that direction and that it would surely carry with it the unwelcome reminder of what lay in the house. The apple orchard, indeed, would be free of the smell. It must have been immediately apparent to Sergeant Callahan. Watching the lanky officer lead them to the orchard, Solomon had a hunch that most things were immediately apparent to Wilfred.

Callahan stopped at the edge of the orchard, kicked aside some dank leaves and twigs and rotting apple cores, then laid his jacket on the ground.

"That's good wool," he said to Kendal. "Ought to keep you dry." He flicked his gray handkerchief out of the jacket pocket and laid it flat on the ground. "Not much," he said to Darby, "but you're a little thing." Again, Solomon was conscious of the quick, private look exchanged between his daughter and the policeman. He had a sudden feeling that he was going to get to know Callahan much, much better and, studying the man, the thought did not displease him.

"Wilfred," Solomon said. "That's an unusual name, isn't it?"

"It means 'resolute peace,' " the sergeant said. "My father had Jesuitical leanings. That is to say, he could be profoundly subtle about matters of conscience and it struck him that he had a duty to name his son in a manner applicable to the future planned for that son. He wished me to enter the priesthood. There are some who think that in naming me, my father was overzealous in his logic. I'm one of them. Do you object to a man who chews?"

The non sequitur made Solomon blink. He was confused already by the seeming learnedness of the sergeant's rhetoric, and he was trying to find the link between Jesuitical logic and Callahan's last question. It became somewhat clearer when the officer removed a short cigar from his shirt pocket.

"Please," Solomon said. "Go right ahead. Kendal and I both smoke."

"Well, sir," Callahan said, "I don't smoke. I just chew these things. That is —" He glanced at Darby. "— most of the time."

"I suppose," Darby said, her eyes glinting, "that sometimes you just can't resist temptation, so you do actually smoke 'em. Would I be right about that, Sergeant Callahan?"

"Yes," Callahan said, and the corners of his mouth twitched. "But mostly I just chew these damn things and that offends a great many people. I don't know if it's the waste that bothers them or the fact that the end gets somewhat mushy. Raunchy, you might say." He held the cigar in his fingers, obviously waiting for their permission.

"Please," Kendal said.

Callahan removed a small bone-handled penknife from his trouser pocket and carefully cut a cross into the closed end of the cigar.

"If you're not going to smoke that thing," Solomon asked, "why bother to do that?"

Callahan shook his head as if he were a little puzzled at his own action. "My father," he said.

"The Jesuit." Solomon had begun to doubt that they would ever get to the matter at hand.

"Yes," Callahan said. "My father was a highly disciplined man who respected the nature of temptation. He felt it a constructive force if applied to the learning process. In short, if men fight temptation, it enhances character." For just an instant he looked toward Darby, then looked away. "Now if I cut the end of this cigar, I cannot obscure the fact that it's ready for smoking. It gives me a chance, don't you see?"

"Wilfred," Kendal hunched forward, her body curved with curiosity, "may I ask you why you didn't join the priesthood?"

"Oh," Callahan said, "I did." Well, he thought, there it is. He wondered what Darby was thinking.

You are, Darby thought, the most surprising man I've ever met.

The silence in the apple orchard was punctuated by tree branches clicking against each other in the wind. Solomon had the crazy thought that the trees were applauding the sergeant's startling statement. He looked at his wife and daughter and saw that they were both immensely intrigued with the man who quietly chewed his cigar; and Solomon realized with sudden clarity that Callahan's rambling had been with purpose. It had been a diversionary tactic to put distance between the Moon women and the horror of the night. It had succeeded. And Solomon was grateful.

"Sergeant," Solomon said, "your father would have been proud of you."

Callahan's reaction was unexpected. He spoke so quietly that it was difficult to hear the words. "I don't think so," he said. He put the birchbark on the ground in front of him. His fingers traced the black letters inscribed on the bark. He looked at Solomon. "I don't believe you've seen this, sir. Perhaps you'd care to read it."

Solomon held up the birchbark so that lights from the laboratory truck faintly illuminated it. He read the inscription aloud.

" 'Thou art in trouble today, I too; another is in trouble tomorrow, I too; after this generation other descendants who succeed your descendants are in trouble; I am in trouble down to the end of the world.' " Puzzled, Solomon replaced the bark on the ground. "I don't understand it." His fingertips felt gritty, and when he looked at them he saw a residue of powder.

"Charles dusted it for prints," Callahan explained. "Wasn't much use; material's too rough. What's on it, the words, I mean, were written many years ago by a remarkable man. A Doctor of the Church. Saint Augustine. He's considered by many to be the father of theology."

"And the father of a bastard son," Kendal said.

"Ah, well, now," Callahan addressed Kendal. "You know him.'

"No. Not really. Not the way I should. I remember a little from school. We read his *Confessions* and the other one. You know, the one with his views on history."

"*The City of God,*" Callahan said. "Are you familiar with it, Mr. Moon?"

"No."

"Augustine believed that, in God's foresight, he made two mystical cities, one or the other of which will claim the allegiance of all men. The City of God, and the City of the Devil."

"That seems an extreme point of view," Solomon commented.

"Among those who study divine things," Callahan said, "there is a great deal of controversy regarding Augustine's suppositions. Such as . . ." He paused. He picked a fleck of tobacco off his lips.

"Such as?" Solomon asked.

"Such as Augustine's view that man is corrupt and helpless."

For a moment no one spoke, and Solomon was certain that each was weighing Augustine's philosophy in terms of his or her own life. He realized that during the last few years he'd felt helpless to change the conditions of his own frustrations but he no longer accepted his inability to alter that course. The adrenaline of his anger had renewed his strength and all he lacked was a target for its expression. In the silence he became aware of a distant sound, faint, from somewhere high over the land. He saw Callahan cock his head toward the sound, too.

"Strange," Callahan said. "Don't usually fly at night."

"What?" Kendal asked.

"Crows. That's a crow calling."

"About Augustine," Solomon asked, "do you believe that? Do you believe that man is corrupt and helpless?"

"I believe," Callahan replied after a pause, "that the wind has shifted. We would do better in the truck." Without waiting for an opinion from the others, he rose. Gracious as before, he helped Kendal and Darby to their feet, holding Darby perhaps just a little longer then was needed. When Callahan retrieved his jacket and handkerchief they were both stained with mud but he paid no attention to that. He shrugged into his jacket and replaced the handkerchief in his pocket.

On their way back to the farmyard they passed the house. The door and windows were open and in the bright interior light Solomon could see that Charles, the lab technician, was moving about, dusting various objects with a fine gray powder. Solomon assumed that he was dusting for fingerprints and he wondered why he had such a strong sense of *déjà vu*, then he realized that the actions of the man, and the interview with Callahan, were reminiscent of a hundred movies he'd seen. Their celluloid quality was already coating reality with abstraction. That this abstraction softened shock was no consolation, for it reminded him that his own profession made him an accomplice to the lie.

He thought of Wilton Forest's offer. The head of TransGlobal had, Solomon knew, been sincere in his wish to make films which explored the religions of the world, and yet he had not been willing to go forward with *Shadow on the Grass*, which dealt with the compromise of a man's soul. Solomon wondered if a bargain could be struck and whether he really wanted to participate in such a bargain.

The conversation about Augustine, interrupted only by the cry of the crow, had been as civil as a seminar but as he'd listened to Kendal's recollections of early teachings, Solomon had thought how little they shared in background and how seldom they had explored the differences. He found himself observing her as he might a stranger: admiring her, respectful, but strangely detached. He recognized that they both were keenly aware of the recent tension between them and that because of their mutual respect for privacy neither had wanted to air their grievances before Callahan. But he felt that their lack of communication was based on more than marital misunderstandings. He wondered if what separated them was the past or the future. He knew that they would have to confront the answer.

Callahan led them into the laboratory truck. While the others leaned against various steel shelves and sinks, Callahan hoisted himself up onto the edge of the table and sat there, slowly swinging his legs back and forth as casually as if he were an observer of a game. Solomon could not determine whether he liked or disliked this strangely relaxed man. The sergeant asked Kendal to relate to Solomon and Darby her introduction to the baseness discovered.

"There isn't much to tell," Kendal said. "You've seen it. I drove up this evening and . . ."

"Why would you do that? I mean knowing about the tongues and everything?" Solomon asked. Both Callahan and Darby were aware of the edge to his voice and of the quick look exchanged by Kendal and Solomon.

"I got out of the car," Kendal continued, "and walked to the house. When I reached the door . . ."

"You didn't see anyone?" Callahan asked.

"I've already told you," Kendal replied. "I saw no one. Nothing. I reached the house and this awful smell . . . this awful . . ." She stopped and took a deep breath. She pointed to the birchbark, which rested on the table next to Callahan. "I saw that thing on the door but I didn't really pay any attention to it because I wanted to get inside. I wanted to know what in God's name was causing that —" She stopped again. "Do you have anything to drink in here?"

"Yes," Callahan said, "of course."

Opening a cabinet, he took down a bottle of brandy and four little medical beakers, poured a drink for each of them, and passed them around. Kendal took a long sip, then continued.

"Anyway," she said, "you know what I found. It was . . . it was terrible. It frightened me. I couldn't figure it out . . . couldn't understand it. Christ, I couldn't believe it!" She took another drink, and in the silence Solomon shuddered suddenly, both frightened and angry at the outrage to his house. Kendal continued. "I tried to call Jabez but no one answered so I drove down there. The door was wide open. I saw glass all over the floor, and some . . ."

"Feathers," Solomon said. "Bird feathers."

"Yes. And there was blood. That's when I called the state police. I remembered that Darby was going to meet the Mouse tonight and . . ."

"Mousey Blum," Solomon explained, not knowing, of course, that Callahan knew who the Mouse was. "He's a friend of mine." He glanced toward Darby and smiled slightly. "A friend of all of ours. A very good friend."

"They were going to celebrate Sukkot," Kendal said. She looked quickly at Solomon, then looked away.

"The Feast of Booths," Solomon said quietly. "It's a holiday."

Kendal stared at Solomon and her daughter. They looked suddenly as if they were tied together by some invisible wire. What was going on between them?

The sergeant dipped the bitten end of his cigar into his beaker of brandy and let the tobacco absorb the sweet alcohol. He put the cigar back into his mouth and rolled it between his lips. He sighed contentedly. "That's a real treat." He removed the cigar from his mouth and studied it thoughtfully as he addressed himself to Solomon. "When headquarters received Mrs. Moon's call they assumed this was a simple ten-fourteen. Breaking and entry. A trooper responded to the call. You may have seen him up at Tuttle's."

"Yes," Solomon answered tartly. "You could say that. Sort of a Nordic type. Blond. Aryan, I guess you'd call it." He was surprised by his own descriptive words and pleased by them. Suddenly, he wanted Callahan — and Kendal, yes, Kendal, too — to know that he was not aligned with the Anglo-Saxon pure.

"Havermeyer," Callahan said. "John Havermeyer. He's a good boy. He saw the unusual aspects of this thing and he called for the BCI. That's where I came in."

"Sergeant," Darby asked, "do you have any idea why something like this was done? Or what's happened to Jabez?"

"No," Callahan said. "I can't say that I do. Now I don't subscribe to the theory that the pastoral beauty of this land is without violation. We don't live apart from the world. We have our fair share of vandalism and burglary, and there are times, mostly during the hunting season, when some Green Mountain boy who suspects that a neighbor has more than a passing interest in his wife will conveniently mistake that neighbor for an eight-point buck. But I have never encountered anything as — as exotic, if you will, as what we've seen here tonight. I guess the ways of the city have been brought to the pasture. I do wish we would learn to deal with Castro."

Solomon was, once again, caught off guard by the final non sequitur. Although he would be damned if he would make further inquiry to the sergeant's reference to Castro, his confusion was apparent and Callahan immediately responded to it. He withdrew the cigar from between his lips and held it out for Solomon to see.

"These things," he said, referring to the cigar, "used to be made in Cuba. Best damn things you ever tasted. Now they come from the Canary Islands and they're not the same. No, sir, they're not the same. It has occurred to me that if more of our statesmen smoked cigars, we would have found a way to make peace with philosophies divergent from our own."

"Wilfred, you talk too much." The words were spoken by the lab technician. As he came into the truck, Charles held four plaster-of-Paris molds in his hands. He set them onto the table next to Callahan, who instantly stood up and began examining them. The Moons moved from their positions and joined the two men. Two of the molds held footprints, their markings different. Imbedded in two other molds were the prints of tire tracks. They, too, were dissimilar, their patterns differing.

"What we've got here," the little man said, "is nothing. This one tread matches the lady's car and 'tother come from Tuttle's pickup we seen down to his place." He turned to Kendal. "Be obliged you'd set your foot into this one." He placed one of the footprint molds on the floor of the trailer and Kendal lowered her foot into it. Her low-heeled shoe fit perfectly. "Ayuh," Charles said, "it's what I figgered." He held up the other mold. "Now this one, she's a puzzler. That ain't from any kinda shoe I ever seen. Ain't no markin's 'tween heel an' toe. It's all smooth like. Maybe some kinda moccasin, but if it is, the feller what wore it, he's got the goldarnedest toes this side of New Guinea or wherever it is they keep them aborigines." He moved down the length of the table until he stood under a strong overhead light and placed the mold directly under it. He pointed to the unusually deep indentation which marked the placement of the toes. "You can see how deep them things dug into the ground. Them toes are prehensile, that's what they are. Prehensile. By God, they're big enough to strangle a —"

He never finished his thought. A sound cut through the windy night. Low. Undulating. Mournful. As if someone were blowing a strange horn. Or as if one animal were calling to another.

It sent a chill through all those in the trailer. Quickly, Callahan stepped to the doorway, the rest moving up behind him; but none of them could see any shapes moving in the darkness, and the sound faded away. In a protective gesture, Callahan moved the others back further into the truck and his manner became suddenly brusque, as if he wanted to shake off any sense of inexplicable mystery.

"Is that it?" he asked Charles.

The little man ran a finger down the length of both sides of his walrus mustache. He wasn't listening to Callahan. He was staring through the open doorway.

"What do you figure that was, Wilfred?" he asked nervously.

"I don't know," Callahan said sharply. "You know the woods. Could have been anything. An animal. The wind. Anything. Now let's get back to business."

Solomon saw that Kendal and Darby had moved closer together and that like himself they did not believe the sergeant's easy answer. But what? When he glanced around the interior of the trailer he realized that he was looking to see if there was a weapon nearby and that his hands were opening and closing with eagerness.

Charles descended the lowered steps at the rear of the truck, leaned down out of view, then reappeared carrying two more molds. He reentered the truck and placed the molds on the floor.

"I took these in front of Tuttle's place. One set was in front of 'tother." He stared at the two molds. His lower jaw protruded and he caught the scraggly ends of his mustache in his mouth and he bit into it, his teeth clicking in irritation. "Now why in tarnation would a man leave his house on all fours, and it rainin' an' all?" He lowered himself to his hands and knees. He placed his knees into the rear mold and, by stretching full length, he was able to place his hands into the forward mold. "Tuttle," he said. "I seen him here an' there. He was a tall feller, weren't he?" He looked at Solomon for affirmation. Solomon nodded. "He'd just about fit these prints," Charles said. He moved out of the molds and rose from the floor but he continued to stare intently at the hand and knee patterns frozen in plaster. "Thing like this," he concluded, "it fair bedazzles you."

"Where do the tracks go to, Charles?" Callahan asked.

"They don't. These here, they're all I could pick up. Rain washed everthin' out. Might be you could try the hounds, but a night like this, I don't figger they could pick up nuthin' but a skunk, an' him only if he broke wind."

"You find any blood outside?" Callahan asked.

"I tole you, rain washed out the kit an' kaboodle. You got to listen, Wilfred. You got to learn to listen."

"What about the blood in the trailer?"

"It ain't dried but a little while. I got me some scrapin's so's we can check it out agin Tuttle's. John Havermeyer, he already spoke some to

Ray Poole down 'tother end of the road. Ray, he tole him that Tuttle done some time in the army so we ain't gonna have no trouble findin' the blood type an' everthin'."

"Ray say he saw anything? Heard anything?" Callahan wanted to know.

"Ray's too far away," the technician answered. "He said he didn't hear nuthin'. 'Sides, he was too busy tyin' them little bitty midges he swears by." Charles shook his head in disgust. "Damn fool, he ain't goin' to catch nuthin' on them midges. Ain't gonna be no more hatches this time of year. Man's gotta go deep for them trout. Damn fool." His condemnation of Ray Poole seemed to rush adrenaline through the little man's system. He clapped his hands sharply together and turned to the Moons. "All right, let's get on with it. Ain't gonna hurt you none."

Charles stepped briskly to a table alongside of the truck's wall. He yanked open a drawer and took out an ink pad and some special paper. He laid them on the table and turned back to the Moons. "I'll need your prints so's I can match 'em with the ones I got from your house. Could be we'll find us an extra set belongs to whoever dunged up your place, but it ain't likely so don't excite yourself we're goin' to catch the feller which if we do ain't goin' to make much nevermind anyways, seein' as how all them judges we got sittin' today can't hardly wait to set all the perverts free to rob, rape, and mutilate. I'll tell you true, the world ain't fit for hogs. Right hand, please."

As, one by one, the Moons stepped up to the table, rolled their fingers on the ink pad, then placed their prints onto the special paper, Callahan resumed his study of the birchbark square inscribed with the strange warnings of a dead saint.

His prints taken, Solomon stood at a sink and scrubbed his fingers but his gaze was on Callahan. It puzzled him that the sergeant's attention was so focused on the small square of bark. It seemed to Solomon that both the disappearance of Tuttle and the vile defamation of the farmhouse demanded priority. Solomon had been struck by the words of the sergeant. *The ways of the city have been brought to the pasture.* Solomon had silently agreed. During his morning walks from Grand Central to Trans-Global Films he constantly encountered the parades of young men and women chanting the litanies of Hare Krishna. At airports, time and again, he had been accosted by some militant youth demanding that Solomon purchase a religious tract that guaranteed salvation. But the wild-eyed zealot was content no longer to address himself to metropolitan sin. He had invaded the rural lands of America. Backpacks were crammed with the literature of God and the songs sung on the Appalachian Trail reflected a newfound faith in Christ. What bothered Solomon most was that the new legions of believers were not satisfied to praise the Lord; the legions angrily demanded the conformity of others. Bigotry's insidious claptrap permeated society, its verbal seeds broadcast across the valleys and into the mountains of the land, and those who gave it credence were constant in their actions. The dialectics of their creeds disallowed debate and stigmatized the nonbeliever. This loathsome form of proselytizing had been one of the reasons for Solomon's remaining distant from his Judaic past. He had thought of himself as a modern man balancing disputation with the sanity of logic and remaining coolly uninvolved with credo. And yet, now, remembering the murder of Brindig, and the joy of his daughter as she sat at Sukkot, he felt confused by his past removal. He looked at Darby as she rolled her fingers across the inked pad and he heard her voice echoing again.

I'm the best there is at being alone and it's no good, Daddy, it doesn't work. It's a lousy place to live!

His glance moved to Kendal. She leaned wearily against one of the sinks, her eyes closed, her fingers stained black from the pad, her shoes crusting with dung. There was something unfamiliar about her pose, her attitude, her look. It took Solomon a moment to realize what it was. She looked vulnerable, as if her weariness came not from any loss of physical strength but from indecision. It surprised Solomon, for in all the years he had known her he had thought of Kendal as a woman of immense control, resolute in her actions, her goals never shadowed, her desires unobscure. Waving confidence like a banner, she enjoined against crisis.

Watching her now, Solomon had the strange sensation that both he and she had been partners, waltzing to the tunes of a masquerade ball, and that now the music had stopped, midnight had chimed, and their masks had slipped.

The twin beams of a car's headlights swept across the rear doorway of the truck. Squinting against the lights, Solomon heard the squeal of brakes. He saw the gold-and-green Plymouth Fury slide sideways through the mud and then stop. John Havermeyer, the Nordic trooper, leaped out of the car.

"Sergeant Callahan!" Havermeyer shouted.

As Callahan looked up from the birchbark, Havermeyer, ignoring the steps, vaulted into the truck.

"Down the rise," Havermeyer said, his breathing hard and fast, "in the mowing. I left Tuttle's and come up the road here and it just sort of flashed up. Damndest thing you ever —"

"Take it easy, John," Callahan said, "take it easy."

"She's burning now. You got to see it!" Havermeyer said. Without waiting for a reply, he turned, leaped out of the truck and started across the farmyard. Swiftly, Callahan and the Moons followed. Havermeyer was running now and the others sped after him. They crossed the yard as Havermeyer's figure disappeared below the rise that led to the mowing where Solomon had practiced his shooting. In just a moment, the others, too, were slipping down the wet grass of the rise. Then they saw it.

At the far end of the mowing, near the treeline, imbedded in the rain-soft ground, was a small wooden cross. It blazed in green flame. Sparks spattered the dark night, and above the crack and pop of burning wood came another sound from somewhere in the distant woods. High and thin and wailing, it could have been an animal in agony.

Or a howling man.

29

Havermeyer carried buckets of water from the stream and doused the fire of the burning cross. Their hands wrapped in towels, Callahan and Solomon pulled the smoldering remains from the ground. Silently, Callahan examined the threads of salt-encrusted wax that had flamed so greenly. Solomon noted that the sergeant suddenly looked tired and that his eyes were strangely sad. Callahan ordered Charles to store the sodden cross in the laboratory truck so that it and the tire molds, the footprints, the fingerprints taken from Tuttle's trailer, could be studied more carefully, could be filed for evidence, could, perhaps, clue the state police into more specific discoveries. Then he led the Moons back into the kitchen of the farmhouse. It was the one downstairs room which had not been dunged. The windows and the doors had been flung wide open and the cold night wind had somewhat alleviated the odor in the house.

When they sat around the kitchen table, all of the Moons were aware that Callahan had something to say, that his attitude had changed from natural curiosity about a crime to an attitude of remorse. They felt that he was struggling with something private and that if they spoke they would endanger the process with which he wrestled. They waited. They saw the laboratory truck leave, followed by Havermeyer in his patrol car. They glanced at each other but still did not speak. They heard the hoot of an owl and they listened to the wind. Abstractedly, Callahan reached for his cigar. Abstractedly, he pushed it back into his pocket. He pulled up his sleeve and scatched the bullet scar on his arm. He pinched the flesh until it was white. He pulled the sleeve down and looked up, his eyes moving from one Moon to another. His gaze lingered for a moment on Darby then shifted to Solomon.

"During your novitiate, when you must decide whether to consecrate yourself forever to the ministry of the Gospel," Callahan said finally, "you must study a great many things, both spiritual and temporal. The history of the Church is no less important than its teachings; indeed, it would be difficult to separate the two. Not all novices come to the same conclusions, regardless of their desires to become ministers. The knowledge they acquire tests them, for they discover that acts performed in the name of the Church have not always reflected the true intention of the Church. Notwithstanding that I chose to leave the priesthood, I still believe that the intentions of my religion remain pure and just. But I am aware of past injustices. I have knowledge of . . ." He paused and again pinched his scar. "Of horror. I have knowledge of horror. Are you acquainted with the period of the Spanish Inquisition, Mr. Moon?"

"Only in a general way," Solomon said softly. The claw of *the thing* within him twitched.

"The Inquisition imposed its will on those they judged to be heretical," Callahan continued. "In extreme cases, they created autos-da-fé to recapture the sinner. They burned them at the stake. These punishments were made public so that all who witnessed the burnings would be terrorized and in that way stay firm in the true faith. It was, of course, a twisted logic. In order to inform the people that an auto-da-fé might soon be upon them, the Inquisition devised a formal procession in which they lighted the Cross of the Holy Office. It was called the Green Cross."

"Because of the color of its flame?" Solomon asked.

"Perhaps," Callahan said.

"And those who were burned — those heretics, as you called them," Solomon said, "were Jews."

"Among others," Callahan said. "Yes."

"But we're not concerned with the others, are we?" Solomon asked. He knew his voice was trembling. "I mean, Wilfred, your history lesson has a point, does it not?"

"Yes."

"Sergeant," Kendal said, "aren't you being a little farfetched? I mean, really, we all know there are narrow-minded people, but they don't go around killing others indiscriminately."

"Don't they?" Solomon asked quietly.

"You're suggesting," Kendal said directly to Callahan, "that some-one has a personal vendetta against us."

"Not us," Solomon said. "Me." He stiffened suddenly and looked at Darby. He reached out and took her hand. "And maybe someone else."

Kendal winced at her exclusion. "I think it would be easy to get para-noid, don't you agree, Sergeant Callahan?"

"I think," Callahan said, "that you should not stay here tonight."

Solomon folded his arms across his chest. It looked as if he were try-ing to warm himself. He was not. He was hiding the fact that the animal inside him was thrashing wildly. He did not want the others to know the excitement he felt. "He's right," he said.

Callahan suggested that they all spend the night with him. He would drive them to his house and they could return in the morning for Dar-by's truck and Kendal's car.

"All right," Darby said. "Why not?" Solomon thought her eyes were particularly bright as she looked at the sergeant.

"Sergeant," Kendal said, "Solomon and I can take our own car. If you'll just give us directions, we —"

"You can follow me, Mrs. Moon."

"Well," Kendal said, "just in case."

Instinctively, Solomon knew that Kendal had no intention of imme-diately following Callahan, that she wanted to be alone with him, Solo-mon. After giving directions, Callahan and Darby left. Kendal saw them to Callahan's car, then returned to the kitchen. Solomon was no longer at the table. Kendal walked into the living room. Although a fresh wind still blew through the open windows, the odor of cow dung remained. Solomon was staring at the shotgun on the wall. He spoke without turning.

"We have to talk."

"Yes," Kendal said. "Let's go to the stream."

Regardless of the chilly night, both were drawn to a favorite place, a place where they'd enjoyed cool mornings and midnight swims and where, often, they'd sat back to back, propping each other up, and day-dreamed. Together, side by side, but not touching, as if neither felt he or she had the right, they skirted the apple orchard and walked across the meadow by the stream. They sat on the soft horsetail fern beside the stream and stared into the water, neither knowing quite how to begin, or what it was exactly that had to be said. Kendal was surprised at the brightness of the landscape and then noticed that the clouds had swept clear of the moon.

"The moon's out," she said.

"Yes," Solomon said. "It's very bright."

"Yes." Kendal tossed a pebble into the deep part of the stream and watched it ripple the surface. "It must be nice to be a beaver."

" 'It must be nice to be a beaver,' " Solomon muttered.

"I hate that," Kendal said quietly. "Did you know that? Did you know that I hate it when you do that, when you repeat what I say?"

"No," Solomon said. "I'm sorry, I didn't know that. I think there are a lot of things neither of us knows."

Kendal knew that Solomon had spoken with no rancor, no accusation, but suddenly she felt that if they probed each other too deeply some wound would be exposed, some wound that would fail to heal, and it frightened her, for it seemed so final.

"Do Paul Henried," she said.

Solomon fished two cigarettes from his pack, put them into his mouth, lighted both of them from a single match, then gave one to Kendal.

"Were you in love with Paul Henried?"

"I think it was more like lust," Kendal said. "Yes, it was definitely lust."

"I'm sorry it didn't work out," Solomon said, smiling a little at the game.

Kendal inhaled deeply on her cigarette and blew smoke past a pool of moonlight and watched it drift away into the darkness. "I wouldn't have married him. Henried, I mean. I never wanted to marry anyone but you." She waited for his response but Solomon didn't speak, so when Kendal continued, she tried to keep her tone light. "I'd have lived with him, of course. You know, in sin. That might've been fun."

"They wouldn't have approved," Solomon said. His tone was not light.

"Who?"

"The church. Your Church of England."

"Good Lord, darling, you're not serious!"

"Yes, I am. Before we were married, when we lived together, did it ever bother you? I mean, how did you square that with the way you were brought up?"

Kendal was sure that their early sexuality was not what bothered Solomon, that he was getting to something else. But what? "The same way you did, Solomon. We accepted what was right for us. It wasn't anyone else's business. We never questioned that, did we?"

"We didn't ask questions about a lot of things."

"Such as?"

"A lot of things."

"Go on." Kendal felt herself growing tense.

"Doesn't it seem strange to you that we never really talked about . . . about . . . the . . . the difference . . . between us? Shouldn't we have come to grips with that? Did we purposely avoid it? Is that what we did?"

"Avoid *what?*" For a moment, Kendal was genuinely bewildered; then she remembered the secret smile exchanged between Darby and Solomon when he had mentioned the Feast of Booths.

"My God, Solomon," she exclaimed, "you don't mean religious difference? You can't mean that!"

"Why not?"

"Because we never gave it a thought. It didn't mean a damn thing to us. It's not part of our lives."

"Isn't it?" Solomon whispered.

He looked at the ground before him to make sure that in the dropping moonlight he could still see the shadow of his head, for he remembered the alarm voiced in the legend of the Seventh Day of the Willow. The shadow seemed to undulate over the stream's dark edges and over the pickerelweed, which looked like white knives rising from the water — and then he knew that the white knives were tongues, tongues of *the thing* that crawled inside him. The tongues of the animal. He felt the now-familiar heat rise within him, and the breath of the scratching animal scalded his lungs, his throat, his mouth, his lips, and he leaped from the wet ground, pacing in small circles, kicking at the damp vegetation around him, his breath popping from his mouth like puffs of smoke exploding in the cold night air and he screamed:

"I'll kill him!" And because he didn't know who he meant, he screamed again. "I will kill them! I will kill them all!"

Frightened by his seeming hysteria, Kendal jumped up, ran to him, and when she saw that he was shaking she slapped him hard across the face, trying desperately to shock him.

"Don't!" she cried. "Don't!"

She grabbed him and they slid on the wet ferns, fell, and rolled into the stream.

Momentarily submerged under the icy water, her hands and feet flailing, Kendal reached out and her fingers curled through the broad leaves of arrowhead. She used their stiff stems to haul herself to the bank of the stream. Spitting dank hair from between her lips, she crawled to the muddy ground above, spun around on her hands and knees, and looked over the dark water. Solomon was nowhere to be seen.

"Solomon!" she shouted, fear swelling in her throat. "Solomon!"

Squinting through the pale mist rising from the water, Kendal saw him. He was in the deep middle of the stream, his hair and face streaked with weeds, treading water.

"Boy," he called to her, "you got some left hook!"

"Solomon Moon," Kendal shouted, choking a little on her own laughter, "you get your ass out of there!"

Solomon plunged out of sight. His underwater passage was defined by the straight, quick ripples of the water above him and then his head broke the surface of the water and he was only a few feet from the bank below Kendal.

"Five more minutes in here," he said, looking up at her and wiping weed from his face, "and a guy could come out a soprano."

"Not you, love," she said, "never you." She reached down and clasped his hand and pulled hard, and he rose out of the water and climbed up the bank. Gasping from the shock of icy water, he flopped on the ground next to her and as he pulled her over him, Kendal could not remember when she had wanted him more. She knew it was reciprocal because she could feel the sexual tension in his body as he arched toward her. He bit into the fleshy part of her lip and she could taste blood and she felt his hands tugging hard at her skirt, ripping at it, pulling it down over her buttocks and thighs, and then he ripped her panties. His body lunged upwards and she toppled to the earth and he rolled on top of her and she felt him enter her, thrusting, pumping. The weeds clinging to his hair fell into her eyes, and her lip was still caught between his teeth. She wrapped her legs around him and pulled him deeper into her and she was weeping as the fire rose in her belly, and then they both cried out, the sound as high and wild as loons lost in their rising flight.

The night wind gusted softly and carried with it the sweet, pungent smell of swamp rose and winterberry. A frog croaked.

"Boy," Kendal whispered. "Boy, oh, boy, oh, boy."

"Ummmm," Solomon said.

"It's been a long time."

"Well," he said, "it's like riding a bicycle. You don't forget."

"Listen," she said, "could you move just a little?"

"Now?"

"Uh-huh. Just a little."

"Why?"

"I've got a thorn up my arse."

"That's what I like about you," Solomon said. "You're always so elegant." He rolled off her and felt his body sink into the leafy mold of rotting vegetation. He was suddenly so cold that he wondered if the ferns would freeze to his skin.

"Solomon," Kendal said quietly.

"Uh-huh." He tried to keep his teeth from chattering.

"I never did that before. I never hit anyone before. Never. I'm sorry. I'm truly sorry. It was a dumb, uncivilized thing to do."

"Maybe," he said, "maybe that's our problem."

"What?"

"Maybe we're too damned civilized."

Kendal turned on her side and inched closer to Solomon, and as he held her she began to pluck wet weeds from his hair. "During the Middle Ages," she said, "there were wild men. They were covered with hair and leaves grew out of their noses, and everybody was frightened of them because they crawled like animals and they stole children and when they bled, their blood was black. People thought they were mad."

"Well," Solomon said, shivering, "I can see why."

"But they weren't mad. They were only grieving."

"For what?"

"For something they lost."

"What was it?"

"No one ever knew."

"That's a very sad story," Solomon said. He shivered again.

"God, you're freezing," Kendal said. "Come on."

They rose swiftly from the stream bank, their clothes soaking wet, ran through the apple orchard and entered the farmhouse.

"I'll get a fire going," Solomon said. He remembered the condition of the living room. "Upstairs."

As Solomon moved upstairs Kendal rummaged around in a kitchen cabinet. She found a bottle of brandy and followed Solomon. When she entered their bedroom, Solomon was kneeling before the raised hearth of their small fireplace, his hands stretched out to the fire he'd started. Kendal thrust the open bottle of brandy toward him.

"Here," she said, "take a good belt."

"I'm okay, honest."

"Listen," she said, "I don't want that to be our last lovely fuck. Drink."

She pulled off her wet clothes, letting them drop to the floor, wrapped herself in a blanket from the bed, and took the bottle from Solomon's hand.

"Fair's fair," she said. As she took a long drink she felt the warmth of the brandy spreading through her and it reminded her of the previous fire in her belly. She watched as Solomon stripped off his clothes. He, too, wrapped himself in a blanket.

"Très chic," Kendal said.

"For a wild man, you mean."

He laughed.

Kendal shuddered at the sound. It was high and thin and filled with anguish and just as suddenly as it had erupted, it stopped. It was, Kendal thought, as if something inside Solomon, something alive, had severed the sound. As if an animal had bitten it in two.

"Solomon," she said urgently, "we've got to get out of here. We've got to go home!"

"Yes," he said in a strangely distant voice, "we've got to go home."

He rose abruptly and, still wrapped in his blanket, made his way downstairs. Kendal moved to the bedroom hallway. She crossed to the stair landing. She looked down. Solomon was on the telephone. She moved back into the bedroom. What was wrong with him? What was happening? Silently, she lifted the receiver of the bedroom telephone. She heard Wilton Forest's voice. It was the voice of a man awakened but immediately alert.

"And there are no conditions?" he asked.

"There are no conditions," Solomon said.

"Remember, Solomon, a simple story. A man, a woman, a child. A family story."

"Yes."

"Do you have something in mind?"

"I will tell the story of a family," Solomon said. "A family from Seville. I'll leave tomorrow."

"Ah," Wilton said, "a Spanish family. A Catholic family."

"No," Solomon said, "Jews." He hung up.

Slowly, Kendal replaced the telephone receiver. She felt cold and hurt, for she knew she was no longer Solomon's home. He had chosen a past to which she no longer belonged. She wanted to cry out to him; to warn him that whatever answers he sought for his despair were here, now, with her. Quickly, she moved back to the stair landing but she stopped when she saw him.

Still huddled in his blanket, Solomon sat in his rocking chair. It was placed in front of the door. The door was wide open. In Solomon's lap was his shotgun. He stared into the dark night, his body bending as if he were keening. What Kendal could not know, what he was unable to explain, was that as his eyes pierced the darkness he saw the entrance to unseen roads, all of which beckoned him toward a mysterious choice. He knew now that the earlier roads down which he'd walked had been paved with his father's fears of a Judaic past, and with his own appeasements. His life, he felt, had been a fraudulent journey through which he had traveled incognito, conciliating all those around him. Perhaps, he thought, in Seville, I will meet the ghost of my father. Perhaps, he thought, tonight, here, in this darkness, I will meet the man who slew the heart of my father.

Motionless, he waited.

Kendal quietly retreated to the bedroom. She lay on the bed. She listened to the slow rocking of Solomon's chair.

She prayed that nobody would come.

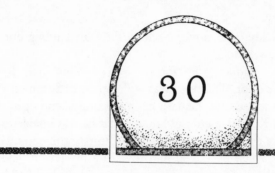

30

H e must be very sick," Darby said.

"Who?"

"Whoever's doing this to us. He must hate us."

"We'll find him," Callahan said. "I promise you."

"He's like some awful kind of ghost, isn't he? A secret man moving into our lives, not really telling us what he wants, just scaring us, scaring the hell out of us. God, I hate secrets!" She saw Callahan wince. "Oh, Wilfred, I don't mean you. I don't mean what you told us about being a priest. That's none of my business."

"Yes," he said quietly, "it is. What I was . . . what I *am* . . . is your business. I want it to be. Have you finished your chocolate?"

"Yes." She licked her lips. "It was terrific."

Callahan took Darby's hand, led her out of the kitchen area and across the room to a wrought-iron staircase that rose to the loft above. The balcony was about eight feet wide as it projected over the living room and what Darby saw surprised her. Running the entire length of the floor, jutting out from the wall, were iron bedsteads. They looked like army cots. Each bed was unmade, its clean mattress ticking exposed; folded neatly on each bed were sheets and khaki woolen blankets.

"Who sleeps here?" Darby asked.

"Whoever needs to," Callahan replied.

"Curiouser and curiouser," Darby mumbled as she followed Callahan down the length of the balcony then turned the corner to another section. This, too, was furnished with the cots. They turned another corner and stood on the long balcony across from the first one. It was here that the four Ryder forgeries hung. There were no cots. Suspended from two metal tripods at either end was a rope hammock. There were two bentwood rocking chairs, both adjacent to end tables of natural rattan. Along the wall under the paintings were unpainted pine shelves that held a miscellany of books and bottles, pipes and phonograph records, and the components of a sophisticated stereo system. There was a faint scent of good tobacco and smoky scotch. It was, Darby thought, a place for a man to enjoy many pleasures. She glanced again at the hammock and wondered what it would be like to make love in one.

Callahan moved to a panel of rheostats on the wall. He dimmed all the overhead lights except those focused on the forgeries. He moved away from the wall and sat in one of the rockers. He motioned Darby to take a seat in the other. She did. After a long silence, during which both studied the paintings, Callahan spoke.

"Do you know much about Ryder?" he asked.

"No, not really," Darby replied.

"Like most men who are obsessed, he took risks."

"How do you mean?"

"No matter what he painted, regardless of the subject matter, and almost incidental to the depth and balance of his design, he kept reaching for one thing: the mystery that exists between what is human and what is superhuman. He wanted desperately to find that thing which is of a higher nature than man."

"That's not so unusual, is it? I mean, isn't that what drives many artists?"

"Yes, of course. But the risk Ryder took involves the paradox of his methods. Here he was, trying to capture, trying to give permanency to something terribly elusive, and yet he used methods which could guarantee only the *im*permanency of what he recorded. Time and again, he painted over his still-wet canvases and he used strange things to paint with; things like a mixture of alcohol and candlewax. Because of that, there is an extraordinary deterioration of his canvases, and therefore it's very difficult even among professionals, to determine whether many of the paintings are, indeed, Ryder's or are very clever copies. In point of fact, the forgeries outnumber his genuine works. These were done by my father. Look at the painting, the figure of Death. Do you know where he came from?"

"No."

"Ryder heard about a waiter in Brooklyn who spent as many hours as possible at the racetrack."

Darby nodded. "The horse that Death's riding is racing around a track."

"Uh-huh. And the figure of Death is that waiter. He killed himself because of gambling losses. It's rather a mundane background, isn't it? — for such a — such a fierce painting. It haunted my father because what he saw in the painting, what he was quite certain Ryder meant to explore, was the absolute helplessness of man."

"And your father did these four paintings, these forgeries?"

"Yes."

"I don't understand. If he was right, if he was so disturbed by what Ryder was saying, then why did your father keep painting the same thing?"

"By reproducing the painting, over and over, my father kept hoping he would find the flaw in what it said." Callahan paused. "Or, perhaps," he continued, "my father wished to show me that the painter's vision was correct, that man is forever helpless."

"Do you believe that?" Darby asked, aware that he had not earlier answered the question when they sat in the apple orchard. "Do you believe that man is helpless?"

"We're taught that such is the case, without external intervention, without salvation from without."

"And?" Darby asked.

"And what?"

"And do you believe that?" Darby persisted.

"If I did, I wouldn't have left the priesthood."

"You no longer believe in God."

"Oh, yes, I believe in God. And I still consider myself a good Catholic. The Church didn't fail me, you see. I failed it."

"And your father?"

"I think in any failure there is mutual blame. In our case there was an artificial imposition. He wanted me to become something for which I was not suited, and in my desire to please him I undertook the role. I presumed that it would be as easy as pushing the peas around on my plate. What we did together, my father and I, was to make a mutual mistake, and we both suffered the consequences. I broke my father's heart."

"You're awfully harsh on yourself."

"I'm stating a fact. I believe in facts."

"I remember," Darby smiled. "It's why you became a cop."

Callahan rose and moved to the pine shelves across the balcony.

Fitted under the bottom shelf was a small, office-sized refrigerator. He opened it and removed a bottle along with two small cordial glasses. Both the bottle and the glasses were frosted from cold. He poured colorless liquid into one of the glasses and placed it on the table next to Darby.

"You can't find this outside of Ireland. Some say that Saint Patrick made it to chase the snakes away. It's really quite special."

"What is it?"

"Cork Dry gin."

"Oh, no," Darby said quickly. "No thanks."

"I think you'll like it."

"I know I'll like it," Darby said, "but I'd better not. Gin does strange things to me."

"Does it make you sick?"

"No, Wilfred. It does not make me sick. It makes me sexy."

"Oh," Callahan said. He started to remove the glass from Darby's table. But her hand closed over his wrist.

"Oh, well," she said. "What the hell."

He poured a glass for himself and leaned back in his chair. "Now," he said, "it's your turn. You told me about the time when you were a little girl in the playground, but you said something else."

"You have very beautiful eyes, Wilfred," Darby said.

"You'd better take it easy on the gin." Callahan was studying her carefully. "What other things, what other crazy things did you do?"

"When you were a priest, were you celibate?" Darby asked. "Or did you cheat?"

"What other crazy things?"

"Listen, would you like some scrambled eggs? I make great scrambled eggs."

"I think you'd be better off getting some sleep."

Darby picked up the decanter. She poured herself another gin. "In the hammock?" she asked. "Are we going to sleep in the hammock?"

"Let's do the scrambled eggs," Callahan said. "Ray Poole raises chickens," Callahan continued. "The eggs are very fresh." He rose and adjusted the rheostats so that brighter light flooded the house. Carrying her gin, Darby followed him across the balconies to the stairway. Going down the staircase Darby stumbled slightly on one of the iron treads.

"Whoops," she said. Callahan turned quickly and, reaching up to steady her, brushed his hand against her breast. Each was conscious of the touch. Neither said anything.

"You sit," Darby said when they entered the kitchen. "I can find everything."

Callahan sat at the butcher-block table and watched as Darby rummaged around and found eggs and milk and herbs and mixed them in a bowl. Despite the gin she continued to sip, she was very efficient.

"Those other things," she said, her back to Callahan, "the other things I did. It was really just one thing. It was what you might call your basic disaster." She poured the mixture into a skillet which rested on the stove and turned up the burner. "The thing I did, I screwed a lot. You see, the tongue thing didn't really work. I mean, the kids hated all the blood and everything, but they still didn't leave me alone. So when I was a little older I tried something else. I thought if I made love to any boy who wanted to, then they'd say, wow, she's really a good kid. I mean, even if she is a Jew. Where's the paprika?"

"On the second shelf."

"Thank you."

"You're welcome."

Darby sprinkled paprika on the eggs and used a spatula to lift them from the skillet to two plates. "At least I told myself that I was making love. I wasn't, of course. I was just screwing. I told Mouse that, too. It's funny, isn't it? There are people you can tell anything to. I guess it's because you know they won't judge you. I think you're one of those people."

She turned toward him, both plates in her hands, and she was crying. There was no choke to her voice, no sound of sobbing, just a trail of tears down her face. "Shit," she said as she saw the tears drop onto the plates of scrambled eggs. "I hope you're not on a low-sodium diet."

Callahan smiled and spoke gently. "I've always thought that one of the finer things in life was to meet an unpredictable person."

"Boy," Darby said as she placed the plates on the table and wiped the tears from her face, "you've just hit the jackpot."

Callahan tasted his eggs. "Wonderful. What's in them besides the paprika?"

"Tarragon and a little curry powder." Darby shook her head and smiled ruefully. "Goddamn gin. I didn't mean to tell you the story of my life."

"I wish you'd tell me more."

"There's nothing special. I grew up — well, older anyway, and I don't feel that way anymore. I mean angry or resentful at being a Jew. I guess if I still resent anything at all it's the way my parents handled the whole thing. They were always so damned careful."

"You mean protective?"

"Well, more than that. It's hard to explain. Maybe because I was a mistake, unplanned for. They'd tried to have children for a long time and nothing happened and then, one day, when I'm sure they'd given up, powie! — out I popped."

"That's not unusual."

"I know. But I think something happens then. They always wanted to make sure they didn't overreact to having a child. They didn't want me to feel I was something special. I guess they were afraid of spoiling me. But what they did was wrong, too. From the time I was a little girl, they made sure they didn't lay anything on me, didn't impose any arbitrary ideas of their own. They figured that way I'd have to learn for myself what was right or wrong, how to behave, what to believe in. I mean, my father didn't seem to believe in anything, anything at . . ." The look on her face changed, the memory of her adolescent despair gone, replaced by a slowly growing delight. "Oh, God, Wilfred, I think it's happening. I think maybe it's really happening. Dad was so different tonight."

"You mean at the house?"

"No, no, no. Before. When I met him at this little synagogue Mouse is fixing. Daddy was really excited. He was . . . he was so touching, so open . . . so lovely . . . so . . ." She stared at Callahan and her eyes were very dark. "So are you. You're a lovely man."

"That's the gin," Callahan said.

"No, it's not. You know it's not."

"Yes," Callahan said.

"You don't have to worry," Darby said. "I'm not going to seduce you. I don't do that any more. I mean, the penis is not a magic wand, is it?"

"No."

"And that's really what I'm looking for. Magic."

"There are very few wizards left."

Darby laughed. "I don't mean that kind of magic. I mean mystery, mysticism, something unexplainable. Something different from the respectable conventions we live with. Something bigger. A miracle, maybe. Name me a miracle, Wilfred."

"The justice of God."

"Oh!" Darby exclaimed. "You've got to see my play. The one I'm going to stage-manage. Do you know *The Dybbuk*?"

"No."

"It's an old Yiddish play and that's what it's about. The justice of God. And obligation. The obligation we have to each other, that we can't escape. It's another form of miracle really. The miracle of sharing, of people coming together, of . . ." she faltered and then continued softly, her eyes shining at him. "Of two people coming together. That is a miracle, isn't it, Wilfred? Isn't that a miracle?"

"Yes," he said quietly, "that is a miracle."

Silently, they looked at each other. Callahan rose from the table and walked out of the kitchen. He began to climb the circular stairs to the loft.

Darby followed him.

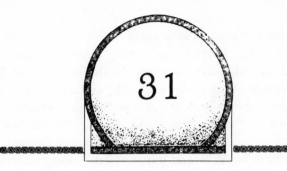

31

Solomon stood at the window in room 310 of the Residencia Dona Maria and listened in awe to the twenty-five clamoring bells of the Giralda. The bell tower, part of the enormous Gothic cathedral in Seville, was all that remained of a mosque which had once graced the square. A simple bronze statue of Faith turned at the apex of the tower. It was as if the figure were wincing from the bell's reverberations and trying to find some restful space within the palpitating air.

Solomon was sympathetic to Faith's plight. He, too, was weary of reverberations — and, he thought, weary of flight. No, not weary; unhappy, tense. He was not inwardly referring to travel; he was referring to the process of people moving away from each other. It was what was happening to him and Kendal.

Yesterday morning, Callahan had driven Darby back to the farmhouse. He had not come in, and when Solomon saw the reflection of sunlight in Darby's eyes, he suspected he knew why the sergeant had not wished to confront him. Darby had said little, announcing only that she was driving her pickup back to New York, where she would meet with Rena to continue work on the forthcoming production of *The Dybbuk*. Solomon explained to her that he was leaving for Madrid that night and would be in Seville the following night. He did not know the length of his stay.

It was then that Kendal informed them both of her plans. She, too, was leaving. She was going to England to visit her father.

"I am," she said to Solomon, her eyes cool and direct, "going home."

He said nothing.

"For how long, Mom?" Darby asked.

"Oh, you know," Kendal said vaguely, "for whatever it takes." Darby wasn't sure what Kendal meant. Neither was Kendal. Solomon made no comment. Made awkward by the excruciating politeness between her parents, Darby departed. But not before Solomon's warning.

"Listen, love," he said sternly to his daughter, "while we're gone, don't do anything foolish. Whatever's going on here, in the house, it's not a good place to be. Whatever son of a bitch is doing it is crazy. He's dangerous. I don't want you here. Let Callahan take care of it. That's his job. Understood?"

Darby nodded silently. It was a way of not quite agreeing. She knew she didn't want to be away from Wilfred too long.

Solomon and Kendal drove back to Westport together. They talked very little. There seemed little to say. Solomon contacted a travel agency which was often used by TransGlobal and arranged his trip. He would leave that night and fly directly to Madrid.

Next, Solomon called Wilton Forest's secretary. He knew her to be a woman unfazed by any request. He told her of his plans and asked that she use the good offices of TransGlobal's Madrid branch to contact someone of learning in Seville, someone who would be familiar with the religious history of Spain and who would have access to records and files of Jewish migration. He suggested that if she were, indeed, able to reach the man or woman they wanted, she might mention that Solomon would be extremely grateful if there were any records of a Rafael Fernandez Muñoz. Certain that she would be successful in this search, Solomon asked her to leave word with the airline in Madrid.

As Solomon packed for his journey, taking particular care to check that his camera had film, he asked Kendal when she planned to leave for Bagshot.

"Tomorrow," she said. "I have things to do today." She didn't, but she had no wish to go to the airport with her husband.

"Shall I call the travel agency?" Solomon asked politely.

"No thank you."

"Well," he said. "Well. Give my love to Oliver."

"Yes," she said. "I'll do that."

He left the house in a local taxi, which drove him to the airport. There he bought a guidebook to Spain. He checked again that his camera had film. On the plane, he spent a long time reading the guidebook, paying close attention to the information about the Jewish quarters in both Córdoba and Seville. He took two 5-milligram tabs of Valium. He slept the rest of the flight.

The next morning in Madrid, there was a message saying to telephone a Professor Rubio Alcalde in Seville. Although he spoke with the quiet formality of a Spaniard, Alcalde's voice was tinged with an Oxford accent. He explained that he had once been a professor in one of Spain's great universities but that he had been dismissed during Franco's reign. Ever since, he had made himself useful as a consultant to those foreigners who wished to learn about the history and glories of Spain. Having been contacted by the studio he was now pleased that he could be of service to TransGlobal and to Solomon.

"Am I to understand, sir," Alcalde said, "that your family name is Muñoz and you wish to learn more of them?"

Although this was not exactly as Solomon had explained it to Forest's secretary, he acknowledged that it was so, and that he wished to trace his family if at all possible and to learn of the conditions of Jewish life in Seville, conditions which might have affected his family.

"Permit me to interrupt, señor," Alcalde interjected. "The name Muñoz is most common. I have in my possession many, many documents. These documents have been authenticated by official sources and each has been stamped with the name of a family to which they relate. I can assure you that the name of Muñoz is often seen. Are you quite certain, Señor Moon, that your family did not leave Spain earlier than the nineteenth century?"

"I'm not certain of anything," Solomon replied, recalling his father's reticence to discuss any matter Judaic.

"I would remind you," Alcalde said, "that the great diaspora occurred in the year 1492."

"Are you saying that you cannot trace the history of a Jewish family?" Solomon tried not to reveal his irritation.

"My dear sir," Alcalde said, "I suggest that the names are of little importance." He paused. When he spoke again, his voice had lost its resonance. It was the voice of a tired, old man. "The stories are the same."

"Well," Solomon said, "do the best you can."

"It goes without saying, sir," Alcalde replied. "May I inquire when you will arrive?"

"Tonight."

"And where will you stay?"

"At the Dona Maria."

"Splendid," Alcalde said. "It is close to my home in the Barrio de Santa Cruz. Perhaps you will do the honor of dining with me."

"That's very kind," Solomon said. Alcalde gave Solomon his address, and they arranged to meet at the professor's home at ten o'clock that night. Before concluding the conversation, Alcalde asked a strange question.

"Do I have permission to ask you something of a personal nature?"

"Yes, of course," Solomon replied.

"Have you — how do you say it in English? — *un estómago fuerte?*"

"I'm sorry. I don't understand."

"*Estómago fuerte,*" Alcalde repeated. "I believe it is what you call a strong stomach. I speak, of course, not in the literal sense."

"Yes, sure, I've got a strong stomach. Why?"

"You will read things, sir," Rubio Alcalde said. "Until tonight."

Solomon wondered why the professor had asked about the state of his digestion. Surely he would read nothing as upsetting as the incidents of the past few days. He put it out of his mind as he ran to catch the connecting flight to Córdoba. It was a short flight and after he landed, airline people helped him find a driver to take him to Córdoba's Tiberiades Square, and then on to Seville. The girl at the desk suggested that Solomon might want to spend more time in Córdoba so that he could tour the Great Mosque but Solomon explained that he had only one mission in the city and then would have to depart immediately for Seville.

The driver of the car spoke little English, and Solomon's Spanish was limited to what he'd studied many years ago at school. Each found it easier not to engage in lengthy discussion. At Solomon's request, the driver parked on a narrow street adjacent to the Jewish quarter. On foot, following a map in the guidebook, Solomon headed for Tiberiades Square. Everywhere he looked were small courtyards, their tiny gardens open to view through black grillework gates. Most of the courtyards were bright with geraniums, and many had decorative fountains, the sound of their splashing waters soothing to Solomon's ears.

When he reached it, Solomon was surprised at the smallness of Tiberiades Square, but he had not come in search of size. He had come to see what sat in the middle of the square. A large stone base rested within a small garden of flowers. The flowers were confined by a single row of bricks. Sitting on the stone base was a carved figure, one hand balancing himself on the seat, the other holding a book folded in his lap. The head of the man was turbaned, he was bearded and his stone eyes were closed in contemplation. It was a statue of Mouse's hero: Moses Maimonides.

As Solomon studied the gentle visage of the stone face, he thought of the tribute Mouse had spoken about the great Hebrew philosopher. *From Moses unto Moses there arose none like Moses.* Solomon wished that Mouse were here to finally touch the cool stone and watch, forever if need be, until the philosopher opened his stone eyes and smiled upon the man who loved him.

Solomon withdrew his Instamatic camera from a pocket. Slowly circling the sculptured figure, he took one photograph after another until only one shot remained. He saved that. He had a special purpose.

He returned to the hired car. His pulse beating a little faster, tingling with anticipation, he asked the driver to go into the country. The driver wanted to know if Solomon had an exact place in mind.

"Wherever there are fields," Solomon replied, mostly describing with gestures. "A field and an olive grove. And a man, a working man."

The driver laughed and said that was easy. Wherever you look there are fields and there are olive groves and men work. It's how they live. But he spoke in Spanish and Solomon understood little of what he said.

They journeyed through small villages and past small olive groves, but Solomon urged the driver on until, at last, they moved through brown Andulasian hills. On either side of the road, Solomon saw men working in the fields but he did not ask the driver to stop until in the distance he saw a field in which only one man worked. The man wore rough black clothing and a white shirt. And the field was ringed by the silver-green of olive trees. Quickly, Solomon ordered the driver to pull over.

Solomon jumped out of the car. He raised the Instamatic to his eye. He called to the man in the field. Startled, the man wheeled around and squinted into the sun. Solomon snapped his picture.

I don't know your name, Solomon said silently to the man in the field, but you're mine!

On their way to Seville, Solomon and the driver lunched in an outdoor café in one of the villages through which they drove. The table was set in the shade and a warm wind blew down on them from the hills. It carried the scent of oranges and, although the two men didn't attempt to converse, they smiled a great deal at each other as they drank from earthen jugs of cold wine and picked from generous platters of grilled sardines and black olives and coarse bread. When they set off again, the heat had intensified and Solomon dozed in the back of the car.

At the Residencia Dona Maria, Solomon tipped the driver grandly, thanked him, and called him *amigo*. He meant it.

Now, listening to the final clapping of the bells of the Giralda, Solomon again wondered what he could possibly read that would oblige Rubio Alcalde to warn him of the consequences. He wondered what the polite professor would think if he learned of the violent obscenities Solomon had encountered recently. Checking his watch, he shrugged into his jacket of the one suit he'd packed. He polished his shoes on the corner of a bedspread, something he hadn't done since he was a boy. He brushed his teeth again. He was, Solomon admitted to himself, nervous about the coming encounter. He doubted that Alcalde would have had the time to discover specifics about the Muñoz family, but he presumed the professor would have data about a typical Jewish family in Seville. Certainly, that would suffice in terms of the necessities involved in developing a story line for Wilton Forest. Then why was he so tense?

Hastily, Solomon left his room and walked out of the Dona Maria. Soon Solomon was threading his way through a maze of twisting, narrow streets and alleys. The barrio was an ancient part of the city, and, as in Córdoba, its small whitewashed houses were elegantly adorned with black wrought-iron filigree and window-boxed with bright flowers.

Although Alcalde had given him precise directions, Solomon found the streets wandering in haphazard directions, some turning in on themselves, others ending in blind alleys, many changing their names as they crossed minuscule squares. Planted in one of the squares was a pomegranate tree. Solomon paused and touched its leaves. He glanced at the painted street sign. *Calle de la Muerte*. The Street of Death. He hurried toward the professor's home.

Rubio Alcalde was a tiny wisp of a man whose curvature of the spine was so severe that he was forced to walk with his gaze on the floor. What little hair remained on his head was clipped neatly short, and ancient scars could be seen through the sparse gray mat. A small gray beard was scissored to a point. He wore immaculate white linen and a high, old-fashioned celluloid collar around which was knotted a narrow, black tie. His suit was black mohair which, although obviously expensive, showed years of wear at the elbows and knees. His black ankle-high boots were polished so brightly that Solomon couldn't help but wonder if they served as a mirror for his downthrust face.

"Welcome to my home, sir," he greeted Solomon at the door. He had to bend his knees and rock back on his heels to look into Solomon's face. When they shook hands, Solomon was surprised at the strength in

Alcalde's fingers. He looked at the man's hand and saw that the fingers were terribly crooked and the knuckles so flat that they had lost all definition. He thought of Mouse and wondered if the professor kept bees.

Alcalde led him across a small, white room sparsely furnished with pieces of ornately carved dark oak and lighted only by eight candles, two in each corner. They walked under a curved archway and into the dining room. There was a long rectangular table, just as ornate as the living room furniture, and around the table were high-backed oaken chairs upholstered in dark red brocade shot with golden thread. This room was considerably brighter than the other, for a massive black wrought-iron chandelier was suspended over the table, holding at least forty blazing candles. For a moment Solomon was puzzled. How could such a tiny man light these candles? Then he saw that a heavy chain could lower and raise the chandelier. Neatly arranged at one end of the table were books and folded documents, paper-covered manuscripts and note pads. Each had a place marked with a ribbon. At the other end of the table was an exquisite crystal decanter half filled with a golden amber liquid, and two delicate crystal sherry glasses. Two embroidered lace place mats had been set out. On them were silver settings for two diners.

"May I?" Alcalde asked as he moved down the length of the table and lifted the decanter.

"Thank you," Solomon said. Alcalde sat at the head of the table and motioned for Solomon to sit at his right. As Solomon took his seat, he realized that Alcalde's chair was fitted with plump cushions so that when he sat his crooked body was higher than the table and he could lean back comfortably. Alcalde poured the sherry.

"To your well-being, sir," he toasted. Both men sipped from their glasses. The sherry was delicious, dry and nutty, its fragrance holding merely a hint of smoked wood. Alcalde's eyes were on Solomon. He raised his glass again. "And to the Jews of Seville," he said. "To the mules they sold."

Solomon was too interested in his own question to inquire about the seeming frivolity of the reference to mules.

"Are you a Jew, professor?"

"Only in the sense that I am among men who continue to search."

"For what?"

"For the way out of the wilderness in which we all dwell," Alcalde said quietly.

Solomon was startled. These were the words he'd heard spoken by the Mouse. "I'm sorry that you don't know a friend of mine," he said. "He believes the same thing."

"To pronounce him a wise man," Alcalde smiled, "would be to compliment myself, which would be unforgivable, no?"

"I think you would like each other a great deal," Solomon said. "He is . . . he is a . . ." Solomon searched for the right word. He found it. "He is a good man."

"There are not many," Alcalde said quietly. He held up his glass and twirled it slowly under the candles. "This inquiry in which you have enlisted my aid — is it for professional reasons or do you have a personal purpose?"

"Both, I think," Solomon said. "Yes, both."

"Does one have priority over the other?"

"Yes." Solomon's eyes met the professor's but he said no more.

"Do you wish me to guess?" asked Alcalde.

"I suspect you know," Solomon said.

"Sí," Alcalde said softly, "I suspect I know." He lifted the decanter. "With your permission."

"It's fine sherry," Solomon said, "but perhaps we should get to the matter at hand."

Alcalde rocked back on his cushions so that his gaze could meet Solomon's at eye level. "Some fortification would not be harmful," he said, and he poured each of them another small glass of sherry. "We live in a peculiar time, Señor Moon. There is a great interest among many men to reexamine the codes by which they live. It is understandable, of course. Like a king devaluating the coin of the realm, man has depreciated the price of life. We look for bargains in morality, so to speak, but when we find them we are displeased, for when one purchases nothing one becomes nothing. *Yo soy Yo y mi circunstancias.* I am I and my surroundings. Sadly, rather than attempt to change our surroundings — and by that I do not mean the external space which walls us; no, I refer to our interior architecture, our hearts, our souls — rather than attempt to change the innerness of ourselves, we seek to quiet our unrest by reaching for the magic of the past: a past, we assure ourselves, in which men lived with honor and nobility. Surely, we say, our fathers must have been wiser than we. As an historian, sir, I assure you that such is not the case. You frown, Señor Moon. Do I not make myself clear?"

Solomon rolled the little sherry glass between his fingers. "I think,

Professor Alcalde," he said, "that this is the second warning you've given me."

"*Es verdad,*" Alcalde said. "It is true." He put down his glass, spread his hands flat on the table, and stared at them. "During the conflict, the Falangists broke my fingers. They were strong men. They snapped the joints one by one. They used a hammer for my knuckles. It took a very brief time but it was painful. I did not tell them what they wished, so they cracked my spine. That was more painful. I thought myself a very brave man. Perhaps it was only stupid. I no longer know. I know only that I do not wish to contribute pain to another man."

In a quick little motion, Alcalde edged himself out of the chair. He moved to the other end of the table, his head only inches above the massed books. His fingers played with the ribbons protruding from the marked passages.

"How like Spain," he said, "to mark blood with silk." With surprising agility, he climbed onto a chair at the end of the table and reached out to the heavy chain that secured the chandelier. He lowered the chandelier so that light shone brightly on the books. He rehooked the chain and climbed down from the chair. "Are you aware of the Archivo Histórico Nacional in Madrid, Señor Moon?"

"No."

"A remarkable place. One can find things of rare value. Among these things are the publications of unusual trials."

"What kind of trials?"

"The original trials of the Inquisition, sir. Of the Spanish Inquisition. Of Tomás de Torquemada's Inquisition. I have, over the years, made many transcripts. Of necessity, due to their historical importance, I have acquired considerable addenda."

Solomon felt a drop of sweat roll from his armpit. Something about the manner of Alcalde excited him. "Such as . . . what?" he asked.

"Such as diaries," Alcalde said. "And letters. Many letters have survived. Among them is a letter from a Jew who sold his mule. It is a common name, of course. It is probable that coincidence merely mocks us."

Solomon's mouth was dry. But he couldn't lift the sherry to his lips. "What," he asked slowly, "is the name of the Jew who sold his mule?"

"Rafael Fernandez Muñoz." Alcalde said.

Solomon nodded. He was unable to speak.

Alcalde's fingers tapped the cover of a book. "He was a Marrano."

Solomon cleared his throat. "What is a Marrano?"

"To be literal in my language," Alcalde said, "*marrano* means swine.

It was applied in a pejorative sense to those Jews who became Conversos. Jews who betrayed themselves and accepted baptism into the Catholic faith but who, after publicly accepting Christianity, continued in secret to practice their true beliefs. If the continuance of Judaic ritual was discovered, the Marrano became a guest at Torquemada's autos-da-fé."

"You mean he was burned at the stake?"

"And other things," Alcalde said. He slid a thin, leather-bound volume from underneath a stack of books and opened it to its ribboned place. "The Muñoz letter is here. I have translated it. Do not thank me." He turned and started through the archway.

"Professor Alcalde," Solomon called. "Perhaps you would prefer that I take this back to my hotel?"

"Please," Alcalde said, "you are my guest. Do not hurry. We dine late in my country. Should you still wish to dine after . . ." He glanced down at the open manuscript. "I, myself, have reading." His mouth twisted into the faintest of smiles. "Today in Spain, there is much to learn of a new fascism. Small groups, you understand, with a certain impunity from active prosecution. The National Revolutionary Youth. The New Force Party. The Spanish Club of Friends of Europe. Exotic nomenclature, is it not? I enjoy reading of their activities. It accentuates the enigma of broken fingers."

He bowed and left the room.

Slowly, Solomon circled the table, his eyes on the open manuscript. He stood in front of it. He touched it. He walked away. He poured another sherry and drank it quickly. Solomon returned to the end of the table, sat down. He removed the ribbon from the manuscript and smoothed the pages. The chandelier was so low that he could feel heat from the candles. He put on his glasses and turned a few pages. They were of a modern, good grade vellum. What must have been a handwritten letter had been transcribed on a typewriter. The left-hand pages were in Spanish. The right-hand pages, the corresponding text, were in English. He turned more pages and saw that finally the letter ended. On the last page of the Spanish text was a duplicate signature of the writer. Rafael Fernandez Muñoz. No attempt had been made to copy the signature for the English translation. The signature was written in a graceful hand, the individual letters examples of learned calligraphy, the strokes firm and bold. Lightheaded, Solomon turned back to the beginning of the letter. There was no salutation. The body of the text began immediately.

It is my largest hope that my son will have a son and he another son and he another and that one of these sons will read of my infamy. I dare dream that at such time of revelation the blood of Muñoz will have been cleansed. It is the one dream left. There is nothing more.

It is known that my grandfather died in "a wilderness of rocks, glory of Spain and light of all her cities." I must be pardoned for borrowing Cervantes' words about the great city of Toledo. One must capitalize on the beauty of language in order to preserve one's sanity. It was in this wilderness of rocks, while the convent bells tolled the Angelus, that the great Dominican Vincente Ferrer inspired the good citizens of Toledo to drag the Jews of the city to the promenade that overlooks the Tagus river. They cut the Jews' throats and threw them onto the rocks below. It was not determined if my grandfather was dead before he hit the rocks or if he died with his head in the waters of the Tagus. It is a small point. This was *She'at ha-Shemad.* A time of persecution. My mother died with him, which I feel certain contributed to her happiness.

My father, also called Rafael Fernandez Muñoz, is a practical man. Forgive me. *Was* a practical man. It is too recent to hold. After the festivities on the promenade, my father and I, his only son, were offered baptism into the true faith. We took the waters together. Later, we participated in the blood and body of Christ. We became *conversos.* In doing so we were untouchable by the Inquisitor and his familiars. This practical step by my practical father allowed us to journey to Seville, where we lived for many years and where, mark you this, in secret we remained Jews. It makes little difference in which city a Jew dwells. They will find you. They found my father.

It happened in this way. For the last fortnight as of the writing of this letter, Tomás de Torquemada has honored Seville with his presence. Many trials have been held. They continue. The Inquisitor is clear in his purpose. He will destroy all heretics. He has a particular fondness for Marranos, among whom can be numbered my father and myself. No. My father no longer can be numbered. He is gone. I will become familiar with it. Believe this. My father is, *was was was,* a man of great age. He had upon him a sickness. Perhaps he was merely tired. His heart made dim sounds. There was much pain. Many nights ago, he decided to die. He made an error.

He turned his face to the wall.

And he was seen! Surely, you must understand the consequence. The Dominican scholars are learned men and they have at hand important manuals which purport to describe the rituals of a Jew:

"A Jew buries his fingernails in the earth so that they may be gleaned on the Day of Judgment. A Jew's chimney does not smoke on Saturdays for he will not have cooked on his Sabbath. A Jew drains all fowl of blood. On the seventh night after an infant has emerged from the womb, a Jew fills a bowl with water and into it he drops barley and a pearl. A Jew crushes Christians like grapes in a winepress. *A Jew who is near death turns his face to the wall so that he may weep for his sins.*"

I do not wish to burden you with more. It is sufficient to know that when one of

Torquemada's familiars spied upon our house and saw that my father had turned to the wall for his death, my father's secret and continued belief in Judaism was established. It was duly reported to Torquemada who, because he is a thoughtful man, gave my father a short period of grace in which to repent. Such is the custom of the Inquisition. They do not speed you to the fire.

Numbed by pain, his ribs cracked from the weight of the stone slab, his eyelids lacerated from where the slab had grazed, Tuttle was grateful for the warmth of the sanbenito cloak they slipped over his body, and even the conical hat was comforting for the cold air of the cave enveloped him. His eyelids stung terribly and fluttered against the yellow light of candles and he was only dimly conscious of being lifted by the boy. He didn't care where they carried him so long as they stopped asking him questions he could not understand and could not answer. He welcomed the soft leather loops through which they thrust his hands and from which he could hang with ease. They crossed his ankles and tied them loosely with a thong but he didn't mind for his feet rested on a stone ledge which was cool and damp and soothed his crushed feet.

He did not know that he was suspended within the niche of Judas.

Idly, he wondered about the silence of the cave and he forced his eyelids open. He saw that the boy sat crosslegged on a stone table, an Irish harp cradled in his lap as he watched the old man stir an enormous pot of honey. He used a narrow wooden paddle to mix the sweet substance, dotted with bits of waxy comb. The old man twisted and turned his paddle, scraping the sides of the pot, lifting the spatula occasionally so that he could test the consistency of the honey rivers which flowed down its length.

Perched on its ledge, Brother Death's black eyes gleamed. The bird stared at the honey pot. Its wings vibrated.

During this period of grace, the familiars contributed their usual kindness. They did not separate me from my father. As I was of his blood, they considered me, also, as one who might have relinquished the true faith and returned to the beliefs of a Jew. Of equal importance, they looked upon me as a witness to his lapse of faith and informed me that it was my obligation to speak. The kindness extended to the knowledge that it made little difference whether I spoke before or after he was *relaxed*. They adorned us with the hated sanbenitos, which they assured us they would hang in the cathedral to perpetuate our shame should we not repent; and so all that passed our home would be warned that inside these walls dwelled the infamous, they attached to our door two red tongues, and they manured our house.

"Jesus!" Solomon whispered. He leaned forward, his eyes close to the pages, and continued to read.

Many days passed, and during all the hours my father did not speak. Nor did he hide. From his secret place, he removed the Torah and books of the Talmud and he dressed himself in *tefillin* and *tallit*, the little square box of the *shel rosh* worn high on his forehead, the *shel yad* around his left arm. The prayer shawl over his shoulders, he pulled at the fringes as if he were counting the commandments of the Lord.

Only after many days did he utter his final words to me. "A Sephardic rebbe asks this question," he said. "How shall one take vengeance on one's enemies?" And my father answered the rebbe's question. "By increasing one's good qualities." Having so spoken, my father closed the Torah and smiled. He was smiling when they came for him.

Riordan lifted the wooden paddle and held it over the pot. Honey and comb coalesced into a syrup that formed globs on the paddle and then ran thickly into the pot. Riordan speared a tiny wet globe of the liquid and let it rest on his finger. He held it up for the bird to see. Brother Death lifted one clawed foot and its beak opened but the old man's eyes narrowed and his gaze held the crow steady. Jubal stared at the drop of honey on his father's finger and he began to breathe quickly. The old man smiled at him and held out his finger. The boy licked up the honey.

Carrying the pot with him, Riordan moved across the cave and stood in front of Judas' niche. He dipped his fingers into the pot and when they were covered with the sweet liquid he raised them and began to paint Tuttle's eyelids with honey. The sticky substance clung to the lacerated skin and calmed the sting, and Tuttle savored the kindness of the act. Just before his eyelashes glued together and as he lost vision behind the honey, he heard the high humming of Jubal's voice and the even higher notes of the harp and, tasting the sweet syrup that dripped across his lips, he almost imagined he was in the presence of angels. If he'd known Tuttle's fleeting thought, Riordan would have been pleased; but he did not know, so he raised his voice and addressed the farmer.

"Through the darkness in which you walk," Riordan intoned, "no longer can you wash your hands among the innocent."

"Amen," sang Jubal.

"You have falsified among the priesthood of believers."

"Amen," sang Jubal.

"Nor can you receive the gift of salvation unless your soul release its content, which is the darkness of which we speak."

"Amen," sang Jubal.

The droning voices of the old man and the boy, the light melody of the harp, the sweet taste of honey on his lips, the linen warmth of the sabenito, the soft rustle of the crow's wings, the dull pain of his wounds — all these things brought a great drowsiness to Tuttle and his chin rested low against his broken chest. He sighed once and his body slightly shuddered.

"And so let light come to the sinner," Riordan said. "For by the death of One was the world redeemed."

He turned toward Brother Death and whistled.

We walked in a parade of the unrepentant. The sun was bright. We could hear horns of the revelers and we could hear the soft clapping of unseen hands, which is the sound of Seville. We turned into the Calle de la Muerte. It seemed a natural progression. We entered a great street. The balconies on the little houses that lined the street were filled with spectators. They were gay. We arrived at the public square. Heavy wooden crosses protruded from their piles of wood and vine branches and straw. A great crowd surrounded them and above their talk and their laughter could be heard the trumpets and the drums summoning all the faithful to the auto-da-fé.

I looked up and noted that crimson damask was draped over a balcony where Tomás de Torquemada stood. Purple cloth hung from the rostrum where sentences were to be read. The marshal, representative of the secular, began the reading. As he named men's names, they were pulled from among us. They were informed of their sentences. They were to be *relaxed*. The Church was merciful. Any who wished to repent at this moment would be put to death before the fire was lighted. Some chose to do this. They were strapped to the crosses. They were strangled. They hung in peace.

Rafael Fernandez Muñoz was named. Before they could pull his chains, my father stepped forward. He refused the mercy of the Church. They strapped him to a cross. Two more men refused the offered mercy. They were tied to crosses on either side of my father. Like my father, they, too, wore long beards. The marshal signaled. The hooded executioner moved to them. He lighted the beards of the two men. He waited until he heard their shrieks and their faces turned black before he lighted the wood at their feet. I do not know how soon they found the true mercy. God's mercy.

The executioner stood in front of my father. He held a little leather sack in his hand, its neck tied with a thong. He opened the sack and filled it with gunpowder. He closed the sack and tied its thong around my father's neck. The crowd shouted its approval. They knew what I knew. When the flames reached my father's neck, the gunpowder would explode. My father would lose his head.

I come now to the difficult part. To my confession. To my infamy. I watched the flame bite his ankles and sever the tendons of one knee. When the fire reached his manhood he screamed. He screamed so loudly that his throat burst and blood ran from his mouth and out of the corners of his eyes, and then he was devoid of sound. And still he screamed. Silently. His eyes were filled with such terror that I prayed for the explosion.

I prayed for more. I prayed for forgiveness. I prayed for the chance to repent. I prayed to be accepted now and forever into the true faith.

I prayed not to be a Jew!

Flying above the burning candles on the table, his wings shadowed on the stone ceiling of the cave, Brother Death attacked his feast of honey. He sank his beak deep into Tuttle's eyelids and pierced the crusted honey.

"Oh, God!" the farmer shrieked. "Oh, God!"

"Yes!" exulted Riordan. "Yes!"

Again and again the bird struck, filling his beak with honey and flesh and mucous membrane, devouring the farmer's face until all that was left were strips of cartilage and bloodied skin and a single drop of honey melting within an eyeless socket of the skull.

They took the shattered skull of my father and placed a pearl inside his mouth. They had been informed that all Jews did this thing for their dead. They threw the skull into my house. They knew that I would understand that when I saw the skull it signaled that my death was next. It amused them not to tell me when.

For some days now, I have wandered the streets of Seville, dressed still in the yellow sanbenito so that I might please Torquemada and his loyals. I beg on the Street of Jews but there are no alms, for there is none that will acknowledge me. Neither Christian nor Jew. They do not see me for I am as nothing. I have betrayed all that is man. I take refuge in corners, hiding from the sunlight that illuminates my shame.

The bishops confiscated my home. The Inquisition is a costly procedure. The sale of this house will help defray expenses of the Church. *Ave Maria.* They are as practical as my father. They left me my mule. I sold him. He is a sweet animal, uncomplaining. I have another use for the money I received. I bought a little glass bottle. It is of rare beauty. Under candlelight it glows a dark red, much like the blood that first comes when one scratches oneself. I have use for it.

I know now why my father decided to die. He understood that the first assassin is always oneself and that self-assassination is a way of life. Such daily dying is the penalty when we betray ourselves. After my father lost his head, I understood that I had lived one day too long.

This morning I walked into the Andulasian hills. I took with me only my pretty little glass. I sit now in the dust of an olive grove. I look at the sky and see a southern shearwater on the way north from Africa. He will find nothing of value. I look at the ground. I admire the talons of a praying mantis. He is fearless. I am not.

I break my little bottle. I chew a piece of glass. It cuts my tongue. My mouth is filled with blood. I swallow the glass and the blood. I eat the remainder of the glass. It is like an animal in my belly. I am dying.

Son of my son, I beg you to open your Torah and read well the lesson of Deuteronomy: "Do not forget the things your eyes have seen, nor let them slip from your heart all the days of your life; rather tell them to your children and to your children's children."

And to he who may be kind enough to knock on the door of my grave, I will say all that I know. Learn to live with the knife at your throat . . . but do not smile.

I sign my father's name. He lives.

Rafael Fernandez Muñoz

But Solomon could not read the signature. Blood rose behind his eyes, his rage blinding him as he released the sorrow of his own betrayals. His body hunched in pain, his mouth twisted open and as he heard his own thin wail he knew it was the cry of an avenging Jew, and that he, Solomon Moon, descendant of all Jews, was the Angel of Death.

CONNECTIONS

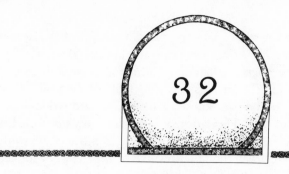

3 2

They dismembered Jabez Tuttle and buried all but his head and hands under the soft clay of the riverbank. The old man was in a strange humor. Although he had seen Tuttle's soul escape from his eyeless sockets and rise to heaven, Riordan was not satisfied that he had served God fully. Since the night he had hidden on the mountain rise and watched the woman clean the farmhouse of its dung, and, later, seen the Holy Cross pulled from the ground, he had felt a terrible anger.

He knew now that the police officer, regardless of his attendance at the Catholic church, only pretended to embrace the true faith. And the Jew made war on God. They had behaved with the arrogance of infidels. They had ignored the warning from his own hand, which was His hand, and so he knew that the Lord was waiting for him to act further.

His unrest was heightened by his concern for his son. Jubal had developed a chill, and his rasping cough was a worrisome counterpoint to the night's soft sounds. The old man made Jubal strip himself of his outer garments. He wrapped him in a bearskin blanket. He placed the boy in between a high rise of rocks and the river.

Riordan set about making a fire which would heat the front of the boy and whose reflection on the rocks behind would warm his back. The wilderness site around the cave was still damp from the rain, so the old man had to forage for kindling. When he returned to his son, he dug a pit. He layered the bottom neatly; first with blue jay down taken from a fallen nest, then fuzzy cattail heads he'd collected, and finally the inner strippings of birch bark.

He lighted his fire. When the dried material was burning well he tossed a number of flat stones into the pit. Unmindful of the heat or flames, he pressed the flat stones deep into the burning material.

Riordan walked through the hawthorn bush and entered the mouth of the cave. A mound of short logs was alongside a stone wall. He selected some hickory and apple, knowing that their hard wood would burn long and hot and well. He returned to the fire and slanted the logs over the heating stones. He motioned to the boy to move closer to the fire. Jubal did so and Riordan thought how like an angel the boy looked, his face a golden sheen from the flames.

It was not long before Jubal loosened the bearskin, let it slip around his shoulders. Riordan could see the sweat rolling down his son's face, onto his neck, and down his chest. But still the boy coughed.

Riordan's cooking utensils had been salvaged from Down Derry's dump. He placed a radiator grille over his fire. He dipped a dented hubcap into the river, filled it with fresh water, put it on the grille to heat. He walked deep into the woods until he came to a partial clearing. He searched for mustard plant, picked a handful, and returned to fireside. The old man crouched by the stack of stones and ground the mustard plants between two of the flatter stones until seeds spilled forth. He tossed the seeds into the hubcap and as the water boiled he stirred the seeds rapidly until a thick mustard paste evolved. He removed the hubcap from the fire and dipped a long piece of flannel into the pot until it was saturated with the hot paste.

"It'll sting some, boy," he said to Jubal, "but you'll be the better for it."

Riordan wrapped the steaming flannel around Jubal's chest. The heat brought tears to the boy's eyes but he said nothing. He could not control his coughing, however and, listening to it, Riordan shook his head. "Steam," he said, "we'll steam it out of you."

Quickly, the old man began to tear wet grass from the ground, and swept up armfuls of moldy leaves and dank moss. He filled the firepit with them, partially smothering the flames, causing thin tendrils of hot vapor to rise. He pushed the boy forward and made him bow his head over the steam. The boy opened his mouth wide and let the vapor enter. He sucked it deep into his chest.

Riordan moved to the river and, using a bowl made from children's bones, scooped out sandy loam. His intention was to layer the fire with loam and then drive a stick into the smoldering mass to create a hole down which he could pour water and thus control the flow of steam for hours. But as Riordan started back toward the fire he became aware of a cloud sliding across the face of the moon and, because he knew that the moon was God's eye, he stood very still and looked toward heaven. The cloud drifted slowly until the white orb was in shadow, then dark, then gone. The old man continued to stare at the sky. He wondered why God no longer looked upon him. He understood that it must be a signal of reproach but it puzzled him. Had he not let light into the eye of the sinner? Had he not inscribed Augustine's warning for those who mingled with the heretic? *But the warning had been removed. The tongues had been removed. The dung had been removed. The flames of the Holy Cross had been extinguished.* The fact that the farmer had been too terrified, too writhed in pain, to do other than babble had not deceived Riordan. Fear and pain silenced only the unrepentant.

Speak to me, Riordan whispered to Him, speak to me!

And the wind that was God's breath blew the cloud from the face of the moon, and when the white disk shone on Riordan's face he knew what he had to do.

He returned to the cave. A small charcoal burner rested on the stone table, its bowl filled with glowing embers. Standing on the grille was a dented aluminum pan. It was filled with boiling sassafras root whose spicy fragrance pervaded the cave, soaked into the limestone walls, drifted into the niche of Judas, where Tuttle had hung, and obliterated the awful smell of death.

Propped on the seat of Saint Bartholomew's niche was Tuttle's severed head. Riordan had placed it there as an act of homage to the legend of the saint's beheading, of his martyrdom. Riordan lifted the head and left the cave.

Jubal was bowed over the fire, his mouth sucking in the steamy heat. His face was fiery red and his eyes watered fiercely, but when he coughed Riordan was comforted to hear the looseness of the phlegm; he knew the boy would soon be rid of his disease. Riordan crouched by his son. He placed Tuttle's head in the firepit and covered it with steaming vegetation. He poured the sandy loam he'd collected over the head and the vegetation and packed it firmly. He used a leafless branch to poke a deep hole through the layers of smoldering material. A thick column of steam rose from it. It smelled sickly sweet. Involuntarily, Jubal pulled away his head, but when he saw the old man eying him, he bowed his head again and said three Hail Marys as he prayed for strength to resist the terrible smell of the steaming skull.

"It's around the corner, boyo," Riordan said quietly.

"What?" Jubal asked, slightly alarmed.

"Winter," the old man answered, and Jubal saw that Riordan's head was cocked toward some sound. "The sweet little things are slow in singing."

"The crickets!" Jubal said quickly, for he wanted Riordan to know that he had not forgotten what had been taught. He imitated his father, cocking his head at the same angle and listening. But he heard nothing.

"I don't hear 'em," the boy said.

"It'll come," Riordan said.

There was a single chirp and then silence.

"What happens to the sound, Riordan?" Jubal asked. "From when you hear it an' when you don't? Where's it go in the in-between? Where's it end at?"

"There is no end, darlin'. There's never any end. There's just the interval, the waiting. God, He holds the waiting in His hand, squeezes it some, don't you see, gives it shape, bounces it like a little rubber ball, and then whooooosh! — Here it comes!"

And sure enough the cricket chirped again.

"Dang!" said the boy, his voice filled with wonder, "if that ain't fuck-all!" Willingly, he bent his head and sucked in vapors from the skull. He licked sweat from his lips and thought how much he loved the old man's stories. He wondered if the old man would tell another one. Or blow a melody on the cow's horn. Or maybe both. He notioned that a story might be best.

"Riordan," the boy asked, "what for are we cookin' that sinner's head?"

"Well, now, we've got to strip the flesh and sinew from it. The bones got to be white and shine like the moon so's the folks inside can get their trepidation from its dazzle. Surely, darlin', it's clear to you that those in the farmhouse have displayed a disorderly life?"

"They have." Jubal nodded slowly. He thought of the picture of the girl. He had hidden it in the cave and touched it only when Riordan was not in sight. He could not understand how the girl had allowed the dung to be shoveled from her home or had stood by as the Holy Cross had been pulled from the ground.

"It is so," Riordan said. "And what does the great Tomás bid us do on such occasion?"

Jubal knew that the old man was referring to the infamous Inquisitor, Tomás de Torquemada, but it was difficult to remember all that Riordan had taught him. He had told him so many things. The boy scratched himself under the hot flannel still wrapped around his chest and he drove the stick deeper into the smoldering mass in the firepit so that more hot steam would rise. He hoped that would please Riordan. But it didn't.

"What does great Tomás bid us?" the old man repeated. He spoke in an ugly whisper, his voice as metallic as if he'd swallowed steel shavings.

"Mustard's burnin' me, Riordan. Mustard's burnin' me fair through!"

"Give me the head," Riordan said.

"Huh? What? Give you what?"

"I want the head."

Jubal feigned confusion. "You want my head?"

"I want the head of the heretic," Riordan said with the awful reasonableness of a madman. "Now."

The lessons received from the old man whirled inside the boy's head. He desperately wanted to recall what Riordan had told him about Torquemada's instructions, but all he could remember was Riordan's constant refrain about spiritual debt. Time and again, the old man had reminded Jubal that a child's obligation was to his father, as all men's obligation is finally and forever to *the Father*. According to Riordan, this debt of child to father could never be defrayed and any who were casual about the obligation must suffer the consequences. The consequences were painful. There was no way that Jubal could erase the memory of the old man's terrible bramble whip. Now, sitting at the lip of the firepit, he dreaded the thought of those stinging thorns, but he knew that he would be the recipient of that lash unless he could remember his father's lessons. Unable to hide his anticipation, he glanced quickly at the old man's hands, expecting to see them inside the great coat, sliding the length of bramble free. But the old man was stirring the fire. His motions were not made at random. He was deliberately making a trench around the steaming skull and, under the fiercely burning embers, its roundness was clearly marked.

Then Jubal knew what was expected of him. The punishment for his forgetfulness was to be a terrible test. With his bare hands he was to lift the head of the heretic from the fire.

"Great Tomás . . . Tomás . . . he . . ." Jubal stammered in despair. If only the old man would wait, would give him time, would wink and pronounce this all a game.

"Now!" whispered Riordan.

Jubal sat very still. He heard the chirp of the tree cricket once again. He wished it were cold. He wished the world were made of ice. He wished the world were without fire. He wished his father dead. But because he knew the world was without end and wishless, he plunged his hands into the fire.

Recklessly, his teeth sawing into his lips to stop himself from crying out with pain, he tore through the terrible coals until he felt the hard bones of the skull under his hands, and, thrusting his fingers through the eyeless sockets, he raised the heretic's head and placed it on the ground before Riordan.

The old man stared at the skull. The high heat of hickory had burned flesh away from bone and what little fat or muscle or sinew remained of the face had been steamed loose. The connective tissues had melted. The plates and roof of the skull were hairless.

"Ah," said Riordan. Then he looked at his son. Jubal sat motionless. A thin streak of blood stained his chin. It had run from his torn lips, and because the boy's mouth hung open slackly as he pulled breath into him Riordan could see that his front teeth were stained with blood, too. Jubal held his hands in front of him, high and outstretched, as if they were resting on a shelf. His fingers trembled and their skin was as darkly red and wrinkled as dried poppies. Straining with the effort, he tried to flex his fingers as if he were strumming his harp, but he could not move them. It was only then that he moaned.

Silently, Riordan rose from the ground and entered the cave. When he returned to the fire, he carried with him a deep bowl of honey and placed it before the boy. He held Jubal's wrists and lowered the boy's hands into the bowl of honey until all the flesh was covered. The old man waited until he saw a slight sign of relief in the boy's eyes, and then he spoke softly.

"The great Tomás," Riordan said, "was a man of huge wisdom. It came to him that there are certain precautions to take if we are to protect the City of God. He understood that there are those who walk the streets of the Devil and that it is our obligation to provide terror for them. Do you follow this, Jubal?"

Jubal nodded. He was beyond words.

"These terrors," Riordan continued, "are the instruments of the saved, and they take many forms." With his fingertips he touched Tuttle's skull. The bones were cooling. Riordan picked up the skull and set it in his lap. He seized a corner of his great buckskin coat and crumpled it in his fist. He used it to scrub thin shreds of blackened skin from the skull; as they flaked off, the whiteness of the bone was revealed. "But the infidel must know he is to die. And this is our sign!" He caressed the skull.

Jubal lifted his fingers from the honey bowl and watched the syrup drip from them. He wondered why a father would burn the flesh of his child.

Riordan thought the frown on his son's face was because the boy had not understood. He rose. He lifted the skull high in his hands. The moonlight gleamed whitely on its bones.

"Oh, darlin'," he cried to his son, "we shall hang the Jew on His cross!"

But Jubal still failed to understand why a father would scorch the skin of his son and he wondered if he would ever again play the songs in which people drifted within the circle of their affections.

Once more the cricket sang. Once more Jubal wished his father dead.

33

The FBI identified Tuttle's fingerprints. The penitentiary where
Jabez had served his prison term corroborated that the scrapings found
in the mobile home matched his blood type.

These things did not surprise Wilfred Callahan but he was disappointed that the investigation into Tuttle's background provided no logical clues as to what had been an apparent act of violence. But Callahan's
experience and instinct made him certain that Tuttle's disappearance
was related to the phenomena of Solomon Moon's experience. What
struck the sergeant was how hideous the acts were; hammering two
cows' tongues to the door, dunging the house. Callahan felt that the per-
petrator of these things must be one and the same man, and he was convinced that the saint's words inscribed on the birchbark was a warning
to which grave attention must be paid.

He had no theory regarding the discarded black bird feathers.

At the state police headquarters, Charles, the walrus-mustached lab
technician, informed Callahan that the plaster molds of tire tracks had
led to nothing and that a check of all fingerprints taken from the Moons'
farmhouse had revealed only two sets which were unidentifiable. Although this clue indicated the presence of strangers, Callahan recognized
they would be difficult to trace. Trooper Havermeyer, along with fellow officers, had enlisted the aid of a bloodhound pack to scour the
woods, but the rains had washed out all trace of human scent.

Because of the preposterousness of the events, Callahan decided to
search the police records of earlier years in hopes of discovering some
modus operandi that might hint at this aberrant behavior. He did not
think he would be successful. He was wrong. He had skipped lunch and

was chewing through his third cigar when he came across the curious report of a skeleton found in a beaver pond. The discovery had been made many months before Callahan had been transferred from Montpelier to the more southern Springfield area. The skeleton had never been identified, nor had the killer. What fascinated Callahan was the sketched position of the body. The bones, locked in their beaver traps, lay in the position of a crucifixion. It would be hard, Callahan thought, to imagine that such a deathly pose was accidental.

He copied an inked map of the site and left police headquarters. In his car, he changed his gray suede shoes to high waterproof boots. Checking the coordinates on his map he saw that he could drive some miles west on Route 103 and then turn north on an old logging road, which would bring him within just a few miles of the beaver pond.

As he drove west on the highway he debated whether to ask Darby if she would like to accompany him. She had surprised him with a phone call last night. She told him that, due to lack of financing, the production of *The Dybbuk* had been temporarily postponed and that she had decided to return to Vermont. She had already contacted Andy Poole, and he had agreed to help her finish cleaning up the farmhouse. She wanted to surprise her parents when they returned from Europe. She liked surprises. Callahan assured her that he did, too, but he did not think it wise for her to stay in that house.

"Wilfred," she said, "I don't like people who run."

Although he had tried to dissuade her, she had remained adamant, and when he realized that his protests were to no avail he asked her to call him if she needed anything, anything at all.

"I'll do better than that," she said. "I'll come to dinner tomorrow. Andy and I should be done by then and I'm dying for a brioche."

"They're better for breakfast," he said.

"I know." Her voice was wicked.

Now, driving west in his search for the beaver pond under whose waters a man had died, Callahan realized that taking Darby to such a place would be foolish. It would only accentuate the ugliness she had already encountered and, because he was a scrupulously honest man, he admitted to himself that his motives were personal and not professional. He knew that the attraction he felt for her was reciprocated. She had demonstrated that with vivid sexuality in the hammock, but even then, even during the course of their fervent lovemaking, he had been aware of her sense of independence and he found it marvelously appealing.

And so when he drove by the farm road which led up the hill to the Moons' house he accelerated and passed by.

He found the abandoned logging road and drove north until, because of fallen trees, he could proceed no further. He left his car and walked into the woods. He was a man whose spirit was replenished by nature, a major factor in his decision to settle in the mostly unspoiled, verdant hills of Vermont, and even though his motive for this walk was catalyzed by crime, he allowed himself to luxuriate in the clean smell of pines and wildflowers and in the sound of flickering leaves. Moving leisurely through a forest whose leaf and moss bed was hardly touched gave him the same sense of peaceful isolation he had experienced as a young seminarian. But even as he dwelled on that he found himself fighting through bramble tangles and the tears in his skin were not unlike the rents in his soul when he had acknowledged his doubt and abjured the priesthood.

As he worked his way toward the bed of a stream which he felt certain was the source of the pond he sought, he thought again of Darby and how wonderfully giving she was. The thought made him short of breath and he paused, smiling inwardly at his own foolishness, yet not believing it was foolish at all. He sat on the stump of a broken fir and in the distance he heard the faintly comical hoo-hoo-hoo of a rambling bear. Or was it an owl? He looked up and let his gaze sweep across the higher branches of the surrounding trees. Callahan was surprised to see how deep he'd walked into the woods, how the trees were closely knitted into mysterious touching shapes, how their thick branches veiled the sunlight. It was cold and quiet. The absence of birds, of which he only now became conscious, startled him.

He rose from the tree stump and picked his way through the heavy foliage down to the streambed. The water was only inches deep, but that was enough to offer a home to minnows, which darted over the mud and gravel bottom. The low water made the streambed an easier passage than the woods, so Callahan followed it for some distance. When he rounded one of many curves in the stream he saw the beaver dam. From its disrepair it was obvious that the meticulous animals no longer dwelled there and he saw that the dam had eroded, split, drained, and that what had once been a fresh pond was now just mud, a dank breeding place for insects. He checked his map and verified that the sketched pond was similar to the site he beheld. All that was missing was the shadow of a crucifixion.

Slowly, he walked around the circumference of the small drained pond. He did not delude himself into assuming that he would discover some specific clue that would magically open the avenues of investigation, but the nature of the violence that had occurred here was so extraordinary that he hoped some resonance of the act might still quiver in the air. He was not a man who disbelieved in psychic perception.

As he ambled around the sides of the pond, Callahan saw that a number of nearby trees had been uprooted by storm and that others had been charred and split by lightning strikes. Only the trunks of many trees remained standing and most of these trees were barkless. Seeing this, Callahan knew that what he had heard earlier must have been an owl, for this dreary landscape of hollow trees was a natural habitat for those strange birds. He examined the ground over which he walked and kicked idly at objects in his way.

And then he paused. He crouched. In front of him was an old squirrel's nest. It was remarkably well preserved and must only recently been wind blown from one of the hollow trees. Callahan realized that after the squirrels had abandoned the fire-blackened tree, the nest had been usurped by a family of owls. He lifted it and marveled at the intricate weaving of twigs and bark, vines and feathers, all encased in a hard bowl of dried mud and as well preserved as if it were Etruscan pottery. He was about to throw it away when something caught his eye.

There was a black sheen within the mud. Slowly, Callahan picked the nest apart. It crumbled in his fingers. He separated little clumps of bark and browned moss and thumbed away bits of mouse fir. Finally, only one thing remained in the palm of his hand.

The feathers of a black bird.

Callahan stared at them. He told himself to be a reasonable man. He reminded himself of Jesuitical logic. He weighed the odds of probability and coincidence. He closed his eyes and pictured the lands that surrounded the swamp and the deep forest through which he'd traveled. He opened his eyes and his gaze slowly swept the area.

This was not a feeding ground for crows.

He felt very cold and the rank gasses from stagnant water filled his nostrils. He put the feathers into his pocket. He began the long walk back through the woods.

Jubal lay on his belly along the grassy bank and slowly lowered his hand into the stream Although the pain in his right hand had been alleviated by the previous night's honey cure, his left hand was still badly swollen and blistered and the skin was stretched so tight that he was unable to extend his fingers. He sucked in his breath when the icy water rushed over his burned flesh. Curled under the water, his fingers looked like dead nightcrawlers, the worms he dug from moist ground to use as bait. He wondered if trout would rise from their gravel bed and nibble at them. He didn't much care. He wasn't sure that he would ever again have use of that hand. No matter what the old man said.

He turned on his side and stared backwards toward the cave from where he heard the dissonant notes of the cow's horn. Riordan was playing an ancient Irish ballad. It was a militant melody. Jubal squinched his eyes shut to better concentrate on the sound. The music was familiar to the boy but he could not remember where or when he'd last heard it. He grunted and opened his eyes and stared into the stream water at his burned hand. He shivered as he thought of the cost of forgetfulness.

And then he remembered. Riordan had sounded that song before they entered the woods in pursuit of the sinner they'd crucified in his own beaver traps. The music had been a call to arms. It meant the old man was preparing for battle. Someone would die. What dismayed Jubal was that he knew who the victim was to be. It was the girl in the photograph he'd stolen; the girl with bright eyes who sat on her pony.

Earlier in the day, after daybreak, Riordan and Jubal had stolen down to the farm. Riordan carried Tuttle's gleaming white skull. Glued between its teeth was the pearl he'd found in the dump. The old man had intended to toss the skull through a window of the farmhouse, but when he and the boy had arrived, they'd discovered the girl and boy hard at work. The hunter who had killed the wood thrush had been nowhere in sight.

The old man and the boy had retreated and returned to the cave. Riordan's eyes burned fiercely. He genuflected among the brambles and tore at his beard and howled at the mountains and not until he'd flagellated himself with the whip of thorns did he quiet. And even then there was a terrible light in his eyes when he spoke in an awful whisper, his breath as hot as a cat's, and he called out:

O Lord, thou knowest; remember me, visit me, and revenge me of my persecutors!

"Jeremiah, chapter fifteen!" Jubal had blurted, praying that he would win favor. But the old man gave no sign that he was impressed. Instead, he ordered Jubal to bring two shovels to the stream. The boy did so.

"I want his bones," Riordan said. Together, the boy wincing from the agony in his fingers, they dug into the soft clay of the streambank. As they uncovered the severed parts of Tuttle's body the old man talked ceaselessly about the penalties for obstructing the Inquisition. At first, Jubal thought the old man was preparing something special for the hunter.

"S'posin' he got fear in his belly and run to ground?" he asked. "S'posin' he's in the woods now, right now, his eyes on us, lookin', knowin'?" Jubal almost enjoyed frightening himself.

"Then we shall select from his conspirators," Riordan said, and he pulled Tuttle's thigh from the streambank clay.

It was then that Jubal had understood who was to be the victim.

When all the random pieces of Tuttle's body had been collected, the old man severed them into smaller parts. He ordered Jubal to prepare a burning pit. Fearful of complaining about his hands, Jubal dug a large hole and layered it with stones and brush — the pit where they'd steamed the skull was not large enough to hold all of Tuttle's remains. When it was done, the old man appraised it. He dug tunnels all around it, their paths radiating from beneath the pit in all directions, and at the far end of the tunnels he dug deeper holes. He set the brush on fire and fed more branches into the pit. When the wood and vegetation had burned low and hot on the layered stones, he tossed all the pieces of Tuttle's body into the pit and covered them.

Riordan and the boy returned to the cave. The old man, Brother Death on his shoulder, candlelight throwing his and the bird's shadows on the wall, opened his Bible and began to read from the Book of Revelations, his eyes burning fiercely. Gradually those eyes closed and his head sunk onto his chest, but even in his sleep his lips continued to move.

Jubal pulled a bearskin from one of the stone shelves and left the cave. He wrapped himself in the skin and lay down along the stream and watched the fire. But not until he saw the melt of human flesh, a hot and waxey river running into all the tunnels beneath the pit, did he fall into a restless sleep. He dreamed he cut off the old man's hands and burned them in the pit and fed the charred remains to the black crow.

When the morning sun was high, he awakened to a familiar grating sound. He turned toward the burning pit. It was uncovered and empty. Riordan sat on the ground. In front of him was a huge stone mortar; a stone pestle was in his hand. He was grinding Tuttle's bones into a fine powder. Turning a little on the ground, throwing off the bearskin, Jubal saw that Riordan had already mixed some of the powder into his raw clay.

He watched now as the old man's fingers delicately molded the clay into exquisite shapes of bowls and bottles, wind chimes and woven trivets, his long fingers kneading, pinching, smoothing. Jubal was truly bewildered. How could his father take such care with his creations and yet be immune to the pain he'd caused his son?

As each design grew more beautiful, Jubal's resentment grew. He rose from the ground, stripped off his clothes, and plunged into the stream. The chilling water refreshed him. He dressed and picked a handful of berries and, turning his back on his father, he munched their sweetness. He heard footsteps and then felt the old man's hand on his neck. He turned.

"You'll want some rest before this evening," Riordan said. But the touch of his father's hand only angered the boy more.

"I seen me some bear spoor over to the ridge," Jubal said, wanting terribly not to be with Riordan. "Mr. Bear, he's just waitin' on me."

The old man studied his son for a moment and then nodded. He walked into the cave. Jubal followed and, in the cave, he took a handmade crossbow and two arrows from the wall. Quickly, before his father could change his mind, he left.

He didn't hunt the bear. He had seen no spoor. He moved through the woods until he was a distance away from the cave and then sat quietly among the trees. He spent the hours desperately trying to flex his fingers, fearful that never again would he play his harp. When, at last, he found response in the fingers of his right hand, he almost sang for joy. Just before dusk he returned to the campsite. Riordan's pottery was displayed on the ground but the old man was in the cave. Jubal lay by the stream and bathed his hands. It was then that he heard Riordan's horn.

Riordan crawled out of the tunnel entrance and struggled through the hawthorn bush. He carried a burlap bag. And Jubal's harp. He placed a few pieces of the pottery in the bag then slung it over his shoulder. He gave Jubal the harp, nodded to the boy and then started through the woods in the direction of the farmhouse.

"Hallelujah," Riordan said.

Dreading what was to happen, the boy walked behind his father.

It was dusk when Andy Poole and Darby completed their chores. They had worked mostly in a companionable silence, each content to wash and scrub and polish until, room by room, the farmhouse was restored to its pristine condition. The farmboy was impressed with the vigor with which the city girl attacked her work and that she did not seem to care how sweaty or grimy she became, nor that she split her nails and stained her jeans. One wall of the living room had been stained too severely to wash clean so, together, they had applied a new coat of paint to it. Halfway through the afternoon, Darby had driven down the hill to Down Derry's village store and returned with a six-pack of beer and two enormous hero sandwiches. Andy approved of the way she drank beer straight from the can but he was too shy to comment. They finished the last strip of wall and both stepped back to admire their handiwork.

"Ayuh," Andy said, "she looks good."

"Ayuh," Darby said, smiling, "she does. Let's finish the beer."

She popped open two cans, gave one to Andy, stretched to relieve her muscles, and suggested that they sit outside and enjoy the afternoon's fading light.

Side by side, they sat on the wide, flat rock that served as a door stoop and sipped their beers. Pink streaks in the west gave balance to a sky already disked by a pale, rising full moon. A pleasing fragrance of rotting fruit drifted from the apple orchard and the occasional chirp of a cricket accentuated the pre-evening silence.

"You must love living here, Andy," Darby said quietly.

"Ain't never been anywhere else," he said.

"New York or Boston?"

"Don't see no need," he answered. "I don't hold with noise."

"Don't you ever miss the excitement?"

"I go bowling over to Bellows Falls. And there's the deer time. Last winter I got me a six-point buck. Had to reach out some, too. That ole boy was two, maybe two-thirty yards, and me with a Winchester seventy didn't have no scope. I got good eyes. Don't mean to brag none. You ever hunt?"

"No."

"You agin it?"

"No. I just don't think I could kill anything."

"They gonna die anyway, one thing or 'tother."

"I know." Darby took another sip of beer. "You ever get close enough to see their eyes?"

Andy drained his beer and then crushed the can between the palms of his hands. He bent the flattened aluminum in two, pressing the sides together as tightly as he could.

"I don't look at 'em," he said.

"Oh," Darby said. She sipped her beer. "There's another one in the fridge."

"Grateful," Andy said, "but I'd best be gettin' home." He made no move to go. "Come a bad winter," he said, "deer, they like to starve in the woods. They gonna die one way or 'tother."

"Yes," Darby said gently and she touched him lightly on one knee. "I know."

He nodded. "It's a natural thing to do, is what it is. Huntin' an' things. It's what a man does. What he's got to do."

Darby said nothing.

"It's part of a man. It's in him." Andy's work boot tapped restlessly on the ground and he turned his head from side to side, scratching his neck against his collar. He looked up into the sky. "A twenny gauge, now, I'd take him right outta the sky."

Darby glanced up to follow his gaze. A bird circled high in the sky, its flight a series of floating circles, the centers of which remained so perpendicularly similar that a pole could have been dropped through the imaginary rings without ever touching a side.

"A hawk?" Darby said.

"Nope," Andy said, "just a crow. A big, black crow. Ain't nuthin' special. Just a big, black crow." He squinted into the fading light. "Pow! Pow!" he said. "He'd drop for sure. Dumb ol' bird, he got hisself sumthin' he likes an' that's for dang sure. See, there, how he moves up an' down but don't go nowhere? Yes, sir, he got sumthin' below tickles him."

Darby and Andy watched the bird flying slowly round and round. Andy rose from the stone stoop. "Well, it's past time. You was to like, you could have supper with my granddad an' me."

"Thank you, Andy," Darby said, "but I have to meet Sergeant Callahan."

"Wilfred," Andy said, "he's a nice feller." He stared down at the ground and frowned. "Might be, come this winter, I'll take Wilfred huntin' with me." He looked up sharply to judge Darby's reaction but she just smiled. "Well," Andy said, "we'll see ya." He flipped his hand at Darby and started toward the road home. Just before he passed out of sight, he leaned down and picked up a large stone. He hurled it at the high-circling crow. He turned quickly and grinned at Darby and then went on his way.

Darby sighed. She was tired. She would have liked to soak in a hot tub but even as she contemplated that she knew that she was more interested in seeing Wilfred. She wondered if he had learned any more about

Tuttle and about the strange violation of the farmhouse. And then, of course, there was Wilfred himself. He was a provocative man who, in the most gentle of ways, seemed able to elicit secrets from those who had remained silent too long. Wistfully, Darby thought how fine it would have been if, when she was a young girl, she'd been able to converse in a similar fashion with her father. She was grateful for what had happened at Mouse's synagogue. She had seen a receptivity and excitement in her father that had previously been alien. She suspected that the long years of his passive dismissal of Judaic matters were coming to an end and she hoped that he would be as enriched as she. Even now, she did not pretend to herself that she fully comprehended her own feelings about being a Jew; she knew only that the recognition of it gave her an inner focus not unlike the core of Catholicism which still centered Wilfred. She smiled to herself. She wished she had some gift to give Wilfred, some small thing, some object that would amuse him or please his eye.

"Well," she said aloud, "you don't."

She drained the last of her beer, rose, and turned toward the door. Behind her, faintly, she thought she heard music. It startled her. It resembled the thin, high keys on the last right-hand octave of a piano. It sounded like . . . like what? She knew even before she asked herself the question. She remembered.

It was an evening long, long ago. She was a little girl and she'd been allowed to take the train from Westport to New York all by herself so that she could meet her father and mother at Emilio's and join them for a night at the theater. Filled with the sense of adulthood and daring, she'd walked up Lexington Avenue in the twilight — the evening the same color as now — and turned into the deli. Em, busy at the counter, had pointed to the back room. She'd been delighted by the beaded curtain that separated the rooms and had been very careful to part the strands. Peeking through them, she saw her father. She heard her father. Sitting at the piano, in profile to her, her father was bent low over the instrument, his left hand dangling free, his right hand quietly toying with the keys. He looked like a stranger; a man who lived in a place she'd never been. She felt that if she spoke he might never forgive her. And she felt that he would be right.

She retreated slowly from the curtain and asked Emilio if she could help him until her mother came. She wanted to cry. She didn't understand why.

Again, she thought she heard the music. She paused on the threshold of the farmhouse door and turned but saw nothing. She started into the house. The music resumed. It was lovely. It was the music of a harp and its song was so melancholy that it was as if the strings were plucked by wounded fingers. The light was falling fast now, the sky losing its striated radiance and dimming into such a dull gray that the horizon was lost and the world seemed flat. Darby peered toward the road and then lifted her gaze to the woods beyond. The music was louder.

A boy playing a lyre emerged from the woods. He played awkwardly, favoring the fingers of one hand. A man walked behind the boy. He moved slowly, each foot so carefully planted one before the other it was as if he were afraid of shaking the earth under him. He looked, Darby thought, like an Old Testament prophet. She was enchanted with their presence and stepped down from the stone stoop and started forward slowly so that she could see them better. They crossed the road and entered the farmyard and continued to move in her direction.

"Good even —" Darby started.

"Shhhh," the old man said. He held up a massive hand to silence her. The gesture was made with tenderness as if he wished to save the harp's music for her, present it to her, make her a gift. Darby dared not move for fear that she would break the spell. She stood very still as the boy finished his song but when the last notes had trembled into silence she could refrain no longer.

"Oh, how beautiful," she cried. Impulsively, she reached out and cupped the boy's face in her two hands. "Thank you," she said. "Thank you very much!"

Jubal trembled. A hot flush burned his face and neck. Never, not once, not a single time, had he been touched by a woman. He could scarcely believe the lightness of her fingers, the softness. He felt as if he'd been brushed by a baby chick or an aspen leaf maybe, a leaf newborn in spring, still green and dewy. He wished she would cup his face forever and on the final day of whatever forever was, maybe she'd touch his wounded hand, because if she did he knew without a trace of doubt that his flesh would lose its burning. Speechless, he stared at her, and when she smiled at him he felt there would be no more winters in his life.

The old man unslung from one shoulder a small burlap bag. He placed it on the ground at Darby's feet and untied the neck. He removed a few objects neatly wrapped in pieces of soft cloth.

"Do you like pretty things, then?" he asked Darby.

She laughed. "You make me sound like a child."

"We are all children," he said. "Children in the eyes of God." His massive hands worked with the delicacy of an artist's as he pulled an object free of its cloth. He held his hand high and let the object dangle from it. A slight breeze shook it and Darby heard the thinnest of silvery tinkles. It was a wind chime, its numerous blades made of the most beautiful pottery chips she'd ever seen. The blades were tied together with gossamer wire and they overlapped each other in a descending cascade. Each blade was glazed, some in a cobalt blue, some in the green of the sea, others in hues so pale it was as if the potter had lost the colors in a dream. The wind stirred the overlapping blades once more and the chimes sounded like distant temple bells.

Darby was incredulous. "Did you make this? Did you make this yourself?"

"Aye," said Riordan, "and me boyo. He's got the gift of hands, don't you see?"

Jubal said nothing. He was perplexed at Riordan's lie. Why would the old man say that he, Jubal, had helped create such a thing? He felt certain that the old man had a reason but he dared not inquire now. Nor would he ever. There were things best left unsaid. What confused him even more than the lie itself was his feeling of resentment. He did not wish this girl with the magical hands to be told untruths.

"Where do you come from?" Darby asked, still unable to remove her gaze from the wind chime.

"Here and there," Riordan said. "Where every man comes from. Here and there."

Darby watched as he pulled two more things from the burlap bag and unwrapped them. There was a single vase and a single bowl. Each was as originally designed and as beautiful as the wind chime. Darby suddenly knew what gift to bring to Wilfred Callahan.

"Do you sell these?" she asked. "Would you sell one of these to me?"

"Ah, well, now," the old man said. He scratched his white beard. "I would if I could but I can't. 'Twould be unfair to the boy, and that's the truth of it."

"Oh," Darby said. "I'm sorry. I thought maybe that's what you did. You know, go around the countryside and . . . and . . ."

"Peddle?" asked Riordan. "You have in mind that we're peddlers?"

"There's nothing wrong with that." Darby was distressed at offending such quixotic strangers. She blushed furiously.

"Look there, Jubal!" the old man said and pointed at Darby. "She's got a garden in her face!" He laughed and did a little dance on the ground and his great coat flapped around him. Darby saw that the interior of the coat was lined with pockets and that something was written on each one of them but he swirled so swiftly that she was unable to read the words. "It's what we are indeed, indeedy," Riordan chortled. "Peddlers. Potters if you want the right of it. We take clay from the earth and mix it with this and that, and whishhht! — here's a pretty in your hand. These, though," he pointed at the wind chime and the vase and the bowl which rested on the ground, "these are for the showing. These are the boy's pride." His eyes sparkled as he looked at Darby. "There's others though. There's others."

"You mean you have others that you'll sell?" Darby asked eagerly.

"Oh, aye," the old man nodded vigorously. "There's many others."

"Do you have them?" Darby pressed.

"We do."

"With you?"

"Not with us."

"Where?"

"In the kiln."

"In the kiln?" Darby asked. "Is your kiln near?"

"How far is near?" the old man asked.

"I mean," Darby said slowly, "could we go there? Would it take long?"

The old man turned to Jubal. "Would it take long, darlin'?" He asked innocently. For the first time since he'd come upon her, Jubal averted his gaze from Darby. He stared at the ground. He wished he didn't have to answer. He knew he did.

"No," he mumbled.

"Oh, please," Darby said. "We can take my truck."

"There's not a proper road," Riordan said. "Would you walk, now? It's a wee walk, that's the thing of it."

"That's okay," Darby said. "Honest." She looked at the sky growing grayer. "It won't take too long, will it?"

"How long is too long?"

"I mean, I have things to do."

"Oh, darlin'," the old man said softly, "we all have things to do."

When Darby followed the old man and the boy out of the farmyard and into the woods, the day was darkening so quickly that had she glanced up she would not have been able to distinguish the crow's wings as he tracked them in the sky.

She did not glance up. She was too excited about the beauty toward which she walked.

34

After arriving at Heathrow in the late morning, Solomon went immediately to an airport pub and ordered a double Johnny Walker Black. He sipped it slowly, allowing the smoky whiskey to trickle down his throat as if he were feeding fire to the wonderful beast that lodged in his belly while he debated his next course of action. He came to certain conclusions. He would call Darby to reaffirm that she had not been foolish enough to go alone to the house in Vermont; and he would call Callahan to tell him that the burning of the green cross, the tongues on the door, the dunging, and the warning of Augustine had not been acts general in nature. They were deeds of a terrorist who hated Jews, and if Callahan could not find those who were responsible for the infamy he, Solomon, would. Solomon would not explain to Callahan that the anticipation of confronting those who tormented him, thrilled him.

He was, therefore, secretly excited when, after calling the Vermont State Police, he was told that Callahan was not in. I have done what I should, Solomon thought, and now I am free to proceed on my own. He decided to leave no message.

His call to Darby was unanswered. He thought Rena might know where she was and the thought pleased him. He had something to say to Rena Nussbaum. He asked the operator to get her number. After only a few minutes, he heard a muffled voice on the other end of the wire. The connection was not good. It sounded as if wind were blowing through a tunnel and when Solomon spoke he could hear the echo of his voice.

"Hello?" he said.

"Jesus Christ!" Rena's voice was filled with fog. "You know what time it is? Who is this?"

"Solomon. Solomon Moon."

"God," she said, then had to stop speaking while she coughed. Finally, her voice was clear. "What do you want? Where the hell are you? Afghanistan?"

"It's a lousy connection." He heard his voice swallowed in its own echo.

"We're what?" she asked. "We're a lousy connection? You called all the way from Afghanistan to tell me we don't connect? Jesus, Solomon, you made that clear. Don't waste money."

"I'm sorry to wake you up," Solomon said. He had forgotten how early it was in New York and it caused him to worry about Darby. "Do you know where Darby is?"

"You mean now, at this hour? If she's got any sense she's asleep."

"I called but no one answered."

"She's a very sensible girl, Solomon. She usually turns her phone off at night. Too many obscene phone call these days, you know?"

"Oh, right, right." Solomon was relieved. "If you talk to her, tell her that I'm coming home and tell her that . . . that I miss her . . . that I love her. I love her very much."

"That's nice, Solomon," Rena said softly. "You guys are getting together, huh?"

"We are together," Solomon said gruffly, emotion thickening his voice. He cleared his throat. "Listen, you still need financing for *The Dybbuk*?"

"I don't know. I'm trying to sell a Giacometti. It ain't easy, pal. Times are tough."

"Don't sell the Giacometti. You earned it."

She laughed harshly. "Boy, you really zing it to a guy."

"No, I don't mean it that way. I mean, you did what you had to do. I don't think there's any right or wrong to it. It just is, that's all."

"Don't be nice. It makes me horny." And then quickly she added, "I'm just kidding. What happened was dumb. I'm sorry about that. I really am. Hey, listen, where are you, really?"

"London. What about *The Dybbuk*?"

"Sure. Damn right. I could use the gelt. Why? You got somebody hot over there?"

"Yeah."

"Who?"

"Me."

"You're kidding!"

"No."

"You mean your company."

"Yes. I'm going to insist they coproduce it with you. I'm going to insist on a lot of things." Charged with new energy, Solomon had little doubt of coming victories. For a long time there was just the echoing wind in the telephone connection and then Rena spoke.

"Solomon, I want you to know something," she said quietly. "If you're doing this because you feel sorry for me, don't. Just don't. I couldn't stand that."

"I wouldn't do that, Rena. I promise you."

"Then why?"

"Because it's a helluva play. If I remember correctly, a man gets rid of his ghost and that interests me. I'd like to be part of that. Okay?"

"Okay. And, Solomon, what happened before, you don't have to worry. It won't happen again."

"I know. I'll call you when I get back."

"Gotcha."

Solomon made one more call. It was to Bagshot; Kendal's father, Colonel Oliver Darby, answered.

"Darby here."

"Hello, Oliver. It's Solomon."

"Well, bless my puddin'! Where are you?"

"I'm at Heathrow."

"Bloody good. Do you want to be picked up?"

"No, no, I'll take a taxi. I can be there in less than an hour. I just didn't want to surprise Kendal. She is there, isn't she?"

"She's in the village at the moment but she'll be back shortly. *Merde!*"

"What's the matter? She's all right, isn't she?"

"Yes, yes, one could say that. I mean to say, she's in good health and all that sort of thing."

"Has she said anything about. . . ."

"You? Oh, yes. Oh, my, yes. She's said a good deal about you."

"Oliver?" Solomon paused. "You don't mind if I do come out?"

"I shall cut off your head and post it on the gate if you don't. That is, if I had a gate. Which I don't. Why is that, do you suppose? I mean to say, the chap next door has a gate, why shouldn't I? Bloody fellow keeps it locked all the time. I think he's frightened that one day the peasants will advance with their petitions. Lot of riffraff around these days, don't you know, Solomon. Everybody's on the fiddle. Sod them, is what I say. Now get your arse out here. I've got some super single-malt scotch that I've been . . . blast!''

"What is it?"

"I've dropped the ice."

Solomon checked his watch. "You into it already?"

"No, not what you think. I've bloody torn up my knee and the sodding doctor has me in a wheelchair with my knee packed in ice. Now listen to me, you bloody rascal, Kendal and I are due later on at Sandhurst Chapel. Do you remember Kendal's friend, Penelope White?''

"Yes." Solomon had met Penelope many times during the early days of his and Kendal's marriage. Whenever they'd gone to London, Penelope had spent a great deal of time with Kendal. They had been close friends at Upper Chine and, mostly through correspondence, had maintained their friendship. She was a tall woman with lanky hair, flat-chested and heavy-thighed, with the red blotched skin of one who suffers from weather.

"She's Brown now," Oliver said.

"I beg your pardon?"

"It's all right, she didn't diddle the natives."

"I didn't think she'd ever diddled," Solomon said.

"She married this chap, Brown, and he has a son who's a captain at Sandhurst. He and his wife have just popped one from the oven and the thing's going to be baptized at the Memorial Chapel. Kendal and I are invited. So you see, there's your baggage."

Solomon laughed. There was little question of why Kendal had fallen into the habit of non sequiturs.

"Do you mean," Solomon asked, "that you want me to meet you at Sandhurst after I drop my bags at your house?"

"Yes, of course. I thought I'd made that quite clear."

Solomon hesitated. "I don't want to intrude on . . ."

"On your wife?" Oliver asked. "What a bloody fool you can be. No worse than she, I daresay. You're both bloody fools. Time you pulled up your socks and got on with it."

Solomon smiled. "Sounds so simple."

"Solomon, do you remember the tree Kendal wouldn't let us cut down?''

"Yes."

"She cut it down."

"I don't understand."

"Think about it. Now get your bloody taxi, there's a good chap."

As the taxi drove through the countryside, Solomon puzzled over the colonel's words. Many years ago when Kendal had been playing on the West End, she and Solomon had spent almost every weekend in Bagshot with Oliver. He lived in a small, unpretentious house just outside the village. Although he enjoyed gardening, he had an absolute loathing for the numerous weed trees which he insisted blocked his view to the heath and cast his garden into cold shadow. On one autumn afternoon, Solomon trained down from London. Kendal was to follow after her evening performance. When Solomon arrived, Oliver handed him a portable gas chain saw. Oliver had another one. The colonel announced that, together, they would cut every bloody sodding tree to the ground. They worked all afternoon and into the evening and by nightfall only one tree remained. They decided to take that down in the morning. But when Kendal arrived she was appalled. You are, she stated simply, murderers. There was no appeasing her and she stormed to bed. The single tree had remained ever since.

Why now had she cut it down? What implication did it have?

When they reached Oliver's house Solomon was not surprised to find the front door open. The colonel was not a man who anticipated intruders. Solomon wondered if Kendal had told her father what had happened in Vermont. He shoved his bags inside the door, then walked around to the back of the house. In the garden, flowers had been cut back, bushes neatly trimmed.

A tall holly hedge bordered the entire lawn. It surprised Solomon, for he remembered the reason for cutting the trees had been to retain a view of the heath. The view now was blocked by the hedge. In one corner of the lawn was the stump of the single tree that had remained. Solomon stood on it and looked toward the heath. He saw only the roofs of new houses. So that was why the holly hedge was planted, to hide the ugliness of the surroundings.

Oh, Oliver, Solomon thought, you cannot fence out those who wish to violate you.

Solomon returned to the taxi and drove to Sandhurst. From somewhere behind the buildings of the Royal Military Academy he could hear the sound of marching men responding to the crisp orders of a drill instructor. It reminded him of his days at Fort Riley, the hours when he had engaged in moonlight combat with Emilio and the Mouse. He drew in a deep breath so that he could give air to *the thing* within him, nurture it; for once again he felt like a fighting man.

Because it was a warm day, the door to the chapel was slightly open and Solomon could see a passage of sunlight on the floor. He moved closer, careful not to disturb the ritual indoors. He heard the padre's baptismal blessing and then the soft rumble of Oliver's voice.

"He's going to drown the little bugger!"

The group inside laughed and then was quiet. As they joined in the Lord's Prayer, Solomon stepped closer to the door and looked in.

It was a small gathering around a silver font. He recognized Penelope and assumed the man in uniform next to her was her husband. There were two other couples, one younger than the other. The older woman, who Solomon guessed was the godmother, held an infant in her arms. The younger woman gazed so tenderly on the infant that Solomon thought she must be the mother. Kendal stood next to Oliver in his wheelchair. As they all recited the prayer, their eyes were closed and their backs were to Solomon.

Solomon's gaze slowly swept the chapel. He had been here once before, the same year he and Oliver had cut down the trees. Oliver had arranged that they all attend Christmas service. Although Solomon had no real desire to do so he had not wanted to offend either Oliver or Kendal. But he had not been prepared for his reaction. When he stepped inside the chapel he'd been struck by what he'd considered the militaristic nature of the place. Built into the stone pillars were panels donated by individual regiments of the British Army. Regimental badges in full color decorated the top of each panel and below them were inscribed the names of the officers of the regiment who had been killed in wars. The ends of the pews were carved with more heraldic badges representing regiments or corps. Everywhere Solomon looked hung tattered banners and regimental flags and the walls of the chapel were filled with more plaques listing the names of officers and men who had died for their country. Above the altar was a large cross shaped like a Crusader's sword, and imposed on a cross of bronze and steel. Even the stained-glass windows, representing the interpretation of the Book of Revelation, were designated by their bestowers: the Rifle Brigade, the Brigade of Guards, the Fifth Fusiliers, the Hampshire Regiment. Solomon had been particularly surprised at the coloring of each regimental plaque. They were of white marble framed in bronze. The regimental crests were carved in gold. All this seemed natural enough, but the names of those who'd fallen were treated hardly in a somber fashion. They were in green with initial letters in red. If there was symbolism to this scheme, Solomon had missed it. Later, Oliver had explained that the architect who had designed the color patterns had felt that those young men who had chosen a military career and, attending Sandhurst, would become most familiar with the chapel, should worship the Lord in an ambience of life's spirit so that they would understand that all who had met a fair and honorable death still lived.

During the Christmas service Kendal had kneeled as naturally as a nun, and her voice had lifted triumphantly in hymn. Rejoicing in the Lord in the sight of tattered flags and surrounded by the names of the dead had irritated Solomon, then angered him. He had felt a total outsider and so remained sitting; did not kneel, or sing. What bothered him most was that Kendal, her eyes bright with childhood remembered, took no notice. He had not understood his anger but felt that in some strange way he had reason to be upset. He could not explain, nor had he tried.

Now, many years later, standing silently outside the open door of the chapel, staring at the sword above the altar, he realized what had made him so unquiet. As a Jew he had felt that his enemies were those whose ancestors had marched in the Crusades and that the killing in the name of the Lord had been obscene. Now, with the new allegiance to his past, Solomon stared hard at the sword, and, his rage swelling, he felt the clawing of *the thing* within. And when his gaze returned to Kendal he heard the echo of Rubio Alcalde's words. *Yo soy Yo y mi circunstancias. I am I and my surroundings.*

The professor's words and Rafael Fernandez Muñoz's shocking letter had seared Solomon's soul as surely as if a hot iron had flamed his flesh. He wanted terribly to put self-betrayal behind him. That he had denied his past and, on a simpler level, a more mundane level, had sought to accommodate the world around him, had been his own failures. He was eager to redress them.

The Lord's Prayer concluded, the baptismal party listened to the padre's thanksgiving and then the service was over. Voices rang with gaiety and celebration, and the members of the party moved together. Kendal spun Oliver's wheelchair around. She saw Solomon.

"Darling!" she cried. It was a spontaneous reaction and Solomon's heart leaped. He knew he could not bear to lose her.

Solomon started forward, but before he reached his wife, Penelope enthused her greetings and introduced him to the others. Their welcomes precluded Solomon and Kendal from anything but a perfunctory kiss and it took some moments before Oliver and Kendal and Solomon could extricate themselves. Oliver surreptitiously groaned about his knee and the baptismal party quickly sympathized. With much patting of the baby, hugs all around, promises to call soon, Oliver and the Moons took their leave.

The wheelchair was folded and placed in the back of Oliver's station wagon, and as Solomon helped him into the front passenger seat he saw that the colonel had had no need to feign his pain. Solomon sat in the rear seat and let Kendal drive them home. On the way, Oliver seemed unnaturally garrulous, regaling them with a story of early Sandhurst when cadets, rebelling against strict discipline, had defied the commandant and his troops, pelting them with loaves of bread. Silently, Solomon wondered how many names of those spirited young men were listed on the plaques in the chapel, but he said nothing for he understood that Oliver was trying to alleviate the tension between his daughter and Solomon.

When they arrived at the house in Bagshot, Oliver announced that he was going to get a little kip and that they should feel free to do as they pleased. He suggested they wake him for a cold chicken, previously prepared, and a bottle of chilled Chablis. He retired to his room.

Alone, Kendal and Solomon stood across the living room from each other, each wary as they watched the other.

"You look tired," Kendal said.

"I've covered a lot of ground."

"Was it a lousy flight?"

"I don't mean the flight. I mean I've covered a lot of ground."

Kendal wasn't sure what he meant and was even less sure she wanted to know. "Would you like a drink?"

"Yes, please."

"Shall we have it in the garden?"

"That would be nice."

Solomon opened the French doors and stepped into the back garden as Kendal went to the bar. He stood there staring at the tree stump. She joined him and gave him a whiskey. She held no glass of her own.

"Not for you?" Solomon asked.

"No. Not yet."

"Penelope looks well."

"Yes."

"Oliver doesn't."

"He tore a ligament in his knee. He doesn't like to complain but it was really rather nasty. Be another week, ten days, before he's out of that bloody sodding chair, as he puts it." She shifted her weight from one foot to another. "Would you like to sit down?" She looked around. "I'll get some chairs."

"Grass is all right. If it won't stain your dress. It's very pretty."

"Thank you."

"You're welcome." He pointed to the tree stump. "That's a good seat."

"Yes." Kendal sat on the stump. She crossed her legs and carefully arranged her skirt. "Well."

"Well." Solomon took a sip of whiskey. "Good. Damn good."

"Single malt."

"Yes."

Each stared at the ground. They looked at each other. They looked away. Solomon cleared his throat. In a reflex action, Kendal did the same.

"This is ridiculous," Solomon said.

"I know."

"I mean, we haven't just met, have we?"

"No."

"We've known each other a long time."

"A very long time."

"Do you want to know something funny?"

"Yes. I could use it."

"I'm afraid if I start," Solomon said, "if I start to tell you everything that I'm thinking, everything that I want to tell you, I'll never be able to stop. I mean, I'll just go on talking until the world ends."

A small smile crossed Kendal's lips. "I'm in no rush. I'm not going anywhere. Are you?"

"No." He sat down on the grass only a foot from the stump. Gently, he placed a hand around Kendal's ankle. He felt her quiver. "Why did you cut down the tree?"

Kendal's hand moved to the back of his neck. She let it rest there. "It's complicated, I think."

"Well," Solomon said, "we've already said we're not going anywhere."

Kendal's hand moved from his neck to his cheek. Her fingers felt very cool and he leaned back so that his head rested against her knees. And she continued. "When I was a little girl, Dad used to take me to the circus. I loved the clowns. I liked to watch them jump through a hoop.

Sometimes on one leg, sometimes a somersault, even backwards. And there was this big fellow who dressed like a lion tamer and he'd flick his whip at the other clowns, just tickling them, and one by one they'd jump through the hoop for him.

"But each year that I went back to the circus, each year as I got older, it got less funny, because I could see that under the paint, under the red noses, were men, just ordinary men. Men like Dad or Mouse or Em. Or you. And I stopped laughing. I didn't like to see men jumping through a hoop. It was a rotten act.

"The last time I went, I kept watching this one clown going through the hoop. He was faster than all the others. I mean, he sprang through and then raced back in line ahead of all the other clowns so that he could go through twice as many times as the others. He just loved jumping through that bloody hoop. When the performance was over, I asked Dad if we could go back and meet the clown and, of course, he took me. The clown was scrubbing off all his face paint and I could see that he was just a little old man. I asked him why he liked to jump through that hoop. He looked at me as if I were dumb, as if there were something wrong with me, and he said, 'Why do I like to jump through the hoop? I like to jump through the hoop because that way every day I know where I'm going.'

"I thought it was the most terrible thing I'd ever heard and I started to cry. I cried all the way home. Poor Dad. He kept asking me what was wrong, and when I finally told him I don't think he really understood."

"What did you tell him?" Solomon asked quietly.

"I told him that I thought if someone always knows where he's going, then maybe he's already there. There's nothing left to find." Kendal leaned over and rested her chin on Solomon's head and cupped his face in her hands. "I think a man who lived that way would be unhappy. Terribly, terribly unhappy."

"You were a wise little girl."

"Only I forgot. As I grew up, I forgot." She slid off the stump and sat on the grass in front of Solomon. "And I'm sorry about that. I am most awfully, awfully sorry about that."

Solomon placed his whiskey tumbler in the grass and held both of her hands. "Listen to me, darling. If I've jumped through hoops, if I've done things I haven't wanted to, it was because I chose to do them. For the wrong reasons, God knows; but I did the choosing. I've been so damn busy not offending anybody, trying to please people, that I lost track. I lost track of . . ." The words of the letter jumped at him. "I lost track of the first assassin. I lost track of me."

Kendal kneeled now and words rushed from her. "I wanted to cut the tree down because I stopped you before. I don't want to stop you, Solomon, from doing anything, anything at all. Be whatever you want to be. Be whoever you are. Be a rinky-dink piano player if you want. Only let's do it together. Oh, God, darling, we were an awfully good act!"

"Are," Solomon said. "We *are* an awfully good act!"

He pulled her to him and they held each other tightly and then slowly separated and leaned back against the stump, holding hands. After a moment, Solomon spoke.

"Do you remember when we were kids and lived in the Village and every night we read to each other?"

"Yes. God, we read everything then, didn't we? We were always so excited. Why does that go away? How do we all let that happen?"

"I think we stop taking risks, stop believing in possibilities. You know, reaching for divine discontent."

"Divine discontent?"

"What Jung talked about. He felt that all of us reach a stage in our lives when we face a basic conflict. I mean, everything in our lives — all the forces we listen to, our fathers, our schools, everything tells us that if we want to feel secure, I mean emotionally secure, we have to operate in a disciplined fashion. The paradox, of course, is that this same damned self-discipline can backfire. It can make us lose any sense of freedom, any feeling of adventure, and when we lose our sense of daring, our risk-taking, we've really lost something of ourselves, haven't we?"

"Maybe it's the part that makes us human," Kendal said. "But it's not a conflict that ends, is it? You can't just turn it off."

"No, you can't turn it off. The trick is to find a way of living with it, of not letting it defeat you."

"That's a neat trick. How do you do it?"

"I think," Solomon said slowly, his voice hard, steely, "you stop weighing the odds. You take risks. You take any goddamn risk that comes your way."

As Kendal watched, Solomon's fingers dug into the lawn, ripped grass from it, tore loose a chunk of sod, then plunged deeper, his hand closing around the moist earth below, clenching it into a ball, grinding it. It frightened her.

"Solomon," she asked softly, "what happened in Spain?"

"I found out that Darby was right. I found out that I'm a Jew." He looked at Kendal and his eyes gleamed. "And I like it. Oh, I like it! It tells me what to do!" Angrily, he hurled a clump of sod into the holly hedge, and when his fingers returned to the grass they were trembling terribly.

Kendal had the awful feeling that Solomon's whole body was a bomb ready to explode. What dreadful thing had he learned?

"Darling," she said gently, carefully, wanting terribly to touch him, not daring to; needing to make him understand. "I love you. I need you. I'm not whole without you. Only half of me's there. I want us to be together now, tomorrow, always."

"We are together."

"No. Almost, but no. Whatever's made you angry, this terribly angry, doesn't let me in, doesn't give us a chance. You've got to get rid of it, Solomon, you've got to do something. Please, darling, for our sake!"

"Oh, I'm going to do something," Solomon said, his voice terror-striking. "Yes. Yes. I'm going to do something all right. Oh, yes!"

He had spoken not to her but to the sky as if, Kendal thought, he were promising something to God. Something awful. And his voice was cold as a blade of steel.

Kendal shuddered.

3 5

Slowly, he circled the truck. The bright October moonlight pierced overhanging trees, and shadows from wind-gusted branches moved across the costumes of *The Dybbuk*. Tiny particles of silver frost, like white rolled-up eyes of the dead, glistened among the tattered clothing. Arms and legs appeared to tremble, as if long-silent men and women sought to breath once more.

Wilfred Callahan did not believe that Darby would have abandoned this, her fictional family.

When she arrived in Down Derry, Darby had called saying that she and Andy were going to clean the farmhouse, but not to expect to see her until night. For dinner, please, she'd said. Respecting her wishes, he had decided not to intrude on her plans. It had, in a way, made his anticipation of her arrival for dinner on this night more pleasurable. He had lost himself in the never-ending details inherent in cases pending at the Bureau of Criminal Investigation, and he had savored the waiting.

Earlier this evening he had sat on his balcony loft and read matters of theology, particularly the works of Augustine. He was certain that the saint's words inscribed on the birchbark were a clue to what had happened at the Moons' farmhouse. He found nothing pertinent to the occasion. Displeased with himself, restless, he paced the loft. He returned to his books, skimmed a number of volumes relating to myth and ritual, symbol and folklore, hoping that somewhere within the texts he would find a reference to black birds.

Occasionally, he became aware of the sound of a car's engine and he would lift his head and listen, waiting for the crunch of tires in his driveway. But the cars passed. Absorbed in his fruitless reading, some time passed before he began to worry about Darby's absence. Had she forgotten that she was to be his dinner guest? Or had she changed her mind? Was she reluctant to risk the possibilities of their relationship? The thought depressed him.

Callahan studied the pale figure of Death in the forged painting. Ryder had believed that man was forever helpless. Perhaps he was right. The sergeant's annoyance at succumbing to a nihilism that contradicted his own life was interrupted by the sound of a car. He hurried to the front door and opened it. The car drove by. Callahan immediately thumbed through the local telephone directory and called the Moons' farmhouse. There was no answer. He walked out of his house, got into his car, drove off. Swiftly.

When he entered the farmhouse, it was dark. He snapped on a light and called to Darby. No reply. Although instinctively he was prepared for silence, he felt somewhat ridiculous as he walked through the house, quietly turning on lights, edging open doors. But foolish or not, his uneasiness increased when he saw Darby's purse on the kitchen table. He opened it and fingered through the contents, smiling at the lack of cosmetics. Her address book was in the purse. Printed on the flyleaf was a request that any finder of the book please contact the owner at the following numbers. Her New York apartment was listed; so was her family's number in Westport.

Callahan took the book with him to the living room, which still smelled faintly of fresh paint. With no anticipation of success, he called Darby's New York number. When there was no answer, he called the Westport number. No answer there, either. The odor of paint reminded him that Andy Poole must have been at the house during the last two days. He put the address book in his pocket and left the farmhouse.

Now, outside, he lifted a torn blouse out of the truckbed. Because it was, indeed, a costume, it had been deliberately abused so that it might reflect the wear and tear of clothing worn by equally abused people. He thought of Darby's story about placing her tongue on the cold steel of the children's slide. He felt anger rise in him. He did not want her to bleed again.

He drove down the road to Ray Poole's place. Knowing that the farmer would have retired early, he was surprised to see a light through the living room window, but as he approached the house he saw that Andy was hunched forward on a couch, absorbed in watching television. Callahan knocked softly. Andy darted a nervous look at the door, then glanced back quickly to his television set. The boy rose and crossed the room.

"Ayuh?" Andy asked as he edged open the door.

"Evening, Andy," Callahan said.

"By Jesus," Andy said in a tone of relief. "Things goin' on round here, Tuttle gone an' everthing, I didn't know who 'twas. Git in Wilfred, an' shut the door."

As Callahan entered, he saw that a video tape recorder was plugged into a television set. The cassette it was playing was a pornographic movie.

"You mind turning that thing off for just a minute?" Callahan asked.

"That feller," Andy said, his attention once more on the screen, "he ain't reached glory yet."

"I need some information," Callahan said tightly.

"I ain't never seen such a big dong," Andy said.

"Listen to me," Callahan said, and the way he said it made Andy listen at once. Callahan stepped over to the television set and turned the tape off. "You with Darby Moon today?"

"Said I'd clean the house, didn't I? Did what I said. Cleaned it, painted it."

"You spend the whole day?"

"Ayuh."

"She with you all the time?"

"Ayuh."

"When did you last see her?"

"When I went home."

"I mean, what time?"

"Don't wear a watch."

"Goddamn it, Andy, was it dark? Was it late?"

"No need to get angry, Wilfred," Andy said.

Callahan drew a deep breath. "Do you remember what you were doing when you last saw her?"

"Wasn't doin' nuthin'. Jus' sittin' a spell, is all."

"Where?"

"We was outside on the stoop takin' a beer. Wasn't doin' nuthin' special. Jus' watchin' things an' everthin'."

"What do you mean, 'watching things'? Watching what?"

"You know, things. Watchin' the day end. Ain't no harm in that, is there?"

"No. No harm at all. Then what happened?"

"Nuthin' happened, Wilfred. Why would sumthin' happen?"

"Did you see anybody, anything?"

"I jus' tole you. Didn't see nuthin'. Now I'd take it kindly, you was to push that thing back on."

"All right, Andy, all right." Callahan sighed. "All right." He pushed the on button and the gyrating figures of sexual acrobats flashed immediately. Disgusted, he walked to the door, but as he opened it, Andy spoke again.

" 'Cept that bird, that dumb ol' bird."

Slowly, Callahan turned back. "What bird?"

"You know, that big ol' black bird, big ol' crow."

"What about him?"

"What I'm tellin' you. He were jus' dumb. Wouldn't go nowheres. Jus' flyin' round 'n round in circles like he got hisself sumthin' dead underneath and couldn't make up his mind should he eat it. Dumb, that's what."

"Where was he?"

"Well, gracious sakes, Wilfred, where'd you be, you was a bird? In the sky, that's where he was. Oh, Lordy, lookit what they're doin'!" The boy's eyes were only inches from the television screen.

"Look at me, Andy."

"Huh, what?"

"Look at me!" Callahan took three quick strides across the room and grabbed Andy's shoulder. He yanked him around. The boy's mouth dropped open in bewilderment. Callahan's voice was low and tight. "Where was that bird? Was it over the farmhouse? Was it near you?"

The boy shook his head and stammered in fright. "It was . . . was . . . it was north some, I guess . . . ayuh, north . . . into . . . into them hills."

"Up where the old logging road runs?"

"Ayuh . . . ayuh, that's her. That's where she was."

"What about the others?"

"Others . . . others?" Andy was obviously confused. "Don't know no other loggin' roads."

"Birds, Andy, birds! What about the other birds, the other crows? They fly in a flock, you know that."

"Weren't none, I swear to God, Wilfred. Weren't no other birds. Jus' that one sumbitch. Honest, I'm tellin' true!"

Callahan released the boy's shoulder. He took a long breath and exhaled slowly. "Yes," he said wearily, "I know. I know you are. Thanks."

Callahan left the Poole house and drove away. He braked his car for a moment under the splintered pine on Poole's land and stared toward the north. Even under moonlight, the mountains were too dark to be clearly outlined. He saw nothing but the vague shape of their rise. He accelerated and drove home. He wanted to study Darby's address book. Perhaps someone knew where she had gone.

He didn't believe it.

"The thing is, Solomon," said the Mouse, "I think he was waiting for you. All these years, he was waiting for you. Fantastic!"

Solomon grinned. They were sitting outside the basement of the synagogue, in the *sukkah*, the booth. Spread before them on the orange-crate table were all the photographs of Moses Maimonides.

Solomon had returned that evening. He'd been unable to reach Darby but his disappointment had been alleviated by the excitement he felt about presenting Mouse with the pictures of his hero.

"Look, see," Mouse continued, pointing at the photos, "see how quiet he is, how he's waiting, a thumb in his book, marking maybe something wonderful for you to read. He's going to teach you, boychick. Hoo ha, is he going to teach you! But be patient, my friend, it will take time, maybe all your life and then some. Don't be in a rush, believe me!"

"But I am," Solomon said. "I am in a rush."

"A starved man, he eats too quickly, he can't keep the food down."

"I'll take an Alka-Seltzer."

"You think I'm kidding, huh?" The Mouse looked seriously at Solomon. "You're a beginner, Solomon, a beginner."

"What do you mean, a beginner?" Solomon asked. "Wasn't it you that said we're all Jews?"

"Philosophically, maybe. Morally, maybe. I didn't mean it word for word. You don't have to be a Jew in the formal sense. I'm not even sure that's what you want. It's not like you're Darby."

"I don't follow you."

Mouse was silent for a moment. He poured a glass of wine for each of them. "You don't mind my saying, Solomon, all your life you been looking for someone you could have a dialogue with. Maybe it's God but I don't think so. Darby, she wants a partnership with God; but you, I think you've been looking for something else."

"You think I want something less?"

"Not less. Different. I think you never felt you belonged anywhere, belonged with anyone. You know, like a group. Listen, I'll use a word, you won't hit me it sounds too heavy."

"I won't hit you."

"Community," Mouse said. "That's what you've been after. Community. But you didn't know how to go about it. I think you tried in your own crazy way."

"What do you mean?"

"Things you told me. Like the games you play with the window washer. Or the game on the library steps with that guy and his lady. You know, the tie people."

"You think those are games?"

"In a way, yeah. I'm not sure about the washer guy. Maybe 'cause he's black and you know the shit they go through. But the tie people, oh yeah, I'm right about that. They're like you. Like you were. They don't belong anywhere. I mean, in their minds they don't belong anywhere, and so you felt they were like you, and you could be easy with 'em. You see what I'm saying?"

"I never thought about it that way."

"You never thought about a lot of things. You're just gearing up, and I love you for it, shmuck."

"Christ, it's taken me a long time."

"Hey, listen, who's holding a clock? I was a kid, I used to go to Rockaway and watch the ocean, the waves. Up on the beach, back in the sea. Up and down. Forward and back. We're no different. We just keep moving, looking for the high tides in our lives, but each time we reach it we flow back a little. Where is it writ that we gotta keep count?"

Solomon had shown the Muñoz letter to Mouse, and Mouse had wept. Solomon touched his jacket pocket. "I'm glad I went back."

"Maybe," Mouse said.

"Now what kind of Talmudic crap is that?"

"I just said 'maybe.' I say anything else?"

"Yeah, I think you're saying something else, only I don't hear it."

"All right. What I'm saying is this. Sometimes when we uncover something, when we find out what happened a long time ago, it grabs us. But that's not always good. We look at it the wrong way, it could burn us. History, who you are, it ain't always pancakes an' peachy pie."

"Are you being deliberately vague, Mouse?"

411 • WILLIAM DARRID

"No. What I'm saying, Solomon, is that a guy can mix up his choices."

"What choices?"

"Obligations is better. What we have to understand is that we don't owe our fathers. We owe our children. That's what you have to get out of what you learned, what you found out. The shit that went down in Spain was terrible but it's too late to do anything about it. You can't bring it back and turn it around."

Solomon felt the animal in his belly. "Maybe I can."

"No," Mouse said. "That's the point. That's the whole thing. You want some kind of revenge, revenge against a whole, huge past, and that's just what a Jew isn't. A Jew is justice, Solomon, justice. I'll tell you something. There was a guy lived long ago, Babylonia. Hillel he was called. He said it best. 'In a place where no one behaves like a human being, you must strive to be human.' You want more? Read Ethics of the Fathers, the Pirke Avot. 'Do not separate thyself from the community.' You see what I'm saying? You're just a beginner."

"What about Vermont? You saw the letter I brought back. You read what Muñoz wrote about the tongues. It's clear, for chrissake. Some son of a bitch up there is doing it all over again. You think he shouldn't be stopped?"

Mouse was very aware of Solomon's cold rage and it worried him. "Listen, Mr. Moon," he said, "I don't like where you're going."

"I'm not going anywhere."

"You know what I mean. I don't like where your head's going. It could be dangerous. Very, very dangerous."

"I don't know what you're talking about."

"Bullshit," said the Mouse. "Level with me, Solomon. You're not thinking of going up there, are you? I mean, you're not crazy enough to try to find that guy, are you?" When Solomon didn't answer, the Mouse spoke more urgently. "Let me ask you a question. You ever come across that guy, you do something bad to him, what happens? They find you and burn your ass. You think you're a Jew? Then read the Torah. 'A man is to *live* by God's commandments, not *die* for them.' "

Solomon thought of Rafael Fernandez Muñoz. Who had not been avenged.

The telephone rang in the basement.

"That's Em," Mouse said. "I told him he should come down and bring a little whitefish, it shouldn't be a total loss."

"Let me get it," Solomon said.

He left the booth and went into the basement. He picked up the phone. "Mouse's place," he said, imitating Emilio. "The borscht is terrific."

"Is Mr. Blum there?" The voice sounded familiar.

Solomon covered the mouthpiece of the phone and called to Mouse. "It's not Em. Some fancy talker wants Mr. Blum." He spoke again into the phone. "May I ask who's calling?"

"Is this Mr. Moon?"

And then Solomon recognized the caller. "Sergeant Callahan?"

"Yes."

Why would he call here at this hour? Solomon's knees were suddenly made of water. He knew it couldn't be good. "What is it, Sergeant? Is something going on? Something else?"

Callahan came right to the point. He told Solomon of finding Darby's truck at the farmhouse. And her purse. Her address book. He made no attempt to make light of Darby's disappearance. He did not hide his own fears from Solomon.

"Jesus," Solomon whispered. "Jesus Christ. I'll get a car. I'll come right up."

Callahan suggested that nothing could be done that night and that it would be wiser for Solomon to wait until the morning. Callahan was going to organize a search through the woods and into the mountains. He would use a number of his own troopers and volunteers from the village. He had also contacted the trainer of a pack of bloodhounds. The pack was working in upstate New York but would be available within forty-eight hours. Meanwhile troopers would comb the woods. Callahan emphasized that the search would be more efficient with the dogs.

"Yes," Solomon said. "Yes. All right. Okay." He spoke carefully for he felt the hotness of his breath and he knew *the thing* was pulsing. After the call, he returned to the booth outside, and when he told Mouse the story he averted his face. He was certain that his breath was rancid.

"Tomorrow morning," Mouse said. "We'll go together. I want to help, Solomon."

"Yes," Solomon said. "Yes. All right. Okay. Sure."

"Callahan's right," Mouse said. "You need some sleep. You want to come up to my place?"

Solomon stared slowly around the booth and when he saw the hanging pomegranate he also heard the words of the dreamed Jew. *We shall meet from time to time.*

"If it's all right with you," Solomon said, "I'd like to stay here."

"Yeah, sure," Mouse said. "You going to call Kendal? England, it's already morning."

"No. When we know more. It'd be better then."

"Okay. There's some old blankets in the closet. We can use the benches inside."

"Mouse," Solomon said, "I'd like to be alone. Do you mind?"

"How could I mind? I'll go upstairs."

They went to the basement; Mouse pulled blankets from a closet and placed two of them on one of the benches. He took another and started toward the small staircase to the main room of the synagogue. As he passed the small black square on the wall to remind all Jews of the bad days of their lives, he muttered softly:

"Barukh dayan emet."

Solomon heard him and asked what he said.

"I said," the Mouse answered, " 'Blessed be the true judge.' " He climbed the stairs and left Solomon alone.

After only a few hours dawn broke and the Mouse, his body stiff from lying on the sawdust floor, awakened. He went down to the basement.

Solomon was gone.

36

S urely, you can see that?" Riordan asked. He brandished the pillow from the farmhouse. His hands moved gently over the needlepoint design of the saint. "That you lived in a house of Jews and lay down with a saint passes all understanding."

Darby could not answer. The terror of the last two days had given way to exhaustion. She did not know if it was night or day. She did not know how long she had been strapped into the cold stone niche of Judas. She knew only that the old man was ceaseless with his questions. And she understood none of them. Endlessly pacing the earthen floor of the cave, he demanded her confession, but because he refused to say what she was accused of, she had no reply. She pleaded with him to tell her what he wished to know but he simply repeated that it was the duty of the sinner to reveal his sin.

When fear had loosened her bowels, she fouled the ledge below her and begged to be taken outside. At first, unmindful of the stench, the old man had denied her request. He told her that it was the obligation of a heretic to humble himself. On the second day, he had instructed the boy to clean her, saying that only in such a condition could she meet God.

Darby had been surprised at the boy. He had unstrapped her, carried her over his shoulder and washed her in water from the stream. Even in her alarm, she had been conscious of how gentle he was when his hands lingered over her flesh. He had done a strange thing. He had brushed his crippled fingers against her lips as if he thought her mouth could heal them. He had removed his hand and stared at his fingers and she saw the puzzlement in his eyes when the deformity remained. During the few times that the old man left the cave, and she heard his awful howling, the boy had made her a mixture of honey and water but, always, he hid the bowl before the old man returned to resume his questioning.

Riordan placed the saint's pillow on the stone table and turned to Jubal, who sat in a corner of the cave.

"Bring me the Augustine," Riordan said.

Quickly, the boy went to the ledge of books and pulled out a leather volume. Above the ledge, Brother Death opened and closed his beak. When Jubal handed the book to Riordan, the old man opened it to a passage and returned it to the boy.

"Read truth to the child," he said.

Never lifting his eyes from the page, fearful that the hate he felt would be disclosed to his father, Jubal quietly recited.

" 'To be gone from the Kingdom of God, to be an exile from God's city, to be without the . . . the " Jubal stumbled.

" 'Manifold,' " Riordan said.

" '. . . the manifold sweetness of God is so mighty a punishment that no torments we know can be compared to it.' "

Listening to his own words, the boy surged with hope. Did this mean that the old man had softened? Did it mean that the punishment to the flesh of sinners was no longer of merit? Jubal's glance flicked quickly at the girl. He dared not speak but he wanted terribly to reassure her and in that way reassure himself that her hands which had so lightly touched his face would move again like birds and in their flight return to the wonder of affection.

But when he heard the whispered scratching he knew he had misunderstood. He turned to Riordan. Slowly, the old man was pulling his bramble whip from under his cloak. The thorns softly ripped the cloth.

"It is not a personal matter," Riordan said to Darby, whose chin rolled on her chest, saliva leaking from her lips. "It is only our obligation to the Lord to see that you reenter His city. There are rules, don't you see? We must offer you a hand of holiness." He nodded at Jubal. "Dress her."

The boy moved toward a yellow sanbenito that hung from a wire in the cave. But the old man spoke again.

"No," he said. "Clothe her for Redemption."

The boy froze. He knew the meaning of his father's words. He turned for just an instant but when he saw the old man's eyes burning at him he removed a different sanbenito from the wire. It was black, painted with the Devil's flames. It was worn by those hopelessly condemned to the fire. Jubal understood that the old man's auto-da-fé would be carried out. Handling Darby as if she were a doll, he slipped the black sanbenito over her, carried her across the cave, and laid her face down on the great stone table. Riordan slipped the pillow under her face so that her eyes bored into the eyes of the saint. His huge hand stroked Darby's head.

"The flesh, the matter of the body," he said softly to the girl, "is Satan's work, and only when the flesh is gone can you find the world of light, the world of the Lord." He turned and handed the whip to Jubal. "Only through vexation can understanding come."

The crow cawed.

The old man removed his cloak and spread it on the floor before Jubal. "For each stroke, let her hear the names of those who came before, those who are with us now, those who will lead her to Grace."

Riordan left the cave. For a moment, the boy was still. Then he crawled through the tunnel of the cave and, staying within the shadows of the stone, peered out. His eyes closed, his face reflecting his inner peace, Riordan sat quietly in the clearing. Jubal quickly retreated back into the cave and, crouching on the floor, removed Riordan's beaver-toothed knife from the cloak. He raised the cloth of the sanbenito which Darby wore so that it no longer touched her back, then his knifeblade flashed again and again, slitting the cloth but never touching Darby's flesh. He returned the knife to the cloak but he removed the leather-thonged bola from its pocket and stuffed it under his shirt. He knew that the old man expected him to whip Darby, so he raised the thorny lash. But he did not touch her. Each time he snapped the whip he struck the cloak on the floor of the cave and each time he cried out a name of an Apostle.

He rolled Darby off the stone table and into his arms. He knew that Riordan would see the knife slits in the sanbenito, but because there were no signs of blood he, Jubal, would have to move swiftly past the old man. Carrying Darby, he crawled out of the cave, and as he rose with her in his arms he cried out the words of Revelation.

"They have shed the blood of saints and prophets, and thou has given them blood to drink!"

Wildness in his heart, the boy bolted past Riordan and down the clay banks of the stream and then plunged into the icy water. As the old man watched in wonder, Jubal immersed Darby three times and as they rose together from the water he made a sign upon her forehead and under the darkening sky his voice lifted boldly.

"Receive the sign of the cross," he cried, "which you have lost through being deceived!"

Seeing the girl cleansed in the waters of her baptism, the old man almost wept with joy.

Later, while the girl slept on the stone table, her head still resting on the saint, the old man and his son sat in front of the cave. In Riordan's hands was Tuttle's skull with its round white pearl, and what the old man said made the boy hug his sides, for he did not want to reveal his frightened trembling. He knew the success of his deceit had been without meaning.

Riordan's gaze moved slowly around the campsite. He explained to the boy that where they sat was consecrated ground, made holy by the heirs of God. It was, therefore, unsuitable for the fire that would consume the sinners. He told Jubal that the Jew in the farmhouse must follow the girl to the flames but that he must be advised of this; such was the nature of mercy. He lifted the skull and turned it in his hands, and said that he would carry it to the Jew. Jubal must carry the girl.

"Where at?" Jubal asked. "Where at do I bring her?"

"To the sweetness of her death," the old man said. "To where I will burn the Holy Cross. To where the earth stinks and to where hosannas will be cried by rats."

The auto-da-fé would be held in the dumpground of Down Derry.

Riordan stood. He whistled softly. Brother Death flew through the cave's tunnel and landed on the old man's shoulder. Riordan smiled at Jubal, turned, and melted into the dark woods, indistinguishable from the descending night, silent, shapeless, gone.

Jubal stared at his withered hand and knew that the music of his harped dream was ended. He rose and started toward the cave.

When Callahan hurried into the farmhouse, Solomon was painting a square of black on the the eastern wall, the wall closest to Jerusalem. Next to the square, a photograph was tacked to the wall. It was a black-and-white picture of a man in a field. It was totally unfamiliar to Callahan.

"Who is that?" he asked.

"Me," Solomon said. Before Callahan could inquire further, he gestured to the painted square. "And this, this is to remind me of the bad days of my life. Mouse taught me that. He called you, didn't he?"

"Yes," Callahan answered.

Solomon turned. He looked terrible. His clothes were rumpled and he was unshaven, the grizzled stubble of whiskers accentuating his pallor. Under his eyes were deep black rings. There was a fustiness about him, a smell of stale tobacco, sweat.

He placed his can of paint and his paintbrush on a newspaper-covered table. Callahan saw there were other things on the table. A double-barreled shotgun. An open box of shells. The sight of these things made Callahan uneasy.

"We've searched the woods around here but so far, nothing," Callahan said. "Maybe we'll have luck with the dogs. We'll start at dawn tomorrow."

Solomon picked up a kerosened rag and carefully wiped his hands. "How will they know her scent?"

"I took the liberty of removing clothes from her suitcase. And we'll use some of the other things."

The sergeant pointed out the window. Darby's truck and Solomon's car were parked in the farmyard. The *Dybbuk* costumes still rested on the bed of the truck.

Solomon moved to the window. He stared at the crumpled clothes. "Have you found out anything, anything at all, anything that will help?"

Callahan told Solomon about the case of the crucified man in the beaver pond and about finding the black feathers, which resembled those in Tuttle's mobile home, and about the crow that had circled the sky above Andy Poole and Darby. "The crucified man, the piece of bark with Augustine's warning — there's a strange consistency to it. Even the bird fits, though I don't know what the hell it all means."

"The bird?"

"It's the story of Benedict. When he hid in the caves of Subiaco, a blackbird fed him. He flew bread to the hermit and saved his life. He was as benevolent as the saint."

"We're not dealing with a saint, Wilfred! We're dealing with a crazy son of a bitch who should be blown —" Solomon stopped. He turned from the window and moved to the table. His fingers lightly touched the twin triggers of his shotgun, then rested on the cold barrels.

Callahan spoke quietly. "I don't want to sound pretentious, but I'd like to remind you that I am an officer of the law. You are not. If we . . . if we run into trouble, I'd appreciate your keeping that in mind."

"Logical," Solomon said. "Very logical. Neat. They specialize in logic at the college of Jesuits, don't they? I mean as opposed to the more tender leanings of the Dominicans. Torquemada's boys."

Callahan frowned. "Torquemada? Why do you refer to Torquemada?"

"Oh," Solomon said, "he interests me."

Troubled, Callahan studied Solomon, glanced for a moment at the black square on the wall, then back to Solomon. Darby had said that her father had given little credence to Judaic ritual, had seemed divorced from the history of persecution and yet he had painted the wall and now referred to the infamous Inquisitor. What had moved him in this direction? What was he not revealing?

"I can assure you," Callahan said quietly, "that my Jesuitical instruction does not affect the common interest we share."

"My daughter."

"Yes. Darby told me that you were a very private person, a guarded man; that it was not easy for you to . . . to open up. I think you're hiding something, Mr. Moon. I want to know what it is."

"I love Darby," Solomon said. His voice was just above a whisper. It was ugly. "I love her very much. I love what she has learned and what she's tried so hard to teach me. So understand it, Wilfred. Understand it and live with it."

"Understand what?"

"I will hurt anyone who has done her harm."

Callahan stared at the shotgun. He tried to keep anger out of his voice. "I want you to put that away, Mr. Moon."

"Is there a new law, Sergeant, prohibiting a man from owning a shotgun?"

"There is an old law that prohibits a man from using a gun in the wrong way." Callahan thought he had never seen a man so wired with tension and he chose his words carefully. "Doing harm to someone . . . hurting them badly . . . killing, perhaps . . . is not an attitude that would fill Darby with pleasure. Nor does it please me."

"Call it instinct."

"The dinosaurs are gone, Mr. Moon. It's time to come out of the caves."

Solomon said nothing.

"On a more personal level," Callahan finally said, "I suggest that you bathe and shave and get some sleep. Tomorrow will not be an easy day. It's highly probable that even you will have to come out of hiding."

Solomon smiled to himself. He felt the wonderful *thing* clawing within, the animal's sweet breath hot in his lungs. Ah, Wilfred, he was tempted to say, I no longer hide. Not now. Not ever again. But he said nothing. Frustrated, Callahan turned and walked out of the farmhouse. He moved quickly to his car. He wanted to reach his home, his books. He wanted to read about Tomás de Torquemada. He wanted to learn why a Jew raged today, here, now, and he wondered where that rage would lead.

He wanted to be there.

37

Solomon stood in the farmyard. Under his fisherman's sweater he shivered against the vision of the rising moon. He thought of the legend of the Seventh Day of the Willow and understood that it was a moon under which a man might stand to receive the final judgment of God; a moon under which a man might die.

Returning to the farmhouse, he removed the curtains from every window on the lower floor. He opened the windows, the kitchen door, the front door. Moonlight glowed faintly in the house. Remembering what Mouse had explained was done on the day of Hoshana Rabba, the day a man's fate is sealed, he removed a jar of honey from a kitchen cabinet, a spoon from a drawer, and walked into the living room. He pulled a Bible from the bookshelves, then placed his rocker so that when he sat, moonlight would pass over his shoulder. He placed his loaded shotgun on the floor next to the rocker, sat, the Bible on his lap, the honey jar in his hand.

As he fed himself from the jar of honey, he opened the Bible to the Book of Deuteronomy as Rafael Fernandez Muñoz's letter had instructed and read the admonition. *Do not forget the things your eyes have seen, nor let them slip from your heart all the days of your life; rather tell them to your children and to your children's children.*

Solomon had studied Muñoz's letter, read it over and over again, immersed himself in the experience of the Jew, felt as the Jew felt, thought as the Jew thought; became the Jew. And like Muñoz he believed deep in his blood that the hunt for Jews never ceased. The warnings were clear. Tongues on his door. Dung in his house. He had little doubt that somewhere in the woods, or on the mountain, in dark fields, a new Inquisitor was at work and that the man who burned the green cross was responsible for Darby's disappearance. What Solomon desperately prayed was that even as Tomás de Torquemada had offered temporary mercy to the child of a Jew, so too would the new tormentor. There was an ugly logic to it, for Solomon suspected that he was the real prey.

It was, therefore, that the words of Deuteronomy became sweeter than the honey as Solomon read those passages that talked of a stranger within the gates, and he felt more certain than ever that the stranger was the one who had defiled his house, had taken his daughter, and was a prophet of other gods, a prophet about whom the Lord commanded:

Thou shalt not consent unto him, nor hearken unto him; neither shall thine eye pity him; neither shalt thou spare him. But thou shalt surely kill him; thine hand shall be the first upon him to put him to death.

Solomon closed his eyes and prayed for the stranger to come. He listened for any sounds that might indicate the presence of an enemy. But all he heard were the night sounds of his house: The toneless scraping of hemlock branches. Wind dusting the roof. The hum of a refrigerator. A field mouse scratching at a pantry bin. There was a faint click of a motor and a soft droning filled the house. The oil burner had turned on. Warm air from the floor vents flowed around Solomon's ankles. He heard the intermittent tiny poppings of floorboards contracting in the night's cold air.

He opened his eyes and looked at the floorboards; what he saw amused him, for he knew it was a lie. Moonlight over his shoulder had cast his shadow upon the floor. The rockers of the chair severed his shadow's head. He did not doubt the legend's truth that if a man failed to see the shadow of his head he would meet his death. What entertained Solomon was the knowledge that it was not he who was fated; it was the stranger within his gates.

He closed the Bible, rested it on the floor. He picked up his shotgun and returned to the kitchen. He placed the jar of honey back in its cabinet. From the front a northern wind gusted through the house. And with it came another sound.

Soft. Smothered. A slithered hush.

Instantly, Solomon thought of leather moccasins whispering across the ground and he remembered the strange footprints found outside the house. He turned swiftly, his hands tightening on the gun. He moved to the living-room door. The moon's ivory beacon tracked through a window, blotching the floor with its whiteness. Solomon skirted the brightness as if he were afraid that the light striking him would diminish the heat within. He did not want his wrath corrupted. A board creaked under him. He removed his shoes, inched forward, hugging the wall of the room, his eyes narrowed against the night.

Something darker than the night stirred outside. It moved forward, closing steadily toward the house, and as the wind gusted once again it carried the scent of an animal.

In front of the window an eyeless skull floated in the air.

And like a wild man grieving for something lost, Solomon raised his gun and fired.

The skull was blown away. Solomon heard a howling cry. He rushed outside, his finger on the second trigger. The remains of the skull were splattered on the stone step, the slivered bones whiter than the moon. Among them rolled a pearl. Solomon leaped off the step, his glance snapping from left to right. The barn. The orchard. The woods. Moonlit shadows quivered on the ground below a hemlock. The tree's lower branches trembled.

Solomon ran across the farmyard toward the woods. The sock on one foot caught on a rock. He stumbled. He tore off his socks and raced for the trees, where he was certain the stranger had run. He was keenly aware of the pungent fragrance of the landscape, the pleasing sourness of rotting vegetation, the smell of autumn's death. He heard the snap of hidden explosions: the night frost splitting seeds, white-footed mice attacking grass, beechnuts falling. The moon's pale path was fragmented by the jutting shape of trees and boulders, but Solomon saw the bronze sheen of beeches, the gold of sycamore, the dark green lacework of hemlock needles. His senses were as alive as wine on fire.

As he entered the woods, sweat rolled down his sides, and when he smelled himself he breathed in the odor of a beast and laughed. He ran through the trees as lightly as a boy, taking infinite pleasure in the stones and twigs that stung his bare feet, resenting the occasional path of soft moss. He sped through the woods, no longer able to live safely. The sounds of the woodland were diminished by the thumping of his heart and each time he heard its swiftly measured beat he felt more alive. He yearned to pull the trigger.

But there was no target. He had lost his prey. He paused and listened. He held his breath so that he could more acutely hear. The wind. The leaves. Nothing more. He imagined a map. On the other side of the woods was a pasture. Surely his enemy would not risk the open ground? But what if he had circled like an animal trapped? The orchard; he would return to the orchard! Solomon headed in that same direction.

Soundlessly, he glided into the orchard. For a moment he was bewildered by the darkness, for the apple trees were more widely spaced than those trees of the woods he'd left. Wind-blown clouds masked the moon. Solomon cursed. He pulled long deep breaths into his lungs, quieting himself until he could no longer hear the pumping of his heart. He tried to remember what he'd learned from Mouse so many years ago on the flat plains of Kansas. He thought of the night bivouacs when he'd been taught to scan enemy territory. He closed his eyes, squinting against the darkness behind his lids. He counted slowly to ten, opened his eyes. The night was no longer black. He became aware of the gradations of light, the landscape no longer an amorphous black but distinguishable pockets of striated grays through which he recognized the familiar tapestry of tree and bush and rock. He forced himself to scan the ground from left to right and then back again to see if he could discover some alien shape. There was nothing.

The passing clouds streaked the moon like the final fingers of a closing fan and in the tree behind him Solomon heard the cadenza of an owl. Four hoots. A pause. Four more hoots, the last note dying. Silently, he turned and looked behind him. At the rear of the orchard was a line of pines. His gaze lifted to the treetops silhouetted against the sky. He studied the angles where branches joined a trunk. He saw the bird.

Unlike other birds, which rested in the night, the owl now sat silently, slowly swiveling its head so that the great round eyes, fixed forever in permanent position, sought whatever prey moved below the tree, a mouse or rabbit or chipmunk that might rustle among the leaves. The owl's silence was a preface to assassination.

As he contemplated his own desire, Solomon felt a warm kinship with the bird.

He heard the soft banging of a door. Eagerly he leaned forward, his eyes bright and hard. He stared through the darkly filtered light, studying both doors of the farmhouse. Neither moved. Was the stranger in the house?

He sprinted out of the orchard, not caring now if he were seen or heard, racing toward the farmhouse. The barn door banged. Solomon whirled. Behind the window of the barn he saw a shape, a shadow; something moved, was gone. Solomon pounded across the farmyard. He reached the barn. He lunged through the open door. In front of him a figure swiftly rose. Solomon slammed the shotgun to his shoulder. His finger quivered.

"Oh, God!" a voice cried behind him, "don't! Please don't!"

He spun around. Darby lay in the shadows of a corner, her arm raised toward him, her eyes moonlit. A glass shattered. Solomon whirled. The figure he had seen crashed through the barn window and dived into the night. Solomon ran outside. He spun in circles, his eyes searching wildly for the figure. There was no one; not the shadow of a man.

Quickly, Solomon reentered the barn. He crouched next to his daughter. Her eyes were closed and she moaned softly. He cradled her in his arms, he stroked her hair. He hugged her to him, then lifted her. He carried her back into the farmhouse, climbed the stairs and laid her on his and Kendal's bed. Dreading what he might see, he turned on a lamp. When he touched her face, she opened her eyes. They were blacker than Solomon remembered. Blacker than anything he'd ever seen. She looked as if she had been fitted with opaque shields to protect her from some vision she dared not face, or as if what she had seen was seared on her corneas for the remainder of her life. But when she blinked Solomon caught his breath, for he saw that light was returning to her eyes. She moistened her lips. Miraculously, she smiled.

"Through . . . the whole . . . world," she said haltingly.

"What, darling? Through the whole world what?" Solomon leaned close to her.

"The boy," she said. "He carried me through the whole world."

Solomon didn't understand her; nor did he try. He wanted only to comfort her, to soothe her, to make her quiet. He spoke softly to her and knew that he would never remember what he said, only that he made small unintelligible sounds as if he were inventing a new language, a language of assurance, of promises and dreams; and as he spoke, whispered, hushed, his hands moved gently over her body, pulling the sanbenito from her and wrapping her in a soft, warm blanket, marveling that her body was unwounded, praying that she would fall quickly into sleep.

But she did not sleep at once. Although she moved very little, she could not stop talking. She spoke in disjointed sentences, her words tumbling incoherently, her thought without logic. She did not address Solomon. She addressed herself, as if she were looking for some reasonable explanation of what had happened.

Solomon left her only once. He warmed some milk and dissolved two sleeping pills in it. As she sipped from the cup she continued talking. At first Solomon paid scant attention, content to let her rid herself of whatever vision had darkened her eyes, but as she continued he came to understand that her rambling was not disjointed, that she was relating some incident that had happened or was going to happen, and when she talked of a burning cross his attention sparked. He gently questioned her, guided her, led her to what she had learned from the boy who had carried her through the world and perhaps beyond. She told Solomon of the old man who waited among the rats and of what he planned, and in the recounting of her story, gradually succumbing to the milk and pills, she was partially released from her pain. Her speech slowed. Her words faltered. She closed her eyes. Darby slept.

Solomon watched her for many minutes to be sure that her sleep was sound, then he turned off the bedlamp and left the room. Downstairs, he hesitated by the phone. Dare he leave Darby alone? Should he call Callahan or maybe Ray Poole to stay with her? He glanced toward the stairs. He knew the sleeping pills would not let Darby wake. She would not leave the house. Solomon gambled that he could reach the terrible stranger who waited before he moved again.

He replaced every curtain and drew them. He locked the windows. He locked the front door. He removed his scattershot shells from the shotgun. He opened a drawer of a chest and searched for what he wanted. He pulled out a small felt bag clasped like a woman's purse. The heaviness of the bag pleased him. He removed four deer slugs from the bag. They were shaped like bullets, thick rounded lengths of lead made to slip easily through the smooth-bored barrels of a shotgun. At one hundred yards they could punch out the heart of a ten-point buck. Solomon intended to be closer to his quarry. He wanted nothing left of the body of his prey: not bone, not sinew, not flesh. He had other plans for his head. He carried the shotgun, a box of scatter shells, the deer slugs, and the small felt bag into the kitchen.

Working at the kitchen table, he dismantled a dozen scattershot shells. He discarded the wadding and the shot, the paper cylinder, the metal firing cap. All that was left was gunpowder. He scraped it from the table into the felt bag.

He searched for a flashlight but couldn't find one. There were candles in a drawer. He removed one and stuck it in a holder. Shielding the candle from the wind, he left the kitchen and walked outside. He crossed the farmyard to Darby's truck. He was glad he'd brought the candle. The gusting wind pushed clouds across the moon. He held the light closer to the truck, moved it over the jumbled costumes. He saw the tattered blouse. Next to it was a pair of nondescript trousers, patched, and with a clothesline belt running through their loops. There was a battered peaked cap, its lining ripped loose. There was a pair of soft, badly scuffed, leather boots, the felt soles so misshapen they would form to any foot. Solomon took all of these things.

Before returning to the kitchen he moved to the front door. He held the candle low over the front stone stoop. The blast of his shotgun had pulverized Tuttle's skull. What was left looked like chips of marble. The pearl was gone, lost in its roll to the ground.

In the kitchen Solomon dressed in a manner of revenge.

He dressed like the dreamed Jew.

Solomon sat at the kitchen table, his back to the door. Only the candle cast light in the room. He raised his hands and placed them above the candle. Slowly, he lowered them over the flame. He felt the heat burn his flesh but held his hands steady. He wanted to experience the pain he intended to deliver.

He was going to set the Inquisitor on fire.

The wind was blowing away from the house, so Solomon could not hear the footfall outside. He felt tears running down his face and he licked at his own salt. When he could no longer stand the pain of the burning candle he removed his hands from the flame. He was ready. He closed his eyes. He whispered aloud.

"*Al kiddush ha-shem.* For the holiness of God."

He reached to pinch out the candle, but —

"Jesus, Solomon!"

Solomon spun around in his chair. Mouse and Emilio stood in the kitchen doorway. Mouse's glance flicked between Solomon's strange dress and the single, flaming candle.

"What the hell's going on?" Mouse asked.

"You didn't have to come up," Solomon said quickly. "It's okay. Darby's okay. She's upstairs. She's asleep."

"Thank God," Mouse said quietly.

Emilio stepped forward. He ran his hands over the shotgun on the table. He gave it to Mouse, who broke open the chamber. He slid out the two deer slugs, weighed them in his hand. He replaced them in the gun. "Nice. A real nice load." He reached under his jacket and removed an Army .45 from his belt. He put it on the table. His eyes never wavered from Solomon. "The forty-five, it's easier to carry but it wouldn't work for you, would it? I remember back at Riley, you were lousy with it. Em, though — he was great."

"It's all the baking," Emilio said. "You get real strong wrists from baking."

"What do you think you're doing with that?" Solomon asked. "Where are you going?"

"With you," Mouse said.

"I'm not going anywhere."

"Really." Mouse smiled. "The cop, Callahan, he figured maybe. You know, just maybe."

"And what do you figure?" Solomon spoke tightly.

"I figure he was right."

"Could we sit with you?" Emilio asked. Neither he nor Mouse waited for an answer. They drew chairs up to the table.

"The cop," Mouse said, "after we shmoozed a little, Em and I thought maybe you could use a little company. You know, while we looked for Darby."

"I told you," Solomon said. "Darby's okay. She's here."

"Callahan know?" Mouse asked. Solomon didn't answer. "No. Of course, Callahan wouldn't know. How'd she get here? You find her? She come on her own? Somebody bring her? What?"

"Somebody brought her," Solomon said.

"Uh-huh," Mouse said. "That somebody, he have anything to do with what went down?"

"Yes."

"And where is that somebody?" When Solomon remained silent, Mouse continued. "You're going after him, aren't you, Solomon?"

"He's mine, Mouse," Solomon answered softly.

"Jesus, Solomon," Emilio said, "you gotta call Callahan. Believe me."

"Listen to me," Solomon said, his voice urgent, passionate, as his glance moved back and forth between his two friends. "I have to do this. I have to do this my way. Just this one time, my way. You guys can call Callahan. You can blow the whistle on me. You can take it away from me. You don't owe me anything, not anything. But if we mean anything to each other, if we have something together, don't. Just . . . please . . . don't. I need this, Mouse. I need it!"

Mouse and Emilio looked at each other. Each knew what the other was thinking. One day, Mouse had said during their time at Fort Riley, he's gonna carve a shape for himself. Yeah, Emilio had answered, and we'd better be there. There were so many years of deep friendship that neither could deny Solomon, but they both knew that he must be accompanied on his search, for their objective would be different from Solomon's. They wanted to find a man and bring him before the law.

They did not want to kill him. They nodded at each other and turned back to Solomon.

"Okay," Mouse said.

"I think I know where he is," Solomon said. He gambled that neither Mouse nor Emilio would suspect what he had in mind.

"We all go," Em said.

"No," Solomon said. "Someone has to stay. Darby's here. Suppose he doubles back?"

"All right," Mouse said. "I go. Em stays."

"Hey!" Emilio said.

"Hey what?" Mouse asked. "Either of you guys ever do this?"

Solomon and Emilio knew what the Mouse meant. Although many years had passed, neither of them had forgotten Mouse's stories of the war. Among the three of them, only Mouse had crawled through darkness on his way to danger.

"Yeah," Emilio said reluctantly. "Yeah, I guess it has to be you. Yeah."

"Okay," Mouse said. "Where do we go?"

"North," Solomon lied. "Up the mountain."

"You're sure?"

"I'm sure."

"How do you know?" Emilio asked.

"Darby told me they put her in a cave. The caves are at the top of the mountain. I'll show you."

Solomon took a pencil and paper from a drawer. He spread the paper flat and began to draw a map. He sketched the logging road and the brook that wound down the mountainside. He drew pasturelands, and thick stands of birch and pine. He penciled in the fence of stump roots where he'd killed the thrush. Beyond the fence he smudged in a shaded area.

"What's that?" Mouse asked.

"Nothing," Solomon answered.

"What do you mean, 'nothing'?"

"Nothing. Just woods. They're heavy. Never been timbered. No roads. Nothing. It goes straight up to the caves."

"It'll be a bitch," Mouse said softly, "but that's where we go." He studied the map. He frowned. "These woods, they steep?"

Keep going, Mouse, keep going! Solomon was counting on his friend's concern.

"Yes," Solomon said, his voice worried. "They're goddamned steep."

Mouse looked at him. "The way you drew this map, it looks like the brook curves around to the other side of the mountain."

"Yeah."

"Easier to go up that way, right?"

"Right."

"It's too early for snow," Mouse said. "Couldn't have been any melt. The water's gotta be pretty low."

"Yes," Solomon said. "It's pretty low."

"Okay!" Mouse slapped the table. "You take the brook. I'll go up through the woods."

"Whatever you say," Solomon said. *Oh, Mouse, you sweet son of a bitch, you took the bait!*

"Now get this straight, Solomon," Mouse said. "Whoever gets up there first, we wait for the other guy. You got that?"

"I got it."

"All right," Mouse said. He rose from the table. He checked the clip of his .45 and shoved the weapon into his belt. "Let's do it!"

"Listen," Emilio said, "don't be no heroes, okay? I mean, you know."

"You got it," Mouse said. "We take this bastard and we bring him back. Right, Solomon?"

"Right." Solomon picked up his shotgun.

They left the house together. They moved across the farmyard through the orchard and up to the stand of conifers on one side of the stream. Solomon stared at the water. He didn't want to look at Mouse for fear his deceit would show. Behind him, Mouse spoke.

"Remember, Solomon, we bring him back."

Solomon turned. But Mouse was gone. He had disappeared so silently that not a leaf rustled, not a pine needle moved. Solomon remembered the legend of Fort Riley.

Don't fuck with the Mouse.

Swiftly, Solomon turned back to the stream. The broken branch of a pine tree raked his face, puncturing the skin. He felt the pain and he felt the blood running. He reached up and rubbed the wound. His fingers came away warm and sticky. He licked them, swallowed the blood. He felt the wild thing within him and rubbed harder at the wound, drawing more blood. He streaked his face with it. He prepared himself to kill.

His plan was simple. His instructions and map would lead Mouse in the opposite direction. Solomon had not forgotten the boy who had run into the night. He did not know where he lurked. He could not be certain whether the boy had returned to the old man or if he waited somewhere in ambush. He knew only that he had to avoid the boy, for he was not the target. He wanted the old man. He suspected that whatever passage the boy had chosen it would not be the long, wet journey through the stream. And so he stepped into the water.

The water was cold and quickly seeped through the broken boots of his strange costume but he was indifferent to it. He was warmed by the hot breath of the animal in his belly. The felt soles of his boots absorbed the slipperiness of rock and gravel over which he walked. Gradually, he assumed the rhythm of a stalking man, gliding effortlessly through the low water, bending so that he would not be snagged by branches of willow and adder which umbrellaed the creek. He moved downstream and the gentle current pressured his stride. It made him aware of his muscles at work which pleased him for he felt that nothing could tire him.

He became part of the night's landscape, sliding like an eel over fallen logs, sniffing the wind, pausing momentarily when he needed to refresh himself, lowering his face to the creek and, like a bobcat, lapping at the water, then moving on. Always moving on.

The creek narrowed, broadened, narrowed again; turned and twisted across the land, skirted old mowings, then rippled back into the woods, became pondlike at times, waist-high. It made no difference to Solomon. He had the eyes of a wildcat. He smelled like a cat. He was an animal crouching, sliding, slipping through water, floating almost, as he moved closer to Down Derry.

He was exhilarated by the specter of his coming kill. He knew now who he was. The rage within defined him. He, Solomon *Muñoz*, raced toward the war he craved, and when he faced his Inquisitor he would vindicate the dreamed Jew, Rafael Fernandez Muñoz — all Jews who had died for what they were.

He reached the bridge. The moon was lower in the sky. Soon dawn would break. Would he be visible if he crossed the bridge? Solomon studied the water before him. The stream narrowed here and the water ran fast, frothing, hissing over jagged boulders. Because the stream was squeezed between two high banks that held the pilings of the bridge Solomon knew that the water would be higher, deeper than before, its cascading force more severe than where it ran behind him. If he continued to wade, his balance would be threatened. Should he fall, his shotgun would be submerged, and when the final moment came it would not fire. He decided to cross the brook and make his way along the bank until he reached the cemetery. He would have to leap from rock to rock. Holding the shotgun high in front of him, he jumped for the first rock. He landed safely. He sprang again. Again, he was safe. He examined the next rock in front of him. It was three feet away and its granite contour was like a cone, its peak a foot above the water, smooth from erosion. Solomon crouched, breathed deeply, sprang. His feet hit the crest of the boulder and he pitched forward, hoping to encircle the boulder within his arms. His feet skidded off the rock and into the rushing water. The current tore him loose. His shotgun slammed against the rock and fired.

Even under the swirling water where he'd been carried, Solomon heard the thunderous blast. As the gun plunged past him he grabbed frantically, but his hand cracked against another rock. The gun sank. He thrashed wildly toward the bank of the stream, was somersaulted by the current, and then his foot hooked a root and he jackknifed over a fallen tree trunk. He seized a branch on the tree but it was rotten and broke away. He clawed further up the trunk until his head broke water and he hung there gasping, spitting sand and mud, water pouring out of his mouth. Using the fallen tree trunk as a ladder, he inched his way up the bank and flopped forward, his face buried in marigold and pigweed, mud plastering his eyes. He dug his hands into the soft earth and pushed himself up onto his elbows. His vision was blurred by the mud on his eyelids. He pulled at the tail of his wet shirt and scrubbed at his eyes and then could see again. He saw two things.

He lay on the edge of the cemetery.

And across the river a single light now burned behind an open window in the square. Framed in the light was Wilfred Callahan. Callahan peered toward the bridge, then turned and looked across the square, stared in the direction of the cemetery.

Solomon sank behind a tombstone. He knew the sergeant must have heard the shot. For a moment Callahan was still. Then he moved away from the window. Solomon rose to a crouch. Callahan returned to the window. Again, Callahan looked toward the bridge, then leaned down and was momentarily lost from sight. When he appeared again he was pulling on a sweater. He stepped away from the window. The light in the room went off.

Christ, Solomon thought, he's coming out! He slithered across the cemetery grass, hid behind another marker. The sound of a door closing carried across the river. A bobbing flashlight moved toward the bridge.

The sergeant was only a silhouette now. He played his light on the bridge and then underneath and across the pilings and over the water that hissed softly in the night. He turned and walked slowly across the village square but as he moved toward his house his pace quickened. The beam of his flashlight swept across the squad car parked on the road. The light went out. Solomon heard the engine start. Headlights were snapped on. Callahan shifted into gear. The car rolled forward, its twin beams sweeping for just a moment toward and then across the cemetery, brushing past. The car turned the corner of the square. It picked up speed. It was moving toward the road to the farmhouse. It disappeared.

Solomon prayed that Darby still slept and would not be able to reveal his destination. He moved from tombstone to tombstone, hunkering for an instant behind each one, then lunging for the next. He no longer had time to circle the dump from the riverbed. He left the cemetery. He reached the road to the dump and began to run. The wet trousers clinging heavily to his legs, his feet pounded the asphalt pavement. Just when he thought his heart would explode he saw the high leaning fence of the dump looming ahead of him. He sank into a ditch, his head lowered close to the rubbled ground, and he pulled deep gulps of air into his lungs while he waited for his body to cease trembling. He blinked sweat from his eyes. He lay on his back in the ditch and he was deaf to all but one sound. The echo of his gun reverberated. He could see the gun descend below the water. How was he to kill? He groped in his pocket for the small felt bag, pulled it out and unsnapped the clasp. He tilted the bag, but nothing ran out. Reaching into it, he felt the wetly glued gunpowder. He wondered if it would explode when the flames reached it. He felt the weight of the two deer slugs in his other pocket and again mourned the loss of his gun. He stared at the descending moon. It was flat, cold, ice-dusted. Solomon shivered. He reached behind him, placing a hand to push himself upright. His fingers touched something in the ditch. It was hard and smooth. He lifted it. It was a bottle, thrown perhaps from a passing car. Its neck was broken. It was small, prettily designed. It was red.

He knew now how he would kill the old man.

He held the bottle in his hand, the broken neck protruding wickedly from his fingers. Quietly, he rose from the ditch. He slid along the board fence, looking for the gate. He saw it. It was unlocked, slightly ajar. He stepped toward it. He heard a sound from within the dump. Soft. Rhythmic. Tapping. And then a voice. A whispered song. He heard

Judem. He moved swiftly to the gate. He edged into the opening. He paused when he saw the faintly moonlit ground. Splitting the earth was the shadow of a cross. Solomon's gaze traveled the upright shadow post on the ground and then he saw the crossbar, too.

And the old man.

In profile to Solomon, Riordan stood on a mound of debris. Covering the debris were crumpled newspapers and torn rags and a pyramid of splintered wood — all things that could easily be set afire. Planted in the center of the mound was a makeshift cross of heavy broken boards. Using a rock, Riordan was tapping a last nail into the center of the crossbar, from whose ends dangled loops of rope. As he sang his Gregorian chant, Riordan's white beard quivered.

Slowly, Solomon pushed against the gate. The rusted hinges creaked.

"Sweet Jubal," the old man said. He turned.

He stood in awe. The rock dropped from his hand.

From the time of his childhood when he trembled at prayer with his whoring mother, throughout the early manhood years when he wandered the dark corners of the earth, ravaging men and women and animals alike, in the course of that time on the lonely beach fornicating with the woman whose life ended as fish feasted on her tongue and, finally, in these recent years of apostlehood which justified the kind murders to which he attended — throughout all these preambling years of faith, he had awaited the final signal of His acknowledgment. On those occasions when he had flagellated himself with the terrible whip of thorns or encouraged Brother Death to peck at his flesh the old man had known that Christ still bled and that his wounds would be forever raw unless appeased by some miraculous sacrifice. He did not question Jubal's absence. To do so would be to question the wisdom of the Lord; and he realized now that the girl had been a sinner without merit, unworthy of Riordan's mercy.

God had sent the Jew.

Riordan kneeled. He crossed himself. "Oh, God, I thank Thee!"

He stood and smiled at the man, who had not moved. His arms outstretched, he moved one step toward him.

"Welcome, Jew," he said. But slowly his smile faded. He was riveted by Solomon's eyes. They looked like circles of transparency, as if the iris and the pupil had fused into a translucent membrane of infinite thinness behind which a red flame rose. His eyes looked ready to explode. Softly, Riordan whistled.

Solomon heard a harsh rustle of wings and from a shadowed place a black bird rose from the carrion on which he fed. The flesh of a rat dangled from his beak. The bird flew to the old man's shoulder.

"To bring hate to His Holy Cross is sinful," Riordan said, still mesmerized by Solomon's eyes. "God prepares for those who do not know Him, as I prepare for those who do not know me."

"I know you," Solomon said, his voice tremulous with rage. "I have known you all my life."

"You have lived in error," Riordan said. "You must die in grace. There are rules."

"Yes," Solomon said. "There are rules."

"Made by the Lord," Riordan said.

"And men," Solomon said.

"You have gone the way of evil men," Riordan said. "You have walked the path of the wicked. If you walk with the wicked, you become the wicked and your heart is filled with wrath."

"Old man," Solomon said in a terrible whisper, "my heart is filled with wrath!"

For just an instant the two men were silent, weighing each other's death; then Riordan's great head lifted and he howled. Trembling in the sight of his target, Solomon's mouth opened and his rage exploded, and in the path of his own sound he saw at last *the thing* was free, its fleshless shape carrying skyward on the hotness of his breath, spreading blackly on the moon, darkening the night. Solomon raised the broken bottle in his hand and charged the planted cross.

The old man whistled shrilly. Brother Death soared from his shoulder. The bird plunged at Solomon, its wings a frantic beat, slashing at Solomon's face, black feathers blinding him. The bird's beak thrust for his eyes. Solomon stabbed upwards with his bottle. He heard a terrible cry, shrilled, cawed, dying, and his hand was flooded by the blood of the bird. The jagged neck of the bottle impaled the breast of Brother Death.

Solomon heard the old man roaring toward him, the vermined earth shaking from his speed. Riordan's arm shot out and his massive fist slammed into Solomon's mouth. Solomon dropped, rolled, spitting blood from his mouth as he tried to claw away from Riordan. He heard the squeal of rats.

The old man's foot lashed out and Solomon felt his cheekbone crack. He was stunned by the pain. He saw the foot come down again. He flung his arms out and grabbed Riordan's leg. He twisted sharply. The old man stumbled, fell. Solomon whipped the deer slug from his pocket. He curled it in his fingers. He slammed his fist into the old man's eye.

He pounded the old man's face. Riordan shrieked. His massive hands closed around Solomon's wrist. He pried at the fingers which held the slug, twisted them, bent them, forced them loose. Solomon dropped the slug and tore his hand away.

He scrambled away, his eyes searching for a weapon. Metal glinted. Blood pounding in his ears, he dived toward the metal. His body slammed across a pile of refuse, slid on the slime of garbage and rotting meat. His foot caught in the twisted coils of a bedspring. He yanked at it. He could not set himself free. He heard the awful breathing of the old man and saw that he was lurching forward. Solomon's hands thrashed out, grasped for anything, and found the glinting metal. His fingers closed on a long steel spring from a screen door. He felt the old man fall on him. He whipped the spring across his face. He felt the rip of flesh and the old man leaned away, then thrust forward again and straddled Solomon, held him in the vise of his knees. Solomon lashed out with the steel spring. He slashed it back and forth, raking it across Riordan's face.

But Riordan's hands rose and he caught the spring and he laughed as he tore it from Solomon's grip. His weight crushed Solomon and as his knees squeezed tighter against his ribs he bent forward, the ends of the spring held in either hand. He placed the spring across Solomon's throat. He leaned his weight against it.

Solomon heard the wheeze of his own breathing and then not even that. Strangely, he felt little pain. He felt weightless, drifting, calm, as if he rode the lowered moon. When he tasted blood in his throat he thought it must be the red glass he'd swallowed under the olive trees in Seville. The blood rose behind his eyes and dimmed his vision, and through his fluttering eyelids, he saw the man above him, black against the white moon, and that shocking portrait of Solomon's past was calling to him . . . *come* . . . *come with me* . . . *come* . . . but Solomon heard a different voice. He heard the Mouse. *It is our children we owe, Solomon, our children!*

The shadow on the moon, fleshed, was no longer faceless. Dying, Solomon understood at last that the rage he'd waited to release was as nothing compared to the sorrows of obligations lost. He reached for Darby. He failed to find her. He closed his eyes.

Riordan dropped the steel spring. He clenched his hands. He lifted them high over his head to hammer them between the eyes of the sinner. Then he heard the whistle of approaching death.

The bola burned the air. Its leather cords scissored the old man's neck. Strangling, he fell from Solomon. On his back, his hands ripping at the thongs, he saw Jubal.

"Wasn't nuthin' left to do, old man," the boy whispered. "I had to get my hands back. Had to. Jus' had to!"

Dimly, Solomon watched as Jubal disappeared through the gate of the dump and he listened to the boy's feet racing down the highway. His numbed body slowly tingling back to life, tears stinging his eyes, Solomon marveled at the boy's act of mercy and he knew his final obligation, the act that would welcome him to the community of men.

Slowly, shaking his head to clear his vision, he rose to his knees, then struggled to his feet, pulled air into his lungs until he felt his strength return. He heard the ugly gasping of the old man. He saw Riordan pull weakly at the thongs around his neck. Still not steady, swaying a little, Solomon leaned over the old man, loosened the thongs, slowly stripped them away. Bracing himself against the quivering of his muscles, Solomon placed his hands under Riordan's arms. Painfully, he began to pull him across the ground. He dragged him over the bedsprings and wet garbage and through the shadow of the cross and then to the crest of the mound of debris. He propped him against the crude cross. He lifted him until he stood against the cross. He slipped Riordan's hands into the loops at either end of the crossbar.

The old man hung there like Christ.

Riordan began to sing. His voice was weak, raspy, raw, but it was filled with a happiness he'd never know, for at last he understood. He knew now what the grandest of all sacrifices was to be. He was to be martyred for the Lord; and when the flames expired he would no longer be the heir to God. He would be God.

His head rolled on his chest, the beard fluttering a little like the wings of Brother Death, and he looked with love at his tormentor. But what he saw paralyzed him with fright. His executioner had stepped away. He stood some feet from the cross. He smiled at Riordan. With an awful certainty, the old man perceived the truth.

The Jew would not accommodate him!

Solomon spoke softly, as if inside the old man's head.

"A Jew," he said, "is justice."

Choked with wrath, his mind whirling with obscenities and epithets, the old man screamed the filth of his accusation.

"Jew!" he howled. "Jew! Jew! Jew!"

"Yes," Solomon said. "Yes."

He turned and walked along the shadowed path of the cross and through the rubble of the dump and out the gate and onto the road, where he began to run. He ran toward his friends, his family, toward all men, and toward himself.

ABOUT THE AUTHOR

WILLIAM DARRID was born in New York City and spent his early years on Long Island. After graduating from high school in Manhattan, he studied acting at The Neighborhood Playhouse School of the Theater. During World War II he served almost five years in the army and then returned to New York and his acting career. From ten years of acting he drew the foundation of his next career—producer of Broadway plays like *The Disenchanted* and *The Andersonville Trial.* He then joined M.C.A. as the Executive Head of the theater department and the New York story department. Now a free-lance writer, he is the author of *The Blooding* and *Solomon Moon* and a number of screenplays. A third novel is on the way. He is married to actress Diana Douglas. Having spent most of his life in New England, Darrid now lives in Sherman Oaks, California—and continues to miss New England.